TOM CLANCY'S
Net Force®

SPRINGBOARD

TOM CLANCY'S
Net Force®

SPRINGBOARD

created by
Tom Clancy and Steve Pieczenik

written by
Steve Parry and Larry Segriff

This first hardcover edition published in Great Britain 2006 by
SEVERN HOUSE PUBLISHERS LTD of
9–15 High Street, Sutton, Surrey SM1 1DF,
by arrangement with Penguin Books Ltd.

British Library Cataloguing in Publication Data

Perry, Steve
    Springboard. - (Tom Clancy's Net Force)
    1.   Computer war games - Fiction
    2.   Suspense fiction
    I.   Title II. Segriff, Larry III. Clancy, Tom, 1947-
    IV. Pieczenik, Steve R.
    813.5'4 [F]

    ISBN 0-7278-6334-7

Printed and bound in Great Britain by
MPG Books Ltd., Bodmin, Cornwall.

Acknowledgments

We would like to acknowledge the assistance of Martin H. Greenberg, Denise Little, John Helfers, Brittiany Koren, Lowell Bowen, Esq., Robert Youdelman, Esq., Danielle Forte, Esq., Dianne Jude, and Tom Colgan, our editor. But most important, it is for you, our readers, to determine how successful our collective endeavor has been.

—Tom Clancy and Steve Pieczenik

PROLOGUE

Hollywood, California
August 2014 C.E.

"Ladies and gentlemen," the tour guide said, "this is the original Paramount Studios wrought-iron gate, built in 1926. Those of you who are movie fans have undoubtedly seen this entrance a number of times. It has been featured in many pictures, most notably *Sunset Boulevard*." She paused for a moment to give everyone a chance to take photographs, or to merely admire the historic structure, then went on. "Sound stage number four is just ahead there. The newer gates, modeled on this one, are over there."

The guide was a beautiful, perky, large-busted blonde who might have been twenty. The day was warm and sunny, and the air not nearly as smoggy as the tourists expected.

Walter and Maybelle Perkins, from Pine Ridge, Alabama, stared at the studio gate. "Get another picture, Walt," Maybelle said.

Walt already had his new Canon multi-megapixel electronic camera raised. He framed the image and snapped the photo. While he was at it, he snapped one of the guide, too.

She *was* gorgeous, after all. Probably be a movie star someday.

Their guide went on. "It is called the Bronson Gate, from the avenue that leads to it. Some of you may have seen old films with the actor Charles Bronson in them. Not many people know that the actor, whose real name was Buchinski, took his movie name from this very gate."

After another brief pause she added, "Paramount is the only major motion picture studio still in Hollywood, and the oldest continuously operating one, as well. Now, if you will follow me, we'll begin the tour inside."

Walter glanced back over the lot. Los Angeles was a lot noisier than he was used to. Its cars, trucks, loudmouthed people, construction, and helicopters all combined to make it louder at midnight than Pine Ridge was at noon on Saturday down at the Safeway.

As Walter turned to follow their guide there was a flash of light, and Walter, Maybelle, their tour guide and tour group—and a good section of noisy Hollywood—got blasted by a man-made sun and crisped in a heartbeat to radioactive ash.

The ballistic missile was a small one, in that the atomic bomb it carried was no more than three or four megatons. The fireball and mushroom cloud were fairly spectacular when viewed from the hills east of Malibu, since, until that moment, the air had been relatively clear—you could even see Catalina Island from the shore.

The initial death toll was just under 300,000. The weapon was a dirty bomb, however, so at least that many more could be expected to die from radiation in short order. The toll would increase even further because of the usual secondary effects of a nuclear bomb, including falling buildings, ruptured gas lines, and rioting.

The second bomb hit near Coit Tower in San Francisco. Only a couple hundred thousand died in that impact. The buildings of San Francisco, designed to withstand earthquakes, proved even sturdier than expected. Also, though no one could explain it at the time, more of the blast channeled out to the bay than toward the suburbs.

The third bomb struck the water just short of the ferry docks in downtown Seattle. A freak effect of the explosion tore the top of the Space Needle loose and spun it away like a giant Frisbee.

Four hundred thousand souls perished in that strike.

The Star Wars umbrella stopped all nine of the remaining missiles. Before the first missile had hit—moments after the initial launch, in fact—the United States had blown through Defcon One and responded to the attack.

Ohio-class ballistic missile submarines of SUBCOMPAC's Group Nine, already on station in the South China and Yellow Seas, unleashed barrages of the new Tomahawk Block VI Nuclear variant (TLAM-N-VI) with its INS/TERCOM/DSMAC/KSA systems, each carrying a standard W80 nuclear warhead. The USS *Henry M. Jackson* (SSBN 730) was the first to fire, but not the last, and four other boomers let go half of their missiles within moments.

Every known major military base in China got a fiery wake-up call.

ICBMs that had stood quietly for fifty years in silos hidden around the United States lifted and sped halfway around the world.

Beijing became a pile of glowing rubble—as did every other targeted major city on mainland China.

Navy troop carriers bearing thousands of Marines—led by MAFORPAC's 31st MEU—headed at full steam to China's shores, to open the door for a full-scale invasion.

B-52 bombers based in NATO-allied European and former Eastern Bloc countries rumbled into the air to rain more atomic grief on the Chinese, who must have had a collective suicide wish—

At that moment, the entire United States military—

submarines, carriers, aircraft, ballistic missiles, Marines, and all—vanished.

Along with China. And the rest of the world . . .

Four-Star Army General Patrick Lee Hadden, Chairman of the Joint Chiefs of Staff, leaned back in his chair in the Pentagon's VR-SYSOPCOM Virtual Reality Theater. "What just happened here, Major?"

Major George Bretton, U.S. Army Computer Corps, shook his head. "The VR shut down, sir."

Hadden glared at Bretton. "I can see that, Major. What I want to know is why the exercise shut down."

"Unknown, sir. The system seems to be running fine, mainframe is on-line, all hardware systems check out. It would appear to be a glitch in the software."

The general frowned. "Major, the United States military does not abide glitches. Find out what happened and fix it."

"Yes, sir."

"And, Major," the general added, "lose the hillbilly tourists. Alabama has electricity and flush toilets these days, and since my wife's family still lives there, I don't find it amusing."

"Yes, sir."

The general and his aides left, and Major Bretton stared at his console. This was bad. This was end-a-career bad. He needed to do something and do it quick.

1

Net Force HQ
Quantico, Virginia

Thomas Thorn was reviewing personnel files when his intercom lit up.

"Commander Thorn? I've got General John Howard on line one."

Thorn looked at the speaker box on his desk. It still surprised him that Net Force, of all places, didn't have something more high-tech—maybe even something virtual—in place of their old-fashioned intercom system. Maybe he would speak to Jay Gridley about that one of these days. "Thanks," he said. "I'll take it." He waved his hand over the phone back and forth twice. The phone came to life.

"Commander," the general said.

Thorn looked at the image of John Howard, a forty-something African-American who had run Net Force's military arm since its inception. Howard had left to take a job as a consultant at the same time that Thorn had taken over the organization last year.

Howard was a good man, and a good general. Thorn had been sorry to see him leave.

"General. How are you?"

"Fine, sir."

"Still enjoying consulting?"

"Yes, sir. Or at least I was."

"Sounds like one shoe dropping, John," Thorn said with a small smile. "Want to let the other one go?"

Howard's image nodded. "Commander, I understand Net Force recently received a request by the Army for help regarding an unexpected problem with the military's VR exercises."

"That's correct, General," Thorn said. "We were up to our ears in work—somebody in the Internet Fraud Complaint Center and the National White Collar Crime Center dropped a ball and asked us to take up the slack."

"Yes, sir. Well, the problem has gotten worse, and the Army's experts haven't been able to pin it down."

"I've heard that, too," Thorn said, frowning. After a moment he added, "So why are you calling about this, John?"

Howard hesitated, then said, "An old friend in the Pentagon thought I might be able to help."

"Is lobbying part of your consulting now?"

Howard smiled. "Personal touch never hurts."

Thorn smiled, too. "True," he said. "I'll see if I can shake some help loose to take a look at the military's problem. I can't promise anything—seems as if we are being nibbled to death by little fishes here lately."

Howard didn't reply, but he didn't move to break the connection, either.

"Something more, John?" Thorn asked.

Howard nodded, all trace of humor gone from his face. "Sir, the powers that be at the DoD were concerned that Net Force might not consider this a priority item."

Thorn sighed. "What can I say? You worked here, you know how it goes. Running errands for the DoD is not in our mission statement. We're a civilian organization under the direction of the FBI, with a little National Guard in the mix."

"Yes, sir, but the Chairman of the Joint Chiefs is involved with this. The man is used to getting his way."

It wasn't the most subtle threat Thorn had ever heard. He felt an immediate, almost reflexive, pulse of anger.

"Well, I appreciate the heads-up, and General Hadden certainly has the clout to make us dance. It wouldn't be a good idea for him to thump us too hard with it, though. Unhappy workers don't always do the best job."

"No, sir." Howard paused again, but not quite as long this time. "Commander," he said, "I think it would be a good idea if we met. There are some things I know that you need to know—material I would rather talk about face-to-face."

Thorn felt a sudden chill. That didn't sound good.

"Okay. What's good for you?"

"I can be there in an hour."

"That fast?"

"Yes, sir. Some grains, the military grinds slow and fine. Some, they chop quick and coarse. Bread is about to be baked, and in your oven."

"Come on in, General. And, John?"

"Commander?"

"Thanks again. I appreciate it."

Howard discommed and Thorn sat back in his chair, staring at the blank screen. He didn't like the sound of this at all. Maybe he had time to step down the hall to the gym and do a little épée work before the general arrived. Never hurt to be relaxed when problems arrived, and he had a feeling one was about to do just that. . . .

People's Army Base HQ Annex
Macao, China

Comrade General Wu stood in his office, staring out the window. From here you could see the lights of the casinos. Tonight's rain turned them into blurry, distant smears of neon and glare.

A pretty sight, but Wu hated them.

Billions of dollars ran through those buildings each year. Like it or not, capitalism was here to stay. Even many of the hard-liners had agreed when the concept of property rights had been put into the Chinese constitution a decade ago. Wu shook his head. Only a fool could still pretend that Communism was going to win out in the end, and whatever else Comrade General Wu might be, he was *not* a fool.

His secretary buzzed him on the intercom.

"Comrade General, Comrade Shing is here."

"Send him in."

Wu went back to his chair and sat, keeping his back straight, his posture that of a soldier. Shing was a civilian, and while he was Wu's man for a number of reasons, not the least of which was money, civilians were unpredictable. Wu needed him, no question, but he didn't have to like the man. Shing represented much that Wu detested.

Not that Wu would ever let even a hint of his feeling about this shine through.

"Comrade General," Shing said, offering a cursory military bow.

"Comrade Shing," Wu said, staying in his seat and returning the nod with just a hair less angle. "Please, have a seat."

Shing sat. The chair facing the desk was comfortable, excessively so. Wu knew men of the old school who thought a hard wooden chair or even a backless bench was better for visitors, to keep them on edge, but Wu was not of that mind. A man who was comfortable and relaxed was more apt to reveal his true nature.

One did not have real power without access to truth.

Shing was a computer expert, in his twenties, educated at MIT in the United States, and as sharp as a master butcher's favorite boning knife. Shing had gone to America young, learned the language, the culture, and, more importantly, as much about the computer business as anybody. Wu did not trust him as far as he could spit against a cyclone, but he needed good tools, and Shing at least was

Chinese, of a good family, and somewhat loyal to the homeland. He was also a genius in the ways of modern electronica, and that was a prime consideration.

Wu hated computers and the cultures that had spawned them. The West was corrupt in so many ways a man could spend half his life just listing them aloud. They had no tradition, no honor, no *chi,* nothing that set a truly civilized society apart from the barbarians. Yes, yes, Communism was a bankrupt philosophy, Wu knew that, but the vestiges of it continued in China, and if you wanted to be a force, you had to deal in it and with it. It would not always be so. Fifty, a hundred, two hundred years? Mere heartbeats in the dragon's breast. China herself abided, she absorbed all, in time.

Wu intended to help China recover her glory and status. She was well on the way, but he would provide a small boost.

History was full of men who, when they acted at the proper moment with the proper motion, had swung the course of events in new directions. Wu would be one of those men. He had spent half his life gathering the proper tools, and if he had to use one such as Shing, so be it. There were times when you fought fire with water, and times when you did it with fire. However distasteful Shing's manner and mores, he was what Wu needed to go up against the Americans.

One did not need to love the arrow one shot into the enemy's heart. . . .

Wu initiated a few minutes of polite civility, Shing responded appropriately, and eventually they came around to the reason the younger man was here.

"Things are progressing well?" Wu asked.

"Oh, yeah," Shing said. "The U.S. Army hacks don't know what happened. Can't find how I got in, haven't a clue how to keep me out or undo what I've started."

Wu kept his polite smile fixed firmly in place. "There will be no problems with keeping to the schedule, then?"

"None I can see."

"And the . . . other thing?"

Shing raised his eyebrows. He gave away entirely too much on his face—more of the legacy of all those years in America. "Well, that will be trickier—CyberNation's security ops are the best. Our attacks there must be flawless. Still, I can do it. And set them against each other."

"Good. Well, then, I will let you be about your business."

Shing nodded. "Thank you, Comrade General." He paused. "Do you suppose I might have another . . . small advance on my . . . stipend? There is, ah, a young woman I have met I wish to take to the casinos." He smiled.

Wu's answering smile was genuine this time. "Of course. Youth should not be wasted entirely in rooms full of computers." He opened his desk drawer and removed from under a file folder a plain manila envelope containing a thick stack of Japanese yen. He handed it to Shing, who probably thought that the comrade general's smile was there for reasons other than it really was.

Shing did not know that the young woman he had recently met was one of Wu's agents. The woman, named Mayli, was beautiful, accomplished in many things—not the least of which were the erotic arts—and she had been instructed to do whatever was necessary to keep Shing happy. If that included marrying him and bearing his children, so be it. Wu already knew all about Shing's favorite foods, the football team he rooted for, and his rather pedestrian sexual preferences. A handwritten report from Mayli detailing those—and much more—was in his desk drawer. He'd just moved it to retrieve the envelope of money he'd given to Shing.

The report was the reason for the smile.

Shing thought Wu a fossil, old, out of touch with modernity, and as a result, weak. Wu knew this because Shing was vain, egotistical, and prone to pillow talk, and Mayli's memory was excellent. There was an old proverb Wu recalled, from his visits to the Middle East. It was Persian. One of the fighting instructors he had sometimes worked with there, Mushtaq Ali, a graybeard Sufi, had passed it along one day over thick, black, bitter coffee in some Turkish-style restaurant: "The young mouse thinks he can bite the lion's tail because the lion is old."

Wu's grin was one of knowledge.

Mayli seemed to be doing her job properly. She had a watcher about whom she did not know, of course. Mayli's watcher would eventually have one of his own, too.

Wu was not a man to trust anyone blindly.

Once Shing was gone, Wu walked back to the window again, to stare through the rain at the neon lights in the distance. Great plans took time, but this one was nearer the end than the beginning. Destiny was not that far in the distance.

Wu smiled.

He returned to his desk, and touched the intercom button.

"Locke?"

"Here."

"Join me."

"What did you think?" Wu asked. He now spoke in Yao, with bits of Sho thrown in, dialects Jack Locke had learned in Hong Kong while running with the street gangs. There were a lot of southern boys in the gangs, and Yao was a favorite dialect. Locke was also fluent in Cantonese, Putonghua, Guoyu, English, and a little Spanish. He was working on German.

Locke, sitting in that same chair in front of Wu's desk, shook his head. "The boy is an idiot savant. He has the touch with computers and can make them sing and dance, but outside that . . ." He shrugged.

General Wu nodded. He leaned back in his chair, and steepled his fingers. "And our plans?"

"On target. If Shing does half what he claims he can do."

"You foresee no problems."

Locke laughed. "Oh, I foresee problems. Scores, hundreds, *thousands* of problems, crouched and hidden like hungry tigers, waiting for us to stumble. A misstep, and we'll be eaten, our gnawed bones left to bleach in the sun. But I'll deal with those." He paused. The general was a fan of Sun Tzu and of the Japanese swordsman, Musashi, and Locke had made it his business to learn their work. He said, "What is it Musashi says? When faced with the ten thousand . . . ?"

"Fight them the same way as one," Wu finished. He smiled slightly. "I am trusting you with a great deal," he said.

"Comrade General, you don't trust me any farther than you can see me," Locke said. "Instead, you recognize that our interests lie on the same path, and you trust me to travel that way until we achieve our common goal."

Wu smiled again, but did not speak.

It was a slight risk, tweaking the general's nose this way, but Locke also knew that the man respected ability, and Locke would not be sitting here if Wu didn't believe he had the skill and talent to do what the general wanted. Plus, toadies were easy to come by—to impress a general, you needed to show some starch.

Jack Locke was aware of the file on Shing in Wu's desk. And he was certain there was a file on him somewhere— Wu never chose to be sightless when there was any way he could see.

Locke also had a pretty good idea what was in Wu's secret file on him, and what was not. He knew he was not a particularly impressive or handsome man, at least not as he understood the words. Too many angles and planes in his face, nose a little too long, lips too thin, and almost-black eyes that, to him, seemed a bit bug-eyed from within deep sockets. His hair was black, with a sharp widow's peak, and while he was in excellent shape from swimming and lifting weights, he was only average height, and not so muscular or broad in the shoulders as to draw attention. Most men looking at a crowd would pass over Locke without a second glance, just another Eurasian face, nothing to mark him out of the ordinary.

Most women, however, saw something there. He had tried to get them to explain it to him, but no two answers were ever quite the same, and there was a vagueness about them when pressed. The most consistent comment women offered was that he looked "interesting." And that part of that look included a hint of cruelty.

Women were ever attracted to bad boys.

Wu would know all this, and more.

Born in Hong Kong, Locke was a mongrel foundling who had been dropped off at a British orphanage forty years ago. He had some Chinese in him, some European— probably English, given where he turned up. He had run away from there at sixteen, and they hadn't made any great effort to find him and drag him back.

He spent some time learning how to live in the mean, crowded streets of Hong Kong, learned how to fight with a knife and his hands while in the gangs, and was certainly on the short road to jail or an early grave when he had been found by a high-born English woman, Lady Patricia Knowles. Patricia—one never called her "Pat," even in bed—had thought him a diamond in the rough. She was richer than the Queen, thirty-six years old, and married to a dotty English lord who was pushing seventy-five and beyond Viagra's help.

She cleaned Locke up, gave him his new name, installed him in an apartment in a good neighborhood, and taught him all manner of things, ranging from how to dress, eat, and behave in polite society to most of the positions found in the *Kama Sutra*. Patricia had been that classic storybook woman—a proper English lady at a formal dinner—and a shameless whore in bed. He could barely keep up with her, even though he was half her age.

After five years, she and her husband had returned to England, but by then Locke was more than a little adept at pleasing a woman, and polished enough to pass for a gentleman. Patricia had directed him to one of her friends, Martha, and he hadn't even had to change apartments.

After Martha, there had been other women eager enough to pay for his company. Sometimes he was merely arm-candy, most times he earned his way in private, but there was always another woman waiting. He had learned his lessons well, and he knew that his appeal, whatever it was, was something upon which he could depend.

He supposed he could have lived that life for a long time. But one can only lie in so many beds, drink so much expensive champagne, attend so many tuxedoed parties before those things begin to pall.

So Locke had turned to crime.

Not because he needed the money—his benefactors had been generous enough over the years, and he was well enough off that he could live on his investments. No, it was the challenge, the spike of adrenaline that let you know you were alive—but that death was coming up just behind you.

Locke's talent here had not been in strong-arm robberies, but in setting up heists worth small fortunes. He traveled in circles wherein there were rich people with cash, jewelry, and art in their homes. That was the beginning. From there, Locke had gone on to bigger things: galleries, jewelry merchants, museums. He had scores all over the Orient, and even into Europe.

If one moves in certain circles, and becomes expert in them, word gets around. Even though Locke hadn't been looking for a job, Wu had found him. Wu had a proposition. When he had put it to him, Locke had been surprised, but intrigued. What Wu could bring to the table made the venture not quite as impossible as it seemed on the face of it.

Locke had said he would consider it. He spent a week mulling it over, then went back to Wu. He was in.

And Wu had known that, too.

"What next?" Wu asked.

"France, then America," Locke said. "Shing's mastery of the virtual does not extend to the real world. There are things that must be seen in person to be known."

Wu nodded. "Yes."

"I will keep you apprised."

Locke stood. The two men gave each other military bows. Locke made sure his gesture was deeper than Wu's. The general would notice. Locke considered himself an equal in this project, not an employee, but it never hurt to be well mannered. Patricia had taught him that. Bless her, wherever she might be.

Route du Parc
Near Nice, France

Charles Seurat exited the A-8 toward Sophia Antipolis, accelerating into a tight, controlled turn in the little Peugeot he'd rented at the airport in Nice. The car was a natural-gas/electric hybrid and had surprising power.

Not too bad.

Still, he missed the larger engines and power afforded by *essence*—gasoline.

C'est la vie.

It would have been gauche to drive anything else to this particular meeting, however. It certainly wouldn't do to drive up in one of his restored Porsches—particularly not when the meeting was in the very PC, cutting-edge environment of Sophia Antipolis.

The small town had started off as little more than a research park in the 1970s, and by the turn of the century had grown to be one of the largest tech centers in western Europe. With streets named after famous scientists and artists: Rue Albert Einstein, Rue Dostoievski, Rue Ludvig Von Beethoven, and the like, it was *the* place to do business, particularly if you were CyberNation.

Art and science coming together, the height of French ambition.

So a PC car: French, and enviro-friendly. All for the movement.

The early morning sun painted the trees with golden light as he drove along the Route du Parc. A heavy cloud layer was coming in, but it didn't look like rain yet. With any luck the weather would hold, and he could make an outdoor dinner this evening with some of CyberNation's friends in Cannes, a little farther north on the A-8.

But first, business.

Today he would meet with Michael LeBathe, CEO of Azure Telecommunications. They manufactured new optical-gate switches and routers that could vastly improve throughput on CyberNation's net backbones. And if his information was correct, LeBathe was a believer, one of the CyberNation faithful, even if the company he led remained publicly neutral.

It is up to me to give him a reason to change that.

He drove across a roundabout with some older statuary in the center, surrounded by lush flowers. The stone faces looked like they might have been prerevolution, possibly brought in from somewhere north, or taken from an old estate.

Revolution.

It was what he was about, the revolution of the world, its essence expressed by the slogans of two centuries past: liberty, equality, fraternity. Only this time it wasn't just for France.

It was time for a change—the nations of the world continued to grow faster and faster, populations skyrocketing, and still they did not yet possess those three key traits. Fraternity, certainly not. Fighting in the Middle East continued, ethnic cleansing, religious rivalries. Liberty? Only in some countries, and even there, true freedom did not ring. Most nations traded freedoms for security, all to protect their territories, arbitrary lines on a map.

And of course there was no equality. The world had shrunk in this day of instant communication, the stage dominated by the greedy West, countries like the United States taking the role of a deranged Sun King, gobbling everything it could to keep its excessive lifestyle and feed its overweight children.

The parallels to the French Revolution were there if you but looked. Seurat had been looking since the early days of CyberNation.

He did not plot to take over the world, no. He did not

need to. When CyberNation gained power, when they began to have the political clout they needed to give their citizens new freedoms, there would come a time when enough people were a part of things that there would simply be no need for any other government.

There would be no need for the seizing of a Bastille, le Guillotine, the Terror, or bloody guerrilla war. Instead, there would simply be a critical mass of desire, an acceptance of the equality of peoples from all over the world who could join an ideal world of no poverty, physical equality, and no language barriers by stepping into CyberNation. True liberty, equality, and fraternity.

Given this ultimate freedom, the ability to live in a world of platonic ideals, where everything could be the best, the most stylish, who would want to settle for less in their own homes and towns? Even dictators had to answer to the people at some point.

And that point was coming.

But first there was work to do.

As a child, Charles had studied the famous paintings of his distant ancestor, Georges Seurat, the Impressionist. The huge canvases were filled with static and serene images that had comforted him throughout his turbulent childhood. Because of his link to the artist, he'd looked beyond the paintings themselves, researching the techniques and methods by which the man had worked.

Months of preliminary painting on smaller canvases had gone into the creation of each great work, extrapolations of how colors would visually mix from a distance, the calculated effect of a tiny yellow dot and a tiny blue one side by side making green, the position of a figure lying down or standing up—all to a purpose.

This understanding had shown him a method for dealing with the complexities of the world through careful planning, research, execution, and a purpose.

Today, for instance.

LeBathe, the man he was going to see, was the CEO of

a publicly traded company: He had to explain his decisions to shareholders, to justify his actions based on profits alone.

One of CyberNation's key selling points to its erstwhile citizens had been the eventual cessation of taxes. The advertising from major corporations would pay for everything, and it would all be free.

Seurat knew this was more marketing than reality: No company would want to foot the bill for the web access of an entire nation. And for now, at least, there was no way he could extend any taxation benefits to a corporation, even if they did agree to join CyberNation as an entity.

But, like his ancestor, he had made careful studies and plans; there were other considerations.

He would offer LeBathe a possibility: supplying the switching gear for the entire CyberNation network. He happened to know that Azure Communications had not yet distributed their gear to major clients; their work was still new enough and untried enough that most corporations didn't want to bleed at the cutting edge.

Such a large order would give publicity to Azure, and would make other clients sign up. Certainly there would be an immediate benefit from this that the CEO could sell to his board of directors. Perhaps throwing in some extra equipment for nothing would seal this exclusive deal, no? Economies of scale, *oui*?

And then Seurat would wave another banner for LeBathe and the board of directors: patriotism. The management at Azure was known to be extremely nationalistic. Seurat might point out how the expansion of French technology could impact the world now, and the possible world offered by CyberNation in the future.

Where the Toubon law from the last century had failed to stem the influence of the outside world on France—by removing words like "cheeseburger," "jumbo jet," and "e-mail" from the language—the expansion of French technology into a new nation would succeed. And if Azure were to get in on the ground floor, why, perhaps it would have more say in the shape of things to come.

Vive la France.

Of course, if Azure's equipment hadn't truly been the fastest his team could find, CyberNation would have gone with another supplier, whether it be Japanese, Chinese, or American. But CyberNation had to have the best, and in this case, that was French. Charles's patriotism, his loyalty, was not to France, but to the dream that was the heart of CyberNation. Eventually, there would be no borders, only a single, unified, information-based world. What was the phrase? Geography was history?

He looked forward to the day when he could dispense with the machinations and sleights of hand he was required to perform to achieve this glorious end. The men at Azure would of course never be allowed to impact the shape of CyberNation with their own biases; but their believing so was necessary. For now.

Ahead, Seurat saw the turnoff to Rue Albert Einstein. He smiled as he drove toward Azure's building, imagining the future, a huge canvas made from carefully worked-out plans and studies, each one helping build a masterpiece that would change the world. It was still a ways off, but it was coming.

It was a heavy responsibility, the future of humanity, but he accepted it gladly.

Vive la CyberNation!

2

Chang Han Yao sighed and shook his head at the image on the computer screen. Pornography, and from a Chinese website no less. At least the server was in Beijing, thousands of kilometers away from him.

It was not particularly inspired, the picture, a plain-vanilla Chinese man and woman, both naked, coupling, nothing perverse about it. They appeared young, but they were not children. They might even be married, so that what they were doing could be perfectly legal in and of itself, although the posting of it in public to drum up sales for more of the same was certainly not.

Chang ran the simple backlook bot he had gotten in England the last time he'd been there, a basic, no-frills, easily fooled piece of software he'd been using for almost a year—a lifetime in computer circles—and it took all of two seconds for the program to render the address of the person who had posted the image of the young couple. A telephone call, and the People's Police would drop round and gather up the sleaze artists. And that would be the end of that—at least as far as Chang was concerned.

If only all his work was this easy.

Fortunately, most Chinese were still not as sophisticated as the rest of the world when it came to computers, and that made some of Chang's job relatively simple.

Unfortunately, that was changing. Once his people had gained access to the international net, the home-grown product had started to improve dramatically. Now there were people in his country who would not be caught so easily as this would-be smut peddler, those who could rascal their addresses from all but the most cutting-edge hunt-bots. Chang's generally superior software and abilities were constantly being overtaken by a new breed of operator, and his goal of running a Chinese agency at the sophisticated level of the United States' own Net Force was a very long way from being realized.

Still, if one reached, one should reach high.

Pandora's box had been opened, the cat allowed to escape from the bag, the thousand-year-old egg hatched—and there was no turning back. This new breed of hackers and sysops was smart. More, they had grown up enjoying private enterprise, so they had money, and money gave access to better and better software and hardware, not all of which was legal.

Chang himself, only thirty, had been one of the Xaio Pangzi children—the "small fatties," so called because they grew up in a time when food was plentiful for the middle class. A fat child was a testament to his parents' wealth. Chang knew those with whom he was dealing.

It was a long way from Beijing to Ürümqui. Were it not for the computer school established here only eighteen months past, and the new chip plant still under construction, Chang would not have been sent to this town. Yes, he had others working for him, and certainly they did their jobs as best they could, but the government still did not understand so much. If they would just—

He smiled, laughing at himself. Yes, yes, yes. And were there no sun, it would always be night.

Chang shook his head. There was no point in traveling along the what-if road. It led nowhere.

He constantly had to struggle to convince the powers that be that he needed to upgrade his systems just to keep pace, to say nothing of staying ahead of the criminal elements. As a Muslim who had the right to put "Haj" before his name, having made the pilgrimage to Mecca only two years before, Chang had a strong sense of morality. Evil would ultimately be punished by Allah, but in the meantime, Chang was able to offer his small part in this world.

Getting some help himself now and then would be nice, Insh'allah. . . .

Aboard the Rock Pusher **Bergamo**
The Asteroid Belt

Captain Jay Gridley looked at his crew. They were down a man, the air in the ship was stale and smelled like lube, but the alien that had killed Hobbs wasn't going to get any more of them. They were still more than ten light seconds away from the Mars Skyhook, almost two million miles, clearing the Bussey Cluster with a cruise-ship-sized chunk of nickel-iron on the pusher, and nobody was anywhere near close enough to help them.

"All right," Captain Gridley said, "here's how it is going to be. Everybody is armed at all times. Nobody goes anywhere alone. We stay together constantly, no exceptions. If you hear a funny noise, you don't go to check it out, we *all* go. If you are hungry, we will all go to the galley and have a snack. We sleep in shifts, and you will have a blaster under your pillow. If you see the alien, you shoot it first and tell the rest of us later. If you see somebody start shooting, you aim your weapon in the same general direction and you cook, too."

He paused to let that sink in, then continued. "We aren't going to go into the air duct system looking for this thing, nor are we going to roam around in the storage areas where the lighting is dim. If it wants us, it is going to have to come and get us and we will make it cross empty space to do it. No matter how tough its skin is, it can't withstand the fire of seven blasters hitting it at once. If we see it—when we see it—we kill it. If it is the last of its kind, too bad—it should have thought of that before."

He paused again, making eye contact with each individual member of his crew. "This, people, is how you stay alive when faced with this kind of threat—you've all seen idiot-plot movies and you ought to know by now that the first rule is: You don't do anything *stupid* so the monster has a chance to get you. Any questions?"

There weren't any.

Jay grinned. In the real world, he was in Quantico, Virginia, at Net Force HQ, initiating a virus protection program with half a dozen sub-routines, wired and taped and shrouded in VR gear, running cutting-edge software on the latest hardware. Here in virtual reality, he was on a space tug, protecting it from a nasty alien monster, which was definitely a lot more fun.

Most people didn't realize that specialized computer hacking was normally about as exciting as watching grass grow. With the advent of VR, you could kick that up a bunch of notches, and improve your own effectiveness in the process.

Not that he needed much help in the effectiveness department. The truth was that most computer criminals weren't all that bright, and so far, none of them had been brighter than Jay Gridley, who sat atop Net Force's electronic food chain. This particular virus was only a threat to people who didn't know how to deal with it, and Jay could take care of the beast with one hand tied behind him and one eye closed. . . .

"Jay?"

* * *

Net Force HQ
Quantico, Virginia

The com override cut into the scenario. Only a few people could do that—his boss, his ex-boss and his ex-boss's wife, and Jay's wife. And the voice was that of Saji, his spouse and mother of Mark Jefferson Gridley, the world's most beautiful baby.

Jay killed the scenario. "Hey, babe. What's up?"

"Your son just laughed at me."

"Really?"

"I know he's not supposed to be doing that at two months, but he did. He smiled and he laughed!"

Jay smiled, too. "The boy is a genius, no question about it. He takes after his father, obviously."

"I'll let you get back to work," Saji said. "I just wanted you to know."

"Thanks, sweetie. I'm almost done here. I'll be home in a couple hours."

"I love you," she said.

"Me, too, you."

After she discommed, Jay smiled again. He did that a lot lately. Being a husband and a father had not even been on his horizon a few years back, and it was a big change, but it was so much more than he had ever thought it could be.

He was about to restart the VR scenario, when the com lit again.

It was Commander Thorn.

"Jay?"

"Right here."

"Come by my office when you get a chance, would you? There has been an . . . interesting development here."

"Sure thing, Boss."

Had to be more interesting than this by-the-numbers virus hunting, Jay figured. He switched off the system and began to shuck the VR gear.

*   *   *

Colonel Abraham "Abe" Kent was lying on his back in the Net Force gym with his feet propped up on a chair, his knees bent at right angles, doing crunches. He had done four sets of twenty-five, and figured he needed at least two more before his abs burned enough so he had to stop. It wasn't fun, and it wasn't interesting, but it was part of the regimen. A man his age didn't get to slack off on keeping fit. Once it was gone, he might not be able to get it back. The days when he could party all night long and then run the Marine obstacle course faster than anybody else on the base were thirty years past; now he was happy if he could run the course and beat anybody without injuring something.

He frowned through the ache in his belly muscles, still doing the crunches, alternating now from side to side, touching his left knee with his right elbow, then the right knee with the left. He wasn't standing with one foot in the grave—at least he hoped not—but once you hit forty, you were on the downside; fifty, and the wrinkles started winning. You had to fight to keep your muscles and flexibility. Not that he had to do a lot of running if he didn't want—at his rank he could decorate a chair and no one would think anything about it, though he couldn't see himself doing that.

After thirty years in the Marine Corps, the switch to commanding Net Force's military arm was a big change. Technically, he was working for the National Guard now. Nothing wrong with the Guard, he'd known some fine soldiers from that branch, but nobody did things quite like the Corps did.

And, as it had recently, the memory of the assassin who was also a classical guitarist came back to haunt him. Natadze, the Georgian, remained free, and that grated on Kent. He hated to fail at anything, and even though nobody else blamed him for the man's escape, *he* knew he was responsible. Natadze was *his* job, and sooner or later, he was going to have to do something about it—

His virgil tweeted. He stopped exercising and picked it

up. This was the work phone. Whoever was calling would be more important than a few sit-ups.

"Colonel Kent here."

"Abe, Tom Thorn. Would you drop by my office when you get a minute?"

"On my way, sir."

Thorn sat in the conference room. Abe Kent was already there, and he saw Jay Gridley being directed this way by Thorn's secretary.

When Jay arrived, Thorn nodded at him. "Gentlemen, Net Force is about to undergo a radical change."

Both men looked at him, but neither one spoke.

"A few minutes ago, John Howard came by to talk to me. What he had to say will be made at least semipublic by tomorrow, but he wanted to give me a heads-up, and I wanted to pass it along. I took the liberty of recording General Howard's visit, so it would be easier if you saw it for yourself."

He touched a control, and the table's holoprojector clicked on. The holoproj lit the air above the table, visible from any angle. The image showed Howard and Thorn in Thorn's office.

"Okay if I record this?" the image of Thorn said.

"Fine by me, long as it doesn't leave the building today. By tomorrow, it won't matter."

"Okay. So what's on your mind, John, that you had to hurry down here?"

Howard took a deep breath. "I don't know if you are aware that the National Guard has had something of a budget crunch of late. They've got funds for Homeland Security stuff, and regular operations, but special ops, such as Net Force's military arm, have been cut into deeply."

Thorn gave a faint smile. "Since I go up on the Hill to talk budget more than I like, I was aware of that, General."

Howard nodded. "Couple that with the fact that the Internet Fraud Complaint Center and the National White Collar Crime Center are finally up and running full-bore, and handling a lot of stuff that Net Force used to do. Add to that the fact that the Chairman of the Joint Chiefs of Staff really wants Net Force to put his concerns about his VR scenario problems at the top of their to-do list. Plus the general has mondo clout across the board, and what do you think you get?"

Thorn frowned. "I can hazard a guess, of course, John, you've done all but connect the dots for me, but I don't really like guessing games. Why don't you just say what you came here to tell me?"

"All right, Commander. The Department of Defense is going to take over Net Force from the FBI. Your military arm will be shifted to the Marine Corps, since you're already right here at Quantico. Nobody will be fired, everything will stay pretty much the same, at least for the time being, but your primary mission from now on will be expanded. The military's computer problems just got a pass to the top of the pile."

"No way," Thorn said.

"Yes, sir, that's what I'd say in your position."

"Can they really do this? Something this complex?"

"Sir, I am here to tell you that it's a done deal."

Thorn shut the holoproj off and looked at Kent and Gridley.

"No way," Jay said.

Thorn nodded. "Oh, yes, way, Jay. DoD swings a real big stick these days, and if they want something and can convince the powers that be that they need it? They get it. Which means we have some things to think about."

Washington, D.C.

When Jay got home, Saji was in the rocking chair her great-grandfather had built for her great-grandmother. The old wooden chair was hickory, and the joints creaked a little every time Saji rocked in it, but there was something apparently soothing about the motion and the noise—the baby, even if he was fussy, calmed right down every time.

"Hey," Jay called as he came through the door. "Daddy's home. How's the world's most beautiful boy and his mother?"

Saji smiled. "He's almost asleep."

Jay nodded. "How was your day?"

"Great." Saji kept rocking, slow and steady, as she told him the adventures of Mark Gridley, the brightest, funniest, most gorgeous child who had ever been born. Every diaper change, every burp, every wiggle. What amazed Jay—what had amazed him from the moment he first saw his child—was that he found everything about Mark just as fascinating as Saji did. He could just sit and watch the baby do nothing. Jay's new favorite way to spend an hour resting was to lie down with Mark sleeping on his chest. Jay had never felt anything like this before: He was a father, and he couldn't get enough of it. Had anybody told him even a few months ago that this was how he'd be, he wouldn't have believed it.

"You want to hold him?"

"Yes."

They switched places. Jay put the baby over his shoulder and restarted the gentle motion of the chair. Mark yawned, made one of his funny squeaks, and closed his eyes.

"And how was your day?" Saji asked.

"Not as much fun as yours." He explained about the changes coming to Net Force. Mark fell asleep in the middle of this, apparently not at all interested in his father's work. He'd sleep for at least an hour, and the drone of their voices wouldn't wake him—once he was out, he slept like, well, a baby. . . .

"So, what are you going to do, Jay?"

"For now, go along and see how things shake out. I can always get another job if the military folks turn out to be a bunch of bigger idiots than I think they will be. Though I have to say I would be surprised if that's possible."

The baby sighed, and added a kind of warbling moan at the end.

His parents smiled at each other. What a wonderful child he was.

3

Thorn was in the gym, doing what he often did when life got more complex than he liked—practicing his fencing. The exercises were familiar, comfortable, and worked best when you just did them and didn't think about them. Which was pretty much the way it worked in a real fencing bout, too. Thought was simply too slow. The hand was quicker than the eye, it was true, and the blade was quicker than the mind. In fact, in all the years Thorn had been fencing, he had only ever met one guy who claimed to be able to process each action on the strip as—or before—he made it. Thorn didn't doubt the guy, but he'd never understood how he could do that.

Right now, Thorn was working on a basic footwork drill: lunge, recover; step, lunge, recover, retreat; step, step, lunge, recover, retreat, retreat; and so on. When he'd first started, his goal was to be able to take ten steps, lunge, recover, and then retreat those same ten steps. These days he went for the entire length of the fencing strip, or piste. The idea was to end up exactly where you started. It developed footwork and form on lunges, and also helped with strength, speed, and smoothness.

He gave up after a while. There was just too much going on inside his head to completely let go of it. The exercise was helping, but not enough. He left the strip and went over to an area of the gym where he'd hung several golf balls on strings set at different heights. He began attacking, picking a particular ball and then throwing attacks of varying complexity, from simple lunges to compound attacks involving bastinadoes and ballestras, each one ending with a strike on the golf ball he'd selected.

Another basic exercise, this was aimed solely at the épéeist, and could greatly improve point control, among other things.

He hit each golf ball three times, and then quit, more frustrated than relaxed. He just could not keep his concentration. Too much to think about. Like sleep on a restless night, the more he reached for that no-mind state, the further it retreated.

When he'd taken this job, it hadn't been a step up, insofar as money or his career went. Far from it, in fact, but that didn't matter. He was rich enough from his software creations that he didn't need to work another day in his life. He had taken the job as a personal challenge, and as a way of offering something to his country in return. Not a choice a lot of boys growing up on the reservation would ever have.

But now? With the military taking over Net Force, there would be changes coming. They might say they would leave it alone, but Thorn knew better. The more hierarchy in an organization, the more it had to make things fit. If the military just barged in and said this was how things were going to be, like it or lump it, they'd find themselves holding an empty sack. The people in Net Force who ran things were all adepts—any of them could bail and have another job lined up before their chairs got cold, and even the military, which wasn't always the most forward-thinking of organizations, had to know that. Hardware was easy; keeping people who knew how to run it right was not so easy.

That was one of the first lessons Thorn's grandfather had taught him about hunting: Tromp in too heavily, you spooked the game.

So, yeah, they'd leave things alone to begin with. Except for that edict to shift priorities so their problem came first, there probably wouldn't be much to look at, insofar as changes went.

But it was coming, Thorn knew. He had run his own company, and had been around the block a few times. It might be subtle at first, but there would be policy changes rolling down the pike, and one day the players at Net Force would look up and realize they weren't in Kansas anymore. . . .

The question was, what was Thorn going to do about it?

For the moment, the easiest choice would be just wait and see. He could type up his resignation and be ready to leave if things went sour.

That was the easy way. But he had a responsibility that he needed to at least try and see through; he had come here to help, and as long as he could do that without outside micromanagement, he'd stick around. That was the failing of a lot of bosses—they hired good people, but then spent too much time looking over their shoulders, poking their fingers in where they shouldn't.

Thorn had always been a hands-off manager himself. He figured that if you laid out good money to hire an expert, you should stay out of his way and let him do his job. An unhappy worker didn't do as good a job as a happy one, and nothing made a skilled hand unhappier than a boss who didn't know when to shut up and mind his own business. Especially when his help made things worse . . .

Thorn had bought out a small software company once for less than a third what it was worth, because of that very situation. The company made a communications package, very sleek and functional, tightly written and fairly simple. The CEO, who knew less about computers than he did sales, kept coming to his programmers with demands about how to improve things. The programmers didn't like that at all, of course; worse, when they implemented the demanded changes, the product didn't work as well and didn't sell as well as it had before.

Naturally, the CEO blamed the programmers for his mistakes. People started to quit, and the stock dropped. By the time Thorn got there, there were only a few of the good people left. He bought the company, fired the CEO, stripped out the things that made the product clunky, and sales went back up. Old programmers came back, the ones who were still there stayed, and everybody was better off. Well, everybody except the fired hands-on executive . . .

He hoped the military wouldn't do something like that CEO, but looking at it realistically, he had to consider the possibility. And if that happened, he could either stay and fight or he could walk, but it was his bicycle they were messing with.

He smiled at the punch line of the old joke, one his grandfather had told him back on the rez when Thorn was in his teens:

"So the missionary is walking about the Indian village with the tribe's chief, and teaching him English.

"They pass a dog. The missionary points at the animal. 'Dog,' he says.

"The chief nods. 'Dog.'

"They come to a cooking fire, and the missionary points at it. 'Fire,' he says.

" 'Fire,' the chief replies.

"As they round a teepee, they see, lying in the bushes, a naked couple making love. The missionary, embarrassed, fumbles for words. Unable to bring himself to talk about sex, he says:

" 'Uh . . . man . . . uh . . . riding bicycle . . . '

"Whereupon the chief pulls an arrow from his quiver,

nocks it in his bow, draws, and lets fly. The arrow hits the man in the back of the head, killing him instantly.

"Stunned, the missionary says, 'Wh-what did you do that for?'

" 'Man riding *my* bicycle,' the chief says."

Thorn smiled again at the memory. He missed his grandfather. The man had been a fountain of wisdom and funnier than a busload of drunk comedians.

Well. It was his bicycle, at least for now, and it was what it was. He'd deal with it somehow.

Ürümqui, Xinjiang Uygur Autonomous Region, Northwestern China

Chang stood in the lobby of the hotel, waiting for the Canadian. There was a hint of jasmine in the air, and a murmur of voices in the background, speaking Chinese, English, and even what sounded like Italian.

The hotel, the Flowering Plum, was new, built only a year ago by a Canadian investment group. Ürümqui was a modern city, and not without a certain international flair: There were Holiday Inns, Ramada Inns, and Double Tree was considering putting up a new building. Mexican restaurants. A Starbucks.

People in the West sometimes found such things amazing—many of those who had never been here had the idea that, outside the well-known cities, China was mostly rice paddies tended by old men wearing big straw coolie hats, riding in wooden carts pulled by oxen. He could understand this—once, he had gone to Colorado, and even though he was an educated man, he had kept looking for teepees and buffalo.

Colorado did have some of those, he learned, but only for the tourists. In the same way, China still had old men in straw hats, too. More of them than the United States had bison, to be sure. Then again, China had half as many web surfers as were in the U.S., and thirty percent *more* than Japan.

Of course, when it came to computer commerce, China had constraints most other countries didn't: fewer servers, more regulations, and the *percentage* of the population that was computer-literate was much smaller than in the U.S. China had a lot more Internet cafes and fewer private systems, but still, his job wasn't the easiest in the world. . . .

Admittedly, he was a good four hours away from Beijing by air, but airliners did fly here from the capital regularly, and with well over a million people, Ürümqui was hardly some sleepy village.

Chang glanced at his watch, a Seiko Kinetic. Two more minutes until the Canadian—the man had a name, it was Alaine Courier, but Chang always thought of him as "the Canadian"—was due. He'd be on time—he always was.

The reason for this visit was simple, but important. Courier had access to some cutting-edge software from America. The stuff wasn't supposed to travel outside the U.S., but it had made it as far as Canada, and Chang wanted it in the worst way.

But this wasn't just a simple exchange. Courier wasn't interested in merely selling the software to Chang. No, Courier was looking to establish his business connections in China, and he wanted Chang to help him with that. Which Chang was willing to do. He was ahead of most of the hot-rodders in his country when it came to cutting edge-gear and programs, but the race never slowed. Miss a step, and you'd be behind, and that wasn't where Chang wanted to be.

Chang knew that if he wanted to put Chinese net policing on the same relative footing as the United States had with Net Force, he needed more tools. He would get those however and wherever he could. His masters would turn a blind eye in his direction as long as he got the job done without causing them any loss of face. If he screwed up, well, that would be on his own head.

"Chang!"

There was the Canadian now. Chang smiled.

Net Force HQ
Quantico, Virginia

When the summons came for Thorn to drop by the Director's office at his convenience, it was not much of a surprise. Actually, the most surprising thing about it was how
long it had taken. Still, the FBI kept things on a need-to-
know basis, just as so much of the government seemed to
do these days. Even from their own employees.

Maybe *especially* from their own employees . . .

Thorn told his secretary where he would be, then took a
stroll. It wasn't that long a walk.

There had been a shake-up in the FBI only a couple of
months past, and the former Director, a sharp woman
named Allison, was no longer in charge. The new guy,
Roland McClain, was a long-time friend of the current
President, a former Army lawyer who'd worked in Iraq after the invasion in the early Oughts. McClain had then left
and taken up tort litigation, going on to make millions su-
ing large corporations for his clients. McClain was something of a jock—played tennis and handball and golf, was
a very fit sixty, and a political animal to the core.

As soon as Thorn arrived at the new Director's office,
the assistant showed him in.

"Thomas, how are you?"

The man's handshake was firm, but not threatening. He
had a tan year-round, and lots of leathery smile wrinkles.
The kind of face you'd buy a used car from, if you went by
looks alone.

"Mr. Director," Thorn said.

"Please, Thomas, call me Mac. We're not big on formality around here, you know. Have a seat."

Thorn sat on the couch, a comfortable, Western-style

piece of furniture of distressed leather with a lot of brass tacks stuck into the woodwork.

"Do you have any idea why I needed to see you, Thomas?"

Thorn smiled. "Yes, sir, I expect so."

McClain raised an eyebrow. "Do tell."

"It probably has something to do with the fact that Net Force is being taken over by the military, courtesy of the Chairman of the Joint Chiefs, and pretty soon we are all going to be Marines."

That got his attention. McClain shook his head. "And you came by this how?"

"We are an intelligence agency, sir. We do stumble across things from time to time."

"Would you like to be more specific?"

"Not really."

McClain frowned.

In Washington, even more than in most places, knowledge was power, and a man who ate, slept, and breathed politics like McClain always wanted to be in the know, more so because he was the Director of the FBI. In this case, McClain didn't have much leverage. He wasn't going to fire Thorn, and in a very short period of time wasn't going to be his boss any longer. At this juncture, his options were limited. McClain knew that, of course, and he knew that Thorn did, too.

Thorn said, "Does it really matter? It's true, isn't it?"

The Director nodded. "Yes. I fought against it—I think Net Force is better kept in civilian hands."

For which Thorn, who was also passing familiar with politics and clout, heard: "Better kept in *my* hands."

"But," McClain continued, "I'm a long way from the top of the food chain, and the big carnivores have made a firm decision. Practically speaking, not much will change, at least to look at."

Thorn gave a very small smile at that, but didn't say anything.

McClain ignored it. "You'll stay where you are," he went on, "but instead of reporting to me, you'll be talking to the DoD via a Marine connection. I'm not sure exactly who that will be yet, but if I had to guess I'd say it would be General Roger Ellis, who is the Corps' Special Projects Commander at the Pentagon these days."

Thorn nodded. This situation must have really angered McClain. Only on the job a couple of months and already they were carving away at his empire. Thorn would bet that Mac's buddy the Prez had gotten an earful about this; obviously, it hadn't done any good.

"You'll be hearing from these people soon. Technically, the transfer of command won't happen immediately, but as of now, whatever they want at DoD, you give them."

Thorn nodded again. "Yes, sir." Even though McClain had offered his nickname, he didn't correct Thorn's respectful "sir." The man had came out of the Ivy League, and his just-one-of-the-boys routine was for show. He was not a bad guy, from what Thorn knew, but the story was, he was like a cat—dropped from anywhere, he always landed on his feet, and any business friendships were pragmatic before anything else. Not "What have you done for me lately?" but "What can you do for me now?"

"I'll pass along whatever I hear," the Director said. "Assuming you don't hear it elsewhere first."

Thorn gave the man another small and brief smile and left. It wouldn't be that hard for him to find out about John Howard coming to visit—nobody had tried to hide it. But knowing it was Howard and being able to do anything with that was a horse of a different color. Howard was a private consultant now, not subject to Ellis's command.

As he walked back toward Net Force HQ, Thorn rolled it around in his thoughts. Still too early to tell. He'd have to wait until he started getting calls from the DoD.

When he got back to his office, his secretary, who was on the phone, waved at him. She put the caller on hold. "General Ellis's office for you," she said.

Thorn smiled. "I'll take it."

No moss growing on the Marines . . .

* * *

Department of Defense's High Performance Computer
Modernization Program
New Pentagon Annex
Washington, D.C.

Jay Gridley was annoyed. More than that, he was angry. He drummed his fingers on the clear plastic table in the holo room as he waited to meet the HPCMP's liaison and thought about how irritated he was.

So it had finally happened. Net Force was moving out of the feds' grip and into the military's. Although Thorn hadn't had the details, Jay knew that there had been a major systems failure during big simulations. Apparently the powers that be felt there could have been some outside cause of the crash and had been sweating blood trying to track it down. So much so that they'd arranged to take Net Force under their aegis just to make it a priority. That meant it had to be a truly huge event.

What was most irritating was, he'd had to come over here to meet someone *physically* for a briefing. Hadn't they ever heard of VR and secure channels? He'd be stuck in traffic for at least an hour on the way home.

Plus, once he arrived, he had to walk the gauntlet: metal detector, explosives sniffer, bio-telltale. Had to take off the belt Saji had given him for his birthday and let it be examined by guards who let him have it back reluctantly, watching him as though they thought he planned to throttle their computer scientists with it. This on top of having to carry a smart-card badge that would set off an alarm if he went anywhere he wasn't cleared to go, as well as an armed escort who had walked him to meet the HPCMP's liaison and who was just across the room, waiting. It was like having a baby-sitter, and it was insulting, to say the least.

Jay knew that it had been that way at many military and government buildings since the 9/11 terrorist attack on New York's Twin Towers and the Pentagon, of course, and he could understand that—U.S. security had been very lax in the good old days. Unfortunately, those days were long ago and far away.

He could even agree with the heightened security measures and the extreme caution. What bothered him the most, though, was the baby-sitter. Jay was a cleared, high-security employee and had been checked seven ways to Sunday, so what was the point of putting an armed guard on him? Jay wasn't going to do anything. He was on their side. He was one of the good guys. He was here to help them find a computer breach.

If there had even been a breach. From what Jay knew of the HPCMP's networks, sneaking in would be tough. For the last year or so, the Department of Defense had operated under new network protocols on their high-speed internal network. These were similar to but incompatible with commercial routers and networks. Any connection to an outside network had to be translated to standard packet protocols, and every such translation point was watched very carefully. Since the system was designed only for military projects, the efficiency and incompatibility were both desirable.

All of which made the entire process he was going through now seem like closing the barn door after the cow had gotten out.

Come on, Gridley, cut them some slack.

He smiled to himself, ignoring the guard. It was true that Thorn hadn't given him much background about Net Force's forced move into the military, but that didn't mean Jay didn't have it.

Smokin' Jay Gridley did *not* go walking blindly down the garden path—not when he could find out what kind of grass grew in the garden, the names of the flowers, the name of the gardener, and the pH of the soil. And he could. Several hours of trekking through cyberspace had given him the background of the HPCMP's mission, their current projects, and the name of the man he was going to see, George Bretton.

He knew Bretton, of course—you didn't get to be one

of the top cyber-jocks in the country without bumping into those few who could run with you. Or actually, a little behind you. Bretton was good—more a specialist in simulations and Human Behavior Modeling than security—but he had some chops.

One of the things Jay had found out was that the HPCMP didn't just do sims. They coordinated immense computing power for other uses as well—modeling of new missiles, design of new weapons and vehicles, and other R&D. If there *had* been a break in to their network, the potential for espionage could be serious indeed.

Okay, so maybe they had reason to be paranoid.

He glanced at his watch, which wore an old analog face—an Omega Seamaster Chronograph Professional. When you looked closer, you could see that it was a pixel job—a datastore that also doubled as a watch, the display showing any one of hundreds of styles.

And right now it was showing that he'd been waiting for fifteen minutes.

Which started him fuming again.

Cool down, Gridley.

It was another five minutes before a short, muscular man in uniform who looked like a recruiting poster walked in Bretton.

Jay tried not to let his irritation show. All the agencies were supposed to exude brotherly love these days, however their people felt.

"George—glad you could make it."

Apparently his skills at acting were worse than he had thought, or else Bretton was just as unhappy.

"Yeah, thanks for coming, Jay." Not much enthusiasm there. Practically deadpan.

This was great. All the hassle of getting here and the guy he came to help didn't even want him here.

Jay wanted to sigh, but held it. This was why he liked cyberspace. What was it Saji said? Sometimes the journey of a thousand steps had to go the extra mile? He waited for a few seconds and tried to imagine how he'd feel if Bretton had been brought in to check up on Net Force security.

Not too good.

Let it go. Give the man some face.

"Yeah, well, I don't know why they dragged me over here when they've got you," he said, shrugging. "It's not like I have a bigger hammer."

Bretton grinned and the tension level dropped.

"Thanks, Jay, I appreciate that. The thing is, I haven't found the problem yet, and as much as I hate to say it, I may not be able to. I've looked under more rocks than litter the surface of Mars."

Hmm. If Bretton couldn't find anything, it might be worth looking into.

"You're sure it's a break-in?"

"Yeah."

Bretton tapped on the table and instantly the empty room disappeared. They were on a crowded street, packed crowds of tourists looking up into the sky where the huge flower of a nuclear fire had just begun to blossom. Everything was still; the scene frozen. The light was harsh and actinically bright, and Jay squinted to protect his eyes.

Bretton unfroze the tableau and the people began to die in slow motion, melting into shadows on the sidewalk. Buildings exploded, glass flew, and steel beams buckled and bent. There was no sound.

"You can see the simulation was going okay," said Bretton.

Jay wondered if the man had kids. Watching the families snuffed out like candles, he felt a sense of helplessness and fear he'd never felt before. A phrase his mom used to say popped into his head. "When you love someone, they become a hostage to fortune." He understood that now like he never had before. He had a new son.

Clinically, he noted the accuracy of the physics models. They would be the primary focus of the sim, after all. The orange-red mushroom cloud forming after the initial event was beautiful, though, in its way.

Bretton waved his hand again and things slowed down

even more. The explosions expanded almost imperceptibly, feathers of flame blooming in stop motion. The 3-D imaging in the room was perfect—crystal-clear and sharp. And suddenly the scene started missing pieces. Tourist bodies disappeared, and then part of the explosion vanished, revealing blue sky. Some of the buildings went away, then the cars, and finally the remaining people and landscape, leaving nothing but darkness.

The HPCMP liaison made a motion and they were back to the moment just after the explosion, frozen again.

Jay got it immediately. The sim was so huge that it had to use the power of more than one supercomputer, each running different pieces. At real-time speed, the effect would have been like a light going off, but in bullet-time, it was visible how each piece of the network had failed—had been switched off by *something*.

"Can I see the background AI data?" he asked.

Bretton nodded, a look of quiet approval on his face at the question. Jay had often found it useful to impress people in their own specialties, so he'd done some studies on the background HBM and AI modeling before coming over. The code that appeared to replace the landscape was the inside of the sim model—what made it work, the physics and lighting, the object scripting.

By looking at this information, they could monitor more carefully the impact of the intruding virus.

The lines of code executed rapidly as Bretton took the speed up a notch, rolling upward like parts on a conveyer belt. And then suddenly, they started to change.

"The key modeling factors just went crazy," said Bretton.

Within seconds errors began bringing down parts of the simulation.

Jay nodded. It was a virus all right. Someone had introduced it into the system, it had waited for the right moment, and then, *pow*.

Knockout.

The question was, how?

He looked at Bretton.

"I'm stumped," the man admitted. "I've been all over the I/O going back for the last year, and there's *nothing*. The transducer network routers haven't sent anything across, timed or not. They're clean."

"Physical memory?" asked Jay. "A disk? Flashmem stick?"

"Locked out without authentication and logging," Bretton said. "And smuggling one in or out would be . . . difficult."

Jay stared at the screens, thinking. There was no other way in. But something had gotten in.

The old Sherlock Holmes adage came to mind. "When you have eliminated the impossible, whatever remains, no matter how improbable, must be the truth."

There had to be some other way.

All irritation forgotten, Jay sat down and started thinking.

A locked-room mystery. Oh, my.

This looks like a job for Jay Gridley.

He smiled.

4

Abe Kent stopped at the desk to pick up ammo and head-phones. He set his shooting bag down and looked at the man behind the counter.

"Gunny."

"Colonel. Are you shooting the old Colt today, sir?"

"Yes."

"Is your ring current, sir?"

Kent smiled. "It is." Gunny was referring to the smart-gun chips, which had to be reprogrammed and checked every month. Kent didn't think much of that program. Net Force–issue weapons were all rigged with electronic chips, one in your side arm and the second in a ring, bracelet, or wristwatch. If you used your own piece on duty, you had to have it so wired. Without the ring or watch in close prox-imity to the weapon, it would not fire.

The colonel knew that was probably a good idea in some circumstances. It would sure be nice if your neigh-bor's little six-year-old girl couldn't cook one off if she came across your pistol in the bedside table. Of course, anybody with a brain wouldn't have a handgun where a little girl who didn't know what it was about could come across it. If you had guns in your house, then you needed to make sure everybody who lived there knew the safety rules about them. There weren't any kids in Kent's life, but he still kept his old slabside .45 locked in a box when it wasn't on his person.

Any technology, such as the smart-gun stuff, that added an extra possibility of failure to a pistol when it was in your hand and when you needed it to save your life? Well, that was a bad idea. Even without the smart-gun tech, guns weren't perfect. Sometimes they just misfired or otherwise malfunctioned due to their mechanical natures.

If you didn't know how to use the thing safely and couldn't keep it from falling into the wrong hands, you ought not to be carrying it. No, the only argument he'd ever heard that made even a little sense to him was that these rings would keep somebody from taking your piece off your corpse and using it to shoot at your coworkers. Even that was foolish, though, he thought. If you were dead, somebody made you that way, which meant that not only were they armed, but they were likely to have better weapons than yours, so increasing the chances of yours misfiring just when you needed it to keep them from taking it was just plain stupid.

Kent took the box of ammunition, his hearing protectors, and his gun bag, and went to his assigned lane. There were only a few shooters in the range, most of them using handguns. As he got to his lane, he saw Julio Fernandez in the next one over.

"Captain."

"Colonel. It's just Julio now, sir. I'm a civilian. I appreciate that you still let me come in to use the range, though."

"How is John? I haven't talked to him for a couple of weeks."

"He's fine. I expect you've heard about his visit to Commander Thorn."

"I heard."

"Going to be a leatherneck again," Fernandez said.

"So it seems." Kent didn't want to go too far down that road right now, so he changed the subject: "You still remember how to shoot that Beretta?"

"Yes, sir. I also remember how last time we shot together, I managed to beat you and that antique .45 of yours real good."

"Three-hundredths of a second after five screens isn't what I'd call 'real good,' Julio. I think the word you're looking for is 'barely.' "

"You thinking to win your money back, Colonel?"

"And then some."

Fernandez laughed. "Barnum was right. There is a sucker born every minute. You want to pick the scenario?"

"I wouldn't want to take advantage, since I probably practice more than you. You choose."

" 'Gunfight at Red Rock?' " Julio asked. "Twenty bucks for the match, best three of five screens?"

Kent nodded. "Number of rounds?"

"Let's keep it revolver-neutral. That's what the bad guys have. Six shots per screen."

Kent nodded. He had seven rounds in his piece, one in the barrel and six in the magazine. He had one spare magazine on his belt, his carry backup, and five more already loaded in his gun bag. He pulled the spares from his belt and bag and lined them up on the shooting bench. "Crank it in," Kent said.

He pulled his pistol from his holster, pinch-checked to be sure he had one in the pipe, then popped the magazine out, checked that, and pushed it back in. He reholstered the handgun and adjusted his headphones a little, then nodded.

"Light it when you're ready, son."

Downrange, the target computer generated an image. One moment, Kent's lane was empty, the next, the air shimmered and two Old West gunfighters stood facing him twenty feet away, hands held over their holstered six-shooters. They wore black cowboy hats and boots, black

trousers and checkered shirts, handkerchiefs tied bandanna-
style around their necks, and seemed real enough to look
at. This was a VR holographic projection, and the computer was smart enough to tell where your bullets passed
through them—assuming you shot and hit them before
they did you. Fortunately, their bullets were only pho-
tonic—

"Draw—!" one of the gunslingers yelled. That was the
start signal for this scenario.

Kent was already moving. Before the gunslinger finished speaking, Kent had pulled his model 1911, thumbed
the safety catch off, and shoved it forward, one-handed. At
this range, he didn't need to use the sights, he just pointed
the gun as he would his finger. He fired once at the pis-
toleer on the right, then shifted his arm a hair and fired
again at the one on the left. One, two—!

Both the phantoms had already cleared leather with
their own sidearms, but were still bringing them up as Kent
cooked off the second round.

When you had done this particular action five or ten
thousand times, it was almost a reflex.

"Arrgh!" one of the bad guys said. He sounded more
like a pirate than a Western desperado.

"You got me, you sidewinding varmint!" the other one
said.

Both fell.

Kent smiled. Back in the Old West, especially the frontier towns, the locals had, according to the history he'd
read, cursed worse than fleets of drunken sailors. The
foulest, most Anglo-Saxon four-letter words peppered
every conversation, and linked together in obscene strings
that would singe the hair off a Marine D.I. The image most
people had of cowboys came from old black-and-white
movies, made in the days when such language was not allowed on the silver screen. The Old West was not quaint,
save in fiction.

He checked his score screen. Two shots, two A-zone
hits, time 0.73 seconds. Not that fast for a cowboy action

fast-draw expert from a tied-down holster, but not bad from a service rig in street clothes.

He still had five rounds left, but he dropped the magazine—the floor had a rubber mat here so the magazine wasn't damaged when it hit—and shoved one of the spare magazines home in a tactical reload. He clicked the safety on and reholstered the piece.

Next to him, Fernandez said, "That one-handed point-shooting will get you in trouble at longer range, Colonel."

Kent looked at the score screen. Fernandez had also hit both his opponents, but was three-hundredths of a second slower.

"That may be," Kent said. "But at short range, it beat you."

"It's early. Get ready. Sir."

Kent grinned.

Hanging Garden Apartments
Macao, China

Wu emerged from the bathroom in a thick white terry-cloth robe, feeling cleaner and very much relaxed. The hot shower he had taken accounted for the cleanliness. Mayli, the beautiful and accomplished undercover operative he employed, accounted for the feeling of relaxation. She lay naked upon the bed, grinning at him like a well-fed cat. Her perfume, something spicy and subtle, mixed with the scent of her own musk.

Wu had a family, of course. There was his dutiful wife, who was in Beijing, probably attending to their six grandchildren. He also had two sons and a daughter, each of whom had provided him with the politically correct pair of those grandchildren.

But Wu had needs, and his wife had long ago stopped caring to adequately meet those, so he took his carnal pleasures elsewhere. Mayli there on the bed was able to

handle those needs with one hand tied behind her. Sometimes both hands tied . . .

Wu grinned at the thought. He was not without wit.

"Are you going to shower?" he asked.

"Later."

"Anything new on our computer whiz?"

She shrugged. "Yesterday he was approached by Data-
Soft U.S., via a cutout in Hong Kong, and offered a job.
Two hundred thousand dollars American a year, a car, an
apartment in Renton, Washington, profit-sharing, a medical plan. Help getting out of the country, and resident status once he arrives. A not-unattractive offer. I wouldn't
really mind living in the States as the wife of a well-paid
computer nerd."

"And what did he say to this?"

Wu moved to the bed and sat on the edge. He shucked
the robe and turned his back toward the woman. "Work on
my left shoulder a bit, would you? I strained a muscle during training."

She slid over and began to knead at his deltoid. She had
very strong and skilled hands.

She said, "He has not replied to the offer yet. But he
won't take it."

"And you know this how?"

"I told him not to."

"And he thinks this highly of you?"

"He has mentioned marriage."

"I thought you wouldn't mind living in the U.S.?"

"I wouldn't. But I told him he was worth more and
should hold out for a better offer. I will need a large house,
an automobile of my own, and an extravagant lifestyle."

He smiled. Of course.

Her fingers dug into the muscle, hard. It hurt, but it was
a good hurt.

"Ah."

"How did you hurt your shoulder?"

"Climbing the rope."

"You stay in excellent shape."

"For a man my age?"

"For a man of any age."

"You flatter me."

"Of course. That is part of what I do best. Still, it is true—you have mirrors, you know this."

He smiled. That was the thing about working with a professional. No illusions. His star was rising, and Mayli, nobody's fool, knew it. She would benefit as long as she was of use to him, and he would benefit from her, in a number of ways. It was good to know where you stood in a relationship. He did not trust her, not past a certain point, but until that place was reached, she would serve. It would not hurt to have an agent in the United States, and once he had accomplished his tasks, there was no reason why Shing could not be allowed to chase the American dollar on their shores with his new wife.

"How is that?" she asked.

He turned around and reached for her. "Better," he said.

Rue de Soie
Marne-la-Vallée
France

Merde! Merde! Merde!

Seurat threw his comset across the room, the small device making a muffled *thump* as it hit the soft leather chair he kept in the corner and tended to use mostly for such moments. Only when he was alone did he permit himself such luxury, and even then he mitigated his anger with forethought.

Replacing a comset with every bad piece of news would be shamefully wasteful, even when the news was this bad.

CyberNation had been attacked!

He hurried towards the garage, grabbing his wallet and a set of keys for the old 914 he favored for going into Paris. The small, mid-engine Porsche was easier to navigate in the narrow streets of the big city.

Thousands of CyberNation's residents had been dropped into blackness across Europe, with outages and other interruptions of service. Milo Saens, his chief security expert, had related several disturbing ramifications of the incident in addition to the most important one:

The failure was the result of sabotage.

Seurat slapped the garage door opener and jumped down the small flight of steps leading into what had once been a wine cellar, but which now included a space for his cars.

He opened the door of the 914 and slid in, jamming the key into the slot. He entered the comp code as well; a necessary evil that allowed him to drive on streets with other cars of later make.

Now the car would be recognized by the city traffic computer for what it was, and should he deviate from traffic laws in the presence of other cars, the onboard computer would force him to the side of the road.

A small smile played across his face. He'd be forced over if he *let* the computer do so. Seurat was not one to put his fate into the hands of others, safety laws or no. A carefully hidden switch on the autocomp would disable its ability to override his driving if he so chose. For the moment, he left it engaged. As with so many other facets of his life, it was useful to appear as one of the herd.

The two-liter engine roared and the acceleration pushed Seurat back in his seat as he ran through the first two gears. He lived on the new Rue de Soie—the Silk Road—part of an expensive development of both new and refurbished homes, and none of them cheap. He found it very amusing that his house was but a short trip away from Euro-Disneyland. Had it been possible, he would have bought a home on Rue de Goofy—just to irritate the traditionalists still trying to keep the language "pure."

What a waste of time and effort *that* was.

It had taken him months to find this particular 914, and even longer to restore the car to the condition in which he kept it, but the effort had been worth it.

Patience. It was all about taking the time.

The attack on CyberNation had ended. Saens, who had called on his comset, had explained that the network would be back up in minutes; had Seurat waited but a little while, he could have gotten a full briefing in a secure CyberNation chatroom without leaving his home.

But the drive to the city would give him time to think, to plan out the best response for what had happened. Like his distant ancestor, Charles Seurat liked to work deliberately and thoughtfully.

The attack had been bad. According to Saens, it had blacked out most of the continent, with tendrils of the blackout spreading to the U.S., South America, and Asia. Reports were still coming in.

Worse, prior to the actual shutdown, the attackers had spoofed servers for passwords and had removed some of the careful barriers that separated bits of CyberNation— protected chatrooms had suddenly been joined by on-line sex groups, personal information of all sorts had been dragged out into common areas, and other doors that were normally closed had opened.

It hadn't lasted long, according to Saens, but any amount of time was too long.

Throughout his life, Seurat had found that every strength held a weakness. CyberNation—with true liberty, equality, and brotherhood for all—was a nonphysical ideal. That removed most of the grime and grit of the world and made it impervious to destruction from physical attack, but its noncorporeal state made it susceptible in other ways.

Like this.

The question was not, "Who would do such a thing?" There were many who were jealous, more who were simply malicious, and there were those who were afraid of CyberNation and what it stood for. No, the question was, "Who is *capable* of such a thing?"

CyberNation had security second to none. Whoever had done this thing was more than expert.

The CyberNation leader knew that he wouldn't be

needed to repair the network—his people were already working on that.

But more than the network needed repair. Those who had lost service could lose faith—might even lose belief in the new nation that was supposed to shelter them. If the citizens of CyberNation could lose their perfect world for any reason—well, it wouldn't be perfect, then, *non?*

They would want an explanation—and satisfaction.

And so did he.

Seurat signaled to exit to the Boulevard Périphérique, the ring road that circled the center of the city, and accelerated, overtaking a large hauler. The truck driver shook his fist at Seurat as the little sports car sailed past. It was currently de rigueur to hate older fossil-fuel cars. Seurat didn't know if it was due to jealousy or environmentalism, although he suspected the former. Not everyone could afford to operate an older car.

Once on the ring road, he stayed in the right lane. The Porte d'Orleans was just one exit ahead. Another hauler was ahead of him, this one painted with signs extolling the virtues of fresh produce.

The lingering thread of his thoughts hung there, waiting. *Satisfaction.*

What would be the best way to give his people what they craved? How could he promise safety and freedom for all? He was the leader of something more than a mere nation. For a moment he saw himself on the spectrum of world leaders: How it must have been throughout the ages for such, trying to satisfy the people they led, promising them what they needed, while trying to deny reality. To offer safety, even where it did not exist.

He supposed that they had found what he did: Sometimes it worked, sometimes it did not. *C'est la vie.*

Ah, yes, vive la CyberNation—*when it works!*

This had to be resolved, and quickly. They had an enemy, one who was adept enough to damage them. This could not be allowed.

He must be found.

And destroyed.

Ahead finally sat the Nouvel building, a postmodern masterpiece that he and the other leaders of CyberNation had chosen for its aesthetics as much as for its functionality and fully integrated net-backbone.

Nearby, parked under the light of a street lamp, was a newsvan.

Ah. No surprise there. The media was ever alert. Like sharks, they came at the merest whiff of blood in the water.

Well, no matter. Someone had handed him a sour lemon, and he was going to make a refreshing drink from it.

He slowed his car and, instead of going into his private underground parking spot, he pulled over on the street outside the building. As he stepped from the car, lights came on from near the newsvan, forcing him to squint slightly as he walked toward them. He squared his shoulders and smiled. He would spin them a story, and they would serve him as he would have it.

Hanging Garden Apartments
Macao, China

Lying naked and sweaty upon the bed, Mayli looked up at Locke as he dressed. She smiled. "You know that Wu would probably kill you if he knew we were doing this."

Locke smiled in return. "Me? I doubt it. Besides, I am certain that he does know. General Wu did not rise to his current position by being a fool. I imagine that he is having you and me watched—I would in his place. I'd guess he doesn't care what we do together—as long as we do our jobs."

Her smiled vanished, turned into a pout.

He laughed. "What? You think he is so jealous of your favors that he would kill his partner for indulging in them?

Wu is a pragmatist. Nothing you and I did today will lessen what you and he do tomorrow. If anything, it might make it better—I've shown you some tricks even you didn't know. Those would be to his benefit, no?"

She sat up suddenly and threw a pillow at him. "Beast!"

He laughed as he reached out and caught the pillow in one hand. "That's not what you said earlier."

She smiled. "I cannot stay angry with you, can I?"

"No. I am too lovable."

"No, not lovable. But . . . something."

Locke tossed the pillow back at her, not hard, and went back to tying his tie. He had heard that plenty of times: *Why do you fancy me? I don't know, it's hard to say, exactly. . . .*

As for Wu, Locke was not only sure he was having him followed, he was pretty sure this apartment, for which Wu paid, was bugged. Audio at the least, maybe video. Locke hadn't bothered to look for the microphones or cameras, but in Wu's position, he would have made very sure he could verify what Mayli told him about Shing—at least enough of it to feel some confidence. There was probably a recording of Shing and Mayli rolling around on the bed in Wu's desk, and no doubt he had watched such a thing if it existed.

Locke's own performance with Mayli? Certainly nothing to feel insecure about—and no doubt at all much superior to Shing's rootings . . .

"When will you return?"

He finished the Windsor knot and straightened the gray silk tie. Against the lighter gray of his tailored shirt and darker silk jacket, the tie was perfect. There were still some excellent tailors in Hong Kong, and with the British gone for decades, easier to get one whose work you liked. A five-thousand-dollar suit didn't look that much better than a three-thousand-dollar one to most, but those who knew such things could spot the differences. Clothes might not make the man, but among the rich and powerful, they were badges that identified you as somebody with taste and means.

"I don't know," he said. "But maybe I'll call you when I do. If I can't find anybody better."

By the time she had thrown the pillow at him again, he was already on his way to the door.

5

Jay Gridley sat in the back of an open-wall ragtop jitney with fifty other passengers; an oppressive, cloying, heat and humidity wrapped the bus like a sodden blanket. Had they been moving, there would at least have been some hot wind, but the vehicle was, like the hundreds of others he could see on the road, jammed to a full stop. Even the people on bicycles and Segways weren't moving, and the air was as still as a tomb.

Around him, the passengers talked to each other in Malay or Bahasa or English, apparently unaffected by their lack of progress.

Jay shook his head. Whatever VR scenario he conjured, the military's super-computers were not easy to navigate. The hardware, software, protocols—everything was a pain. Even with full access, delving into these things was as difficult and complex as anything Jay had ever done. The place was a rat's nest of back alleys and twisted roads, with buildings looming over the narrow streets, far too many people—read information packets—and a host of other complicating factors Jay hadn't even begun to sort out.

His respect for Major Bretton ratcheted up several notches. If the man could negotiate this mess at all, he was good.

Next to him a local man, probably seventy, and dressed in a white short-sleeved shirt and a sarong, smiled, showing better teeth than Jay expected.

"Selamat. You Thai?" the man asked. His voice was raspy and full of phlegm.

As it happened, that was partially true. "Yes."

"You have children? I have five—four sons and a daughter, plus nine grandchildren."

"I have a son. Only one."

The old man laughed, a cackle. "You young. Plenty of time."

He pulled a cigarette from his shirt pocket and offered it to Jay. "Smoke?"

Jay declined.

The old man lit the coffin nail and inhaled deeply. Gray tendrils rose in the hot and still air. The smoking explained the raspy, phlegmy sound to old man's voice. Even though Jay had created the scenario, he sometimes fell into a kind of schizophrenic state where things for which he was responsible, such as the old man's voice, came as a surprise to him, as if somebody else had built the program.

"Is it always like this?" Jay asked. He waved to encompass the gridlocked traffic.

The old man shrugged. "This a good day. Some times, much worse."

Great. Just what he needed to hear.

The old man looked out through the open sides of the jitney. "Rain is coming soon. Cool things off."

Jay nodded. How bad was it when a tropical storm, with lightning, thunder, and rain blasting down in sheets angled almost horizontal, was something you were looking *forward* to?

Ick.

This was going to be a long, long day. . . .

DMZ, *Just North of the 38th Parallel*
North Korea

The U.S. Air Force was doing a terrific job—the thousands of smart antimine bomblets, TDO-A2s, known unofficially as "garden weasels," had cleared major pathways in the minefields on the NK side of the wire, so when the new M10A3 gasoline-powered heavy tanks began roaring across the line, they were able to make good speed. The tanks' 105mm cannons added noise and smoke to the already shrouded battlefield, but the tin can drivers didn't need to see anything outside their sensor screens—fog, rain, smoke, darkness, none of these were impediments to the electronic gear the heavies carried.

Overhead, the scores of fighters and bombers continued to roar—no need for stealth now—dropping huge payloads, ranging from the ten-ton BLU-84a "Big Blue" daisy-cutters that would chop down enemy soldiers like a lawn mower in dry grass, to the GBU-27B smart bombs from the F-111s that could find a chimney and go down it like Santa Claus bringing coal to the bad kids, to the BU-28 five-thousand-pound bunkerbusters.

That section of North Korea was, for the moment, the most dangerous place on the planet, more so than an active volcano. You might outrun lava. No way could you outrun 20mm machine-gun rounds from a jet fighter chasing you.

Yes, the North Koreans had a huge army, and much armor and all, but with the full force of the United States military brought to bear all at once, there was no way anybody on this planet was going to stop it—

Except that it did stop.

Just like somebody switching off a lamp . . .

*   *   *

The Pentagon
Washington, D.C.

Thorn removed the VR headset and blew out a sigh, still astonished by the power of the simulation. It was as if he had been there, standing just behind the action, hearing and seeing and feeling the thrum of all-out war, smelling the gunpowder and cooked earth. . . .

General Roger Ellis, U.S. Marines, head of Special Projects Command—SpecProjCom—for the Pentagon, and Thorn's new boss, leaned back in his chair and looked at him.

"Very impressive," Thorn said.

"Yeah, up until the point that it shut down," Ellis said. "That simulation took a boatload of expensive log-in time and the lion's share of attention from a cross-linked pair of supercomputers to run, and somebody killed it like stepping on a fire ant on the sidewalk. It happened yesterday. You can see why the Head of the Joint Chiefs isn't happy."

Thorn nodded. Ellis had a Southern twang in his voice. Texas, maybe. "Fire ant" had come out more like "fahr aynit."

They were in a sim-room adjacent to Ellis's office at the Pentagon, no windows, a bland space done in the same institutional colors as much of the rest of the place. The building was a maze—you needed the guard/guide they issued you at the door to find your way around, even with the flow charts. As dull an office building as there was, and this a room to doze off in, Thorn thought, though certainly not during a VR ride like the one he had just taken.

Ellis was in his late fifties, but white-haired and with a pale, lined face, looking ten years older than he was. He was in uniform, and one that had been well cut by an attentive tailor to minimize his belly, which, even so, was well on its way to winning the war with his trousers. What Thorn's grandfather used to call "Dunlap's Disease"—his belly had done lapped over his belt . . .

"Of course, the expense doesn't hold a candle to what a real-world exercise like this would cost—not to mention that we couldn't hardly practice it against the North Koreans or the Chinese. Still, a million here, a million there, and like Dirksen used to say, pretty soon it starts to add up to real money."

Ellis looked at Thorn. "This is what you people do, run down computer geeks who screw things up. This was a dangerous security breach. Can you fix this?"

Thorn nodded. "If it can be done, our people can do it. Though you are looking at two different problems here, General. Finding and collecting the party responsible is one; repairing the software is another. My people will look for the hacker, and maybe we can help some with the repairs, but it's your scenario programmers who will mostly have to resolve that."

"Commander, I guarantee that if you bring us whoever did this, we'll get him to tell us everything we need to know to fix it. And then some."

"Yes, sir."

"So, you got your techno guys on it?"

"My best man is already working with the project liaison. More people will be put on it as soon as they have something to go on."

Ellis grinned. "Welcome to the Marines, Commander Thorn. Colonel Kent is still in charge of your tactical guys?"

"Yes, sir."

"Tell him to drop by and see me when he gets a chance."

"I will."

"All right. We have some chain-of-command things to hash out—I'll have my paper- and electron-pushers contact yours—and some other miscellaneous stuff, but the main thing is, you jump on this problem like ducks on a June bug and catch this sucker. Everything else we'll work out as we go."

"Understood, General."

"Good. Go do it. Keep me posted."

As the guard escorted Thorn toward the exit, the head of

Net Force considered his first interview with his new boss. So far, so good. How long it would be before the other shoe dropped, he'd just have to wait and see.

Paradise Road
Eden

The temperature was warm enough so that you could take your shirt off and be comfortable, but not so warm that you got too hot just walking around. Maybe around eighty or so. There were some high clouds in the pure blue sky, and a gentle breeze that ruffled the trees a little.

A manicured lawn stretched in front of the cottage, short grass that felt great under bare feet. A white-painted wooden picket fence surrounded the lawn and house. A medium-sized dog, a party-colored mutt, slept in the shade of a big oak tree next to the house, feet twitching as he chased imaginary rabbits in his dreams.

Framed in the big kitchen window, working on lunch, were three gorgeous women: a tall, busty, blonde, wearing a string bikini top; a redhead with hair down to the middle of her back, in a tube-top; and a dark-skinned, curly-haired brunette without any clothes at all covering her perfect breasts. The trio looked out through the window, smiled, and waved.

The hammock was strung between two sycamore trees; next to the hammock was a small table upon which was an ice chest full of bottled beer, an appetizer pizza piled high with three kinds of meat and two cheeses, and a humidor full of good Cuban cigars.

Mounted on the tree above the foot of the hammock was a holoproj set, and the images of the players in the championship American-style football game danced in the shade. Fourth quarter, two minutes to go, and the score was tied, 28–28.

The cheerleaders, young women, all of them flawless—
and bare from the waist up—were going wild. Now and
again, the camera would show them in slo-mo, so the
bouncing was particularly interesting. . . .

Man. Was this heaven, or what?

Bam!

The house, lawn, dog, beer—all of it—vanished. The
idyllic scene went black, in the blink of an eye. A moment
later, the blackness was replaced by flames, and a scene
right out of Dante's Inferno. Tortured souls writhed in the
eternal fires, screams of pain filled the air, and everywhere
was smoke and stinking sulfur. . . .

CyberNation HQ
Paris, France

Charles Seurat shook his head. "Quite a shock," he said.

Georges, the programmer, shook his head. "The kind of
man—or sometimes woman—who usually elects this particular cottage scenario is generally working-class, what
the Americans call 'blue-collar,' and the abrupt shift from
paradise to inferno is particularly scary. Most of them have
had religious upbringings, and in that teaching, the scenario they picked is not, ah, consistent with Heaven. To
have the fantasy replaced with Hell is not only a jolt, it is,
on some level, what many of them believe they deserve.
Despite our assurances that it was a glitch, and even offers
of free time, we have lost customers because of it."

"How many?"

Georges shrugged. "Hard to say for sure. We know
those who complained numbered only in the dozens. How
many just dropped their service and left without saying?
Who knows? Not everybody responds to the exit survey."

Seurat shook his head. "And you have not found the
source?"

"Just like others. The trail bounces from several satellites and then vanishes. He is very good, this hacker."

"Well, we ought to have somebody who is better. This kind of attack is unacceptable. One man!"

Georges was quiet, but Seurat sensed that he had something to say. "Yes?"

"Two things, *mon capitaine*. First, CyberNation is not the only target. We have heard from reliable sources that the United States military's war scenarios have likewise been attacked with some success."

"I have heard these rumors. What of them?"

"It means that we may have a common enemy. And thus, perhaps, an enemy of our enemy who might be of some help."

"And what is the other thing?"

Georges hesitated.

"Go on, spit it out."

"We cannot assume that our hacker is alone. He may be part of a cabal. Or worse."

Seurat thought about that for a moment. "Sponsored by a government, you mean." It was not a question.

"*Oui*. CyberNation offers a threat to traditional geopolitical entities. If we succeed in our aim—*when* we succeed in them—our power will rival that of nation states. No one ever gives up that kind of power willingly."

Seurat nodded. Yes. Georges had a point. A hacker backed by a government would have many more resources than one sitting alone in his room using his personal computer. Now that he thought of it, such a premise made more sense, that the attacks were backed by such resources. But—who? Which country?

The most adept would be, of course, the United States. But if they were being attacked themselves, unless it was a clever feint designed to throw CyberNation off their trail, then that would seem to rule them out. They could be very devious, the Americans, but from what he had heard about the cost to their military due to their computer disruptions, that seemed too steep a price. Even if CyberNation knew the U.S. was responsible, they were in no position to start an all-out computer war.

Not yet.

This needed looking into further. Seurat had contacts in the States, people who ought to be able to find out more. Time to use these contacts. He did not like being a target, no matter who the shooter might be. . . .

Locke sat in his rented truck—one that had been made to look like a plumber's vehicle—and pretended to write a work order. The front door to CyberNation's HQ was visible in the truck's large, outside rearview mirror, and this was what Locke watched while ostensibly filling out the paperwork. The good thing about pretending to be a plumber—and he wore an old coverall with the word *plombier* stenciled on the back—was that people paid you little attention if your truck sat parked in a neighborhood for hours. With the French, if they saw you sitting in the truck doing nothing, they assumed you were goofing off, and dismissed that with a Gallic shrug. Lazy *bâtard, oui?*

Locke smiled at the image. He had little French to speak of, enough to have dinner or catch a taxi, and it would not have mattered if he was adept in the language— the French looked down their long noses at everybody who was not them, no matter how well they might speak their tongue. Them and their foolish quest to keep the language pure.

The CyberNation building had been a hive of activity since he had arrived, and the comings and goings of high-level employees had a certain frantic nature that Locke took to mean that Shing's machinations had, at least to some degree, worked.

Plus he had bribed low-level employees—guards, secretaries, and the man who delivered lunches—and while the precise nature of the problem was not something upon which they could report, they could definitely confirm that something was going on—and that CyberNation's leaders weren't happy about it. No, not happy at all.

Locke had reports from the United States that the military had also suffered under Shing's hand, and he would, in due course, travel there and check it out personally.

He had to give Shing credit, though. So far, it seemed as if he had been able to do everything he had claimed. Of course, that had to continue for the greater plan to unfold properly. If Shing was stopped, there was a backup plan, a more hands-on method that Locke would implement, but he hoped to avoid that. Not because he was worried that it wouldn't work, but the risks entailed would require time and energy better spent elsewhere.

A policeman walked by on the sidewalk. He looked at the truck.

Locke smiled and nodded at the *flick,* then went back to his pretend paperwork. He was obviously not pure French to look at, and the policeman apparently did not wish to talk to him and suffer the expected butchery of speech by a low-life foreigner.

Arrogance was a pain, even if it was useful. Locke could hardly wait to get to the U.S. They were so much more easygoing over there.

He caught movement in the mirror. Ah. It was Seurat, the czar of CyberNation, emerging from the building. As he did, a limo pulled up and the Frenchman entered it.

Locked started the truck's engine. From what he had learned, Seurat was an automobile buff—he liked to drive. That he was not in one of his sports cars probably meant he was, as Locke had also heard, traveling. A fan of fine cars did not leave an expensive vehicle in an airport or train station parking lot exposed to the elements and the possible dings from the carelessly opened doors of other drivers.

Company presidents traveled all the time, and probably this was no more than a business trip; still, given the problems CyberNation was currently facing, it was not a bad idea to at least check it out. Knowledge was indeed power.

The limousine pulled away from the curb, and Locke followed it into the afternoon's commute.

6

The Pentagon
Washington, D.C.

Abe Kent had long ago come to terms with most of his
fears. Not that he had lost them—there were still plenty of
things that could worry him, if he let them: Going blind, or
senile, or stroking out into paralysis, these were fears he
still carried, but he had learned to control them rather than
letting his fears control him.

The way he dealt with them was to pay attention and not
deliberately do things that might cause them, at least as
much as he could. He ate well, stayed in shape, and had
routine physicals. He didn't drink much alcohol, save for a
little wine or beer now and then, and had given up smoking
his pipe twenty years back. There were no guarantees, of
course, and in the end something was going to kill him, but
a quick and sudden end didn't scare him. He had come
close to that often enough that he had been, as far as he was
concerned, living on borrowed time for most of his life.

He had been a good Marine. Would have made general
by now if he hadn't been quite as good—if he'd been pre-

pared to let things slide in ways he hadn't been willing to do. So, the worst thing that Roger Ellis could do to him was kick him out of his job, and when he looked back over his shoulder, there was not a lot he regretted. As a result, Kent wasn't afraid of this meeting.

Still, there was a twinge of . . . unease . . . as he approached the door of the Pentagon office with his guard and guide, who was also a Marine. A kid, maybe twenty-eight, and a sergeant, who knew who he was.

It had started to drizzle on the way over from Quantico. Maybe that was an omen.

"Here we are, sir. I'll be back to collect you when you are done."

"Thank you, Sergeant."

"Semper fi, sir."

Kent grinned at the kid. "You know it, son."

Ellis had put on a few pounds, and looked paler than when Kent had last seen him, about five years ago. Ellis had been a colonel then, making general a couple of months later. Kent had sent him a congratulations card.

Sent him a second card when he got bumped up another star a year ago. No point in being bitter about it.

"Abe, how are you?" Ellis asked.

"Fine, General."

"Come in, have a seat."

Kent did so.

Ellis liked to beat around the bush a little before he got down to business, and the two men exchanged did-you-hears and guess-who-dieds and such for a couple of minutes. Finally, Ellis arrived at the point:

"So, tell me about Net Force. The military arm."

"We have some good people. Lot of regulars from the service. John Howard put together a sharp team. Good training, good gear, good support, both from the Guard and the Net Force Commander."

"Never thought I'd see the day when you'd be in the Guard," Ellis said.

"Well. I'd pretty much come to the end of the road in

the Corps, hadn't I? Another few years as a doddering, su-perannuated colonel, teaching at a college somewhere, running some logistics kiosk, that was how I was going to end my career. When John Howard called me, it seemed like a way to do something worth doing with the last of my active duty time." He paused. "I never was much good as a desk commander."

Ellis nodded. "You angered some very shiny brass, Abe. You know that. What did you expect?"

Kent shook his head. "I knew what would happen, Gen-eral. It's just that I couldn't let the consequences affect my decision. You know what went down, sir. What would you have done, in my place?"

Ellis pondered that for a moment. "Well, I'd like to say I'd have done the same thing. The Marines ought not be baby-sitters for the sons of rich elected officials." He paused. "But I've always been more, ah . . . flexible . . . than you. I think I'd have caught the drift and done some fast talking. Hell, even after you knocked the kid's teeth out, you could have bowed and kissed a ring or two and they would have let it slide."

"Probably."

"But you didn't."

"No, sir."

"If you had it to do over again, you'd do the same thing, wouldn't you?"

This was, Kent knew, a loaded question. Ellis was trying to find out which way he was going to jump if put under pressure. The smart answer would be to say, "No." That he had come to see the error of his ways, and that what the Corps wanted was more important than any sense of per-sonal honor or pride one of its colonels might feel. That was the smart answer.

Kent said, "Yes, sir, I'd do it exactly the same."

Ellis grinned. "I'm happy to see you haven't lost your backbone, Abe. Me, I'm a political animal. I'll bend if the breeze is strong enough, but I want a man with courage in the trenches when push comes to shove."

"It's a risk, of course, using me. You realize that, sir."

Ellis nodded. "Yes. But let me tell you a little story."

The general glanced over at a framed photograph on his desk. From where Kent sat, he couldn't tell if it was a 3-D holoproj or not, but the frame looked like an old-fashioned 2-D still shot. "My parents used to have a dog, a big old German shepherd named King. One night, my father got up in the middle of the night to go pee and he looked down and saw a big splotch of blood on the carpet in the bedroom. He went looking for King and found him in the kitchen, a puddle of blood on the floor."

Ellis looked back at the colonel. "The dog had a nosebleed. My mother got up, and she and my father ran around with towels and cotton balls, wiping things up and trying to get the bleeding stopped. Only they couldn't. There wasn't an all-night vet clinic anywhere around, so they sat up all night with the dog, petting and trying to calm him, catching the dripping blood with a towel. Early in the morning, they took King to the local vet's office, and waited until it opened. My father sat on the stoop outside the office with the dog's head on his lap, the blood soaking into his trousers. The vet finally got the bleeding stopped, but since there was no sign of any injury that could have cause his nose to go off like that, and it had never happened before, he wanted to run some tests. He did. They set my old man back four hundred and fifty dollars."

Ellis paused, then gave the colonel a little smile. "What they found, Abe, was that the dog had had a nosebleed. There was nothing major wrong with him that could have caused it. It might never happen again. A four-hundred-and-fifty-dollar nosebleed."

He smiled again, then shook his head. "But my parents didn't begrudge the money. The dog was part of the family; they loved it in the same way they'd loved the children when we'd lived at home. King slept at the foot of their bed; they took him for walks, and in the back of the car when they went out. As much as they were his pack, he was their dog."

He paused again. "So what I am saying, Colonel, is that it works both ways. When you have people who are loyal, you owe them that in return."

Kent nodded.

"You run your unit the way it needs to be run. We'll do the paperwork, get the chain of command sorted out, all that, but—welcome back to the Corps. I'll try to keep the sticklers off your back as best I can." Ellis stood, and put his hand out.

Kent came to his feet and extended his own hand.

"Thank you, sir," Kent said. And he was surprised at how good it felt to hear Ellis say what he'd said. Back in the Corps.

Home.

Obstacle Course
People's Army Base Training Annex
Macao, China

The day was warm, and made for much sweat. The humidity was such that the sweat evaporated very slowly, offering little cooling.

Wu had never been a gifted athlete; rather, he had been dogged in his determination. He learned how to pace himself. Like the mythical race between the tortoise and the hare, in which the slower creature could only win if the faster one faltered, Wu became adept at being steady. In a short sprint, unless your opponent pulled a hamstring or fell and broke an ankle, steadiness was not enough. But in a much longer contest, the opportunities for an opponent's misfortune were greater.

As Wu clambered up over the wooden wall, using the inset pegs for hand- and footholds, he reflected upon the many pitfalls a smart tortoise could lay for a dull hare.

Wu had read Sun Tzu's *Art of War* enough times that he had much of it memorized. The Japanese swordsman Miyamoto Musashi's work, *A Book of Five Rings,* was another work that Wu knew and understood. A man who stood on a hill and saw danger approaching had an advantage over one who walked around a curve in the road and ran into it surprised. Forewarned was forearmed.

Wu topped the barrier and slid down the other side. Ahead, a long and thick snarl of razor wire covered the ground like a low roof, leaving a gap under it less than a meter from the dirt. The snarl was twenty meters long. One could crawl on one's belly or lie upon one's back and scoot along under it, pushing with one's feet and wiggling. The back method was a hair faster for most, and easier on the elbows. But you could not see ahead as well, and once you cleared the wire, you were, for a few seconds, lying upon your back. Wu attacked this obstacle on his belly and suffered the greater discomfort. He had long ago learned that the first to shoot did not always win. Accuracy was more important than speed.

He smiled as he recalled the recording he had seen of Locke and Mayli making love. There was a man who knew all about sex, Wu had to give him that. He had learned things watching, and it would be interesting to try these techniques out.

But now was not the time to be thinking of such things. A man distracted on the field of battle would likely not live to regret it.

He dropped to the ground and began to crawl. Ahead of him, he saw the feet of an officer essaying the obstacle, toes down, also a belly-crawler.

Being able to see a wide swath, the larger picture, had advantages. There were times when wide and shallow served better than narrow and deep. The ability to see breadth and depth together was Wu's gift. Such was necessary for a general in battle. Small-picture men very often died with eyes gone wide at an attack from an unexpected quarter.

The dirt was hard-packed from all the bodies that had dragged themselves over it. Despite the recent rain, the ground gave not at all. It was like crawling on asphalt. Even under his coverall with its padded elbows and knees, it was not a pleasant sensation.

At the end of the snarl, the ground opened out. You could turn over, but rising any higher than you had been under the wire could be fatal. Today, only the lasers were operating, and sticking an arm or your head up would get you a red dot lighting upon you like a weightless fly. On testing days when soldiers who would join the elite troops crawled here en masse, the laser lights were replaced by machine-gun fire. Every tenth round was a tracer, and you could see how close the bullets passed above you. Over the years, men had died during live-fire exercises.

Wu felt no sympathy for those who had done so. A soldier who panicked here, where the bullets would not drop below a ruler-straight line a meter from the ground? This would not be a man with whom you wished to risk your life in the field where there were no such constraints.

Wu cleared the wire and continued his crawl as if he were still under the jagged-toothed roof. Fifty meters ahead were the ropes—thick hemp lines as big around as his wrist, and you had to climb up them seven meters to reach a platform.

Here was where upper-body physical strength offered an advantage. Wu had long ago learned to use his legs and feet to assist his hands. A strong man could climb the dangling rope using his hands alone, faster than Wu could do his inchworm shinny. There was a time when Wu had done it that way. Even now, he could still manage it—but that was not wise.

Wu had been taking the long view for many years. He had learned long ago there was little value in demonstrating one's abilities to impress others. The ropes ahead were not the last obstacle. Others that needed muscle lay ahead, and pacing was important. Wu had learned how to fight smarter, not harder. Arriving at one's goal first but exhausted was not the formula for victory.

Wu smiled again, and continued crawling toward the ropes.

University Park, Maryland

Thorn's arm and shoulder were already aching, but he still had thirty more cycles to go with the *katana*. He stood in front of the mirror in his home *salle,* the wooden sheath of the Japanese weapon at his left hip placed so the cutting edge was up, held in place by a karate-style cloth belt. The sheath was lacquered a shiny jet; the blade, nearly mirror-bright, had the patterns and clay-temper line that identified the sword as one of the traditional folded-steel weapons lovingly created by a master craftsman. This particular weapon, one Thorn had only just acquired a month ago, wore a handle of pebbled manta-ray skin, under the tradi-tional diamond-wrap silk cord, the butt capped with bronze, and an iron *tsuba,* or guard. It was of the New Sword period—"New" being a relative term, since it had been made in Musashi Province by Korekazu, or one of his students, four hundred years ago.

Under the handle, which was held in place by a bamboo peg, inscribed in Japanese characters upon the tang, was the name of the smith, the year the blade was made, and a phrase that Thorn had been told translated to "one fortu-nate day in February, this blade was made" along with the surname of the original owner. Below that, there was an-other inscription that said "three-body." This latter was, Thorn had learned, the number of men, stacked one upon another, that the sword had cleaved through during its sharpness test. It did not indicate whether those men had been alive or dead when the test had been done; apparently, both were commonly used. . . .

The folded Damascus-style steel was relatively flexible, with the edge tempered to a harder state. This gave the blade great cutting qualities, better than that of many modern steels. Thorn had seen a vid once, an old rip from a home shopping channel, in which the salesman was demonstrating a stainless-steel copy of a *katana*. He talked about how sturdy it was, and to show that, whacked the spine on the table in front of him several times.

On the last whack, the blade snapped in half, and the broken part flew up and stabbed the man in the biceps.

Newer did not always mean better. . . .

One of the big advantages of having money was that you could buy such things as this treasure. It had cost as much as a new Mercedes, and with care could be around another four hundred years.

Thorn smiled. It would be interesting to see how well an eight-hundred-year-old Mercedes ran. . . .

He took a deep breath and tried to ignore the burn in his deltoids. Relaxing as much as he could, he reached across his body with his right hand. He tried to allow his consciousness to expand, to achieve a total awareness the Japanese called *zanshin*. Such was the goal of an *iaido* practitioner using the live blade.

In Japanese, *do* meant "way." This was different from the more warlike arts, which were usually known as *jutsu*. *Iaido* was not an ancient art, according to what Abe Kent had taught him, but a term that came into being in the early 1930s. The parent art, *iaijutsu*, had been around for many centuries, but since, as in Western fencing, killing people with a sword these days was more or less frowned upon in polite society, the killing arts had evolved. . . .

There were all kinds of formalities to *iaido*—ranging from detailed instructions on how to clean the blade, and precisely how to tie the string of the bag in which the sword was carried, to how to stand, sit, bow—everything. But there were only four parts to *iaido* once you were ready to move: the draw, the cut, the shaking of blood, and the return to the sheath. Kent had told him the Japanese names—*nukisuki, kiritsuke, chiburui,* and *noto*—but had also said that the names weren't important.

The goal was simple: A master swordsman became one

with the blade. After countless hours of practice, the idea was that there would be no conscious thought involved when action was required. One moment, you stood facing your imaginary opponents, the next, the sword was in your hand and you cut them down. The moment after that, you shook the blood from your blade and put it away. All without raising your heartbeat . . .

The samurai sword was primarily a slashing rather than a thrusting weapon, though it could be used as such, and very much unlike a foil, épée, or saber in weight, balance, or effectiveness. Yes, a master fencer of the French, Italian, or Spanish schools would almost certainly stab a master *iaido*-ist first, a straight-line thrust being faster than a broad slash. In a match, with buttoned weapons, this would be enough. However, in a real duel, a stab would probably not be instantly fatal. Your opponent could be dying, but still able to move, and the result of such a situation against a man with a razor-sharp *katana* and the knowledge and determination to use it would most likely be *ai-uchi*— mutual slaying. To give that first thrust, you would expose yourself to the return cut. Mutual slaying was an accepted goal for the Japanese—the way of the samurai, the saying went, is found in death.

Historically, Western swordsmen generally wanted to pink their opponents, kill them if necessary, and walk away. If all you wanted to do was commit suicide, you could jump off a high bridge. If a man was willing to die to take you with him, that gave such a man, Thorn thought, a decided advantage.

He drew the sword, brought it up and over his head, and in the doing, grabbed the handle with his left hand behind the right. It was a two-handed weapon, and the pivot-style grip allowed for great power. He brought the sword down in a cut. You could take a man's head off with such a strike. Or, in the case of this very blade, cut through a stack of bodies three deep. An adept with such a weapon and willing to die using it would be a formidable opponent. Not somebody you'd want to screw around with.

Thorn moved the blade to his right, released his left hand's grip, then did a wrist-twirl that spun the sword in a downward circle. He added a snapping, slinging motion that ended the twirl with the blade's tip pointed at the ground.

Still trying to stay relaxed, he turned the sheath sideways with his left hand, brought the blade up and across his body, the spine toward him, and touched the mouth of the sheath with the back ridge just below the guard. He drew the sword across his body to his right, keeping his left thumb and forefinger lightly pinched over the blade—this was to remove any lingering traces of blood—until the point reached the scabbard's opening. He pushed the handle forward, away from himself, and lined the blade up, then gently slid it home, until the brass friction plug just ahead of the guard snugged tight. He twisted the sheath back to edge-up position, removed his right hand, then bowed.

Seventy-one. Only twenty-nine more, this session. And, according to Kent, maybe ten thousand or so repetitions to get to the point where he was beginning to get comfortable with the process.

Thorn grinned. He had a *long* way to go. Still, there was something in the simple motions. Thorn knew that "simple" didn't mean "easy," any more than "complex" meant "hard," but even after only a few months of practice, it was already beginning to feel much more comfortable. Which, when you started waving a razor-sharp blade around, was certainly a good idea. . . .

7

Department of Defense's High Performance Computer
Modernization Program
New Pentagon Annex
Washington, D.C.

For a man of lesser technical skill, creating scenarios for
VR could take away valuable time better spent on the problem that needed to be solved. Jay, who had been among the
best in the biz for years, didn't have that worry. He had a
shelf piled high with stock scenarios, figuratively speaking,
and he could always grab one and plug it in. You built stock
when things were slow and you had time to get it right. And
if you couldn't get it right, why bother? Grab some commercial product, light it, and ride somebody else's train. . . .

Not *this* boy, no, sir, nohow, no, thank you!

Jay grinned as he slipped into the VR gear. The mesh,
the casters, the feelware, it was all getting better and better
every year. A man suited in full sensory mode could see,
hear, smell, taste, and touch things in a VR scenario. It still
wasn't as good as RW in a lot of ways, but some of it came
awfully close.

Jay had brought his personal gear to the military annex—he wasn't keen on wearing somebody else's sweaty,
non-custom-fit stuff. If they were worried about him somehow hiding information in the suit's system, he could leave
it here—he had two more sets just like it, one at home, one
at Net Force HQ.

It was true that the military systems had their private
gestalt, but applying his own scenario to them was doable,
if not as easy as interfacing with civilian stuff. He grinned
again and shook his head. You didn't throw a pebble out in
front of Smokin' Jay Gridley and expect him to trip and fall
on his face.

The biggest problem was, he had to be here physically
to do it, since there was supposedly no way to access the
systems from without. Which, of course, was clearly
wrong, since somebody had apparently gotten in somehow
and bollixed things up pretty well. And if they hadn't gotten in from outside, then there was some social engineering going on, and it had been an inside job. Finding and
closing the open and hidden door was what needed to happen. That was Jay's job. If it turned out the bad guy was
one of the military's own? That wasn't Jay's problem.

Rigged at last, Jay called up a new scenario, one he had
just finished building a few weeks ago. Seemed like a good
time to try this one out. . . .

Aboard the Warship HMS Riggs
Somewhere in the Caribbean

"There she is, sir, off the starboard bow." The first officer's
British intonation was crisp and properly deferential.

The air was full of the scents of salt and sunbaked oak
and warm tar. Well, creosote for tar, actually, which was
close enough.

Captain Jay Gridley, of His Majesty's Royal Navy, nodded. He raised his polished brass spyglass and searched for

the target. It took a while to locate it—the field of vision in
these old scopes was terrible . . . ah, there it was.

The pirate's ship flew the Jolly Roger, the skull and
crossed bones leering in the bright tropical sunshine.

"There's a squall off our port, sir," the officer said.

Jay lowered the telescope. "Yes, Redbeard will certainly
make for that, hoping to hide. Well, we will not allow that
to happen, will we?"

"No, sir. Of course not."

Jay laughed softly. He loved the British Navy. At least
the fictional historical version he had created, which was
admittedly a combination of Horatio Hornblower and Captain Blood. The real Navy during this period had not been
quite so dashing. Men on board a wooden ship in the Caribbean were sweaty, seldom-washed, and brutal. An educated and relatively refined captain, who might while away
an evening playing his violin or with chess, could have a
man flogged for almost any reason, and did so often, from
what Jay could determine. There were times when actual
history was better, and times when the fantasy was more
fun. Besides, in fantasy, Jay didn't have to get the names
and details exact—or spot-on, as the Limeys would
say. . . .

The three-masted *Riggs* had made full sail, and the rig-
ging creaked under the driving, hot breeze, the canvas and
lines stretching and straining as the vessel cut through the
sea in pursuit of the dreaded Redbeard, a man who had
plundered fat merchant ships for far too long. . . .

There had been several nasty pirates called "Redbeard."
Jay had also heard of Blackbeard and Bluebeard. He wondered if there had ever been a Blondbeard? Did they call a
man who shaved Nobeard?

He smiled, then shook his head. No matter. In this scenario, the information that Jay chased lay just ahead, cast
in the form of a pirate ship. The *Riggs* was faster, better
armed, and, because Jay had made it, better crewed. They
would run the pirates down, board and capture them, and
then make them talk.

His first officer interrupted Jay's thoughts: "We'll be within range soon, sir."

The weather was freshening. The salt spray splashed harder, driven by the herald winds of the approaching rain-squall. The pirates were hoping to get to the rain before the *Riggs* ran them down, to hide in the weather.

"Bring her about, Mr. Smee." Jay almost laughed every time he said his first officer's name, but managed to keep a straight face most of the time.

"Yes, sir."

They would line the ship up for a broadside. The pirate ship would strike her colors and surrender, or they would be bloody sorry. Har!

Oops. That was the pirates' expression. British Naval officers were more articulate. They had come up with such terms as "square meal," "son of a gun," and "no room to swing a cat," this last being for the cat-o'-nine-tails used to flog crewmen whether they deserved it or not. Wouldn't be any of that on Captain Jay's ship, by gawd. Nor any "hars."

The sea was choppy, waves driven by the rain and wind growing in size. The *Riggs* drew closer to the pirate vessel, a couple hundred yards away now, parallel and almost even with her.

Jay took the loudspeaker cone from a crewman and aimed it at the pirates.

"Hallo, the Jolly Roger!" he yelled. "Strike your colors and prepare to be boarded!"

For a moment, Jay wasn't sure they could hear him over the freshening wind and chop. Then the pirate ship fired its cannon, at least four on her starboard side. Clouds of dense white smoke belched from the enemy ship's cannon ports.

Fortunately for the *Riggs,* the rough sea must have affected the pirate gunners' aim—the whistling balls fell twenty feet short, splashing white gouts as they sank.

So much for that idea.

"Return fire, Mr. Smee. All port guns!"

"Aye, Captain!"

The officer yelled at a relay, who passed the command on.

Five seconds later, the guns of the HMS *Riggs* spoke as one, and five cannonballs shot through the air, covered the short distance to the pirate ship, and smashed into her. One ball hit a mast, toppling it—lucky shot, that; one ball hit the deck amidships and plowed a splintered furrow in the deck; the three remaining balls hit the hull, one above the waterline, and two below it. The pirate ship began taking on water.

"Make ready another volley!" Jay yelled.

If they wouldn't give up, they would pay.

They would learn, by God, that it was *not* a good idea to defy Captain Jay Gridley. Though he wasn't happy about having to sink the pirates. Satisfying as that might be, it didn't get Jay the information he wanted.

Oh, well. Might as well enjoy what he could . . .

Net Force HQ
Quantico, Virginia

Thorn leaned back in his chair and reflected on the call he'd just ended. The head of CyberNation was coming to the U.S., and he wanted to meet with Thorn. Along with a visit from the head of the Chinese version of Net Force, this was going to be the week for company.

Too bad Marissa Lowe wasn't in town. He'd like to get her take on these visitors. Still, she went where the CIA sent her, and even though she was the liaison from that agency to Thorn's, she had other duties. The world was a busy place for intelligence groups these days. . . .

Well, there might be something he could learn on his own. He wasn't entirely dense. CyberNation's goals weren't ever going to be reached, he believed that, but they did have a very solid network and some outstanding people. Thorn knew guys who had been bright lights in the field who had opted for CyberNation's employ. Good pay, good benefits, access to cutting technology, CyberNation had no trouble hiring first-class people.

And the Chinese were up and coming. Still not anywhere near the level of the United States when it came to computers, hard- or software, but rising, and you couldn't ignore an industrializing country with a billion and a half people in it.

Thorn waved his hand over the intercom, wiggling his fingers for the optical reader.

"Sir?"

"Is Jay Gridley in the compound?"

"No, sir. He's at the Pentagon Computer Annex today."

"Ah. Would you give him a call?"

"Yes, sir."

It wasn't as if Quantico was a million miles from the District; still, making Jay drive out here wasn't necessary. If a phone call with visuals wasn't enough, they could log into one of the secure VR rooms Net Force maintained for more personal meetings. Jay would have his virgil; the call's coded pipe would be more than enough protection. Thorn was comfortable with that.

He smiled. He should be. His company had developed some of the software for such chats. He had written much of the code himself.

He'd get Jay on board, maybe have him show the CyberNation guy around, what was his name? Seurat? Like the painter . . . ?

Net Force VR Com Room

"Excuse me?" Thorn said.

"I said, 'Absolutely no way,' " Jay said.

Thorn stared at Jay as if he had suddenly grown a second head. Disagreement was something he encouraged in his people, but this was too far, even for Jay Gridley.

"Explain," Thorn said.

The VR room was very realistic. It took real-time images from phonecams and used those, so what you saw was more or less real. It was modeled on their RW conference room, just down the hall from Thorn's office.

Jay frowned. "Look, Commander, long before you came on board, Net Force had a major battle against CyberNation. It got real ugly. John Howard got shot because of them. We even got sued by another one of their people, a man who later fired at us himself."

"CyberNation?" Thorn said. "The computer geeks who want to start their own on-line country?"

Jay nodded. "Yeah, that's them. They came at us electronically, politically, and live and in person."

"I don't remember being briefed on this—and believe me, I would have remembered if I had ever heard a word about it."

Jay shrugged. "It's been a couple years and they've been quiet since. This was back when they were trying to get big numbers to join up, and they didn't care how they did it. Part of their scheme was to take down a major chunk of the net, leaving themselves as the only real viable option."

Commander Thorn shook his head. "The net was designed so that couldn't happen."

"The Internet was, yeah, Commander, but that was a long time ago. The World Wide Web pretty much replaced the old Internet a while back, and with the increased ease of use came increased vulnerability. These days, if you know which backbone servers to take out, you could do a whole lot of damage. The net, the web, they are more complex now than ever before, and everything is linked to everything else—communications, servers, private companies, government, military. There were some real bad apples at CyberNation, and it came down to guns and bombs. People died. The government apparently decided it was better to keep most of it hush-hush. Eventually it all got squared away, but not to my satisfaction."

Thorn thought about that for a moment. "So why is CyberNation still around if they are such bad folks?"

Jay smiled grimly. "Good question, Boss. These guys all wear eye patches and pegs legs and carry cutlasses, as far as I am concerned. But the official tale was that a rogue splinter group was responsible for the crimes. We took them down, and nobody could prove it went beyond them, so that was the end of the story."

Thorn shook his head. The concept of CyberNation was like that of Communism—too idealistic to work. The hope that geographical nations would cede the rights and privileges of a real country to citizens of a virtually created one? It would never happen. However much time you spent on-line, you still had to *be* somewhere in the real world, and that spot, if it was on land, belonged to somebody. Nobody had built a giant raft-city way out at sea yet, and if they did, probably not a lot of folks would go live there. You were subject to the laws and regulation of an RW country, and the idea that most countries would give that control up because some net organization paid them taxes on a citizen was simply not realistic.

Oh, sure, there were some poor countries that might go for it. Some Third World spots where the idea of big numbers being able to get wired and on-line was fairly unlikely, which kind of killed the point, but only a relative handful of those would take such a deal. No major country was going to buy into the idea that one of its breathing citizens living in a house on Elm Street would suddenly become a foreign national who had allegiance to a web server and was no longer subject to the local laws, like some kind of diplomat. No way, nohow.

And yet, CyberNation had convinced millions of people to join up in the hope that just such a thing was going to come to pass. In doing so, it had become bigger than AOL and able to offer some very good programs. They had the best VR scenarios available commercially, with a wide range of choices.

Still, Thorn was always amazed at how gullible some people continued to be, even in this supposedly enlightened age. A virtual country? Not on this planet.

"Listen, Jay, we have reason to believe that whoever is attacking our military is also taking potshots at CyberNation."

"Good for them."

Thorn shook his head. It was just the two of them, alone in a VR room. "Things change. Yesterday's enemy is today's friend. You know how that works. At the moment, CyberNation and Net Force seem to have a common problem. We want to solve that. We will take any help we can get."

"It sucks."

"Come on, Jay. That is the way of the world, and you are much too bright to not know it."

Jay didn't say anything.

"We've also got a guy coming over from China, the head of their Internet police agency."

"Chang Han Yao?"

"You know him?"

"I know who he is. He's got a few moves. What's he over for?"

"Ostensibly, to talk about modernizing China's agency, maybe to pick up some tips. The Chinese are our friends these days. Communism is on the way out, and they have become a major trading partner. Have you seen that exhibit from the Forbidden City at the Smith?"

"Yeah, VR. Very interesting. I got no grief with the Chinese."

"And you'll help with the man from CyberNation. A French guy."

"Seurat. I know his work. He wrote a paper on quantum computer applications that was . . . passable."

"I do seem to recall something about quantum computers and Net Force," Thorn said.

"Yep, that was a crazy English scientist and a dotty old lord. They shot at us, too." Jay shook his head again. "You know, for an agency that is supposed to be a bunch of desk jockeys riding expensive chairs in dark and quiet rooms, we seem to get shot at a lot."

Thorn smiled. "Probably that won't happen here."

Jay didn't smile back. "I wouldn't bet on it, Boss. Cy-berNation claimed to have gotten rid of all the bad guys, but it's hard to believe the people at the top didn't have a clue what was going on."

"But you'll help me with this guy?"

Jay nodded, his face glum.

"Thanks, Jay. I appreciate it." Thorn paused. "So, any-thing new on the war game hacker?"

Jay frowned again and shook his head. "I've been run-ning things down, but so far, nothing. The military sysop is pretty good, and the system isn't supposed to be reachable from outside, so it isn't like some wahoo can just dial up and log in, even if he had the codes. We're dealing with somebody who has been very careful."

"But you'll get him, eventually?"

"Oh, yeah. I always get 'em, Boss. It's just a matter of time. . . ."

Pan China Airlines Flight #2212
Somewhere over the Arctic

Chang stared through the window, but there was nothing to see save a dense layer of clouds a few thousand feet below the jetliner. Normally, he didn't take a window seat when he flew, especially on long flights; he preferred to have the aisle, so as to be able to stretch his legs now and then, or at-tend to business in the toilet.

But the flight had been crowded—relations between China and the United States were at an all-time high, and even with a new airline that added several flights a day to the States, the jets were, so he had been told, usually full. Plus, this was a direct flight to Washington, D.C., and much faster than the old ones where you had to fly to Los Angeles, then switch to an American carrier for the final leg across the country.

Cutting five or six hours from your travel time made this

flight much in demand. Normally, Chang would not have had the clout to merit such a flight. Then again, a man who knew as much about computers as he did had some advantages. He had access to reservation codes, and booking his own flight with those had been a simple matter. The state of the industry in China was such that this was not even illegal—nobody had ever worried about it, since nobody outside of himself and a few of his employees even knew it was possible.

He grinned. He would have to plug that hole when he returned home. At least for others . . .

"Would you care for a drink, sir?"

The flight attendant, a pretty, moonfaced young woman with a bright smile, stood in the aisle, leaning slightly over a couple traveling from Beijing to visit a daughter who, Chang had been told, lived in Baltimore. The attendant's chest, completely covered under a shirt and buttoned jacket, loomed over the husband, who had the aisle seat.

"Some club soda, please," Chang said.

The young woman moved on, much to the disappointment of the man seated on the aisle, Chang felt.

The Canadian, Alaine Courier, had provided Chang with some excellent software, and, more importantly, an introduction to a U.S. official who had access to Net Force. As a result, Chang was traveling to Washington to meet the head of the agency, which could not help but be useful. Just to see how the place was laid out, what equipment he could see, anything, that would be wondrous.

There were those in his government who wanted very much for China to be a match for the United States in all things. Properly approached and primed, such men could be most helpful to Chang's desire to upgrade his systems and technicians. *Why, yes, Comrade, I went to Net Force Headquarters. They are so far ahead of us, I fear it will take many years for us to even begin to catch up. Of course, a few million carefully spent would close that gap considerably, if a man knew exactly what to buy and how to use it, but . . . what are the chances of that happening . . . ?*

Chang would rather not play those political games, but in these times, there was no choice—not if you wanted to stay in the race. He did not enjoy such things, but he was learning how to be adept at them. It was, alas, part of the job. Better he know how to do it than not. . . .

Next to him, the woman said, "Did I mention that my daughter and her husband have given us three grandchildren?"

Several times, Chang thought. But he smiled. "Really? How wonderful for you. . . ."

8

Abe Kent was no Luddite—he used VR training for his troops as much as the next commander—it was just that he preferred reality over virtual reality. Unfortunately, the reality was that there were some scenarios you simply couldn't do in the real world. The Iraqis and the Iranians, even the Colombians, tended to frown upon a small military unit taking target practice on their citizens, no matter what their crimes.

The days of gunboat diplomacy and backing up private companies like United Fruit were long past, and Kent had no desire to see them come around again, so when you needed to work in the field against a team of Bosnians or Afghanis on their home ground, you dressed your men— and women—in sensory gear and did it in VR. It worked out all right, for the most part, and it was far better than nothing.

But Colonel Kent never lost sight of the fact that no matter how good the electronic impedimenta, no matter how well the stim units worked muscles, the computer scenario was not reality. You could simulate the feel of crawling over a muddy field, the sounds of gunfire, even the heat of a desert afternoon, but nobody broke an ankle, tore a groin muscle, or got fatally shot in VR.

Yes, there had been a few heart attacks in scenarios that were exciting enough to start the blood pumping fast, though most of these, Kent understood, had been using gear that simulated sexual encounters. Kent had never lost a trooper in VR, and he was in agreement with Bill Jordan, the famous gunfighter who had come out of the Border Patrol in the 1950s and '60s.

Jordan, whose skill with a double-action revolver was legendary—he could pick aspirin tablets off a tabletop at fifteen feet by point-shooting, without scratching the table's finish—had written a book on gunfighting called *No Second Place Winner.* Kent had an autographed copy of that book at home and had read it several times.

When talking about fast-draw experts who popped balloons with their side arm's muzzle blast, Jordan said that in the history of gunfighting nobody had ever died from a loud noise—meaning that you needed to practice hitting a target using a real gun with full-power ammo. Speed was fine, but accuracy was final, and the only way to make sure you had both was to practice using the gun you'd have when the bullets flew for real.

The troops grumbled when Kent took them out to the Marine training field in a pouring rain to practice tactics, but he knew that those experiences would pay off if they ever found themselves in such a situation.

Of course, lying on the sloppy, cold ground in the rain, as he now was, wasn't the most pleasant way to pass an afternoon, but this was how you got real practice. If your LOSIR gear shorted out when it started raining, this was the place to find that out, not on a real battlefield where somebody was trying to shoot you. If you jammed your assault rifle or subgun's barrel into the mud and plugged it, best you learn how to clear that, since firing a weapon with a slug of mud blocking the muzzle could get you a face full of shrapnel when the barrel exploded, as it could. At the very least, that weapon would be useless.

Kent had once seen a soldier on a firing line at a military range in Texas using a .308 assault rifle with a suppressor fitted to it. No way to silence that boom completely, certainly not with hypersonic rounds, but the idea was to quiet it a little, to make it harder to pinpoint the location. The machinist who had made the suppressor, or the shooter who had threaded it onto the barrel, or maybe both, had made a mistake. When the shooter fired off the first round, the bullet caught something in the silencing device, tore it off the muzzle, and hurled it thirty meters downrange.

"Whatcha got there, son?" the rangemaster had called out. "A grenade launcher?"

The .308's muzzle was damaged enough so that firing it again without repair would have been dangerous to anybody close.

Kent smiled at the memory.

If you had to have such an experience, a safe shooting range was the place to have it—not facing a platoon of enemy soldiers with AK-47s that might be old but that worked fine. A man could kill you with a cap-and-ball carbine that had been old-tech during the Civil War. . . .

"Clear," came the voice over Kent's LOSIR headset.

"You heard the mine-finder," Kent said. "Let's move, people."

The team, six troopers and Kent, scrabbled up in the rain and muck and splashed their way across the field. There were AP mines buried here—electronic ones that sent an IR pulse to the receivers the men wore in their SIPEsuits. If you stepped on one, any receiver in range announced it with a loud "beep." To make it more realistic, a small flash-bang in the ground went off, and that was enough to singe your clothes a little, reinforcing the electronic sig in a way that you didn't forget. Scared the hell out of you and stung a little, but a real mine would have blown off an arm or leg or killed you outright, and the little popper reminded you to pay attention.

The scout had located the hidden mines in their path, and electronically tagged them, so the heads-up panes in the unit's helmets, run off the backpack computer, showed the location of each antipersonnel device. As long as the suits worked, you could zigzag your way across the field and not worry about stepping on a mine. If the suits failed, then you had to do it the old-fashioned way, which took a lot longer. Now and then, Kent arranged for the suits to fail, but not today. Today, they would make it across the field before they were ambushed by an automatic motion sensor-operated tracking machine gun that fired either electronic bullets or paint balls, depending on the programming. Today, it would be paint balls, because those left no doubt, even in the rain, as to whether or not you had taken a hit.

Looking down and seeing that bright red splotch on your groin would make the point. Paint balls would sting a little—but then a high-powered AP round, even in good ceramic body armor, was going to seriously wound or kill you if it hit solidly.

The colonel himself didn't know exactly where the gun would be set up. The field sergeant had chosen a spot for it. Kent did know it would be out there somewhere, and he had taught his troops that they should always expect the unexpected, so *they* ought to be looking for it, too.

Kent had always thought the Boy Scouts had come up with the best two-word motto that dealt with this: Be prepared.

Rue de Soie
Marne-la-Vallée
France

Seurat paused to consider which suit he would pack for the trip to the United States. The Versace was a more modern cut, with a rougher tooth to the fabric, but the Gaultier was a more classical "power" suit, with a darker tone.

As he considered the merits of each, he looked, as he often did, at the painting facing his private desk. It was one of his most prized possessions, an original Georges Seurat, largely unknown to the rest of the world.

The painting wasn't as polished as some of the artist's earlier works—certainly not as much as *La Grande Jatte,* which had taken two years and countless studies, but it did bear the Neo-Impressionist pointillist dots of color that had marked his ancestor's later works.

It was small, only three feet or so wide, and more intimate in subject matter than many of the artist's famous pieces: A small child sat on the floor in front of a sofa; behind him was a Christmas tree, and on the right, trailing down from the top of the frame, was an adult woman's arm, reaching down to hold the boy. The tone was dark: a mix of warm ambers and saturated magentas. The colors blended beautifully, each dot giving the painting a vibrancy no solid patch could hope to match. The composition was pure Seurat: static shapes, with little to disturb them. The diagonal of the woman's arm broke the verticals typical of the artist's work, but did not jar the mood.

In front of the boy were some toys: blocks, a top, a small stuffed animal. But the child wasn't playing with them. Instead, he leaned into the arm, and looked out at the viewer, a slight smile on his face. There was a look of innocent awe, thoughtful joy, and the anticipation of something good to come.

The CyberNation leader had always thought the boy's expression was one that embodied the joy of discovery.

He blinked, his eyes warm, as he stared at the painting. The subject was his ancestor's son, Pierre George, and the approximate date of the painting was December 1890. Seurat the artist had died suddenly in March of 1891 of some infection—and his son had followed him the month after, apparently of the same ailment. The juxtaposition of the joy in the painting against the certain death that was coming was powerful.

The painter had not known he had but a few months left to him.

Seurat had known the painting for nearly his entire life. A great-aunt had given it to his parents when he was a young boy, and they had hung it in their sitting room. It had been purchased from Madeleine Knoblock, the artist's wife, just before her death, and kept from the world. She had not been well liked by the rest of the family, and had disappeared for years after her husband's and son's death.

Many times he'd thought about the look of discovery on the boy's face. It had encouraged him to try many new things, to seek out new experiences. He had been the boy. But tonight, he was the adult, reaching down to comfort the boy, to shepherd him from what might come. And the boy was CyberNation.

For him, the lesson was clear: You never see it coming. And it put him on his guard. Surely his ancestor hadn't seen his end approaching—could he hope to do better than his famous forebear?

Perhaps. Then again, no matter what kind of spin he put on it, the truth was the truth:

Not everyone wins.

He exhaled a long sigh, not having realized he was holding his breath. It didn't matter really. Win or lose, one had to do what one could, *oui*?

He would do everything in his power to protect his own curious and thoughtful infant from the dangers threatening it. Which was why he was packing now, to go see the Americans, whose military systems had been attacked by the same person or persons who had assaulted his child.

Considering the history CyberNation had with the Americans, particularly their Net Force, Seurat would hardly have predicted such a trip for himself. But he would climb into whatever bed was required to protect *his* nation.

He grinned. Perhaps he might be able to find a beautiful woman's bed somewhere along the way, eh?

That thought in mind, he considered the suits.

Power, he thought, and carefully folded the Gaultier into the Halliburton travel case on the bed. Neatly stacked socks, shirts, and ties surround it in tightly webbed compartments. These days, luggage was so often opened by airport security that it was embarrassing to pack less than neatly. And Seurat never did things by halves. Anyone who saw his packing in an airport would see the product of an ordered and considered mind.

Yes.

He closed the suitcase and checked the time on his old IWC chronometer. He still had a few minutes until Michel picked him up for the trip to the airport. Had CyberNation invested in its own plane—which it certainly could afford—there would be no need for such scheduling, but the nation of ideals kept one away from the physical world—he had never gotten around to it.

He wondered if the Americans would be able to help. They were smart—or at least they had a tremendous number of resources, which sometimes amounted to the same thing. An army of brutes could accomplish much, if there were enough of them. . . .

Arrogance, Charles, arrogance.

He had to remember not to underestimate them. No matter what he believed of the nation as a whole, there had to be at least a few sharp people keeping the bread and circuses running. Were there not, the last remaining superpower would not be such, eh?

The real question—and his real concern—was whether or not the Americans were responsible for what had happened. A faked incident of their own might have been staged to draw CyberNation in, to deceive them into joining as an ally against a foe that did not exist—the purpose to fuse a partnership where CyberNation would remain a weaker ally, or perhaps to link the two nations symbolically in world opinion.

He didn't believe that, though. If what he had learned was true, such a plot would have cost a great deal, and money was always such a consideration with the Americans that it seemed an unlikely scenario. Still, one had to consider all the possibilities.

America's allies had a tendency to act as ventriloquist's dummies for the huge nation, and Seurat would have none of this to taint the purity of CyberNation. Sooner or later the torch of the most powerful nation would be passed to another—and Seurat did not want to delay this inevitability in any way.

He leaned toward the idea that a government was behind the attack. It seemed unreal that a single man with limited resources could manage to do so much damage on his own. A government could support an apparatus large enough and powerful enough. Too, only a government would care enough to want to bring another government down. It was approaching hubris to consider that CyberNation was worth going to war with, but the evidence was there, *non*?

But could the United States be so worried about Cyber-Nation that they had decided to act?

He didn't know, but as the shepherd, as the adult, he had to find out.

If the Americans planned treachery, they'd find him a difficult target. Years of fencing had kept his body and mind honed to a razor's edge. The lamb might lie down with the lion, but in his case, it was more like a wolf in sheep's clothing lying down with the lion.

He smiled. What was the term they used about the French? Ah, yes, frogs.

Well, this *frog has teeth,* mon ami.

As they would find out, if they attempted to hurt his nation.

His alarm chimed. It was time to go.

*   *   *

Washington, D.C.

It had been a long time since Chang had been to Washington. The place had a charm to it. It was different than New York or Boston or Los Angeles or Chicago. It felt much more like a Southern U.S. town than a big city. As the taxi took him to his hotel, he looked at the people and buildings, recently washed clean by rain and now basking in bright sunshine. Here was the head of the superpower that was the United States, and it looked so . . . ordinary. . . .

Looks could be deceiving, of course. Chang knew this as well as any. He recalled an old joke he had heard as a younger man, here in the States.

A man is walking a tailless little yellow dog on a leash when another man walking a snarling bulldog comes up. The bulldog takes a run at the little dog, growling and snapping. The little yellow dog opens enormous jaws and bites the bulldog in half.

The bulldog's owner stares at the other guy. "Lord, man, what kind of dog is that?"

"Well, before I cut off his tail and painted him yellow, he was an alligator."

Chang smiled at the memory. No matter how you disguise it, an alligator is still an alligator.

Here in this city, this unique district, lived men who had more power than the greatest rulers in all of history. With a spoken command, their leader could more or less wipe out every human being on the planet. There were enough atomic and hydrogen bombs in America's arsenal to directly destroy hundreds of millions, with the resulting fallout killing millions more. And if the scenario of nuclear winter was true—that awful theory that enough smoke and dust in the air would cast a pall over the whole of the world and bring about massive weather changes—it might be that one man could destroy most of the life on Earth. It was a frightening thought. Nobody knew this for certain, and Chang hoped nobody would ever have to find it out the hard way.

Washington might look innocuous to a visitor, but it was, like the yellow dog in the joke, more than it appeared on the surface. Just like the people of this country. Many in the world thought that Americans were overfed and lazy, concerned only with their toys and their easy lives.

That kind of thinking was a mistake. Americans were an affable people, sure enough, but when attacked, they did not shrink from a hard response. Witness what they had done to Afghanistan, to Iraq, and what they were almost certainly going to do to any other nation that was stupid enough to threaten them. To attack such a country was to court a terrible retribution.

Chang smiled. Such was certainly not his intent. The new China was more interested in commerce than war— there were more than a billion mouths to feed, and business was growing better and better.

Before he went to visit Net Force, he had appointments with several software and hardware dealers eager to have Chang's business. There were some limitations on the technology he could legally acquire, of course, and there probably always would be, but such restrictions had lessened in the last few years. Nothing Chang wanted to get his hands on presented a threat to the U.S.'s national security. At least, he didn't think so.

The cab arrived at the Constitution, a small but well-appointed hotel on Chang's approved list. It wouldn't cost much more than staying in a comparable place back home.

Chang alighted, paid the driver, then followed the bell-boy who collected his luggage into the building.

A sunny day in a sunny city, and he was a man about his business. What could be better?

Well, he thought as he approached the check-in desk, a beautiful and sunny woman with which to share it would be nice. He was between relationships at the moment, no girlfriend back home. He had thought to be married and a father by now, but work had gotten in the way. He would have to spend some time in that arena when he got home. A loving and passionate wife, sons and daughters, these were things he wanted. Life wasn't all about work, after all. The Prophet had said so, and Chang believed it.

Paradise Cove
Fiji

The sun was warm on Jay's bare back. He wore a pair of ragged shorts and nothing else. The hot sand made little *chee-chee* sounds under his feet as he walked. A line of breakers rolled sudsy white surf onto the beach. Gulls *crawed* overhead. Palm trees wafted in the gentle breeze. The bananas and coconuts were ripe, you could see fish in the tide pools, and the heady scents of flowers and fruits drifted about him. It was as close to a tropical paradise as Jay could imagine. Because, of course, he *had* imagined it.

In such a place, the set of small footprints on the wet sand at the shoreline was easy to spot and follow. Once Jay caught up with the person who had made those prints, he would have access to a vital bit of information. Which, at this point, would be a lot more than he currently had—which was to say, at this point, he didn't have anything at all.

Jay was not used to being stymied. Part of the problem with being really good at what you did was the realization that a lot of people weren't able to run with you. You started to take it for granted that, when given a problem, not only would you be able to solve it, you'd be able to do it fast. Like being an international chess grandmaster, most of the players you ran into simply weren't in your league. But even the world champion lost now and then—nobody was perfect. Nobody stayed champ forever. Sooner or later, somebody better came along and beat you.

Intellectually, Jay knew this. Emotionally, however, it was hard to accept.

Jay Gridley did not like to lose. Ever.

The track followed the shoreline for maybe a quarter of

a mile, then veered into the dry sand, heading away from the beach. The footprints weren't as distinct here, but still easy to see across the otherwise smooth sand. Two hundred yards away from the water, there was a line of trees and underbrush, and there the footprints disappeared. But even so, there was a trail, narrow and winding, and no sign of broken branches or disturbed bushes leaving the path. A couple years back, Jay had learned how to track a man on foot, even one trying to hide his trail, and whoever this was, he was sticking to the easy way.

There was a gentle rise, and it was cooler here in the trees, but not enough so that Jay needed a shirt. The dirt and moss underfoot were soft and warm. Birds cheeped, some kind of small creature chittered in the trees, and Jay enjoyed the hike.

After another fifteen minutes or so, the animal track widened into a clearing, ringed by banana and palm trees.

In the middle of this glen stood a woman dressed in a sarong, a bright red patterned wrap that covered her from her breasts to just above her knees. She had a Polynesian look to her, silky black hair that hung to the middle of her back, dark skin made darker by the sun, and a flashing white smile. Altogether gorgeous, Jay decided.

He returned her smile. Well. This was easy enough. About time.

He walked toward her. She waited.

Fifteen feet away, he stepped onto a broad palm leaf and felt his belly lurch as he fell into a pit.

He landed heavily on his feet, collapsed, and stood up again, shaking his head, already angry with himself. Fortunately, the trap had not been lined with stakes; but it could have been. As it was, the edges of the pit were two feet above his outstretched hands. He jumped up, caught the edge, and it gave way under his grip. He fell, cursing.

He shook his head again, disgusted with himself. And here he'd just been thinking about how great he was.

Jay shook his head. He would have to dig climbing notches in the dirt, which, with his bare hands, was going to take a while, even in the soft soil. And he knew that the smiling woman he had been following would be long gone by the time he reached the surface.

Gritting his teeth, and biting back a few more choice curses, he got to work.

WTC Airlines Flight #217
Somewhere over the Atlantic

Locke wished that the Concorde SSTs were still flying the Atlantic route between Paris and New York. Yes, he was in first class, and certainly there were things he could do to pass the time; still, commercial air travel was so much less interesting than almost any other mode of transportation. There was nothing to see, just clouds and distant ocean. The air on board a modern jet was dry, stale, and full of enough germs to infect an entire army.

A train, a riverboat, those gave you sights. Even an old prop plane chugging along at low altitude was better. Riding a bike or walking was the best of all—you could interact with the scenery. You saw things while walking you'd miss in a car or on a train, and certainly would miss on a jet roaring along at six hundred miles an hour.

Still, if you needed to get somewhere quickly, the jet was obviously the way to travel. Crossing an ocean on a ship could take a week; flying over it, a matter of hours. One had to balance the means against the end. Too bad there were no such things as matter transmitters, like in the sci-fi stories on television.

Locke had seen those as a kid—with Captain Kirk and Spock speaking dubbed Mandarin. Step onto a pad, Scotty pushes the sliders, and presto! You were instantly where you wanted to be. . . .

Locke sipped at his club soda. When he had been making his living from women, he had drunk alcoholic beverages at social gatherings; it was necessary. These days, he seldom indulged in liquor. He did not like to have his thoughts fuzzed by anything.

In fact, he had found certain smart drugs and mild psychedelics to be enhancing, and he sometimes took these. In competition, with all things else being equal, the smartest player had the advantage. The kind of work he had come to required a sharpness of mind, a concentration, and anything that altered his consciousness and made him feel less clever? No, thanks.

This venture with Wu was intriguing on many levels. If it succeeded, it would be hard to top. The money aspect of it was enormous, the level of detail needed immense, and offhand, Locke couldn't think of any way he could better it. Well, toppling a government, perhaps, and becoming a king himself . . .

Locke smiled, and sipped his tonic water again. He would worry about that once he accomplished the task at hand.

He had come a long way from the streets of Hong Kong. And not just in distance.

9

People's Military Base Annex
Macao, China

Wu hated computers. But then he pretty much disliked high technology in general. Were it not for such things, the Chinese would rule the world. It was a simple matter of numbers, and the Chinese had more of them—more citizens, more soldiers, more weapons, more everything. At least, everything that wasn't high-tech.

But with their electronic smart missiles and radar and sonar and IR satellites that could spot a man smoking a cigarette at night in the fog from hundreds of miles up in the sky, the armies of the West had the advantage. And their superiority in technology more than made up for the Chinese superiority in numbers, the Chinese superiority in tradition, and the Chinese superiority in moral standards.

For now, anyway.

Wu recalled the first American Gulf War, wherein the Iraqi troops had dug in, formed lines as had been done for hundreds of years—and had been whipped like a housewife beating a dirty rug. The Iraqis had been outflanked, outmaneuvered, and outgunned. They sat there in their trenches in the desert while the United States flew over them unseen like a sharp-eyed eagle, watching every move they made. If, in the land of the blind, the one-eyed man was king, then a man with two eyes and high-tech telescopes was a god. The Iraqis had not had a prayer of winning—not using the tactics of the past against those of the future. No chance at all.

Wu sighed. The Chinese could put millions of soldiers onto a field, but today, those numbers were not enough. To win a battle, much less a war, against an enemy with a vastly superior technology, you either had to develop weapons of your own to match his—or you had to somehow take his away.

A smart weapon with its brain removed was no danger. The playing field would be leveled considerably if the West could not bring its toys to the game.

Thus the need for Comrade Shing. Water could defeat fire, but with a large enough fire, water was not the best way—fire itself was.

"Report, please," Wu said, giving Shing his usual enigmatic smile.

"We progress according to plan," Shing said. He was bored with this; it shone from his face. He felt superior to Wu, felt a contempt for him and his oldness, had no respect for tradition. Shing was one of the new dragons of the air, all looks, bright red wings fluttering, pretty to gaze upon, but no substance, no connection to the ground. You must have roots to withstand the cyclone's winds. Men like Shing would be blown around the skies in a moderate breeze. Computers were amazing playthings, smart bombs could not be denied, but their reality was ephemeral. Take those away, and it was the man on the ground who decided the battle.

The pen, in the long run, might indeed be mightier than the sword, but on a street facing a man with a sword, a pen was a poor weapon. There would *be* no long run for the scribe against the warrior in such a situation. Shing did not know this. He had not yet learned that real power always comes down to the sword. All else flowed from that.

Wu knew. Wu also knew that the sword of power must, at times, be taken from those who did not know how to wield it. From those who did not wish to give it up.

Shing was of some value. Locke was worth more.

Men with swords of power were not to be faced directly, however. They might be less than adept with their blades, but even a casual backhanded swipe could behead somebody foolish enough to stand in front of them making annoying noises. One needed to distract them, misdirect their attention, and while they were busy, slip in and steal their weapons for one's own use.

This was Shing's worth. He would be a distraction, though he would have no idea this was the use to which he was being put.

Shing was too full of himself, his own skill and talent, to even consider that a man such as Wu could use him thus.

Pride was both terrible and wonderful—terrible for the man who suffered it; wonderful for one who could use another man's hubris to his own ends. . . .

So, go on, flying dragon, feel superior. Look down from the skies upon lowly Wu, plodding across the ground like a turtle, ancient and slow. Eventually, the cyclone would come, and Wu, safe in his shell, would be here long after the dragons of the air had been dashed against the mountains, their bodies left there to freeze in the chilly heights. . . .

He smiled at the image. Even a poor general could be a poet, if not a great one. But there were other ways to make up for that.

Edward's Park
Washington, D.C.

Jay Gridley, who had survived countless VR battles, a quantum computer-generated stroke, and a brush with Mr.

Death Himself in the form of a bullet to the head, stood at the edge of the sidewalk, worried about crossing the street.

The walk sign had just lit, and bright LEDs gleamed at him, offering the same promise the witch in the fairy tale had offered Hansel and Gretel: inviting, but surely a dark side lay hidden in it somewhere.

He eyed the traffic on both sides of the intersection. All the cars were stopped now, waiting for him to head out into the street. Waiting for the baby.

Come on, Gridley.

He felt a nervous tingle, but stepped forward, pushing the pram. He paused to eye little Mark, who lay quietly, watching the world go by overhead, with seemingly no cares in the world.

If you only knew, son.

Not willing to be distracted from their imminent peril, Jay scanned the street again, looking for signs that the drivers at either side were planning to run him over. Eyes that had been trained to note the slightest change in the hyper-realistic environments of VR scanned every detail. He saw nothing out of the ordinary.

Part of him laughed at his nervousness, but another more primal part nodded, satisfied.

It was okay.

He made it across the street and pushed the carriage toward the entrance to Edward's Park, still not sure this was a good idea. Saji was doing a how-to VR-cast on Buddhist meditation, and had suggested he get out of the house for a while, so she could focus.

"Go to the park, Jay," she'd said. "Have some fun, and show Mark around!"

It had sounded good, but now, alone, without his wife nearby, ready to use her mothering superpowers, he was nervous. Plus, there was the whole danger thing. It was fine to go for a walk by himself—not that he really liked going out in RW that much—but here he was with a little defenseless *person,* and he was completely in charge. What if something happened to him? What would happen to the baby?

Come on, Jay, you can handle a walk in the park.
Well, maybe.

It was a new feeling for him, this responsibility. Maybe it was because he hadn't yet had enough time with his son on his own. Saji was always there, ready to help out. God, was this what she went through when he was at work?

It wasn't that he couldn't handle the physical part of things. He was brighter than most people he knew—come to think of it, brighter than most people he didn't know and would never meet. He could handle a bottle, and Saji had supplied some milk for the one in the little incubator bag at the back of the carriage. Plus he had a binky, if all else failed.

The pram looked like those seen in old movies set in the late 1890s, a big black carriage with huge wheels and a pullover top that protected the baby from the sun and er-rant looks from strangers. He and Saji had looked all over D.C. for one like it. Saji had read somewhere that babies felt more secure if they could look at their parents, so it *had* to be the pram.

No, it wasn't the physical part of things that made him nervous. It was the thought that maybe something would happen from which he couldn't protect his child. It was a heavy weight, and one that explained all kinds of things he'd seen in other people with children. He had been ad-mitted to the secret fatherhood; the fatherhood of knowing just how terrifying the world really was.

Before, when he'd worried about things going to hell, it hadn't been so bad—the world only had to last long enough to see himself and his friends through it. After that, nothing mattered much anyway. But that time period had now been extended another lifetime, and it added a certain amount of pressure.

His son gurgled a happy sound, and Gridley looked down, feeling a warm pleasure run through him. If there was a dark side to these new minefields of responsibility, there was also a light one. He'd never felt such uncondi-tional love for anyone in his life. Whether he was up at five in the morning feeding the boy, or changing a dirty diaper, that pleasure didn't diminish in the least. Part of him knew that this was purely biological, but he just didn't care.

Amazing.

There was a pond at the center of the park, where ducks swam. He'd brought part of an old loaf of bread to feed them, thinking it might amuse his son.

But maybe not. No one had bothered to tell him that babies younger than about six months tended to just *sit* there, not doing anything. Well, if you didn't count eating, crying, and filling diapers. All his life he'd seen pictures and vids of babies crawling or running, or sitting up and playing. He just hadn't been told that there was a time frame around such things.

Oh, well. He could always just sit and hold him.

He glanced down again, and little Mark was looking up at him.

"What are you looking at, little tiger?"

The boy grinned a toothless smile. Daddy was *talking* to him.

Jay wished he could have this much fun at work. He'd been struggling to figure out his latest puzzle. It seemed so *close* sometimes, as if there was something that he just wasn't seeing.

One of his old mentors had said more than once that his intuition was a plus for programming: that it could short-circuit hours of scut work with one sudden realization. This time, though, it just wasn't coming.

Ahead was the pond. He looked at the water. The breeze pushed ripples across it. A pair of white ducks swam sedately along. He noted the details for future VR work, and looked for a likely place to park the pram.

"Wahhhhhhhhh!"

At Mark's sudden wail, Jay went tense.

"What is it, pumpkin? What's the matter?"

He leaned down and sniffed. It didn't smell like a full diaper.

He quickly ran through the list. Hungry? Didn't sound like a hungry cry. He reached in the little incubator bag anyway and produced the bottle, warmed to just the right temperature.

Nope. He didn't want that.

The crying went on. Jay began to feel an edge of panic.

Binky, binky, fallback plan.

He lowered the gemlike plastic pacifier to his son's mouth, which popped open and latched right on.

The crying stopped immediately.

Whew.

He pictured what he might have done if the binky hadn't worked: running full-tilt across the park, heading home to get Saji.

Glad it didn't come to that.

He looked down and saw that Mark had spit out the binky. His little arms flailed around for it in frustration. Jay could see that it had fallen just to the right of the boy's head, and reached down to get it. Mark's hands twitched, trying to find his lost comforter. The boy had such a look of irritation that Jay found himself thinking about his own problems.

Yeah, he thought, *all I need is a little help from someone else, get them to reach down and hand me the solution.*

And then the realization clicked, the situation spun around, and he saw how he might beat the locked-room mystery.

Yes!

Jay smiled at his son again, and stroked his head. Not bad—take the baby to the park, and cut the Gordian knot at the same time.

Mark's eyes started to close. Get a binky, go to sleep. Must be nice . . .

Jay grinned.

Smokin' Jay Gridley was about to ride again.

He turned the pram around and headed home. Saji would be done teaching her lesson by now, the boy would nap for at least an hour, and Jay could get on-line and run with his new idea.

10

Wormwood, South Dakota

Instinct was like inspiration. Neither were things they taught in computer school, though a few of Jay's teachers had spoken about one or the other. Nor were they things you should depend upon with any regularity; then again, they weren't things you should ignore when they tweaked you, either.

Jay felt that tweak again now—a sixth sense of somehow knowing he was close. It was different from wishful thinking—he'd experienced that often enough to recognize the feeling.

The scenario wasn't a complicated one. It was an old standby he'd built years ago, a town in the Old West, with cowboys and shopkeepers and schoolmarms, and that atmospheric *High Noon* twang underlying it. He had changed names and places and upgraded the sensoria, and it was one of his favorites.

Jay strode along the boardwalk, tipping his hat to the ladies he passed, inhaling the odors of dust and horse dung. Tumbleweeds had gathered in the alleyways, and the sun-bleached storefronts and graying wood buildings baked in dryness.

Ahead, at the entrance to the town saloon, the Hickory Branch, a figure suddenly moved from the boardwalk and into the place.

Jay wasn't sure who he was hunting, but he knew, he *knew* that this was his quarry. His realization at the park with his baby son had pointed him in this direction, and it felt right.

He hurried toward the saloon. There were two ways into the Hickory Branch—the front door, which, unlike so many movies, wasn't a pair of useless swinging doors that did nothing to keep out the heat, dust, and flies, but a wooden-framed etched-glass panel that closed just like any other door. There was also a back door, plain old wood, and generally kept locked save for when trash—of one sort or another—needed to be hauled out.

Jay left the walk at the gun shop, went down the alley to the back, and moved two buildings down to the Branch.

He tested the saloon's back door. It was locked. Good.

Jay circled back to the street, passed the hitching post, which was empty—smart men didn't leave their horses tied up there during the heat of the day, even, though there was a trough with water where the animals could reach it. If you lived in town, you walked to the saloon; if you came from elsewhere, you paid the livery stable boy a nickel to put your horse in the shade, and make sure he had food and water.

Jay opened the door and stepped inside.

It was Saturday, and the place was crowded, smoky, and not much cooler than outside. The beer was warm, too, but if you drank enough of it, you didn't mind the heat, and these frontier towns were full of what would later be called "alcoholics"—men and women both.

The piano player didn't pause, but kept on tinkling away at the off-key instrument, playing some kind of New York show tune from the late 1870s.

Jay didn't look particularly threatening. He wore a

shopkeeper's duds—boiled shirt and starched collar over a pair of gray pinstriped trousers and low-heeled English-style riding books. His coat—even in the heat, men often wore coats when they went out—was a cutaway frocklike thing of gray wool. His hat was closer to a derby style than a cowboy ten-gallon.

He didn't want to look threatening, not like some *pistolero* with low-slung strapped-down Peacemakers. More like a mild-mannered shopkeeper.

He had his gun, of course. The coat's right-hand low pocket was heavy canvas stiffened with leather, and in it was a chrome-plated 1877 Colt .38 "Lightning," with a two-and-a-half-inch barrel. The revolver looked like the Peacemaker, sort of, though the butt was rounded. It was a somewhat delicate machine compared to some weapons, but it had the advantage of being double-action, which meant that you didn't have to manually cock the hammer for each shot. You could just point it and pull the trigger repeatedly until you ran out of ammunition. The hammer spur had been removed, so as not to catch on the pocket during the draw.

Billy the Kid had owned a similar gun. Pat Garrett had carried a larger model, the "Thunderer," in .41 caliber. And John Wesley Hardin, one of the meanest of the gun-slingers, had gotten one just like Jay's as a gift from his brother-in-law, Jim Miller.

Definitely not a gun for shooting at targets twenty-five meters away. It was for taking out a bad guy ten or fifteen feet away. The short barrel made it easier to get out and working.

Jay moved to the bar, pretending a nonchalance he didn't feel, while searching the faces for his quarry. The person he'd glimpsed out front had been a man, he was pretty sure—or a woman dressed like a man. That meant he could discount the three trulls in low-cut dresses who worked the crowd, and the woman playing cards in the side room with four men. He could probably eliminate those men, too, since the one he was after wouldn't have had time to break into an ongoing game—there was usually a waiting list for poker on a Saturday.

Jay grinned. His scenarios were a mix of fantasy and genuine history, but when he put real stuff in, he usually had it from two or three sources.

"What'll you have, friend?" the bartender said.

He was, like Jay, wearing a coat, white shirt and tie, and wool trousers.

"Beer."

"Two for two bits, special."

"Draw two."

Jay took his hat off and hung it on a rack mounted on the wall next the bar. There were maybe thirty people sitting at tables or standing next to the long wooden bar, which was made from gleaming and well-waxed hickory, albeit stained and scratched in places. A big looking glass in a horizontal oval frame took up much of the wall behind the bar, and next to that, a painting of, of all things, a sea battle between sailing ships, blasts of smoke from the ships' cannons and a raging fire on one of the vessels giving the painting a sense of action.

The beers came, in heavy glasses. Jay put a quarter on the bar, picked up one of the beers, and sipped at it. Warm, acrid, sudsy, the way beer used to be drunk. He used the mirror to see what he could, then turned slightly to regard the smoky room.

Every other person in here smoked. Hand-rolled cigarettes, cigars, pipes. Some chewed and spit at strategically placed bell-mouthed brass spittoons, and some of the spitters were very accurate, the local equivalent of NBA three-point shooters.

Twenty years from now, if they survived the other ills of the frontier, a lot of these folks would have emphysema, lung cancer, or throat cancer. Jay shook his head.

He started eliminating suspects mentally as he sipped at the beer, which he held in his left hand so as to keep his gun hand free. Just in case.

Anybody who was obviously part of a group that

seemed to have been there a while—easy enough to judge from empty glasses on their tables—was out. Jay's quarry had just come in, so he looked for men with glasses that were mostly full.

That dropped the numbers to maybe six or seven on the floor, and two at the bar besides himself.

Then Jay looked for men who seemed to be alone, not part of a conversation. This wasn't a sure thing, but—and this was where his intuition came in—Jay was sure that the man he wanted wasn't a local, but somebody passing through.

Right away, that narrowed it down to the men at the bar.

Of the two, one was a tall, greasy-looking cowboy with a full beard, wearing leather chaps over canvas pants, a patterned flannel shirt with a dark blue bandanna at the throat, and a short stag-handled sheath knife on his belt. No hat, and no gun, and no place to hide a shooter of any size, at least not that Jay could see. He might have a little revolver or a derringer in his pants pocket, but if so, neither would be coming out with any speed, judging from the cut of those trousers. Six months away from his last bath, easy.

The second man was shorter and paler. He was hunched over his beer so that Jay couldn't get a good look at his face, but from what Jay could see the man looked clean-shaven. Like Jay, he wore a cutaway-style coat over dark trousers, and low-top shoes with buckles.

Jay glanced away, trying to see the shorter man's face by using the mirror. At that moment, the fellow looked up at the mirror himself, and Jay had the feeling he was also using the mirror to check the patrons.

Jay cut his gaze away, so as not to be caught looking. But before he did, he had the impression of something odd about the man's eyes. Nothing he could pin down immediately, but . . . *some*thing.

It was one of these two. He was sure of it.

But—which? Cowboy, or Buckles?

In his quarry's position, Jay wouldn't be going around in any scenario unarmed—in this case, "armed" being a metaphor for defensive programs that would be apparent to anybody bright enough to be here. Since Cowboy didn't seem to be packing—and that knife would only be good at close quarters, unless he was an expert at throwing, and even then, he'd only have one chance—then that pointed to Buckles.

Then again, maybe the quarry was banking on the idea that somebody looking for him would assume he'd be armed, and the fact that he wasn't would allay suspicion.

Buckles could be carrying a hand-cannon in that big floppy coat pocket, or have a hidden belt holster under it, though he, too, could be unarmed.

Jay took another long pull at the beer. It was a problem.

He wanted this guy alive, to question, whichever one he was, and so drawing his revolver and potting them both was out.

If he drew down on the wrong one, the other would be forewarned, and Jay would be behind the power curve.

If he did nothing, eventually one or both would leave, and he would have to choose which one to stay with, since he obviously couldn't follow them both.

Not unless they hooked up, which wasn't likely in *this* scenario. Men who came out of the closet in these times were not regarded fondly in such a town where they'd surely be thought an abomination.

So. Which is it gonna be, Jay?

The bartender came over and wiped at the already clean wood with a rag. "You want some pickled eggs? Free lunch."

Jay shook his head. "You know those two down at the other end of the bar?"

The bartender didn't look at the men, but smiled at Jay. He had a big, droopy moustache stained with tobacco, as were his teeth.

Jay caught the inference. He pulled a silver dollar from his pocket and put the cartwheel onto the bar. He slid it toward the bartender.

The man laid his hand over the coin and neatly palmed it.

"The big fellow is Bob Talley. He's foreman at the Rocking K ranch south of town. I don't know the little Chinaman."

"Chinaman?"

"I'm guessing he's got some Chinee in him. Slanty eyes. Not supposed to be in here, we don't usually serve their kind, but he looks white enough nobody's noticed, and his money is good."

Jay nodded. Being part Thai, he had a little Asian epicanthic variation, too, but in this kind of scenario, he usually altered his appearance to be as bland white-bread as possible. He didn't want to draw any attention.

"You're a bounty hunter, ain't 'cha?"

"What makes you say that?"

"Stranger comes in, you right behind him. You're carrying something heavy hidden in your right-hand coat pocket, dollar to a dime it's a pistol. I don't see a badge on your shirt. Plus you give me a dollar, no lawman would do that. So, bounty hunter. What'd the little Chinaman do?"

"Shot a nosy bartender," Jay said.

The man grinned and moved off. He had his dollar.

Jay took a deep breath. There were times when social engineering—bribing somebody—was the way to go. Not the most elegant method, maybe, but Jay was to the point with this hunt that he was past worrying about elegance. He wanted results and he didn't care how he got them.

He sipped his beer. He had his quarry identified. Now, he'd wait to make his move—

The bartender stopped in front of Buckles and said something.

Buckles jammed his hand into his coat pocket, fast.

Jay knew immediately what had happened. That double-crossing bartender had given him up!

Jay dropped the beer and went for his own pocket. His move was smoother and faster—he came out with his revolver and thrust it toward Buckles, stopped with his arm extended, ready to shoot.

Buckles froze, his own weapon but halfway out of his pocket.

The other man was maybe fifteen, eighteen feet away—
an easy target for somebody with Jay's skill.

"Let it go and put your hands up," Jay ordered. "We'll
talk, nobody has to get hurt—"

Buckles shook his head, grinned, and jerked his gun
from his pocket. He tried to get it lined up on Jay—

Jay squeezed the .38 Lightning's trigger, one, two,
three—!

The bullets hit Buckles solidly in the chest. The man
collapsed.

Jay frowned in disgust. Didn't people know when they'd
been beaten?

As he looked at the dying sub-routine, he had to shake
his head. Apparently not.

Still shaking his head, Jay turned his revolver on the
bartender and shot him, too. The rat.

But at least it wasn't a total loss. He knew something
now he hadn't known before.

Net Force HQ
Quantico, Virginia

Thorn looked at Jay. "Chinese? Are you sure?"

Jay, in the flesh, nodded. "Yep. I did as much backwalk-
ing as I could after the scenario, and knowing better where
to look, I found some signs. He might not *be* Chinese, but
he's operating from there."

Thorn shook his head. This was . . . unexpected. And in
less than an hour, the head of the Chinese version of Net
Force was supposed to be walking into Thorn's office. How
weird was that?

"So, what does this give us?"

"It narrows down the search pattern. I can start the
Super-Cray straining access to the net from China. That's a
lot of hits, and disguised, I'm sure, but it's a place to start.
I can also start checking around. If the attacker is Chinese,

he sure didn't get that good over there, so he must have studied in Europe or the States. I can run sieves on that."

Thorn nodded. "Good. Go for it."

"When is the CyberNation guy getting here?"

"This afternoon, right after lunch. And guess who else is scheduled for a meeting an hour from now—Chang."

"Huh. There's a coincidence." Jay paused. "He could help. He's got ways of getting in and out of Chinese systems we'd have to go the long way to reach. Maybe I could talk to him?"

"I'll let you know when he arrives."

"Thanks, Boss."

"Keep at it, Jay. I have every confidence in you."

Jay grinned. "I wish I did. This one is a bear."

"And you'll hang around for Seurat later?"

"Yeah. If I have to."

After Jay was gone, Thorn decided he didn't have enough time to eat and go work out before Chang arrived. Well, it wasn't as if he didn't have a boatload of e-paperwork that needed attention. He'd simply have lunch at his desk. The Republic had more than one computer problem nipping at its heels, and just because overall control of Net Force had been shifted didn't mean any of those things had gone away. . . .

11

The Garden of Perpetual Bliss

Daytime in the Garden of Perpetual Bliss was usually sunny and seventy-two degrees. It would rain now and again, sometimes a mild drizzle, sometimes a windy storm—but never too windy—and always warm enough to sit in without getting cold. Enough rain fell to keep the lush foliage nourished and vibrant, all the myriad shades of green, all the colorful flowers. Bees buzzed, but never stung. Butterflies danced and flitted by.

Here, a group of Hindus wearing orange robes sat in full lotus, meditating, connecting with the essence of Vishnu, Brahma, and Shiva. Next to them, in the shade of a giant baobab tree, a dozen Buddhists knelt in *seiza*, counting their breaths and seeking no-mind.

A short way down the path, Christians and Jews and the followers of Mohammed sat in a large circle, exchanging prayers and smiles.

In the Garden, too, were those who thought every rock had a soul, that all wisdom came from their ancestors, that the Sun was the ruler of all it touched. And there were others who had no gods at all, but only their common humanity.

In the Garden, there was no dissent, no jealousy, no hatred. All who came here became one of the family of men, and no man's hand was ever raised against another in anger. People dressed as they wished, or went nude.

Sometimes music drifted over the Garden, and such was its nature that the sounds each person heard on those occasions were suited to their personal tastes: Here, it was a raga, there a fugue, and past that, delta blues. People sang or danced or sat quietly and listened, and no one resented another's manner of expression.

Fruit grew on the trees—apples, bananas, pears, coconuts, plums, oranges, every kind a hungry soul might desire was there somewhere. Vegetables, too, and nuts, and all manner of beasts—fish and fowl, even red meat—were available, if that was one's wont.

One could come to the Garden to do, or just to be. It was all the same, and it was all wonderful.

When the dragon came, red-scaled and breathing fire, swooping down from the clear sky, most in the Garden thought it was some new entertainment.

Until it started cooking and eating people.

The Garden of Perpetual Bliss heard its first screams of terror that day. Smelled the stink of roasted human flesh. Beheld fear in a way that had never happened here before.

The dragon landed and stalked, crushing all before him, pausing to bite off a head here, a leg there, hissing with a sound that stirred neck hairs in atavistic panic. The people had no way to stop it, they had no weapons, and the dragon moved through them unmolested.

Some ran. Some stood their ground and waited for their end.

And in a short time, those who did not flee were consumed. . . .

* * *

The Watergate Hotel
Washington, D.C.

"Merde!" Seurat said, shaking his head. He removed the headset and sighed, staring at his portable computer. He was in no danger here in his Washington hotel room. As those in the Garden of Bliss VR scenario had not been in any real physical danger, either. But the assault on their psyches must have been a terrible jolt.

Seurat's anger surged, a hot flush that made him want to scream and hit somebody. CyberNation had created a paradise in that garden, a place where those who wished such a thing could go and bask in an ideal that had never happened in the real world. All men as brothers.

And someone had ruined it. Attacked and destroyed the carefully built scenario, terrifying those tuned to it. Yet another of the hacks that added cracks to the CyberNation's foundation. Small ones, so far, but left unchecked they could grow and threaten the entire organization.

Seurat could not—he *would* not allow such a thing to happen. Not on his watch.

The damage to the program had been repaired, of course, quickly and easily. But the damage to the memories of those who had been in it when the incident had taken place? Not so simply fixed. According to his techs, there had been fifteen thousand people worldwide in that scenario when it was attacked. And while that number was but a drop in the bucket compared to the total membership of CyberNation, some of those people would leave and not come back. Like a small stone tossed into a pond, the stories would spread.

CyberNation? Yeah, I used to be a member, but I quit. They don't have their act together—you wouldn't believe what happened in one of their shared-scenarios. . . .

Worse, what if the attackers chose one of the giant-scale scenarios next time? The Super Bowl 'cast, or the Pope's Christmas message? The latest Hollywood blockbuster on demand?

True, those had gotten increased security since the attacks had begun, but since they still did not have a handle on the hacker, who was to say that he couldn't worm or trojan his way into one of those?

If ten or fifteen million people got a dose of nastiness like that which had happened in the Garden of Perpetual Bliss? That would be . . . bad.

Very bad, indeed.

Seurat glanced at his watch. Almost time to leave for the meeting with Thorn, at Net Force.

CyberNation's past with Net Force had been less than happy, and Seurat could not expect them to welcome him with open arms; still, if they could help, he would welcome it. If he had to lie with the Devil to save his child, then that was what he would do. Whatever it took.

None of Locke's sources at CyberNation in France knew exactly why its leader had traveled to the U.S. Parked in his rented cab near the hotel's Virginia Avenue entrance—that had been a bit of a trick, but at least this way he would blend in—Locke waited and watched. Even with the occupied sign lit, he'd had to turn away people who wanted a ride. Blind fools.

Such a location—a busy hotel with several entrances and exits—was a surveillance problem for an operative alone. You couldn't cover all the ways in and out, and if you picked the wrong one, you would lose your subject.

Not that it was of major concern. Seurat was not much of a threat. And whatever his reasons were for being here, they could hardly affect what Shing was doing to CyberNation, if indeed that was why Seurat had come. Still, Locke prided himself on being thorough, and if you went somewhere to shadow a subject, it was better to stay with him than not.

Fortunately, Locke was experienced enough in these matters to have dealt with such problems more than once. This was one of the easier ones: Seurat wasn't aware he was being followed, nor did he have reason to suspect that he was. He had rented a car at the airport, and that vehicle was now parked in the hotel's lot. Under the rear end of

Seurat's car—a high-end Porsche—was quick-glued a powerful, on-demand radio transmitter the size of a matchbook. Untriggered, the bug did nothing—anybody looking for it using broadband field-strength meters would not find anything. Even a casual visual inspection would miss it, since it was colored to match a car's undercarriage and tended to blend in. But if Locke sent a coded signal to it, the device would begin narrowcasting a GPS signal that would pinpoint its location—if you had the proper receiver.

The device was live now, and it told Locke that the car was in the hotel's parking garage.

It was not foolproof, of course. Seurat could leave by a side or back door on foot, catch a taxi, or be picked up by a limo, and Locke would not know. Still, Seurat liked to drive, and he had not rented a Porsche to let it sit in a parking lot while he took a cab.

It probably wasn't important to any of Locke's plans what the French computer guru did while here, but it was better to know than not.

As it happened, Seurat must have left the building via another exit, for the coded sig from the Porsche began emitting a higher-pitched tone, sending an alert that indicated a change in position.

Locke started his car's engine, and lit the tracker. A map of the city appeared on the screen, and a tiny red light showing the position of Seurat's car blinked on and began to pulse.

Wu might not like technology, but Locke was certainly happy with this little toy. As long as he stayed within fifteen miles of the transmitter, and as long as the battery held out—at least six hours of continuous 'casting—the map would show Locke exactly where the Porsche went, and give him the best route to get to it.

*　*　*

O'Rourke's Brew Pub
Quantico, Virginia

When John Howard called to confirm lunch, Abe Kent suggested they go where a lot of military business had been conducted over the years: a local bar—or, in this case, a brew pub.

Both were dressed in civilian clothes, with one of the pub's own beers, made right there on the premises, in frosty mugs on the table in front of them. Kent and Howard were just two old friends relaxing at the pub. They were trying the new house beer, Heavy Lifting, a dark ale fizzed with nitrogen instead of carbon dioxide—the bubbles fell rather than rose. It was mildly bitter, with a chocolaty, smooth finish. Good stuff.

"How's work going?" John asked.

"Slow," Colonel Kent replied, taking a sip of his beer. "There's really nothing for me to do but training at the moment."

"Something will come up."

Kent nodded. "I expect so. How about you?"

"It's a lot different. Money is better, and Nadine is a lot happier, though there are times when I want to smack some of the people I'm trying to educate. You wouldn't think a man who was head of a major corporation could get there by being stupid, but apparently that's not the case."

Kent laughed. "The old joke about the chain of command only being as bright as the dumbest link."

Howard nodded. "So, how does it feel to be back in harness with the Corps?"

"Honestly? Better than I would have thought. I never really felt as if I had left the Corps as much as it had moved away from where I was standing."

Howard took a drink of his ale and nodded. "Yeah, politics. You have to play if you want to stay. I guess it's always been that way. I've heard stories worse than yours."

"Me, too."

"You think Rog will cover your back?"

"Maybe. But if they boot me out, it won't be so bad. You can only lose your virginity once."

Howard chuckled. "You ought to come by the house now and then, Abe. Nadine would love to cook a meal for you. And she's got a lot of single women friends who wouldn't mind an old boot like you. Come on a Sunday, you can go to church with us, have roast beef for lunch, hang out."

Abe looked at his friend. "I might just do that." He paused a moment. "Can't say I am much of a churchgoer, though."

Howard looked at his beer, then at Kent. "Not proselytizing here, Abe, but didn't you ever feel the need for prayer out there when the bullets were whistling past and calling your name?"

Kent smiled. "Every time. Prayer and pucker-factor go together better than peanut butter and jelly. You know what they say, John: There are no atheists in foxholes."

"So you are a believer."

Kent nodded. "Oh, yes. I believe in God. And I've got no arguments with Jesus being the Son and prophet. I don't even have problems with Allah or Mohammed or Harry Rama, if it comes to that. Everybody has to be someplace. Not my job to tell 'em where."

"I hear a 'but' there."

Kent looked at his old friend, debating whether or not to tell him the story. It didn't come up too often these days, but it wasn't as if it was a big secret—he had told a few people along the way. And here they were, drinking good beer, shooting the bull. Why not?

He paused for another sip, then said, "Well. It goes back a long way. My maternal grandmother used to live down in Lafayette, Louisiana. Every other summer when my brother and I were kids—he was eight years older than I— my folks would ship us to Grandma's for a few weeks to visit. After my brother turned into a teenager, he stopped going, but I still went. And he did wind up going to college down that way later."

He sipped again, then pushed his glass a little ways away from him. "The summer I was ten, I stayed with Grandma. She lived on the bank of a bayou. I think it was the Vermilion River. Water came almost up to her back fence when it rained hard. She had a little dog, a Pomeranian named Dolly, and a parakeet named Pancho. I used to take my BB gun down to the banks of the muddy bayou and shoot at snakes and snapping turtles. For a while, my great-grandfather lived there. He was ninety-something, and he used to sit on the bank with me, fishing with a cane pole. We caught catfish, bream, even a gar, now and then. Had to throw them back. Grandma wouldn't scale and cook them and she wouldn't let me and Great-Grampa in her kitchen to try."

Kent grinned, remembering those days. Great-Grampa Johnson smoked a pack of unfiltered Camels a day, and took nips from a bottle of Old Crow he kept hidden under the bathroom sink. He was a small man, compact, and had served in France in the Great War.

The cigarettes and liquor never did kill him—he died from pneumonia he picked up in the hospital after he fell and broke his hip, at age ninety-three.

Kent pulled his memories back to the present. "Grandma was a bridge player and a churchgoer. Grampa worked on the oil rigs out in the Gulf, he was an engineer, and mostly gone. They were Methodists, which is about as benign a Christian group as ever there was. The main difference between them and the Baptists, my grandfather used to say, was that the Methodists sprinkled, but the Baptists had to dunk, since their congregations needed more water to keep cool during the hellfire and brimstone preaching."

Howard smiled.

"I went to Sunday school at home, and when I visited Grandma Ruth, I also stayed for the church service with her."

Kent paused again, spinning his glass slowly on the table. "This was back in the early sixties, around '61 or '62. The

civil rights movement was going on, and it was . . . turbulent . . . down South."

Howard nodded. "My folks told me the stories of uncles
who went down to Mississippi and Alabama to march. Terrible times."

Kent said, "I was a kid, I didn't have much of a clue about
what all that meant. The schools were segregated, the bus
stations had separate waiting areas for whites and 'coloreds.'
I remember seeing bathrooms at a gas station on one of my
visits once that had three doors on the side: Men, Women,
and Colored. The churches were also segregated. Grandma's
church, Magnolia Methodist, was only a few blocks away
from her house, in an upscale, all-white neighborhood.
Grandma was well off—she drove a powder-blue Cadillac
and had a mink stole." Kent frowned and took another sip.
"There had been some talk about demonstrations. Supposedly, some of the local black folks—called either 'coloreds'
or 'nigrahs,' if you were polite. If you weren't polite . . ."

Howard's jaw muscles flexed. "I believe I know the im-
polite term."

Kent nodded. "So, apparently, the story was, these agi-
tators were planning on integrating some of the local
churches on an upcoming Sunday. Nobody seemed to
know exactly when, only that it would be soon." He
shrugged and went on. "I was probably a typical kid when
it came to religion. I believed what my folks told me, I
earned my own Bible by reading and memorizing chapter
and verse. I wasn't devout, but I liked the stories, and I felt
comfortable knowing that the blue-eyed-blond-haired Jesus was up there watching over me."

Howard shook his head but didn't interrupt.

"So on this particular Sunday, the minister stood in
front of the congregation and said, 'You all have heard
about the possibility that we might have a visit from our
Negro brothers and sisters in the next week or two. I think
it would be appropriate for us to discuss how we might deal
with such a situation.' "

Abe paused again, his eyes staring over Howard's

shoulder, but he wasn't seeing the sparse pub crowd. He was seeing that day long ago. "Now I was just a kid, John, but I knew what Christ's message had been. Love thy neighbor, turn the other cheek, and all that, and I expected that the congregation would hold to those principles. That they would, even if they were a little uncomfortable, welcome anybody who came in—even if they had to sit in the back—to worship in God's house. I was young and unlearned in the ways of the world."

"Let me guess," Howard said. "It didn't go down like that?"

"Fifty-odd years ago, and I still remember it vividly."

The minister, a thirty-something balding man in a dark suit, standing up front, listening to his congregation.

"No way!" a tall, white-hair man in a blue suit had said. "If they want to worship, they have their own little church down the road!"

"I say we lock the door," said a red-faced fat man. "We got enough men here to take care of anybody who tries to force their way in!"

"God doesn't want the races to mix," said a gray-haired woman in a black dress, wearing a little hat with a black veil.

Abe drew in a deep, ragged breath. "It went on like this for what seemed like a long time. Violent action was the predominant voice. If the coloreds came, they'd, by God, be sorry. Even at that age, I knew that this was where the minister was supposed to step up and deliver the lesson. What Christ would do in these circumstances. How a Christian should behave. He was supposed to be the sheriff with only a double-barreled shotgun standing against a lynch mob, do or die. But he didn't. He just stood there, pale, listening, and let the congregation work itself up."

Kent paused again, then gave a little half smile. "As it turned out, our little church wasn't on the list. Nobody ever showed up, so it was all moot. But that's when I stopped going to church. When my grandmother and my parents tried to make me, I refused. I was punished for it—they grounded me, my father took his belt to me, but I wouldn't go. I didn't know jack about integration, but I knew what was right, and this wasn't. I didn't want to belong to that group."

Howard shook his head sadly. "That's a terrible thing for a child to see and hear. But you know, there's a difference between the message and the messenger. Sometimes the man carrying the Word misinterprets it. That doesn't mean the Word itself is wrong."

Kent nodded, frowning. "I know that, John. But look around. There are a lot of bad messengers. More people have been killed in holy wars, in God's name, than for ambition or territory. Christianity against Islam; Islam against Hindu; even Catholics against Protestants. Yes, Jesus threw the money changers out of the temple, but he didn't start a war with the Romans. He never killed anybody."

He paused and sipped at his beer again. "It's just that I don't need somebody explaining things to me that I can read for myself, and I sure don't need somebody getting it wrong. I think the churches have screwed up what was a fairly simple message. 'Churchianity' is a different thing, it has a life of its own. God isn't about buildings and Sunday-go-to-meeting Christians."

Howard started to speak, but Kent cut him off. "I expect you are about to say that it isn't that way at your church. I believe you. But at my age, my connection to God is personal. I believe He hears my prayers just as well on the battlefield as he does in church, and I'm too old to put up with the other bullshit."

Now it was Howard who paused and sipped at his beer, an uncomfortable look on his face. "Abe," he said after a moment, "I appreciate you telling me that. I have the feeling it wasn't easy for you, and that it's a story few have heard."

Kent nodded.

Howard tipped his glass at his friend in a small salute. "Which makes it my turn, I guess. I'm only ever going to say this to you once. What you do with it is up to you. The thing is, Abe, I'm very comfortable in my own faith, and I'm comfortable sharing that faith, but I'm not comfortable *preaching* it, if you know what I mean."

Abe smiled and nodded but didn't say anything.

"You say that you believe, my friend, and it makes me happy to hear that. But belief alone is not enough."

Kent frowned at that. "But the Bible says—"

"I know," Howard said. "John 3:16, ' . . . whosoever believeth in him shall have eternal life.' " He grinned. "I've always been partial to King James."

Kent didn't smile in return. "It also says that 'not through acts shall a man enter the kingdom of heaven, but through faith alone,' or words to that effect."

Howard nodded again. "Yes, but the question is, what do those words, 'believe' and 'faith,' mean? You see, if that's all it is, a belief alone, then it's sort of a get-out-of-jail-free card, isn't it? And that's the way, I'm sorry to say, that a lot of Christians view it: 'I believe in Jesus, I'm going to Heaven, so it doesn't matter what I do here on earth,' and that's both true and false. You're right that our acts here don't earn us any points with God. On the other hand, if we do truly believe in him, if we truly believe in his Son and his Word, then we are compelled to do certain things, to live our life a certain way. We are compelled to acts of mercy and kindness. We are compelled to charity and to a Christian love for our fellow man, to 'love one another as ourselves.' And we are compelled to join others in worship, for as the Bible also says, 'Whenever two or more gather in my name, I am with them.' "

Howard paused for a sip, draining his beer. "I won't preach at you, my friend, and I won't pressure you to come to church. But I will ask you to think about it. And while you're thinking about it, you can still eat lunch with us, can't you?"

Abe smiled and drained his own glass. "Oh, yeah, John. No problem there. As long as Nadine doesn't sneak some widow in on me."

The two smiled.

12

Chang was not impressed. Certainly not with the security at the facility, at any rate. Yes, there had been armed guards at a gate, who had come out and inspected Chang's chauffeured car, looking into the trunk and opening the hood, with a dog sniffing about the tires, presumably one trained to detect bombs.

The guards had directed Chang's driver to a lot several hundred meters away from the building, one surrounded by a tall chain-link fence topped with razor wire.

A small electric cart was waiting to take Chang to the building. The driver looked at Chang's ID, and matched it to a handheld flatscreen before starting off.

At the entrance, more armed guards checked Chang's identification again, and inspected his briefcase. They asked him if he had any kind of computer recording media with him. He did not. He knew that there were computers in this complex that were not connected to any network, inside or out, and that the only way material from those could be transferred was manually. He expected his case would be searched more thoroughly when he departed.

Still, the look into his case seemed cursory, and the guards did not pat him down.

He was issued an identity badge with his picture and a retinal scan pattern upon it. He guessed that if he went anywhere he was not supposed to go, an alarm keyed to his badge would trip.

An armed guard took him to an inner waiting area, where a receptionist placed a call. A few minutes later, a man arrived.

"Mr. Chang? I am Commander Thorn's assistant, Dylan Lacey. Please come with me."

Chang followed the man, looking around carefully as they walked. Yes, he saw carefully placed sensors mounted on the ceiling. No doubt there was some kind of reader there scanning his ID badge.

Still, they had not body-searched him, so he could have smuggled a weapon into the place. Even if there had been a hidden metal detector to ferret out guns, he might have a fiberglass or ceramic knife or pistol. Chang knew there were handguns that contained no more metal than a couple of teeth fillings, and even the cartridges were ceramic and plastic.

As if reading his mind, the assistant said, "Commander Thorn asked me to fill you in on our security systems. Aside from the guards and metal detector built into the door frame, we have IR card scanners in every and all rooms. Our house computer keeps track of everybody's badge. If you remove the ID card and try to move around without it, a silent alarm goes off, and you will find yourself facing some edgy armed guards."

Chang nodded.

"In addition to those, we have also installed the new Bertram Hard Object Scanners at various places—I'm not at liberty to say where."

Chang frowned. "I had thought those were not yet in production."

"You are correct. They are not yet commercially available. But we have a relationship with the maker—Commander Thorn is a major stockholder in Bertram Systems."

"Ah."

That put a different spin on security. The HO scanners used harmless ultrasonic pulses to scan subjects, and worked on density. Anything hard enough to take an edge, or that would withstand the pressure generated by a bullet being fired, would show up, and that would include ceramic guns and plastic knives.

But it wouldn't stop a chemical or biological attack—

"And we have also recently installed sniffers set to detect chemicals used in explosives, plus one of the new Morton bioscanners that can pick up certain substances, like, say, anthrax, down to a few parts per billion."

Chang smiled. Ah. Better and better. Would that his government had such devices. At the offices and plant that he ran? They had some old men waving people in and out at the doors, and one old metal detector in the most sensitive areas.

Of course, terrorists had not targeted his industry in China, and anybody who wanted to steal the latest technology wouldn't be looking for it there, either. You could pick up more advanced hard- and software in an Apple store than you could at most military computer centers in China. . . .

"Here we are, sir. Commander Thorn is expecting you."

"Thank you," Chang said.

Thorn was a tall, well-made fellow, dressed in a business suit that was equally well-made. He stood, came around his desk, and extended his hand for a shake. "Mr. Chang. Welcome to Net Force."

Chang recognized the Native American aspect of him—his coloring and cheekbones, mostly.

"It is my honor to be here, Commander Thorn."

Chang bowed slightly, and they shook hands.

"Please, call me Tom. We aren't big on formality here."

"Thank you. Then you must call me Han."

"Dylan filled you in on basic security?"

"Indeed. Most impressive."

Thorn shrugged. "Would that it was not necessary. We live in interesting times."

Chang smiled. "One of our proverbs."

Thorn complimented him on his English; Chang filled him in on his college, days in the U.S. They visited for a few minutes about people and places they had in common. Someone brought black tea in heavy white mugs. They engaged in small talk, polite, and as much a part of every social function in China as whatever business lay behind those.

After a few minutes, Thorn said, "I know you came here to get an idea of how we do things, and I will be happy to pass along what I can. Our governments seem to get along pretty well these days, and we are always glad to help our friends. But something has come up that we could use your help on."

Chang kept his face impassive, though this was a surprise. "My help?"

"Yes. Let me explain. . . ."

Chang listened while Thorn—who seemed very candid and forthcoming—laid out the problem. He did not get into deep detail, and Chang did not expect to hear those specifics, but even so, even saying this much was astounding. Attacks on a secure network? And from within China?

It was not something from which Chang could turn away. If somebody good enough to attack a closed network—Thorn had not specified what kind of network it was, but had given the impression that it was a significant system—and not be caught by Net Force actually *was* in China and not just spoofing? Chang needed to know who that was. And if he somehow managed to help Net Force solve its problem? They would certainly be grateful. And that gratitude could translate into all manner of things that Chang would give his back teeth to get his hands on.

When Thorn was done, he said, "I would be most happy to offer any small assistance I can."

"We greatly appreciate it, Han. I have another appointment soon, but if I might, I'd like to have my assistant introduce you to our head of computer operations."

"Jay Gridley?"

"You know of him?"

"Commander, everybody in the computer world knows of Mr. Gridley. He is the top dog."

Thorn grinned. "Well. Welcome to our pack."

Washington, D.C.

Seurat drove the Porsche—a new one, with far too many bells and whistles for a man who preferred seat-of-the-pants driving—out of the city and toward Net Force HQ. There had been some changes, or so he had heard, and maybe they could no longer help him—or maybe they wouldn't offer their help even if they *could.* But he would see what he would see.

It was a beautiful country, he had to admit. So huge. The drive to Virginia was short, and traffic heavy much of the way, but there were millions of miles of road in this land, some of which ran through areas where you might not see a house or person or another car for hours. There were states here that still allowed high speeds on highways out in the middle of nowhere, where a man could open up full-throttle and roar along at velocities closer to those of an airplane than an automobile. Too bad he did not have the time to drive across this land—such would be a memorable trip, he was sure.

A slow-moving truck blocked his land, and there was just enough room to whip around it without causing a traffic accident. Seurat gunned the engine and swerved around the truck.

The car in the next lane over honked its horn, and the driver raised his hand and extended his middle finger in Seurat's direction. One did not need to be a lip-reader to see that the man was cursing at him.

Seurat smiled. He'd had plenty of room for the maneuver—at least two or three meters away from hitting the other driver's car. It was the other driver's problem if he could not see that, *no*?

He upshifted into fifth, and even in that gear the car surged forward. Ah, the Germans. Savages, brutes, but they did know how to make fine vehicles—you had to give them that.

Looking at the tracker's map, Locke naturally speculated on Charles Seurat's possible destinations. Where could he be going outside the city?

The map was a good one, and it wasn't long before Locke had an excellent idea where the head of CyberNation was heading. The Marine base, the FBI, and Net Force lay only a few miles ahead.

Of course. Net Force was the world's standard when it came to catching cyber-criminals and -terrorists. Surely the U.S. military would have consulted them about its problems, and it made perfect sense that CyberNation would, too.

Was this something about which Locke and Wu should worry?

Locke was not familiar enough with the organization to know the ins and outs of it, but it certainly bore further study.

If that was indeed where Seurat was heading.

Maybe he was just going for a ride in the country.

Locke smiled. Always assume the worst—that way, anything lesser was a gift.

He would see, soon enough.

Net Force HQ
Quantico, Virginia

Jay had a few minutes before he had to deal with the Chinese guy. And after him, the CyberNation creep.

Might as well keep busy, no point in sitting around stewing.

He reached for the colorful box on his desk, thinking that there should really be a warning on all packaging for new VR tech: *Danger! Sharp edges inside!*

He'd lost track of the number of times he'd crashed his systems with new gear, but playing with bleeding-edge equipment was often worth the risk. This was why he always had at least two computers in his office: one for testing new gear, and one that was a couple months behind the leading edge, but with a stable OS. Should the test box crash, he'd switch, and have one of his guys reformat the crashed one.

He grinned. There were *some* advantages to being in charge of things, after all.

The box showed a close-up of the head of some bird of prey with tiny ones and zeros reflected on the predator's yellow-amber eye.

Raptor 9000X! Soar VR with the Highest Resolution Eyes in Cyberspace! read a yellow banner running diagonally across the face of the box. *New LED scan technology!* announced another.

Well, he'd see. He'd heard something good about this new technology from one of his techs and had arranged to get a working sample. Even though Net Force employees were not allowed to make official endorsements, VR companies back-channeled info to each other and dropped rumors for street cred.

Our gear is used by Net Force VR jockeys. What's on your desktop?

The rest of the world wouldn't see this gear for at least another three months—not long in the RW, but sometimes a three months lead could be a very big advantage.

He opened the box and pulled out what looked like a pair of wraparound sunglasses. A small plastic packet with a cable fell out as he removed the glasses, but he ignored it. Cables were for people who couldn't afford wi-fi.

The glasses were much lighter than the flexscreen LCDs he currently used.

He opened them and looked at the lenses, which were brightly mirrored.

Interesting. They don't look like thinscreens.

The inner surfaces were more curved than even flexible-screen technology was supposed to allow. Jay felt his interest sharpening. At the corners of each lens were tiny little holes. The temples of the glasses seemed slightly thick, and there was an optical output on the right earpiece.

A jack: These things need wires?

He pulled out the installation sheet. Well, not necessarily. If he had an optical repeater, which would pick up tiny infrared pulses from the front of the glasses and run them into the VR input card on his machine, he wouldn't need wires.

Unfortunately, since he'd been using radio-based wireless for the last several months, it looked like he'd have to use the output jack on the glasses.

Crap.

He made a mental note to order a repeater if the new glasses worked, and then bent over to pick up the cable that had slipped out of the box when he opened it.

Wires. I hate *wires.*

He hadn't had to use a cable to connect his VR gear since forever. Yet, at the same time that he was annoyed at having to regress to being tethered to his machine, he was intrigued. To require an optical cable, these things had to be drawing an awful lot of data to them.

He opened the cable packet and slipped one end into the right earpiece jack, then swiveled the end of the test machine around to find its VR card.

Do I even have *optical in?*

He searched the back of the machine, and was relieved to find one where he'd hoped on the VR card. Net Force cards were state-of-the-art with all the latest ICs and inputs. He hadn't remembered the input, but since he hadn't had to use it yet, there was no reason he should have.

He attached the cable to the card, *snick.* He spun up the odorama and pulled on some gloves. The LCD monitor tank he used when he wasn't wearing VR gear lit up: *New Hardware Detected. Updating.*

Since he'd put the driver disc in his computer already, the process was fairly automatic. A calibration screen came up with another message: *Please put on your new Raptor 9000X glasses!*

He put on the glasses and saw his eyes reflected for a second, and then the holes in the corner of the glasses lit up and he gasped.

He flew over a huge plain. He looked down and saw the shadow of a great bird, and then looked ahead. There was movement. His vision zoomed in as he watched, and he saw a tiny field mouse scampering for safety toward a tiny hole that had to be its burrow.

The VR sim was on rails, so he couldn't control where he was moving, but he could look around as he flew. The scene changed shockingly fast, clear colors, realistic mountains and scrub brush rising up to meet him as he landed and pounced on the mouse.

Again he soared, and a tiny translucent window appeared telling him to acquire three more targets to locate extreme eye focal points.

Fantastic.

It was like calibrating an old PDA's stylus. He completed that stage of the calibration, and went to a testing range where his eye movement allowed him to change VR views almost instantly.

Eye movement tracking. That was brand-new. Such technology had been around for ages for helping paralyzed people, but coupled with the sharpness? It was very impressive.

Jay tilted his head slightly and moved his eyes, and the device compensated. Apparently there was some kind of tilt sensor in the glasses as well that read head inclination and mixed the data with the eye sensors.

Nice.

But best of all was the extreme resolution. VR was fairly realistic—at least *his* scenarios were—but this was like when his folks had gotten their first High-Definition TV set. He remembered how amazed he'd been to suddenly see how *sharp* TV looked—the sweat on the announcer's head, the seams in scenery—things had reached an entirely new level of reality.

This is great.

He called up the documentation and checked his suppositions. Sure enough—there was a new Texas Instruments gyro chip that read head movement, and the tiny holes in the lens corners tracked his eye movements, then bounced three low-power laser beams off the mirrors—made by Nikon to the highest standards, if you could believe the rap—into his eye, painting directly on his retina. Things looked real, because as far as his eye was concerned, they *were* real.

Very clever work here.

Time to play.

He called up a favorite test scenario, a glade in Japan looking toward Mt. Fuji, cherry blossoms falling around him.

It looked . . .

It looked like *crap*!

Jay walked over to the cherry tree and peered at it. Had the glasses malfunctioned?

No. There was the texture he'd programmed—it had looked great on his flexscreen glasses because their resolution was so low.

Holy cow.

The resolution on these glasses was so sharp that he could see the edges of the pixels. It was like stepping into a comic book from the real world.

Hmmm, I've got some work to do.

It wouldn't do to have anyone else seeing *his* VR with these glasses, that was for sure. He'd have to amp up the textures, improve the bump-mapping, and double or triple the data throughout for this scene. No way he was going to be caught looking amateurish.

No wonder these things needed optical. It was like giving somebody who had 20/60 vision a pair of glasses that corrected for near-sightedness. They could see all right before the glasses, but afterward would be ever so much better.

Which gave him an idea.

He called up a firewall he'd been trying to break, looking to find the cracks where he could drive a code-breaking spike.

On his older VR visual gear he hadn't been able to see any difference in the smooth, black obelisklike wall. But with the Raptor's resolution, he could suddenly see a pattern of cracks where data structures joined together and made up the firewall. Yeah, sure, it was part metaphor and part construction, but he'd take it.

Just glancing at the wall with these new glasses, and he could see exactly where to crack that wall. He was sure of it.

Now, that *was cool.*

Net Force was going to be outfitted with these within a few days—hours—if Jay had his way. As soon as they hit the commercial market, there was gonna be a boatload of VR reconstruction as other makers suddenly saw their constructs in a bright new light, but until then, wearing these babies would make you at least a prince in the land of the blind, if not the king.

Until these things became common, the bleeding edge of technology was gonna be something with which Jay Gridley could slice the bad guys.

He couldn't *wait* to show this to somebody.

"Jay?"

The voice brought him back to the moment. He looked up and saw his assistant standing there. He blinked at her. "Huh?"

"I have Mr. Chang here to see you."

"Oh. Oh, yeah. Sure. Send him in."

A moment later, she was back, leading a short and definitely Chinese-looking man in a gray suit.

"Mr. Gridley. My honor to meet you."

Jay waved that off. "Mr. Chang." He stood. The two shook hands.

"Cal Tech, right?"

"Class of '03," Chang said.

"Come on in. Take a look at this." He waved at his computer. "You're not gonna *believe* these visuals!"

13

After they introduced themselves and sat back down, and before Thorn could say anything else, Charles Seurat nodded at the corner behind and to the right of Thorn's desk. "You fence?"

Thorn had his gear bags in the corner of his office, and the only way Seurat could have known what was in them was to recognize the logo on the épée bag. Most non-fencers would not have a clue what the name meant. And because he obviously *did* recognize it, then that meant Seurat, too, was a fencer or a serious watcher.

"A little," Thorn said with a small smile. "Don't look for me in the next Olympics."

"Nor me," Seurat said. "Would that I had brought my blades. We could have worked out."

That was a pretty obvious hint, Thorn thought. It was not what he would have expected, even if he had known that Seurat was a fencer as well. Even avid fencers didn't normally throw down the gauntlet within moments of meeting another fencer—and certainly not under circumstances like this.

On the other hand, he had known that Charles Seurat was anything but ordinary—something, Thorn acknowledged, that could be said for himself as well. And the Frenchman did have the right idea. After all, what better way to measure a man's mettle than at the point of one's sword?

"I have extra," Thorn said with another small smile. "Just down the hall. It wouldn't hurt to stretch a little after sitting at this desk all day."

Seurat returned the smile. "Lead on," he said.

The two men went to the gym, which was empty at the moment. Thorn opened his locker, wherein he had an extra set of practice gear—blades, including foil, épée, and saber, along with gloves and a mask, and a variety of jackets. He kept hoping that some of the other Net Force personnel would decide to try their hand at fencing, and so had a small array of gear to fit a variety of sizes.

"Excellent! I see you use first-rate gear."

"What is your pleasure, Charles?"

"Foil, I think. I'm a bit sluggish and out of practice."

"Foil it is. Help yourself."

Thorn smiled again, but privately, when he noticed that the Frenchman chose a blade with a German Visconte grip rather than the traditional—and expected—French grip. *This just might be fun,* he thought.

The two men changed clothes and donned fencing gear. They each went through a series of stretches and warm-ups. Thorn noticed that Seurat moved very well for a man who claimed to be sluggish and out of practice.

Warmed up and looser, they took their places on the piste, or fencing strip, Thorn had taped out on the floor and regarded each other.

It had been a long time since Thorn had fenced foil, and even longer since he'd fenced it for real. It was the weapon he'd first learned, back in high school, and as such it was his first love, but he'd pretty much abandoned it after he'd discovered the épée and the saber. And lately, of course, thanks to the promptings of Colonel Kent, he'd been focusing almost exclusively on *iaido*.

Old habits die hard, however, and he was pleasantly surprised at how comfortable the blade felt in his grip.

He sketched a quick salute, saw Seurat mirror the move, and they both slipped on their masks and came to guard.

"Ready?" Thorn asked. As the host, it fell to him to start the opening touch. He used English, however, since it would feel more than a little awkward using the traditional French *"Etes-vous prêt?"* with a Frenchman.

He could see the small smile that formed on Seurat's lips, and knew that he understood.

"Ready," he said.

Thorn smiled, too. "Begin."

The word had barely left his lips and the Frenchman was in motion. Two quick steps, a liquid smooth—and lightning-fast—lunge, and Seurat's blade was slipping around Thorn's guard.

Except that Thorn wasn't there. At Seurat's first step, he had begun sliding backward, letting the Frenchman close distance, but not, perhaps, quite as quickly as Seurat had hoped.

When the attack came, Thorn was just far enough away to bring his hand back along Seurat's blade, press against it in opposition, and then, swiveling his left shoulder back to draw his belly out of line in case he'd failed in his attempted opposition, send his own point streaking toward Charles's heart.

Seurat countered with a parry four, Thorn pressed back with his bell guard, trying to maintain the opposition, and a moment later the Frenchman recovered backward out of his lunge, retreating out of distance and coming back to guard.

No touch. Neither point had met the opponent, on target or off.

Both fencers smiled and saluted each other.

"Nice attack," Thorn said. "Very quick."

"And an excellent move on your part," Charles said. "I anticipated the opposition counterattack, of course, but I hadn't expected that particular evasion from an épéeist."

Thorn smiled again. So Charles had done his homework, had he?

"Yes, well, I wasn't always an épéeist," he said.

Seurat nodded and tossed Thorn another quick salute. *"Prêt?"* he asked.

Thorn answered the salute. *"Oui, je suis prêt,"* he replied. *"Allez!"*

And they were off once again, a ballet of blades and body, dancing the ancient dance of victory and of death.

Thorn grinned, feeling the adrenaline rush through him once more, the exhilaration of competition, the incomparable thrill of testing oneself against another. Through the mask, he saw an answering smile on Charles's face.

Yes, the Frenchman had had a very good idea indeed.

Jay was ready—as ready as he was going to be, anyway—for the meeting with Seurat. The one with Chang, that had been fine. The little guy from China was sharp and very appreciative, and they'd be getting together again in RW or VR to establish some Chinese connections. Chang was quiet, down-to-earth, had some moves, and deferred to Jay's expertise, which he was smart enough to see, no problem.

But CyberNation's rep coming in? Jay didn't have much faith he'd be so easy. First, he was with the organization that had given Net Force a royal pain in the posterior. Second, he was French, and there was a reason that "snotty Frenchman" had become a cliché.

Jay didn't want to do it, but he had told Thorn he would try to behave in a civilized fashion, and he'd give it a shot. That CyberNation had been responsible for nearly killing John Howard, and had done a bunch of other dangerous and illegal stuff, didn't make it easy. This was going to be like sitting down with a *terrorist,* as far as Jay was concerned.

Sure, CyberNation had claimed no responsibility for the

two incidents—"rogue elements out of our control," and so
on. But, hey, the Secretary always disavowed all knowledge of the *Mission Impossible* team, too, didn't he?

No need to disavow anything that was *successful,* was
there?

The door opened and in walked Seurat. Jay recognized
him from some of the background VR he'd run. Tall,
aristocratic-looking, with dark hair, well-cut and short. Nice
suit. He looked flushed, and Jay understood why—word had
come past Jay's door that Seurat and Thorn had gone to the
gym and danced with those whippy blades the boss liked to
play with, and wasn't that just swell? Fencing buddies.

*Really nice suit, though. Give them that. The French
sure know how to dress.*

The CyberNation leader eyed Jay like a man might look
at a trained chimpanzee, his expression a sort of a wonder-
if-it-can-understand-me look.

Oh, boy.

Could be that Mr. Seurat had what some of Jay's buddies at MIT had called Euro-Q. Back in his school days
there had been a good number of best-of-the-brightest im-
ports from Europe, who had thought that because they
were in the land of the tasteless American, that it meant
they were naturally smarter as well.

But Jay also remembered one of his old college buddies,
a guy named Bernard from Tennessee. Bernard had been
invited to play chess by an Englishman named Sykes.
Bernard, who spoke slowly with a thick Southern twang,
had looked mildly bemused.

"Well, ah'm afraid I barely know the rules of that game,
sir," his friend had said. "But ah'll give it a try, if'n you
want."

Sykes had, according to the story, looked positively
gleeful. He'd been ready for a fine round of pummel-the-
Colonial, but instead had been *destroyed* by Bernard, who
in fact was a ranked chess player and had competed nation-
ally. The lesson hadn't been lost on Jay: Never judge a
book by its cover.

Maybe he's not just an arrogant, well-dressed jerk.

"Allo? You must be Monsieur Greedlee?"

Because he didn't want to be at the meeting, Jay was primed to be irritated, and this was enough to start the ball rolling. "Mr. Seurat," he said, taking care to pronounce the second syllable "rat" instead of "rah."

Seurat's frown was paper-thin and gone in a second, but Jay had seen it.

Jay had played this game before. Guy was gonna have to get up earlier than that to stay ahead of him. He smiled and waved at the chairs.

They sat down at the glossy-finished wood table. The fluorescent lights overhead gleamed upon the thick finish, and Jay could see their distorted reflections as he sat down. Seurat's body language was relaxed, but Jay could tell it was a front. The man's eyes did not match his poise, and while there were no overt signs, Jay thought he could feel the man's annoyance.

He stifled an inward sigh. Better get it started so he could get it over.

"I understand you've had some problems at CyberNation with your networks?" Jay asked.

Seurat's lips compressed slightly before he replied. "Indeed, we have been attacked by a major VR talent, on several occasions. By that, I mean someone very good was involved. World-class, Mr. Gridley."

The stupid-Frenchman accent had vanished. His English was now as crisp as an icicle at thirty degrees below zero, with barely a trace of any accent.

Aha! Shades of the Tennessee chess champion!

Seurat said, "I understand you have some familiarity with VR?"

Some familiarity? Jay wanted to stand and spit on the man. Which was, of course, exactly why the man had said it. *Don't let him get your goat, Jay.*

"Yes, I have some small knowledge of it," said Jay, thinking, *More in my little finger than in your entire programming team.* "Perhaps we can help train your people to

discover what went wrong. After all, the U.S. did invent
VR, and not everyone has the same understanding."

"Or perhaps we might show you a way to keep your military's very expensive war scenarios from going into the
toilet?"

Seurat smiled, his expression as bland as Jay's.

Oh, he wanted to play?

"I don't expect we need any help there. I'm on the trail
of the perpetrator. Only a matter of time until I get him."

"Time is money, is it not?"

Jay smiled. The man was smooth. Butter wouldn't melt
in his mouth.

Seurat shook his head, and the smile, this time, seemed
genuine. "Mr. Gridley, I will acknowledge that you are better than I, better than any of our people when it comes to
chasing VR criminals and terrorists. And that I am an arrogant Frenchman and you have put me in my place. Now
that we have both waved our weenies at each other, perhaps we can get past the posturing *merde* and down to
business?"

Despite himself, Jay had to laugh. The guy had it nailed.
Score a point for him.

"Go ahead, Mr. Seurat." He pronounced the name cor-
rectly this time. "I'm listening."

Seurat continued. "Our most recent incursion was just a
few hours ago, when a VR dragon entered one of our
shared-space utopias and began attacking our citizens."

"A dragon?"

"*Oui.* I was sent a copy of the attack from one of our
VR security monitors on my way to Washington. Here is a
link to a secure CyberNation storehouse where a copy has
been set aside for you."

He handed Jay a slip of paper with a VR address on it.

Dragon. Western or Chinese?

The form of the dragon might add weight to the clue
he'd uncovered at the VR saloon. Jay looked at the address
and nodded.

"I'll see what I can find out," he said, then added, "but I may need unrestricted access to your network."

The unasked question hung in the air.

The Frenchman seemed to reach a decision, and nodded to himself.

"I shall see that you are allowed whatever access you need, Mr. Gridley."

Jay nodded. That was true, the guy had just made a big decision.

Jay made a decision of his own. "Call me Jay," he said.

Seurat nodded. "And I am Charles. I will be at the Watergate until tomorrow morning. Please contact me if you have any trouble with network access."

"The Watergate," said Jay. "Of course." He smiled. This time Seurat smiled back at him.

Of course. What better place for a rival nation's leader to stay than the site of one of our worst scandals?

Jay didn't like CyberNation, but he had to give Seurat points for style. And balls.

But I get more points for getting full network access.

He wasn't sure he'd be able to help the virtual nation, nor even if he wanted to help it, but he was certainly going to enjoy walking through their systems while he tried.

Jay Gridley wins again.

14

Kent attended to his paper- and e-work, always a bigger part of his job than he liked. When he couldn't put it off any longer, he would just plow into the requisition forms, assorted order-postings, and such, and make an attempt to catch up on his perpetual backlog. Much as he hated it, there were times when he had to get into the grind.

While deep in the minutiae of a report on uniform grades and current in-house stocks of same, his computer *pinged.* For a moment, he didn't recall what that meant; then it came to him: It was a searchbot attention-sig.

He had the system set up for voxax, so he said, "Searchbot report."

The file on uniforms collapsed and shrank as if being sucked down a drain, leaving a small icon in the bottom of the computer screen. The bot's report appeared in its place, and the bot started to read it aloud in a voice that reminded Kent of a particularly boring professor whose course Kent had once taken at the War College. "Stop vocal," he said. He could still read.

The report, which on the face of it seemed innocuous enough, was about a classical guitar competition in, of all places, Lincoln, Nebraska. The solo finals were being held this coming Saturday at seven in the evening, and would consist of four contestants. Their names were Emile Domenicio, Sarah Pen Jackson, Richard Justice, and Phillip Link.

None of these names meant anything to Kent.

The listed programs included works by Bach, Rivera, Barrios, Sor, Scarlatti, Berkeley, and Pujol, also names that, until recently, would mostly have meant little to him. But, since the operation in which the Georgian hired killer, one Eduard Natadze, had managed to screw up Kent's initial fieldwork for Net Force, the colonel had made it his business to learn about classical guitars and the music associated with them. That was because Natadze had been, by all reports, a talented amateur classical guitarist. That was in addition to his day job: strong-arm and hit man for the late Samuel Walker Cox, a rich man who'd once been a Soviet spy.

Natadze was a man who had beaten Kent at every turn, always a half step ahead, and who had escaped. Oh, how that had rankled.

It was still impossible for Kent to think about it without building a head of steam that threatened to blow his head off. Abe Kent flat did not like to lose.

The case was officially closed—there had been some high-level sweeping under the rug, for political and financial reasons—but Kent hadn't just smiled and let it go. He might not be able to spend any official energy on it, but he hadn't quit looking.

A few seachbots that kept eyes open for material concerning classical guitar music and instruments didn't cost anything, and there was always the hope something might pop up that would be useful.

Offhand, he couldn't see what it was here, other than the most general anything-classical connection.

But, at the bottom of the scroll, there was a notation that several luthiers would be on hand for a showing of their classical instruments. One of these guitar-builders was Otto Bergman, who, according to the article, hadn't shown his works in public for more than three years.

Bergman. Kent nodded at the name, remembering it.

When they had been searching for Natadze and had a general idea about him, before they had known specifically who he was, they'd been cross-checking guitar-makers who specialized in concert-quality instruments. They'd eventually run the hit man's home address to ground this way, by backtracking an instrument he'd bought from a world-class maker in California, a guy named Bogdanovich.

There had been a mysterious explosion at Natadze's house shortly thereafter, and that instrument, along with several others, had been destroyed. A shame, that. The official line was that Natadze had done it, but Kent had never quite accepted that—a guy who spent that much on guitars and who loved to play them would have pulled them out before he blew the house up.

Later, after the investigation had been pretty much shut down, Jay Gridley had found that Natadze had another guitar on order, which, at the time, had been several months away from completion. This particular one was being built by Otto Bergman, who lived in Colorado, Kent recalled.

Naturally, Natadze hadn't been stupid enough to send in a new address to take delivery of his guitar, even though it had set him back about eight grand, if Kent's memory was accurate. That would be a dead end, except that Kent had an idea that if somebody wanted a handmade instrument bad enough to pay eight thousand dollars for it, he might try to find a way to collect it.

Natadze was on the run, and it would be stupid of him to show up at Bergman's virtual or real door with cash in hand asking for the guitar made for his pseudonym—he'd have to assume that Net Force had made that connection, he was too smart not to figure that.

But Bergman still had that guitar, because Net Force

had paid him the five thousand dollars Natadze still owed on it, and told him to hang on to it. Kent assumed that Natadze knew Bergman still had the guitar, but not that Net Force had paid the tab on it—though he would not be surprised if Natadze had figured that out, too. Nobody had ever called for it, and Kent hadn't really expected that anybody would, but it had been the only bait they'd had for a trap, weak as it was.

Kent stared at the guitar competition notice. Natadze couldn't buy the guitar he'd wanted, not under his name, nor the phony handle he'd used, but if old Otto was showing his wares at a public place for the first time in years, there was no reason Natadze couldn't just walk up and try to buy one on the spot. He liked the man's work enough to have put up three thousand bucks against eight, and he hadn't gotten anything for it.

A man strolls up to your display, nods at the guitars.

Nice work. You have any instruments in stock that aren't spoken for?

Well, yes, this one is for sale.

Put it in the case, sir, I'll take it. . . .

Order anything by mail or the web, there were ways to track you and find out where you were—credit cards, phone numbers, delivery services. Walk up in person, give the salesman a phony name and a sheaf of clean bills, and there was no trail, no way to trace you, or even know you'd *been* there, unless you happened to walk in front of a surveillance cam and somebody bothered to look at the image.

Given the tens of thousands of cams available to Homeland Security, and the millions of images that they provided, the chances of coming across somebody like Natadze again without real specific places to look were slim and snowball.

It would be a smart move, cash and carry, and low-risk, especially if you had any idea the search for you had been effectively shut down months ago.

Kent leaned back his chair. Natadze apparently had enough money so that a few thousand dollars wasn't worth risking his freedom over. But more than the money itself, the passion Natadze felt for his music might make a guitar like this something to take a chance on. And besides, from what Kent had learned about the man, he might be the kind of guy who, once he set his mind on something, kept going until he got it. And it wasn't as if they had anything else that would lead to him. . . .

Kent considered it. It was a reach, a very long shot, but not a costly one. The competition was a few days away, and things were quiet here. It would be on a weekend, too, so he'd be on his own time. And there were a lot of military aircraft in the air on any given day. More than one branch of the service owed him a favor or two, not to mention that he was back in the Corps now. He could snag a flight heading that way, take in a classical guitar competition, and browse the luthier's display afterward, couldn't he? It wasn't like he had a hot date this Saturday, or anything else on his plate he needed to worry about.

And if Eduard Natadze showed up looking for a new guitar?

Boy, wouldn't that be worth the trip?

15

Three Pines Motel
Quantico, Virginia

Locke had spent four days in and out of a motel not far
from Net Force Headquarters at Quantico. It had been a
productive time. Seurat had stayed another day in D.C.,
then gone home, and Locke had stuck around and done research, a bit of social engineering, and had learned some
disturbing information.

None of which was nearly as disturbing as what was
happening in his room right at the moment. . . .

In his late twenties, Locke had had a paramour whose
family had inherited a membership in Hong Kong's Empire Gun Club. The club was made up of well-to-do Brits,
ex-pats, and wealthy Chinese who could afford the five-
thousand-pound-a-year membership fee. You didn't even
have to own a gun to use the place—there was an incredible variety of weapons locked away at the main range that
they would allow members to shoot.

The woman with whom Locke had been having a professional liaison, Rowena, was fifty-something, well-made,

and enjoyed firing off various handguns three or four times a month. She also took it upon herself to teach Locke all about the things: not only how to aim and shoot them, but how to take them apart, the differences between pistols and revolvers, the strengths and weaknesses of the different calibers, and a wide range of ballistic and other information. Locke had shown a professional interest—Rowena got very passionate after a session at the range, and she liked to slake her excitement in bed—but he hadn't thought he would ever have much use for the ability to fire a pistol accurately.

Back in his days in the street gangs, it would have been useful, for those rare times when guns came out. Even in Hong Kong twenty-five years ago, handguns had been easy enough to come by, if you had enough money. But they were bad for business. Most of the boys who ran with Locke used their fists, sometimes augmented with clubs, knives, or even hatchets, but rarely firearms.

In the days before the English pulled out, the police, who might not raise an eyebrow if two rival gangs thumped each other bloody and filled up a local hospital, took a dim view of anything that might threaten tourists. A stray bullet that wounded a rich visitor from Japan would mean a lot of street criminals would be spending time in jail until the police sorted it out.

Many of the gang members had picked up odd bits of Chinese martial arts—kung fu, *wushu*—along the way. The town was thick with old Chinese men who danced those dances, and the techniques that worked on the street were passed along to fellow members. Locke was no Bruce Lee, but he could handle himself, and he'd never played with guns until he'd met Rowena.

It had been a waste of time, insofar as Locke never expected to use the knowledge again. But he'd been wrong.

At this moment, he was glad his former lover had spent all that time showing him what she had—

—because the man sitting in the chair across from him

in the hotel room had a pistol in his hand, and it was loosely pointed in Locke's direction.

The gun was a Colt 1911, a semiautomatic that had once been U.S. military issue, long ago. The man holding it, one T.A. Collins, aged sixty-four, was a former security guard who had worked briefly for Net Force. Collins had been fired for drinking on the job. Locke had poked around and found him, guessing that he would be amenable to selling information. Collins had been open to the idea. The day before yesterday, he had been an asset.

Now, he had become an annoying problem.

"Pointing a gun at me isn't really a good way to cement a good business relationship," Locke said.

Collins was fifteen feet away. Too far to jump, even knowing what Locke knew—which was that Collins apparently hadn't spent much time practicing with his weapon— the thumb-safety was still on. While it would take only a half second to wipe the safety off, it shouldn't be employed in such a situation as this—Collins couldn't know if Locke had a weapon himself, and a half second might be enough for him to seize the advantage.

Collins said, "Yeah, well, let's just think of this"—he waggled the gun—"as insurance."

Locke nodded. "All right. How much?"

"Ten thousand. I go away, nobody hears any stories."

Locke nodded, considering the proposal. He had paid Collins a thousand dollars U.S. and had found out about Net Force's recent transfer to military control, a most useful bit of information. Now the man was blackmailing him, threatening to point him out to the authorities for asking his questions.

Ten thousand would not make a large dent in the operating fund Wu provided. If you could make a problem go away by throwing money at it—and if you had plenty of money—then it wasn't much of a problem. Here, in this moment, it would be the easiest—and safest—action. Buy the fellow off. No muss, no fuss.

But, of course, blackmailers, once you caved in, tended to be greedy. Locke had known a few such men in his former profession, men who slept with married women, then made them pay and pay to keep it secret. More bad business.

Locke might not be in this country but a few more days. Then again, he might be here for weeks, depending on several factors, and if it was this easy for Collins to collect money, he would almost certainly return for more. Even that wasn't necessarily a big problem in itself—the man was greedy, but small-minded. Five figures was essentially pocket change given the scope of the operation Locke and Wu had begun.

No, the real problem was that Collins, who'd been bought, had not stayed bought. True, it was hard to ask for the information he wanted without opening himself to risk, but any further down this road might put the entire plan in jeopardy. It would not do for the United States Homeland Security to be looking at him as a possible terrorist. They had the power to grab him up and lock him away, and while he might eventually get free, he had no desire whatsoever to have to deal with that.

No. Mr. Collins here had made a big mistake.

If there was one thing Locke knew how to do well, it was to massage an ego.

"All right," Locke said. "You got me. I'll get the money."

"You have that kind of cash *here*?"

"In my suitcase, in the closet there. I have about twenty-five thousand." Locke stood.

The flare of greed in the man's eyes almost made Locke laugh. He stood.

So did Collins. "No, I'll get it. I wouldn't want you maybe finding a gun in that case next to the money."

"I don't own a gun." True enough.

"All the same."

"Fine. You'll need a key to open the suitcase. May I?"

Collins nodded. "Carefully."

The luggage was closed, but not locked—these days, too many airports would just break into cases if they were—

and Locke didn't even have keys to his suitcases. But he withdrew the keys to the rental car from his pocket slowly and extended them toward Collins. He took a step. Another.

Collins put his own free hand out to collect the keys.

Locke gently tossed them at the man, aiming to Collins's right. With the gun in that hand, Collins couldn't use it to catch the keys, and the angle was awkward for him to use his left hand, though he tried. It turned him slightly, so the gun swung to his right and toward the floor, where the missed keys fell.

Locke was maybe seven feet away. He took two fast steps and kicked Collins in the groin.

"Uhh—!" Collins grunted and bent over, suddenly in great pain.

Before he could slip the gun's safety off and get the pistol aimed, Locke grabbed the man's head with both hands and twisted sharply, pulling up at the same time. That was the trick—one or the other wouldn't do it, chiropractors twisted necks all the time and made people feel better, but moving in two planes was risky—

Collins's neck snapped. Locke let go, and the man collapsed, paralyzed. Locke squatted, put his hands around Collins's throat, and squeezed. With his air shut off, it was only a matter of a couple of minutes until the man was dead.

Locke stood, feeling the flow of adrenaline ebb. His heart was still racing, his breathing fast, but it was over.

Locke saved by a lock. Ironic.

Now the problem was: How was he going to get rid of the body?

Four Leaf Clover Casino
Macao, China

Wu did not consider himself a gambler. There were times when a man had to take risks—all life had risk—but he came to such times prepared to deal with them as best he could. A

man who wagered much against the roll of a pair of dice or
the fall of a marble onto a roulette wheel, unless he was rich
and could afford to lose, was an idiot in Wu's book.

Unless, of course, he knew the dice were loaded or the
wheel rigged to pay off in his favor.

The line between shrewdness and idiocy was sometimes
thin, but there *was* such a divider, and you wanted to be on
the right side of it.

The slot machines' noises were tiresome, but Wu continued to pull the handle of the one in front of him, feeding
it from a credit card issued by the casino. The room
smelled of stale cigarette smoke and perspiration, despite
the air conditioners that filtered and cooled it. And maybe a
little stink of desperation was mixed in. All around him,
scores, maybe hundreds of people, were losing money they
couldn't afford to lose.

Wu wore civilian clothes. To a tourist, he'd be just another graying local pumping a slot machine.

Wu had more than one reason to be here, but the immediate one was the young Mr. Shing, who sat at a blackjack
table with Mayli standing next to him, one hand on his
shoulder. Shing was playing for small stakes, and was
down a couple hundred. He had, of course, a system. Mayli
had told him all about it, and for a man who thought himself as smart as Shing did, that was incredibly stupid.

The only way to beat the house was to be some kind of
savant who could count cards in your head. Since the
casino used multiple decks, this was more than a little difficult, and even if you could track every card played accurately and bet accordingly, all you did was shift the odds a
little bit in your favor. Play for five hours at a time, and
with good counting skills, you could win six times out of
ten. Not a major killing without a lot of work, but a slow
and steady income.

Of course, the best dealers at most casinos also knew
how to count cards, and if they saw that a player had an increased chance of winning, they could shuffle up and kill
that advantage.

And then there were ways to cheat outright.

A pair of glasses with small television cameras built into them, to send images via radio or cell phone to a partner who had a computer figuring the odds with each hand. Most casinos now ran wideband jammers in their gambling rooms, killing transmitters or receivers, and they had infrared detectors to catch those using line-of-sight IR devices.

Wu knew there were small personal computers you could hide in a pocket that would keep track of the cards and offer advice on amounts to bet. For four or five thousand dollars U.S., you could get one of these, and increase your odds from winning six out of ten sessions to maybe seven or eight. The casinos knew about these devices, of course, and some of them had scanners that would spot them, even in this day of so many personal electronics— phones, personal assistants, and the like.

If you got caught bringing a card computer or spyware into a casino, they'd just ask you to leave. If you got caught using these at the tables? That could get you beaten and left in an alley, and the local police would not be the least bit sympathetic.

Any way a man could think of cheating, the casinos had already seen it and twenty variations. And if you had a system and real money? They would send a chartered jet to pick you up and bring you.

His machine chortled and paid out fifty dollars in credit, and lights flashed and bells rang, to tell other patrons that winning was possible.

Wu smiled. He was slightly ahead and playing on the house's money, not that it mattered. He was more interested in watching Shing and Mayli. He had no worry that the boy would spot him. Shing had never seen him out of uniform, and Wu would bet that the computer expert would walk right past him without noticing who he was. Too full of himself to pay attention to old men on stools playing slot machines.

Mayli would know him, of course. She had seen him out of uniform—out of clothes altogether—but if she did see him, nobody looking at her would mark it. She was a professional. She would know he wasn't here just to play the slots, and she'd probably guess he was watching Shing. Or her. But she would not let on, not even a hint. She knew better.

Wu's machine went crazy. The buzzer buzzed, bells rang, a bank of red and blue lights on top flashed in a rapid sequence.

What—?

He glanced at the screen, and saw that he had just won a five-thousand-dollar jackpot.

Around him, people looked at him, they smiled or frowned, some offering congratulations. Casino personnel headed toward him.

Wu frowned. He didn't need this attention. He turned away from the blackjack tables to make sure his face wasn't visible. Yes, Shing was full of his own ego, but walking past a loser and turning to notice a big winner were different things. Wu had no desire to explain anything to Shing he did not want the man to know.

Osage Motel
North of Lincoln, Nebraska

Getting from Washington to Nebraska had been easy. Colonel Abe Kent had found a military flight headed that way and got himself invited on board. Getting back, however, was proving more of a challenge.

It turned out there wasn't a military flight from Nebraska heading toward Washington/Quantico until Sunday around noon. On top of that, to catch the first available flight he would have to drive to Offutt AFB. Though fairly close, it certainly wasn't walking distance, so he rented a motel room on the highway to Omaha, and went there after the classical guitar competition was done.

Just after midnight, he was lying on the bed staring at the open closet. In the alcove, next to his git'n'go travel bag, was another case—one he hadn't brought with him from Quantico.

He recalled the evening as he lay there. Any of the four finalists had been professional enough to make a living at it, from what Kent could tell—and the guy who had won was maybe not quite as technically perfect as the one who came in second, but he had a more intense connection with his instrument and the audience. Kept his eyes closed most of the time, and given the complex pieces and fingerings, that impressed Kent. Plus, he just seemed to get into the music more than the others.

It was also interesting in that the contestants had played without any kind of amplification, at a university theater with maybe three hundred people watching. They simply came out onto the stage, sat on a piano bench, and propped one foot up on a little footstool. One guy had used a plain wooden chair, and had some kind of prop stuck to his guitar that kept the neck angled up.

You could have heard a pin drop just before the players got started, the quietest theater Kent could remember being in, and despite the size of the theater, which could probably hold twice as many people as were there, the nylon-stringed guitars had enough volume to carry all the way to the rear seats, which is where he'd sat, looking for Natadze.

Kent hadn't seen him, but he had heard the music just fine.

The luthier displays afterward were also impressive. Objects of art, most of them, guitars that looked great and made sweet music—when somebody else picked them up and played them. Kent's musical talent was zero, except that he liked to listen to all kinds—from classical to jazz to rock to country, whatever—if it was done well.

The hunt for Natadze had come up empty. The former hit man for Cox hadn't shown up looking for a new guitar. Kent would have spotted him, even if he'd changed his appearance, he was sure of that.

Well. It had been a remote possibility at best.

He had talked to Otto Bergman, once the makers had

started packing their stuff away to leave. He'd identified himself, and told the man why he was there. Bergman, who was sixty-something, white-haired, wrinkled, and tanned more than Kent would have thought a guitar-builder would be, had pointed out the very instrument that Natadze had ordered.

"I don't have that many at any given time," the man had said. "And since that one seemed destined to stay at my shop forever, I figured I might as well get some use out of it. It belongs to Net Force—you could take it with you, if you wish. It's just taking up space at my place, and if your man was going to try and get it, he would have done so by now."

The idea of hauling an eight-thousand-dollar guitar across country rattling around in the back of a C-130 didn't appeal to Kent. He might hitch a ride on something a little more upscale, a C-40 or maybe even a C-12 or C-21, and that would be more like flying commercial, but still.

As if the man could read his thoughts, Bergman had said, "I outfit my guitars with Josey Herumin cases, Colonel. They are made of carbon fiber and Kevlar, custom-fitted. Josey gives me a deal on them because I buy five or six a year, and they add eight hundred dollars to the price of the guitar. You could drive a truck over one of them and it wouldn't hurt the guitar inside. I have a picture of a Toyota pickup with one of the front wheels resting on a Herumin case, and tire doesn't even dent it."

"How do you know I'm really from Net Force and not some con man trying to steal one of your instruments?"

"How would you know I have one belonging to Net Force? I didn't tell anybody, and I'm assuming they didn't, so if you know, either you are with them or a very clever thief." He paused, and looked at Kent intently. "You aren't a crook, are you?"

"No."

"Good enough for me. Anyway, I've been paid for it. Wouldn't cost me a thing if you swiped it." He grinned, then, his face softening. "Besides, *you'd* be the guy who has to deal with Net Force."

Which was how Kent came to have a very expensive

classical guitar in the closet of his motel room, inside a black case you could use for stopping bullets.

He had a paperback book he'd picked up at the airport, one of those military history things done by some big-name writer and a former general, and he read for thirty or forty minutes before he turned off the light and went to sleep.

Kent came awake in an instant. He'd heard something, some noise in the room with him that ought not to be there.

His side arm was on the floor next to the bed and he reached down and pulled it from the holster. He thumbed the safety off and cocked it. That sound seemed very loud. There was a small flashlight on the bedside table, a butt-button job he carried when he traveled, in case a fire or some other disaster cut the power. He grabbed the light, then carefully rolled over the bed and onto the floor to his left, away from the front door. He crossed wrists so that the light and the gun's muzzle were aimed in the same direction, then he thumbed the light button on.

He did a fast sweep of the room with the light. Nobody there.

The little metal safety loop-latch on the door was still in place—nobody had come or gone that way.

He came up to a low crouch and worked his way to the bathroom.

Nobody in there, either.

He straightened up. Must have been something outside that sounded closer than it was. He switched on the overhead light.

He was only a meter or so away from the closet, and there, he saw two things immediately:

The guitar case was gone.

There was a stack of hundred-dollar bills on the floor where the case had been.

He knew immediately what had happened.

He ran to the door. He flicked off the safety loop and unlocked the door, jerked it wide, jumped outside and dropped low, and spun three-sixty as he looked for a target—

Nothing—

He was in his skivvies, with a pistol in his hand, and fortunately, at three in the morning, no civilians were standing around in the parking lot to have heart attacks when they saw him. He came up from his crouch, all alone.

Natadze!

The bastard had *come into his room*—had to be through the bathroom window—taken the guitar, and left what Kent was sure was going to be five thousand dollars in its place.

Son of a bitch!

After he hurriedly got dressed, Kent searched the parking lot and the area around it. Natadze wasn't there.

Sure enough, his room's bathroom window had been the point of entry—there were tool marks on the frame, where somebody had forced the sliding glass panel open, and what he took to be shoe heel or sole scuffs on the painted wall.

The guy had balls, no question. To break into his room, take the guitar, and then *pay* for the sucker? *That* was nervy.

But maybe worse was, Natadze had spotted him, figured out who he was and what he was doing, and managed to tail him—without Kent having a clue. That *really* galled.

Of course, Kent should have considered that if he would recognize Natadze at first sight, then Natadze might know *him* as well. Back when they'd been after Cox, Natadze could have seen him. Or maybe just found an image of Kent somewhere—a lot of Net Force information was available to the public, and certainly Kent's appointment to head the military wing hadn't been any kind of state secret. Natadze could have found that out easily enough.

Well, that didn't really matter. What did matter was that the guy had been within a couple meters of Kent while he snored away. If Natadze had wanted to, he could have just as easily shot Kent dead as not, and that made him feel worse still.

Why hadn't Natadze shot him? Why had he left the money? What kind of man was he, to do that?

Despite his anger, Kent felt a grudging admiration building for the guy. He had made a couple of big points:

He hadn't stolen the guitar, and he could have iced Kent, but had chosen to let him live.

Had to give the man credit for style.

But that wouldn't slow Kent from trying to find him.

There were two security cams at the motel. One was inside the lobby, set to scan anybody approaching, or at the front desk; the other cam watched the parking lot. Kent waved his ID, made some vague threats about Homeland Security, and the night clerk was only too happy to let him view the recorder.

Natadze wasn't on the hard disk. There was a good shot of Kent twirling around in his underwear, waving his gun, though.

If Natadze had a car, he hadn't pulled it into the lot, so he was thinking ahead.

Half a step ahead, just like before.

For a few seconds, Kent considered calling the state police and trying to set up roadblocks. But what information did he have to give them? Natadze could have changed his looks entirely—hair color and style, could have grown a beard, gotten colored contact lenses, maybe even had plastic surgery.

He didn't know what the fugitive would be driving, wearing, anything. The only certain identification would be the guitar, but Natadze could hide that—under a blanket on the floor, in the trunk, anywhere. Was Kent going to ask the state police to stop and search every car with a man alone? Who was even to say he *was* alone? He could have a girlfriend, a confederate; for that matter, he might be on a bus or a train by now.

Too many variables, not enough information.

So close. But he might as well have been on the moon, for all the good it did Kent.

16

CyberNation

Jay wandered through a cityscape that looked like Metropolis, Gotham, and the *Blade Runner* version of L.A., all rolled into one, with a little Tokyo sprinkled in for flavor. The architecture ranged from modern to Gothic to art deco, from 1890s San Francisco to skyscrapers taller than the twin towers in Kuala Lumpur.

Whatever else it might offer, CyberNation had an infrastructure that was something to see. It was huge. Nothing but city, as far as you could see, farther than you could walk in two days.

And Jay now had the keys to the buildings.

Well, not all of them, but enough to keep him busy for the next couple of years, even if he didn't feel like picking locks or kicking in doors—which he could always do.

It was gigantic, but not evenly built. Most of it looked fuzzy through Jay's new viewer, though there were parts where it seemed as if somebody else had gotten their hands on a pair of those same glasses and started smoothing things. As he walked down the sidewalk, which, in this scenario, appeared to be a lot like Fifth Avenue in New York on a busy afternoon, full of pedestrians, the road clogged with cars, trucks, bicycles, and Segways, Jay tried to take it all in.

He passed sensoria, where customers could step in and experience canned fantasies—be an action hero, a great lover, explore another planet, or whatever struck your fancy.

There were restaurants, bars, schools, stores, everything you'd find in an RW city, plus things available only in VR: sex shops where your partner could be a particular movie star or group of stars; clubs where you could hunt down and shoot the most dangerous game—other humans. Russian Roulette parlors where you could bet your VR life.

Behold the vices for your enjoyment. . . .

Jay hadn't begun to see it all, but he was willing to bet that anything legal in VR anywhere would be available in CyberNation, and probably some stuff that wasn't legal. Kiddie porn wasn't legal, though there were some weird cartoon exceptions to that, but Jay didn't expect to find that here. The whole issue was too emotionally charged, and the chance of it backfiring against them was too great.

Drug-dispensing VR gear accessories for your suit were in the same category—prohibited by CyberNation, he thought—but for different reasons. These actually were legal, but they required a doctor's prescription. Jay knew there were ways around that, and he was sure that Cyber-Nation knew all of them, but he doubted they offered them. CyberNation wasn't strong enough to flout the laws of RW.

Not yet, anyway.

There were any number of other esoteric perversions that CyberNation probably didn't want to risk as well. Other than those, the sky was the limit—or not; you could fly to Mars or Alpha Centauri, if you wanted. In VR.

He passed a huge library with the word "Knowledge" over the door.

He paused in front of a map shop that offered views from spysats—you gave them your GPS coordinates and they could zoom into your backyard with enough resolution to see what newspaper your wife was reading on your deck.

It was easy to see the selling points for a place like this. Why waste your time in the RW, which was messy and dangerous, when you could come to CyberNation and experience everything you ever desired, and all from the comfort of your own home? Don full sensory gear with penile or vaginal accessories—delivered to you as part of your sign-up package—and you could have any kind of sex you wanted with anybody, without the risk of catching some disease.

It was true that VR food didn't offer any sustenance, but that was part of the appeal—you could eat all you wanted and never get fat. Yes, the stims for food weren't perfect yet, the electrode cap that cranked up your brain centers had a way to go, but the wireless taste-bud lozenges were getting up there. They could deliver a fairly good approximation of a lot of things using the basic sweet-sour-salty-bitter tropes, along with the nares odor-gen gear. And CyberNation's proprietary suitware was cutting-edge—Jay had some of it in his own sense-suits.

In top-grade mesh, you could experience tropical heat, arctic cold, or any temperature you considered perfect. With the best sensory-stim, you could feel the sand under your feet, the hard coolness of a rock face you were climbing, or the water around you as you flippered along in your scuba gear to explore for sunken treasure. Still not as good as the RW in a lot of cases, but without the risk—or the discomfort—and getting better all the time. For many, the dream was better than the reality. And Jay was hardly one to point fingers, given the time he spent suited up and in VR.

There was, however, trouble in the city, otherwise Jay wouldn't be here.

He caught a taxi and gave it the location Seurat had provided: "Take me to the Garden of Perpetual Bliss," he said.

The cabbie nodded and turned on his sat-radio. "Any kind of music you wanna hear?"

"How about classic rock, late sixties? Beatles? Rolling Stones?"

"You got it, pal."

Paul McCartney began singing and playing "Blackbird." An antiracist song, according to Sir Paul, and easy to see from a distance, though apparently at the time few had understood the message.

Wasn't that always the way?

Net Force HQ
Quantico, Virginia

In his office, Thorn listened to Abe Kent's report on his encounter with Natadze, nodding but not speaking. When the colonel had finished, Thorn said, "You're sure it was him." It wasn't a question.

"No doubt in my mind. I don't see how it could have been anybody else. Who would take a guitar and leave the exact amount he owed the builder in its place? Who could know how much that was?"

Thorn sighed. "I don't see how there was any way you could have known he'd follow you—I wouldn't have bet a penny against a dollar he'd have even been there."

"I would have won the small bet, but I lost the game."

"Don't blame yourself, Abe."

"I'd love to have somebody else to lay it off on, but it was my mistake. I should have had a contingency plan. It never crossed my mind, and it should have."

"Done is done," Thorn said. "What now?"

"I know where he was, and when. If it's okay with you, I'll get Gridley's people to run a search on security cams in the area—motels, car-rental places, the whole package. He was at the guitar thing in Lincoln, he followed me—maybe he missed a step along the way."

"You think there's much chance of that?"

"Frankly, no. It was a fluke that we tied him to the Cox

deal in the first place. A lucky break that he happened to be passing by a bank machine while somebody was using it, and that some woman ran a red light in front of him and we got pictures. Can't bank on luck again."

"Cox paid for it all," Thorn said. "Blown to pieces in his own car. We've officially moved on."

"Natadze is a loose end. And we're sure he was the guy who took Cox out."

"Depending on how you look at it, he did us a favor. Given the politics and money involved, Cox would have died of old age before we could have put him away, and even that was iffy."

"He's still a killer. And I owe him."

Thorn nodded again. He understood that. "All right. Pass it along to Jay's group and see what they come up with. Good luck."

"Thank you, Commander."

After Kent was gone, Thorn thought about that case. What a mess it had been. Old Soviet Union spies, hit men, a crooked billionaire . . .

His intercom buzzed. "Sir? Marissa Lowe on one."

Thorn smiled. "Got it."

He waved the phone to life and got a visual. Marissa, who did several things for the CIA, including being the liaison between that spook group and Net Force, was a strikingly handsome woman with skin the color of coffee and just a little cream.

"Hey, Tommy."

"Hey, yourself. How's . . . ? Where are you again?"

"Classified, I'm afraid. You don't need to know."

He laughed. She was a funny woman. Smart, too, though she tried to play that down.

"When are you coming back to town?"

"More classified information, my boy."

"But eventually?"

"I believe I can stipulate to that much, yes."

"What a terrible operative you are—see, I just wormed

information out of you. What if I were a spy? I could set up a surveillance, knowing you'd be coming to Washington sooner or later. Catch you, just like that!" He snapped his fingers.

She laughed, and he liked being able to make her do that.

"I want to see the requisition you put in for your surveillance team, Tommy. The little box where they ask for approximate cost and time for the team to be in the field. You gonna write 'eventually'?"

"I'm the boss, I don't need to fill out no stinkin' report."

She laughed again.

"I hear there's a new restaurant opening up in Foggy Bottom," he said. "Italian, being run by the guy who used to be the chef at Gianelli's."

"Ah. And . . . ?"

"Well, if I had some idea when you'd be back, I could make reservations. Treat you to dinner."

"Must be nice to be rich," she said. "But I wouldn't know, being a lowly GS-13 barely scraping by."

"Oh, yeah, rich is good. You could marry me, then when we divorce, you could get half, then you'd see."

"You put that in writing?"

They both laughed.

"Hypothetically speaking," she said after a moment, "if you were to make a reservation at this new restaurant for, say, Thursday, maybe you wouldn't have to dine alone."

"Thursday's bowling league night," he said.

"Uh-huh. I can't even *imagine* you in a pair of bowling shoes."

"I was the lowest scorer in my junior high class," he said. "A solid ninety-six average. Shall I pick you up?"

"Nah. If I'm back, I'll meet you there. Eight o'clock?"

"Assuming I can get reservations."

"Big-time bureau commander and rich man like yourself? No problem. Eight o'clock."

She discommed, and Thorn grinned to himself again. He did like smart, funny, beautiful women. What was not to like?

Paris, France

Unlike some of his colleagues, Seurat didn't mind going into the city when he had a good reason. He left his car at home and took the Metro—nothing of worth in the city was more than five hundred yards from a Metro station, so the saying went, and parking in the city, like a pay telephone, was impossible to find. Nobody with a brain drove into Paris, and since the advent of mobile phones, the government assumed everybody would have one, so why have the clutter of phone kiosks everywhere?

Today was a meeting with a potential new client—a Saudi prince and businessman who was looking to start a new server in that country, and who wanted a link with CyberNation. Being a prince was not as impressive coming from that country as it was, say, from England. There were scores, hundreds, maybe thousands of them down in the desert atop the oil pools, the result of royal families in which the men could have as many wives as they could afford. An oil sheik could afford a considerable harem.

The Saudis were not as pure as they liked to pretend; much of that Muslim strait-lacing offered publicly disappeared in private. Yes, they were currently French allies, of a sort, and there was a quid pro quo, but some of the hardest drinkers, biggest womanizers, and consumers of pornography Seurat had ever met had been Saudis. If you had enough money, there was usually a way to get what you wanted, if you wanted it enough, and to make sure that people looked the other way while you enjoyed it.

And in VR, it didn't count—since you weren't *actually* drinking or screwing around. . . .

He glanced at his watch. Running a little later today than he wished. No time to stop at a museum or gallery. Seurat liked to drop round the Musée d'Orsay every so often and see *Le Cirque*. Georges Seurat had done many drawings, but only a few major paintings, and they were all over the world. *Sunday Afternoon on the Island of La Grande Jatte*, his most famous, and the inspiration for a musical play, *Sunday Afternoon in the Park with George*, was at the Art Institute in Chicago. Others were in London, New York, San Francisco. Too few of them were in Paris. A shame, that, but buyers with enough money to afford such things lived where they lived.

His connection to his famous relative was known and accepted by some, if the legitimacy was sometimes argued by others. Though Georges had died a young man, only thirty-one, of meningitis or diptheria, depending on whom you believed, he had *two* hidden families. Most knew about Madeline Knobloch, of course, but few knew of his other mistress, from whom the director of CyberNation was himself descended. . . .

The day was warm and sunny, and Seurat enjoyed the bustle and sounds of the city as he walked along the Rue Vernet, toward the Elysees Star Hotel. There was a woman he had met there once, a Spanish countess, ah . . .

He saw the Saudi prince lounging in a cast-iron chair at the outdoor cafe down from the hotel, a cup of tea or coffee on the small table before him. Such cafes were traditional in Paris, of course, though Seurat himself thought that drinking coffee and having croissants with a steady stream of noisy automobiles passing by was hardly relaxing. There were cafes on some of the pedestrian malls, streets that had been closed to vehicular traffic but not those on foot, that he found much more appealing. It was hard to appreciate the swaying walk of a beautiful woman in high heels when a moving van with a loud muffler crept past and belched smelly exhaust at you.

The prince was in a business suit that had probably cost

more than the price of the average car. The prince, who liked to downplay that and be called Said, saw Seurat strolling in his direction. He raised his cup in salute.

Seurat smiled and nodded.

A sudden darkness rolled over the street. Seurat frowned and looked up, to see a rain cloud blotting the sun. That had come up fast—

A lightning bolt lanced down from the cloud, struck a group of walkers waiting to cross at an intersection, and scattered them as if a bomb had gone off in their midst.

A demonic voice began to laugh loudly as more lightning played over the street. Hail started to fall, clumps as big as golf balls, smashing down; hurricane winds blew, and people on the street screamed and ran for cover—

Merde! *The bastard whoreson hacker was at it again—!*

Rue de Soie
Marne-la-Vallée
France

Seurat stripped the sensory gear off, still enraged. Losing a potential client was bad, but not major. That the hacker was still able to attack CyberNation seemingly at will *was* major. He had already called his technical people and they were on the hunt, but he did not hold out much hope for a quick taking of prey.

This had to stop. And when the man responsible was caught, Seurat wanted to see him put into a hole so far down that the light of day would never touch him again.

Merde!

17

Quantico, Virginia

Getting rid of a body was not nearly as worrisome as all the forensic television shows and movies made it out to be. The main trick was to make sure the corpse wasn't discovered before you were far enough away that the authorities couldn't possibly link it to you. And not to leave anything really obvious around that pointed in your direction—DNA, fingerprints, or your business card. . . .

All that stuff where they took a hair and put it into some medical machine that whirred and fifteen seconds later spit out a picture of the killer? Total fabrication.

Locke had wrapped the blackmailer up in the bed's top sheet, waited until dark, and taken the corpse to his rental car, where he put it into the trunk. He'd located the motel's cleaning woman, waited until she had gone into an empty room to clean it, and taken a clean sheet from the stack on the cart to replace the missing one.

The next morning—one did not want to skulk around late at night with a body in one's car trunk and risk being pulled over by a bored policeman—Locke drove to a nearby industrial district and scouted it. It took but half an hour for him to find what he was looking for. He found the number of a real estate agent on the sign in front of the building, made a call from a pay telephone, and determined the information he needed. Luck ran his way—the place was perfect.

From there, he drove to a local mall and bought supplies. From a hardware store, he purchased a hand-truck dolly, a battery-powered Skil Saw, a tree saw, and a hammer, along with a small machete, a painter's drop cloth, and a box of green plastic leaf bags. He also picked up a set of painter's coveralls, shoe covers, and rubber gloves, and several bottles of spray cleaner and paint thinner.

At an art supply store, he bought a large roll of plastic wrap and another of white butcher's paper, along with a black marking crayon.

He found a cyber cafe, bought an hour on a computer, and logged on to the Internet. There, he found an appliance store, and using a PayPal account into which he had deposited several thousand dollars under a phony name months before, bought a chest freezer and arranged to have it delivered immediately to the address he had found in the industrial district.

At a long-term parking lot near a new commuter airport, he stole a minivan, swapping the license plates on it with the car parked next to it. He wore a basic disguise when he did this—a hat, a pair of sunglasses, and a fake moustache—and paid the lot fee on the stolen car at an automated exit teller. He drove back to his rental car, parked in a lot next to a cinema complex, and transferred the body and supplies to the new vehicle.

He drove out into the Virginia countryside, found what looked like an old and mostly unused logging road in a pine forest, and drove until he was several miles away from the main road.

He got out, dressed in the coveralls and shoe covers, and put the gloves on.

He carried the rest of his supplies and the body into

the woods. He laid out the drop cloth and unwrapped the body onto it. He removed the clothes and put them into a trash bag.

It took a couple of hours to get the body reduced to packages of five pounds or less, fifteen minutes alone to saw the head into small bits and knock all the teeth out. Each part was wrapped in plastic, then in butcher's paper and marked with a crayon: steaks, roasts, ribs, chops.

When he was done, he rolled the bloody drop cloth up and put it into a plastic bag, cleaned the saws and machete carefully, then loaded these into three different plastic bags. He removed the coveralls, gloves, and shoe protectors, and put them into another bag.

He packed up and left.

Back at the industrial site, which was a recently emptied building, he parked in the back where he'd had the freezer delivered. He picked the lock on the door, and used the hand truck to move the small freezer into the building. He removed the freezer from its corrugated cardboard box, and took the styrofoam packaging out. As the real estate agent had told him, the electricity was still on, and was supposed to stay on for at least a month, because there was a new tenant due to move into the building then. He found an outlet and plugged in the freezer.

He transferred the packages from the van and put them into the freezer, all except the bits of head and fingers, closed the freezer, relocked the door, and drove away. It wasn't recommended, to load a freezer that way before it got cold, but if the meat was burned a little, that didn't really matter. Eventually it would go solid.

At a Dumpster behind a butcher shop, he put the leaf bag with the drop cloth in it.

At an apartment complex eight miles away, he got rid of the bag with the dead man's clothes. He kept the wallet, watch, and keys, along with a ring.

The freezer's packaging went into a different trash bin.

The wallet, empty, and the watch, ring, keys, and saws went into a lake in a park, heaved far enough from shore that nobody was apt to step on them if they went wading, which they probably wouldn't, since there was a sign that forbade swimming. He tossed the teeth into the water, too. Even if somebody found any of them with the fillings, there was no way to put them into context to match a dental chart.

The rest of the supplies went into trash bins or Dumpsters in four different locations. The last bags, containing his coveralls and gloves and the contents of the dead man's wallet, he set afire in an old oil drum behind a junk yard, using the paint thinner to get them flaming good. He made sure the gloves burned—no fingerprints left there.

He drove to a cemetery and found an open grave awaiting a new tenant. He remembered the old joke about graveyards: Why were there fences around them? Because people were dying to get in. He put the bag with the chopped-up head and fingers into the empty grave, covering it with enough dirt so that it wasn't visible. He very nearly was discovered at this by somebody visiting nearby, but managed to finish his chore before they got close enough to see him. He had considered finding a dog kennel or going to an animal shelter and feeding the bits to the dogs, but he remembered the old urban legend about the choking Doberman, and while the brains and skull bits wouldn't give anything away, a finger would, since government security guards had their prints on file.

He returned to the airport lot, put the minivan back in the same slot it had occupied before, switched the license plates to their original vehicles, and left.

As he drove toward a different motel, he considered what he had done. Yes, it had been a lot of work—he could just as easily have buried the headless/fingerless body in the woods, It might not have lain there undisturbed forever, but it probably wouldn't have been discovered for weeks or months, if not years. And once it was found, the authorities probably wouldn't have been able to ID the corpse—most people did not have DNA records on file.

But when the new tenants of the industrial space opened

the freezer, they would either toss the packages of meat, or somebody would take one home for supper. If that happened, unless that diner happened to be a cannibal, there would be an immediate uproar. Such a heinous crime could only be the work of some twisted sociopathic psychotic, a real loon, and the FBI profilers would have themselves a fine time.

And what they would come up with wouldn't bear any resemblance to Jack Locke. . . .

He smiled. He had given them a show, and they would buy it, because they *wanted* to buy it. Locke was, he felt, an artist, and this kind of thing was part of his art and craft. The last person they'd be looking for would be a Hong Kong businessman.

A simple sleight of hand. And clever, too, if he did say so himself.

Meanwhile, he still had to deal with the issue at hand, Net Force and CyberNation, and while that shouldn't take any violence, it was always an option. . . .

18

Space, the Starship Enterprise

Jay was studying the holographic projection on the bridge of the *Enterprise* with Bretton when the alert light and Klaxon began flashing and blaring.

"All hands, Red Alert!" came a stentorian voice.

Jay nodded at his VR companion.

"I'd better take this."

George just nodded, and Jay stepped back into an alcove to take the call, muting the scene with a privacy screen. He could see out, but Bretton couldn't see in. Only Saji and Thorn could intrude on one of his scenarios with this level of urgency, so he knew it had to be important.

"Jay?"

It was Saji. She sounded worried. All of his calm curiosity disappeared when he heard the tone in her voice.

"Yeah, babe?"

"It's Mark."

A bolt of fear stabbed through the VR jock as the words registered.

Mark.

Was he dead? Had someone kidnapped him? Jay had thought his imagination fairly good, but parenthood thus far had shown him that he had entirely new realms of worry to discover.

"What is it?"

"I don't know!" Her voice rose on the last word.

He was unnerved. In all the time he'd been with her, Saji had *never* sounded like this. She maintained her calm, had held her center under the most severe stress. She hadn't even sounded this bad when he came out of the coma.

"We were playing in the living room, and suddenly he started coughing and acting funny. I got worried and called the on-duty nurse, and she said we ought to bring him in."

She paused.

"And then he seemed fine, but he started jerking around like he was having a seizure, and we're stuck in traffic, and he's not getting better!"

Oh, God!

"Where are you now?"

"I'm on—on Sherman, heading towards the Children's Hospital. Traffic is jammed!"

Jay stared through the privacy screen at the quiet bridge of the *Enterprise,* stars flickering on the main viewscreen, the hologram of the Dyson sphere floating in the center of the space. His emotional distance couldn't be farther from the calm scene—it seemed like hours had passed since he'd taken the call. He looked over at the chronometer readout and noticed it had only been a minute. Less.

For a moment he just sat there. Saji's terror and his concern for his son froze him. But only for a moment. He hadn't gotten where he was without being able to work under pressure.

Come on, Gridley, let's get something rolling here!

First Saji: "It'll be okay, babe," he said, not having any clue that it would be. But he had to say *something*. She had to keep it together, and it was the best he could do.

"I'll fix the traffic—and I'll meet you at the hospital as soon as I can. Hold on, babe. How's he doing now?"

Calm, Gridley, radiate calm.

"He seems a little better." She paused. "I love you, Jay."

"I love you, too. Drive. It'll be okay."

He disconnected and broke the privacy screen.

Bretton looked up. "Something wrong?"

"Family emergency. Gotta go—I'll check back with you when I can."

Bretton nodded. "Good luck."

Quantico, Virginia

Jay killed the VR he'd been using to link with Bretton, and shifted his work space from the military network he'd been on to regular VR. Even though they had secure filters all over his link, and the transfer packets were all a different protocol than his regular VR, he was still very careful not to mix his VR access.

And with what he was going to do, he certainly didn't want the military to be able to access him now. Or anybody else.

He tabbed to a different scenario—he was in a large office with filing cabinets all around. He ran to a large green one and jerked open the top drawer. The drawer squeaked as it had since he programmed it years ago as an exercise in office interface, the VR equivalent of an old-school desktop.

From a hanging file folder labeled *Recent* he pulled a thin red folder, opened it, and hurriedly leafed through the pages inside.

He tapped a sequence on the floor with his foot, and a voice-input box appeared by his head.

"Find Saji," he said.

"Acknowledged."

The program he'd called was a subset of a larger FBI

project that had been scrapped several years before. Officially, at least. Through a combination of GPS satellite and ground-based radio repeater triangulation, the software could identify the location of a particular cellular telecom signal, if it was on file.

Ostensibly, the project had been killed due to a lack of interest, but the real reason had been to avoid big-brother backlash—a concern that, unfortunately, was not completely unwarranted. Jay had used the program a few times for Net Force operations, and once, when checking the satellite logs, he'd seen that several other agencies within the alphabet soup of Washington's security apparatus had Lazarused the software more than a few times.

A tiny map appeared, hanging in space where the vox input had been.

There she was—

While the program had been working, Jay found the codes he'd been looking for.

The Greenies were about to ride again.

A few weeks ago, he'd helped the District Public Works Department track down some hackers who called themselves the Greenies. They had been messing with local traffic signals using stolen codes they'd run through VR that could read traffic light IDs and change them at the push of a button.

At the moment, the only buttons they were pushing were on phones at the county jail. Jay prayed that those codes still worked.

He tied the search program to software he'd used once for following money across VR, changing the input parameters to track Saji instead. He tagged a locator for the nearest traffic signal on her route to the hospital, just . . . there, and set the light to go green.

Now, wherever she was, all the lights were going to turn and stay green until she passed them.

For a second, Jay thought about what he'd done. He'd just hacked public transportation for personal reasons—no excuse under the law, and if he was found out, there would be trouble.

True, he'd bounced the program across several hundred VR nodes in the net, spanning the globe several times, with spoofed router codes that would make it virtually impossible to trace. It was unlikely anyone else could catch him, but the risk didn't matter. It was his son's life, and there was nothing—absolutely *nothing* he wouldn't do for him. If somebody was going to be late on their commute because of what he'd done, that was just too bad.

He set the program to dissolve after Saji reached the hospital, and slipped out of VR. He had to get to his car—

He nearly ran over Thorn as he bolted through the door. "Sorry!"

"Where's the fire, Jay?" Thorn smiled.

"Mark's on the way to the hospital with Saji—he's having seizures!"

Thorn's smile vanished. Immediately he said, "We've got a helicopter on the pad. Go there—I'll clear it."

"Thanks, Boss."

Jay ran.

Beijing, China

Now and again, General Wu had occasion to travel, and this time, it was to attend the retirement dinner of his old comrade, General Pei, a salt-of-the-earth fellow who had risen through the ranks from foot soldier to commander. Pei had been a peasant who had joined the army during the Cultural Revolution and progressed quickly in rank. This was due less to his military genius than it was by virtue of his uncanny ability to not offend anyone. Sturdy and steady Pei, he was known as. After rising to the top ranks, he had been put in charge of supplies at a base near Tibet, where he had served honorably for ten years before time to retire.

Now Pei was leaving, probably to go back to his family farm in the sticks, and his friends and comrades were going to raise glasses and toast his departure, knowing their own time would be coming soon enough.

The event was being held at a new military building on West Chang'an, south of Nunhai Lake and near the Beijing Concert Hall.

Since Wu had arrived more than two hours before the dinner was to start, he took the opportunity to stretch his legs a bit.

The area was thick with museums, including Monuments to the People's Heroes, Mao's Mausoleum, and the Museum of the Chinese Revolution, which were conveniently located across from the Gate of Heavenly Peace, which led to Tian'anmen Square and the Forbidden City.

There was also more than a little smog in the air, undoubtedly negating any health benefits the walk might confer. Wu smiled at this thought. He had been living on borrowed time since the riot at Manchu Station twenty-four years ago. A little smog wasn't going to worry him.

The day was warm, with no rain in the forecast, so the air would stay murky for a time. There were more than a few people on the sidewalks, and foreign tourists strung about with cameras in loud shorts and shirts gaping at the buildings and monuments. It was always busy at the main gate to the Forbidden City.

Would that he had lived two hundred years ago, to have been a general in an age when it really mattered.

Even fifty years ago, it would have been a nicer walk. Now, there were McDonalds' and Burger Kings and Kentucky Fried Chicken fast-food places, French bakeries, and signs advertising Coca Cola and The Gap and Ford automobiles. Holiday Inns and Sheraton Hotels. The Olympics in 2008 had left more such dross behind. Like pox sores on a beautiful woman, these things made Wu feel ill to behold, here in the heart of his homeland.

He liked to believe that he was a realist. He knew he could not single-handedly roll back the clock and erase all Western influence here. But perhaps he could undo some of it, and certainly he could make a difference. One did what one could.

And certainly he would do that.

He looked at his watch. Still plenty of time. He might stop in at the new military library, which was not far from Pei's event. Or perhaps he would just walk. It was smoggy and warm, but he was fairly relaxed. He had seen Mayli just before he had left, gotten her report on Shing, along with her more intimate ministrations, plus he had managed to nap for a couple hours on the flight. One thing you learned to do in the military was sleep when the chance came up—you never knew but that you might not get another opportunity for a while.

Yes. He would walk through the city, and try to ignore the Western bastardizations as best he could. . . .

19

Giarelli's Restaurant
Washington, D.C.

Some restaurants you went to for the food, some for the ambiance. A few you went to in order to see or be seen. This one had it all—the chef, Antonio Cavelos, was a master in the kitchen. The decor was low-key, subdued, and with enough sound-absorbing material in the walls and ceiling that the place was relatively quiet, even though it was packed. There were dignitaries ranging from U.S. senators to ambassadors to movie stars. All of whom were interesting, though not, Thorn thought, as interesting as the woman sitting across from him.

"So, what do you think?" he asked Marissa.

"Tony can cook, no questions. Best eggplant parmesan I've had outside the old country."

"Go there a lot? Wait—that's classified, right?"

She smiled. "So, Tommy, how's your love life?"

He blinked. This was a new area of conversation for them. "What love life?" he asked. "I haven't had a date since you and I went to that charity thing in New York."

"That wasn't a date. We were working."

"See?"

"Poor Tommy. Spending his evenings all alone."

Where was she going with this? "I'm used to it," he said.

She smiled. "How's work?"

He paused, unsure whether he was glad she had changed the subject. "The usual. Well, except for us being taken over by the military and given a new mission which we don't seem to be accomplishing at the moment."

"Well, as Dylan said, the times they are a-changin'."

"Was that before or after he started making commercials for Victoria's Secret?"

"Waaay before. And how is that for you?"

He shrugged.

The waiter materialized, holding the dessert tray. He smiled as he lowered the tray.

"Which one has the most fat, sugar, and calories in it?" Marissa asked.

"The triple-chocolate cream cheesecake."

"We'll have two of those," she said. "And coffee, not decaf."

The waiter smiled again and moved away.

"Seriously, Tommy."

"The jury is still out. So far, it's been hands off, but that's because they really need us. The military has a different approach to life than civilians. We'll see how it goes."

She gave him a long, steady look. "Are you thinking about walking if things don't go your way?"

She had a way of putting her finger right on things. More than once, she had looked at him and nailed down exactly what was going on in his mind.

"I didn't sign on to be somebody's lapdog. I've been around too many people who think that everybody who works for them needs to be micromanaged. If I'm hired for my skills and abilities, then I expect to be able to use them without somebody not as good telling me how to do my job."

"Too rich to put up with that crap, huh?"

"In a word, yes. One of money's biggest perks is, you don't have to work with jerks and idiots if you don't feel like it."

The waiter returned, bearing coffee and chocolate cheesecake.

"Lord, that was fast," Marissa said.

"The best people get the best service," the waiter said. "Tony's rule." He smiled at Marissa.

"Lucky I'm with her," Thorn said.

"Yes, sir, very lucky."

The coffee, freshly brewed, and probably from beans roasted in the back and ground minutes ago, smelled wonderful. And the cheesecake looked as if it would make you gain five pounds before you touched it with your fork.

Marissa took a big bite of hers, and moaned. "Better than sex," she said. "Mmmm."

Thorn took a bite of his own cake. Way too rich. Thousand calories in the piece, easy.

"C'mon, Tommy, when I give you a straight line like that, you're supposed to run with it."

"Oh, sorry. What's my line?"

"You're no fun."

They had another bite each. Thorn sipped at the hot coffee. Excellent brew.

"There are some smart folks in the service, contrary to the old claims about military intelligence being an oxymoron," she said.

He waited for her to take another big bite before saying, "Where'd a sweet young CIA op like you learn a word like that?"

Before she could swallow enough of the cake to slap him down, he continued, "I know they aren't all third-grade dropout hawks. I just don't do well with somebody looking over my shoulder. If they leave us alone, no problem." He paused, then said, "Abe Kent is happy, though."

"Oh, yeah, back in the Corps. How's he doing?"

"He's a good man, but he had a nasty experience recently."

He told her about Kent's trip to Nebraska, and the run-in with Natadze, the classical guitarist hit man. She knew who he was, of course, having been a part of the Cox investigation, and her clearance was at least as high as Thorn's, probably higher.

"Interesting," she said, when he was done. "Nobody likes a loose end after things are supposed to be wrapped up tight. I got the idea that the colonel was pretty methodical. I'd put money on him eventually running Natadze down."

Thorn nodded. "Jay Gridley had a little scare, too. His baby son got sick. Boy is in the hospital, but it looks like he'll be okay."

"That's good."

There was a moment of silence, one gravid with . . . something.

"I'll be buying dinner tonight," she said, her voice quiet.

He started to smile and treat it as a joke—dinner would set them back maybe three hundred bucks, more with the wine—but he stopped. "Why would that be?" he said, his voice as quiet as hers.

"Because I don't want you to think that buying me a nice dinner is why I'm going home with you tonight."

Thorn's mouth suddenly seemed very dry. He couldn't find any words.

She smiled. "Cat got your tongue?"

"I hope," he managed.

She laughed.

University Park, Maryland

Thorn woke up to the smell of coffee brewing. A moment later, Marissa came into his bedroom, wearing a thick and fluffy bathrobe he'd gotten at the Tokyo Hilton years ago. She carried two mugs of steaming coffee.

"Hey," she said.

"Yeah, hey, yourself."

Her hair was damp, she must have showered. He'd slept through it. She sat on the edge of the bed and smiled at him, handing him one of the cups as he sat up.

No surprise he hadn't heard the shower running. After last night, he'd have slept through a bomb going off in the front yard.

He sipped the coffee. It was good.

"You a breakfast eater?"

He shook his head. "Mostly not."

"Me, neither. Just as well. I'm not a domestic kind of girl," she said. "I can make coffee and run the microwave oven, but I don't cook to speak of. Lord knows my mama tried to teach me, but I was always more interested in climbing trees and fences and exploring the Two Acre Woods. I can burn a hamburger, and on a good day, make salad."

"No problem," he said. "I'm pretty good in the kitchen."

"And not bad for a white boy in the bedroom."

They both smiled.

She said, "I need to get going, Tommy. Work."

He nodded. "You need a change of clothes?"

She raised her eyebrows. "You have women's clothes here? In my size?"

"I think maybe my aunt might have left some stuff here when she came to visit a while back."

"Uh-huh, sure she did." She grinned again. "I have a fresh outfit in my car, and a go bag."

It was his turn to raise his eyebrows. "Oh, really? You mean you *planned* this all along?"

"Did I say that? I always keep a change of clothes and a go bag in the car. Never know but that you might be caught out on an all-night surveillance or something."

"I thought the CIA wasn't supposed to run ops inside the country."

"Where on earth did you get that notion, sweetie? You need to come to town more often."

She started to rise. He touched her shoulder with one

hand. He needed to tell her how . . . great this was. And maybe see if she felt the same way. And maybe see where it might go. Definitely see where it might go. "Hey, Marissa . . . ?"

She read his mind. Shook her head. "Don't go there yet, Tommy. Let's let it sit for a while and see how it feels. But, yeah, it was a pretty special first date, wasn't it?"

She padded away and into the hall bathroom. He sat in the bed, the sheet around his waist, and sipped at the coffee. She wasn't anything like his usual type of woman—they tended to be intellectual, brainy, and Nordic—blue-eyed blondes with sharp wits and gym-toned bodies. Marissa pretended to be less smart than she was—he'd checked her out and her IQ was higher than his—but she was still more of a heart-person. And given her chocolate skin, brown eyes, and black curly hair, about as far away from "Nordic" as you could get.

He shook his head. And none of that mattered at all. Because what Thorn was feeling was something that hadn't stirred in him for a long time—but not so long that he had forgotten what it was called.

He didn't want this feeling. Couldn't afford it, really, not at this time, but there it was.

Like it or not, he was falling in love with this woman.

20

Thorn sat staring at his computer's holoproj, not really seeing it. This thing with Marissa was definitely throwing him
for a loop. He had to acknowledge it, but it was still weird.
She was so . . . different. . . .

He looked up and saw Colonel Kent standing in the
doorway.

"Abe. Come in."

Kent did so.

"So, what's up?" Thorn said, shifting mental gears.

Kent said, "I've got a line on Natadze."

Thorn blinked. "Really?"

Kent nodded at Thorn's computer terminal. "Log in to
his file, bring up the name Stansell."

Thorn waved at the computer sensors, then said, "File:
Natadze, sub-file, Stansell."

A webpage blossomed in the air, a holoproj showing
several guitars.

"Ask for La Tigra Blanca Tres," Kent said.

Thorn did.

The image changed. A classical guitar appeared, rotating slowly. The instrument was a pale but rich color, somewhere between tan and off-white on the sides and back, and the color of an old manila folder on the front. The sides and back had patterns that looked like tiger stripes on them.

"Looks almost like it's glowing," Thorn said.

"That's called chatoyancy. Same thing you get off a tiger's eye gem, or a piece of fine silk. A characteristic of the wood used."

"Hmm. Interesting."

"The White Tiger," Kent said. "And the third one with the name. Made by a guy named Les Stansell, in a little southern Oregon town just north of the California border."

"Very nice."

"The wood on the front is Port Orford cedar, that on the sides and back Oregon myrtlewood. Neck is Spanish cedar, the fretboard is ebony, if it makes any difference. Runs about five grand and change for Stansell's basic models—he's made a specialty out of these kinds of woods, and the guitars are apparently well thought of by serious players. I checked it out, they go on about tone and sustain and the top opening up fast."

Thorn nodded.

"This particular one wound up in a specialty shop in San Francisco, and the asking price is ten thousand dollars."

Thorn waited. "And . . . ?" he said after a moment.

"Not a lot of people walk in off the street and buy ten-thousand-dollar guitars. I sent a bulletin to every luthier and high-end shop I could find via the Net, asking to be informed of sales where the buyer of a classical instrument costing more than five thousand dollars wasn't somebody known to the seller. I get six or eight hits a day, and I usually am able to run them down and eliminate them—with help from one of Gridley's guys."

"And you haven't been able to run this one down."

"No. The backwalk runs into a dead end."

"Could be a lot of things," Thorn said. "Somebody trying to keep it from his wife, maybe looking to dodge taxes, like that."

"That's true. I ran across that once before—some guy bought a spendy guitar and didn't want his wife to know. But I was able to find him and figure that out pretty quick."

"You think this is our guy."

Kent nodded. "I do. More hunch than anything else. The shop owner was contacted via e-mail, the money was transferred from an account in the Bahamas, and the buyer is supposed to drop by and pick the guitar up tomorrow."

"And you don't want to have the local FBI team check it out."

"No. This is . . . personal. I'd like to be there myself."

Thorn nodded. "Go."

"Thank you."

"Natadze is a bad mark on my record, too, Abe. You need any help?"

Colonel Kent shook his head. "I don't think so. This time, surprise will be on my side, not his."

"Keep me posted."

"I will, Commander." He paused. "How's Jay's son doing?"

"Okay now, so I hear. Not ready to come home yet, but doing better."

"That's good."

"Yes."

Kent went to the shooting range and put in an hour, burning a hundred rounds through his sidearm. He was going after a professional killer who would be armed and extremely dangerous. The least he could do was make sure his weapon was working properly and he was able to shoot it straight.

He cleaned the piece at the range, reloaded it, and headed home to pack a bag.

The smart thing to do would be to get to San Francisco, assemble a team of FBI ops, plus a squad of the local police SWAT team, set it up, and if Natadze showed and blinked crooked, take him down fast.

But: Natadze hadn't crept into somebody else's motel room and swiped a guitar from under their sleeping noses. The man had made Kent look stupid too many times to let it pass into somebody else's hands.

Besides, Natadze hadn't killed him. Could have, no question about it, but didn't, and Kent knew it didn't have anything to do with Natadze being worried about what one more death would do to his jail time if he was ever caught. The man was a professional hit man, and yet he'd let Kent live.

That had to count for something.

No way was Kent going to respond with a posse of sharpshooters.

No, he was going to be on a plane this afternoon, and scoping out the guitar shop as soon as he could get there. Natadze might decide to come a day early—or a day late. One thing for sure: Whoever picked up that handmade ten-thousand-dollar instrument was going to have Abraham Kent on his tail when he walked out of the store. No question about that at all.

Quantico, Virginia

Money could only buy you so much, Locke reflected as he considered the situation. Here he was in a so-so motel in Virginia, in a tiny town that wouldn't exist were it not for Marines and government workers. He had established that Net Force was indeed linked with CyberNation and actively trying to deal with Shing's machinations, and when it came right down to it, that was just about all he could expect to do, wasn't it?

Locke didn't like trusting people in general, and less so those who did things he himself could not do. Shing was a one-trick pony, but it was a clever trick. Locke—and Wu—

had to hope that Shing was sufficiently skilled at it to go against the best security in the world and win. Living on hope was dangerous.

Locke mentally shrugged. His part of this operation was going as he had planned—so far, at least. It would not fail due to mistakes he made. That might not mean much against the loss of the fortune destined for his pocket if it went sideways, but it was the best he could do under the circumstances.

He couldn't get inside Net Force or CyberNation to see what they could or could not do against Shing's attack, not any more than he already had, and the bottom line was, even if he could, what could he do about it anyway?

It was, he decided, time to leave. That there was a frozen body in small packages out there waiting to be discovered did influence his decision a little. He wanted to be far away when it turned up, just in case he had missed something. . . .

People's Military Base Annex
Macao, China

Wu passed the envelope full of currency across the desk to Shing.

The younger man smiled. "Thank you, Comrade General."

Wu smiled in return. "It is nothing. When we are successful, we would not stoop to pick such as this up if it fell from our pockets." He paused. "Things continue to go well?"

"Yes. The Americans and the French still run around like blind men on a football field, bumping into each other, but seeing nothing."

"This is good."

"When we're ready to unleash the dragon, it will damage their houses so badly they will all but collapse. And they don't have any idea it even exists!"

So full of himself, Wu thought. Still, if Shing was correct, it would be a great victory. Wu's heart soared as he thought of how it would be when he made the call to the North Koreans. Not a dragon, perhaps, more like a pack of hungry wolves, but dangerous enough to anyone in their path . . .

"Well. Go and enjoy yourself at the casinos," Wu said. "And say hello to that young lady you spoke of."

"I'll do that," Shing said.

They both smiled, and while Shing's expression was doubtlessly insincere, Wu's was real.

It was so good to be the man who knew what was going on, really it was.

Children's Hospital
Washington, D.C.

The pediatrician, a tall, skinny man of sixty or so named Wohler, spoke to Jay in the hall, amidst that antiseptic smell Jay associated with hospitals.

Saji sat with Mark in the private room behind them. Whatever else you might say about it, Net Force had a great health plan.

"It's too soon to say he's completely out of the woods, Mr. Gridley, but he's responded well to the medications and his fever is greatly decreased. I'd like to keep him here for a few more days to be sure everything goes as we hope."

Jay nodded. "Yes, sure, whatever it takes." Jay wasn't happy with the way doctors hedged everything they said, but he supposed he could understand it. They got sued at the drop of a hat, and it was safer if they never promised anything they weren't positive they could deliver.

Mark's convulsions had been due to a high fever, and that was because of the pneumococcal pneumonia he had suddenly developed. The onset had been faster than they usually saw, the doctor had said, and no, there wasn't anything Jay or Saji could have done to protect Mark from it. Yes, there was a vaccine for some strains, but not the one Mark had. The bug that caused it was common, so much so that probably three quarters of the people walking around on the planet had it or some variation of it in their systems, where it was pretty much harmless most of the time. Nobody was quite sure exactly why it sometimes decided to lodge opportunistically in the lungs and start to grow.

The main thing was, Mark seemed to be okay. No apparent brain damage from the high fever, which had registered 106 degrees Fahrenheit when Saji had brought him in.

After Jay had rascaled the traffic lights, it had only taken her a few minutes to make it to the hospital, and Jay had gotten there in under half an hour—the helicopter pilot was a speed demon in that machine, and he'd put it down on the pad outside the ER like a champion gymnast sticking the landing on a dismount.

"Thanks for your help, Dr. Wohler."

The older man smiled. "That's what I do, son."

Back in the room with Saji, Mark slept. Every time the baby twitched, Saji jumped, but they had him inside a clear plastic tent, she wasn't supposed to touch him, and that broke her heart when he cried.

The last time that had happened, Jay had said, "Enough of this!" He'd gone and washed his hands with the antibacterial soap in the bathroom, put on rubber gloves and a surgeon's mask like the nurses did, and reached into the tent to comfort his son.

As soon as Mark had felt his father's hands and heard his voice, he had quieted, even though Jay must have looked scary in the paper surgeon's mask.

"How's he doing?" Jay asked his wife.

"Better. He seems to be resting more. What did the doctor say?"

"Nothing really new. I think he believes Mark is going to be fine, but nobody around here will commit to that. I did some research, and baby doctors get sued a lot. Obgyns get hit the most, then pediatricians, followed by orthopedists. Nobody wants to say everything is okay and risk it *not* being totally okay." Jay sighed. "He wants to keep him here a few more days," he finished.

Saji nodded. "That's fine."

"Look, why don't you go home, change clothes, take a shower, maybe a nap, get some books or something? I'll stay with Mark."

They had slept on the fold-out couch, which wasn't particularly comfortable, and washed their faces in the bathroom sink, but they were both tired and rumpled.

"No," she said. "You go. I can't leave."

Jay shook his head. "I can't, either," he said.

He took her hand. She squeezed it. They looked at their son, and they worried together.

21

The guitar store wasn't in downtown San Francisco, but in a little upscale pocket neighborhood on the way toward Oakland. This was an area that had been bought up and renewed, old buildings remodeled or torn down and new ones built that looked like those they had replaced. There were shops and businesses within easy walking distance of housing—small apartments, row houses of condos, and even single-family homes. Very nice and, Kent knew, very spendy. Real estate in the Bay Area had always been some of the most expensive in the country, and it still was.

It was late in the afternoon before he arrived at the shop, which was identified simply as "Cyrus Guitars." There was a parking lot across the street next to a deli, and Kent pulled his rented and outfitted van into that. He had food, water, a little portable potty, and assorted other knick-knacks that would make a long surveillance bearable.

He went into the deli and talked to the guy running the place about letting him park there for the next couple of days. His Net Force ID and a few words about Homeland

Security—along with a single fifty-dollar bill—were enough to settle the deal.

With the van situated, Kent walked across the street to the guitar place.

It wasn't particularly impressive from the sidewalk. The sign was low-key, there was one small window with a single guitar on display, and without those to identify it, the shop could have been any small-business storefront.

Inside, it was more interesting. There was a wooden counter, covered with what looked like a sheet of black velvet. Behind the counter, hung on the wall inside a series of rectangular glass or Plexiglas cases, were ten guitars. They were mostly classical models—Kent had become passingly familiar with the design—a couple of steel-string acoustics, and he quickly spotted the one made by Stansell—the color on the sides was unique.

The man behind the counter sat on a stool with one foot propped on the cross-supports, playing an acoustic guitar that appeared to have a stainless-steel clamp on the neck several frets up from the tuning pegs. He wore sweatpants and a T-shirt and what looked like moccasins. His right arm was covered with a long black sleeve. It took Kent a second to realize what the sleeve was for: to keep his bare skin from touching the guitar.

The instrument had a rich, warm tone. As Kent watched, the player squeezed the metal clamp and removed it from the guitar.

"G7th capo," the player said. "Great design. Locking cam, doesn't detune the strings if you're careful, one-handed operation, imported out of the U.K. by John Pearse Strings. Plus the looks-cool factor is still very high even after ten years." He extended the clamp toward Kent, who walked over and took it. He didn't know capos from capons, but the little device did feel very solid and well-made. He said so as he handed it back.

"The euro is down again," the man said, "so they are running about fifty bucks American. I'm Cyrus, what can I do for you?"

Cyrus stood, and was tall—six-five, six-six, maybe, with a one-cut cropped-short red orange crewcut. He wore three or four earrings in each ear, wire-rimmed glasses, and had what looked like some kind of tribal tattoos on the arm Kent could see.

There were several ways to play this, and they usually depended on the guy you were dealing with. His instinct was that Cyrus was a solid citizen. Something seemed familiar about him, Kent couldn't put his finger on exactly what it was. He decided to go for it straight on: "I'm Abraham Kent," he said, "I work for Net Force."

"The net query, yeah. Nancy told me about that. She's my manager—she's the one who does all the Internet/web stuff."

Kent nodded. "You sold a guitar to somebody who's supposed to come in tomorrow to pick up."

"Actually, I have five or six folks dropping by to collect instruments in the next few days."

"You'd remember this one. The guitar went for ten thousand dollars."

Cyrus smiled. "You say that number as if it's amazing. I've got almost two hundred thousand dollars worth of guitars on display here, couple of 'em cost three times that much." He waved an arm at the wall. "But I know the one you mean—the Stansell White Tiger, right?"

"Yes."

He nodded. "Some guy bought it from Nancy, and paid for it up front, a bank transfer. Most of our customers I know personally, or by reputation. Some are referrals. I don't know this one."

"I'm not certain he's the guy I'm looking for, but if he is, he's a bad man, and we need to have a chat."

"What'd he do?"

"Killed some people, among other things."

"Really? Not something serious classical guitar players are usually into."

"He's not your usual player."

Cyrus looked at Kent. He nodded slightly. "Okay. So what do you want me to do?"

The man didn't seem particularly disturbed at the idea that he'd be dealing with a murderer. Kent looked at him with the unspoken question: Why so cool?

Cyrus rolled the protective sleeve down his arm, grinning. The Marine Corps logo was tattooed in blue on his upper arm. "Semper fi, sir," Cyrus said.

Kent shook his head, and returned the grin. "Do I know you?"

"Not personally, but I was in First Expeditionary in Second Iraq—I saw you around a couple of times, Major."

"Colonel, now," Kent said. "Hell of an operation, that."

"Yes, sir, it was. Glad I survived it. What's the deal?"

"This guy shows up, you fill out forms or whatever you usually do and send him on his way. But if sometime during that procedure you could get to this"—Kent pulled a small cell phone from his pocket and put it on the counter—"and just push the 'send' button, right here, I'd appreciate it."

Cyrus looked at the phone. "Yes, sir, I can do that. Then what?"

"Nothing happens in the store. I'll know the guy if I see him. He leaves, I follow him, and somewhere, we get together."

"No problem, Colonel."

Once a Marine, always a Marine.

"Thanks."

"You'll let me know how it turns out?"

"That's the least I can do."

They both smiled.

College Park, Maryland

The driver dropped Thorn off at his house and left. It was only one o'clock, but Thorn had some old business to deal with, business he would rather not do at the office.

He walked to the front door. It was a quiet neighborhood, not far from the University of Maryland. There were a number of college professors and even a dean or two living on his street. The tree-lined roads—mostly pin oak, but some elms and pear trees, too—were shady, the houses big and built mostly in the early part of the last century.

He thumbed the print-reader on the new lock he'd had installed, and stepped inside to do the same to the alarm system control panel, which went from red to green as it disarmed.

He set his case down next to the half-round table against the hall wall, and headed for the kitchen.

Lying on the kitchen counter was a single, long-stemmed rose. The petals were such a dark red that they seemed almost black.

Thorn smiled at the flower as he picked it up and sniffed it.

The rose smelled as good as it looked.

Who did he know who could get past a thumbprint reader lock and alarm system? And who would leave a black rose on his kitchen counter?

His smile got bigger. Oh, this was too much.

He unclipped his virgil from his belt. "Call Marissa," he said.

He held the little device to his ear with one hand, the dark rose in the other.

"Hey, Tommy."

"Hey, Marissa. Thank you."

"For what?"

He held the virgil so that its cam pointed at the flower.

"Very nice," she said. "What's that got to do with me?"

"It was on my kitchen counter."

"And you think *I* put it there? That would mean I'd have to drive way the hell and gone to God's country, then rascal a thumbprint reader lock and house alarm with a security cam, to leave that flower in your kitchen, just to make you smile when you saw it. You think you're worth all that trouble?"

"I hope you think so."

There was a pause. Then she said, "Maybe. We'll just have to see. Where are you taking me to dinner tomorrow?"

"Anywhere you want to go," he said.

"Try and surprise me."

"Oh, I expect I can manage that."

"Want to bet?"

"I'll send a car for you," he said. "Seven o'clock okay?"

"What's the wager?"

"Tell you after I win," he said.

"You're on."

She discommed, and he just stood there smiling at the rose.

San Francisco, California

As it happened, Kent saw Natadze go into the shop. It was just after ten A.M., and while he had camped in worse places than a sleeping bag in the back of a van, it hadn't been the most comfortable night's sleep he'd ever had. It was easier to be a twenty-year-old stoic about such things than it was to be a man his age. . . .

He smiled at the memory that brought up. About the time he'd turned fifty, he had hurt his right knee running an obstacle course. He'd come down off a swinging rope over a mud hole, let go, and hit crooked. Wasn't the first time he'd ever hurt a joint, and he limped through the rest of the course, went home, and RICE'd the injury—rest, ice, compression, and elevation—along with some ibuprofen every few hours, SOP.

After a couple weeks, when the knee was still bothering him more than he thought it should, he went to see one of the base doctors.

The doc, a kid of maybe thirty and a captain, had started his exam, and while he was poking and prodding, asked, "So, how'd you do this, Major?"

Kent told him.

The kid had frowned. "Major, a man your age ought not to be running the obstacle course."

"A man my age? Son, I'm *not* a man my age!"

It had been funny. But in the decade since, he'd noticed that the aches and pains he'd shrugged off even at fifty took longer to get better. Some of them hung around for months. Some of them were still with him for years—that knee injury tended to throb when it got cold and rainy even now.

But that was the name of the game, he knew, and while growing old was the pits, it sure beat the alternative. . . .

Natadze, wearing a leather jacket over what looked like khaki slacks and some kind of soft-soled loafers, was twenty-some years younger than Kent, and a professional assassin. It would be stupid to ignore that. He wasn't going to challenge him *mano a mano,* straight up. They didn't like handguns in San Francisco, but somehow Kent didn't think that meant much to his quarry. He'd be armed—wearing a jacket like that in this heat—and he'd be wary.

Five minutes later, Kent's virgil beeped, but as he reached to shut it off, he heard Cyrus's voice: "Colonel?"

"Here."

"He's gone out the back door. Said his car was parked back there, asked if it was okay."

Kent frowned. More wary even than Kent had figured, and still a step ahead. He reached for the van's ignition, cranked the key.

"The alley is one-way, running east. If his car is there, he'll be coming out on the street next to the dentist's office, unless he goes against the traffic."

Kent was already pulling out of the parking lot by then. "Thanks, son. I'll let you know how it goes."

Kent hurried to the corner, made the turn, and saw the sign for the dentist's. He pulled in behind a bus and past the mouth of the alley.

There was a double-axle truck parked a hundred feet in, the doors open. No sign of a car—wait, there was Natadze—

He was on foot, half a block away, and going in the other direction—!

Kent mashed the gas pedal, lurched around the bus, and sped for the next corner, a one-way street, which, fortunately, was going west. He careened through the turn and roared down the street. Ran a red light and pulled another right turn. The mouth of the alley was just ahead. He passed it, pulled into a loading zone, and stopped, a hundred feet away—

Natadze, carrying a black guitar case, emerged from the alley and looked in both directions. Kent saw him in the rearview mirror. Natadze couldn't see him enough to ID him, he was sure.

Natadze crossed the street, dodging traffic, and went to a late-model gray Toyota parked in a no-parking zone. He opened the car with a remote, put the guitar in the back seat on the floor, and climbed in.

Kent grabbed a notepad and the mechanical pencil on the seat next to him and wrote down the car's license number. California plate, probably a rental. He'd once had a digital recorder for such quick notes, but the battery had died in that at a bad time, and he'd gone back to the old-fashioned way. Not once had the battery run down on a sheet of paper, and he had four extra pencils in case one ran out of lead.

Kent was no expert at surveillance. He had been taught the basics as part of a two-week class in investigative procedures given by Marine Intel a few years back. His and Natadze's noses were pointed in different directions, and that was bad. When Natadze pulled out, Kent would have to hang a U-turn to follow him. Anybody looking for a tail would spot that and mark the vehicle, so you'd start out with a strike against you. The only way around that if you were alone was to wait until the subject was far enough away that he might not notice, and if you did that, you risked losing him. Without an electronic tag on the subject's vehicle, you were restricted to line of sight, and if he got too far out of that, you would almost surely lose him.

But God smiled on Kent this time. It was Natadze who pulled out and made a sharp U-turn, passing Kent's van. Kent dropped in his seat, waited a few seconds, then edged back upright.

Natadze made it to the corner, stopped at the red light, and signaled for a right turn.

Kent let one car get between them, then pulled out.

The light changed to green. Instead of turning, Natadze pulled across the intersection straight ahead, then switched his blinker off. The car between them followed. Kent did too, dropping back a little.

His quarry was being careful, and obviously looking for a tail. If he spotted him, Kent would be burned, and the game would change. It wouldn't be a sub-rosa surveillance any longer, it would be a chase, and that made it real iffy.

Of course, Kent had his virgil, and he could call the local police at any time. If Natadze spotted him and ran, he'd have to do that, since the van wasn't the best car to be drag-racing through the streets of San Francisco. He didn't want to, but his pride wasn't as important as catching this guy.

Natadze made a right turn at the next intersection—another one-way street. As soon as he was out of sight, Kent reached down, grabbed a Giants baseball cap, and put it on. He took a pair of sunglasses from over the visor and slipped those on. He couldn't change the look of his vehicle, but he could alter his own a little, in case he had to get closer.

Kent made the turn.

Natadze was a hundred feet ahead. He pulled the Toyota over to the curb into a loading zone.

Smart.

Kent drove past, along with five or six other cars.

Natadze would be looking for people stopping behind him, so that was Kent's only real choice.

Half a block ahead was a big truck with a piano on a hydraulic lift parked in front of a music store. Kent pulled in behind it.

He saw Natadze edge back out into traffic. Kent slouched in his seat, then lay on his side as Natadze's car approached.

Kent pulled away from the curb, four cars behind Natadze. Too many. If his quarry got through a light turning yellow ahead of him, he'd be screwed.

Kent moved over one lane and sped up.

He passed Natadze on the man's left, got a couple cars ahead, and then pulled over in front of him.

A front-tail was risky, but at this point, it was all risky.

He picked his virgil and thumbed a programmed button. That got him into Net Force's secure database.

"ID Colonel Abraham Kent confirmed," a woman said. "Query, sir?"

"I need information on an automobile license number," he said. He rattled off the plate number. "It's probably a rental car. Renter ID and local residence, please."

"One moment, please."

As Kent approached the next intersection, he watched Natadze in the outside rearview mirror. Kent went through the green light.

Natadze stopped, even though the light was still green.

Drivers behind Natadze honked their horns. Probably called him some foul names, too, though Kent couldn't hear that.

Kent watched the traffic signal and Natadze's car in his mirror. The light turned yellow. Just as it turned to red, Natadze stomped on the gas and burned rubber through the intersection.

Anther smart move. Anybody following him would also have to run the red light and Natadze would be watching for that.

Nobody did, because nobody else was following him.

"The car is an Avis rental, checked out at the San Francisco airport this morning at 6:16 A.M. The driver's license says that his name is Fernando Sor, a Spanish national, and the local address on the rental agreement is the Hotel Alhambra in Lucas Valley. However, a cross-check of the address given shows that there is no such hotel there—or anywhere else in Lucas Valley."

"Thank you." Kent recognized the phony name—a classical guitarist, one whose works had been featured in the concert he'd attended just before Natadze had broken into his room that night.

Not that it was any help.

"Does it say where and when he is supposed to return the rental car?"

A beat, then, "Yes, sir. At the San Francisco airport, tomorrow morning."

"Can you check and see if Fernando Sor is booked on any flight leaving San Francisco tomorrow?"

Kent couldn't stay where he was. Sooner or later, Natadze would turn, and by the time Kent made it around the block to catch up to him, he could be gone. He slowed, and as he did, swapped the Giants baseball cap for a Seattle Mariners cap and a different pair of shades.

Behind him, Natadze had moved into the center lane.

"Sir, Fernando Sor is booked on a Left Coast shuttle to Los Angeles at 9:40 A.M. tomorrow."

Kent nodded. "Thanks again. I appreciate it."

He clicked the virgil off and dropped it onto the seat. Well. That was something. If he lost Natadze, he had a place to look later. Of course, that flight information could be bogus, but it was what he had. If Natadze didn't think anybody was following him, then maybe it was valid.

Natadze passed Kent on the left.

Kent pretended he was a delivery man with a stack of books and magazines in the back of the van, just a guy doing his job. The intel op who had taught him how to follow and spy on people had told him that such an attitude made a difference. If you looked at your subject—or didn't look at him—as an operative following him, a wary man might detect something in your posture. People in the game had a sixth sense, some of them, and by the act of pretending you weren't watching them, they might pick up a subliminal clue that you were doing just that. If you were just a guy on your way home, then you weren't ignoring the quarry or concentrating on him—he was nothing to you one way or the other, and he might believe that.

It had seemed weird to Kent at the time, but the few times he had tried it in practice sessions, it had worked, so he followed that advice every chance he could.

Natadze drove past.

It went that way for fifteen more long and nerve-wracking minutes. A couple of times, Kent was sure Natadze had spotted him, but apparently not, because eventually, Natadze wound up at a Night's End Motel, where he pulled into the parking lot.

Kent parked his van just past the motel's entrance, got out, and quickly walked to where he saw Natadze park and alight from his car. Natadze took the guitar out of the back, then walked to a room, where he let himself in with a key card.

Gotcha!

In the Air over Southern New Jersey

The business jet was fairly quiet for a craft its size, and the air was still, so flight was smooth. It was also still daylight, and, this time of summer, probably would be for another hour or so.

It was just the two of them, plus the pilots. Thorn had thought about having an attendant, but thought that might be too much. They could walk to the plane's bar and get their own drinks.

Marissa shook her head. "I still can't believe you did this."

"You said surprise you."

"Well, I was surprised, I confess. Do you do this a lot?"

"Only once before, after I heard the Elvis story, just to see how it felt."

"The Elvis story?"

Thorn nodded. "Supposedly, Elvis and his crew were sitting around at Graceland and one of them started talking about this place in Denver that made these great sandwiches. So Elvis says, 'Let's go!' They warmed up his private jet, and flew from Memphis to Denver just to get supper."

"Really?"

"That's not the best part. When they got there? They had the sandwiches delivered to the plane. Never got off. Ate, cranked it back up, and flew home."

She shook her head again. "Sounds just odd enough to be true. So, what is this little trip going to set you back?"

He shrugged. "I don't know. Not enough so the accountants will worry."

She said, "Ah. The old Cornelius Vanderbilt line about yachts—if you have to ask how much one costs, you can't afford it?"

He frowned. "Marissa, are you really going to bust my chops for having money? I was lucky enough to come up with some software that people found useful, and it paid real well. I'm not in the same class with Arab sheiks or major rock stars or basketball team owners, but I can live high and not run out in my lifetime. What Sophie Tucker said is true—'I've been rich and I've been poor. Rich is better.'"

She grinned at him. "Relax, Tommy. I'm just pulling your chain."

He smiled back. "And I'm defensive about sitting on a fat wallet."

"Most self-made men are, at least the ones I've met. They feel as if they lucked into it, and on some level don't deserve it."

"Date a lot of rich guys, do you?"

"A few. Rich, poor, you all look alike in the dark."

He laughed.

"So, what's this restaurant you're taking me to, Mr. Moneybags?"

"Ah, that's part of the surprise."

"Okay. You want to get me a beer while you're up?"

"While I'm up?"

"Have to get up to get me a beer, won't you?"

He laughed again. "Not much incentive there."

"Want to join the Mile High Club?"

He stood up quickly. "I'm getting that beer now," he said.

* * *

Macao, China

Locke tapped on the door, smiled at the camera, and waited for Leigh to answer. It was good to be back.

China was not the United States. Locke doubted that there would ever be the degree of personal freedom here as there. Still, it was his home, and he was more comfortable here than anywhere else. Better the devil you know than the devil you don't. . . .

To look at, this house he was visiting was nothing special. A middle-class bungalow, built in the 1970s or '80s, on a street with two dozen others just like it. If you knew how to look, though, you'd spot some differences.

The entrance, which looked like imitation wood, was actually a steel fire door in a steel frame, and probably weighed a hundred kilograms. Locke knew that there were three dead-bolt locks, plus a police brace-bar on the inside. You could ram a truck into the door and it wouldn't go down. The back door was much the same.

The outside walls were brick. The roof was heavy ceramic tile, and there were banks of solar cells that fed enough juice into a dozen heavy-duty marine batteries to run everything in the house for days. The phone antenna on the roof looked like a television satellite dish. There was a gasoline-powered electrical generator in an armored shed in the back, inside a chain-link fence topped with razor wire. Locke also knew that the building's interior walls were wood slats over steel posts and expanded metal sheets, and you'd have trouble driving a truck through them, too.

Not that you could get a truck up the short but steep hill that was the yard, and past the heavy cast-iron furniture—benches, chairs, a table—all of which were bolted into concrete pilings.

The windows looked innocuous, but hidden behind the shades were hardened steel grills that would resist any casual attempts at burglary—or even a would-be thief with hammers, saws, and determination.

The house's power supply and phone landline arrived

via a buried cable inside a steel conduit, and the electric meter was locked inside a steel box. The water meter's valve box was welded shut, and the meter reader had been bribed to ignore it.

There were state-of-the-art alarms and automatic CO_2 fire extinguishers installed in every room.

It was about as secure a place as one could have in this city.

The door opened, and Bruce Leigh stuck his head out, looked right and left to make certain Locke was alone, and said, "Come in."

Locke did. Leigh shut the door behind him and relocked it, clicking the wrist-thick police bar into place. One end of the bar slid into a plate on the floor, the other angled into a second plate welded to the middle of the door. Such a setup would hold the door in place even without locks or hinges. The bar had to weigh ten kilos, but Leigh, a fitness freak, handled it easily.

Leigh, an ex-pat Brit, was short, broad, muscular, and an expert on security computer systems. And also seriously paranoid, if not to the extent of clinical schizophrenia.

Locke doubted that anybody ever gave him any grief about his name.

"You changed cabs?"

"Three times." Three was the magic number. Not two, not four, but three.

Leigh nodded. He turned and walked away. Locke followed him.

The house was filled with computers, at least thirty of them, ranging from some ten or fifteen years old to those still warm from the maker.

Leigh led him through the gym, wherein he had installed a treadmill, a rowing machine, a stair climber, a mini-tramp, a stationary bike, and two Bowflex machines, along with half a ton of free weights on various barbells and dumbbells. Locke had never asked Leigh how often he worked out—you didn't ask the man personal questions—but there was a computer in the room whose screen showed a schedule, and a passing glance once had told Locke that Leigh spent three hours every day in here.

The man worked, and he worked out, and that seemed to be it. If he had women, they came here, as did all his groceries and other supplies. As far as Locke knew, Leigh never went out. He was a serious introvert. And one of the best computer geeks in the world, much less China.

Down the hall, the main computer room had four large-screen monitors and two holoprojectors, arranged in a U-shape.

Leigh sat in a padded leather chair inside the surrounding computers and started waving his hands over various optical sensors.

"I've got the building plans, the communication codes, and the alarm system specs—don't have the codes on all those yet, but I will have them by the end of the week. I have also built the traffic signal program, and the electrical grid system is no problem.

"Do you have a date yet?"

"Not yet."

"Let me know. There's a rotating encrypt on the transfer protocols for the bank's armored trucks, and we'll have to get that no sooner than a week in advance.

"The police systems are nailed."

"Everything seems to be in order," Locke said.

"Yes. Of course."

"There is a new variable," Locke said.

Leigh snapped his head around as if Locke had slapped him. "What?"

"Apparently Net Force and CyberNation have come to some kind of agreement regarding their situation."

Leigh relaxed. "That's Shing's problem. Even he should be able to handle that."

"I just thought you might want to know."

Leigh shook his head negatively. "All I have to worry about is Chang. Not that he's any real problem. Besides which, he's gone to the U.S."

"To do what?"

"Who cares? Probably trying to score some gear. Chang has a few moves, but no real equipment, and his programs are garbage. He doesn't even know I'm out here. Nobody in the world knows I'm here."

Locke nodded. He removed an envelope full of cash from his jacket pocket and handed it to Leigh. The only way the man would accept payment was in small, used bills. He surely had some kind of electronic banking presence, some credit somewhere, to get all the computers he had, but Leigh kept that to himself and Locke didn't know what or where it was.

Leigh stood and the two men headed for the front door.

"I'll see you again in a week."

"Don't forget to change cabs when you leave," Leigh said. "Three coming, three going."

"Of course," Locke said.

Washington, D.C.

Chang had visited the Smithsonian—the Air and Space Museum, some of the art galleries. He had seen the Hope Diamond, and gone to see the copies of the U.S. Constitution and Bill of Rights in the dark and quiet room where they were kept in armored glass cases full of inert gas.

He had gone to pray in some of the larger mosques—Masjid Baitullah, the Muhammad, the Ul-Ummah, Ush Shura, as well as some of the newer ones, the Madjid China, and the Sino.

He had enjoyed a stimulating conversation with Imam Jaseem Yusof at the China Mosque, and with the Chinese-speaking teacher at the Sino, Haji Chan Ho. All who dwelled in Islam were connected; those who had made the journey to Mecca even more so.

He was on his way to meet the software seller the Canadian had steered him to, an American by the name of Petrie, at a restaurant not far from the Mall. Well, not far for Chang, who was used to walking a mile or three to get where he wanted to go back home.

So far, this had been a most interesting trip, most interesting. Jay Gridley, though somewhat preoccupied by his son's illness, had been very forthcoming about many of his procedures. More so than Chang had expected. Of course, the workers in the trenches did not always share the security concerns of their overlords—computer people spoke a language the way that musicians did, and their common interests bonded them. Already, he had learned more than he thought possible. Techniques he could take back home and apply immediately to his own systems. They were so rich, the Americans, and they didn't realize just how much they had. They took so much for granted. Gear that he would have given an arm for, they shrugged off and threw away as outmoded. Amazing.

With any luck, this man Petrie would be able to fill some major gaps in Chang's arsenal. Many of the cutting-edge technologies were proscribed—they simply could not be exported. However, the trade status between China and the United States was, at the moment at least, good, and there were some programs and hardware available now that had not been even in the recent past. Chang did not have an unlimited budget, but a few thousand dollars here would go a long way to help things.

And there was always the possibility of under-the-table deals, for programs that were technically not available, but for which there was no real reason to keep them so. The U.S., like China, had its lists of things forbidden. Often, though, the items put upon these had little or no reason to be there, they were but part of a wide swath that had not been examined against reality.

There was a downloadable anti-viral program, for instance, that was not even as good as the ones Chang already had, that was unavailable simply because of the style of encryption in it. This encryption had been part of Chinese software applications for more than a year, and yet it was still on the list. Nobody had gotten around to updating things, and as soon as they did, this would be changed.

Well. He would do what he could. He was already farther ahead of the game; anything from here on would be a bonus.

The Gridley-Bretton Dyson Sphere
(Formerly the Omega Stellar System)
The Long Spiral Arm of the Military Galaxy

Jay reached out and turned the Dyson sphere, rotating it with arms that spanned the inner orbits of a solar system, searching every square inch of the sphere's quadrillions of square miles looking for the hole from which unauthorized data was coming and going.

It was VR to the max—a distillation of an abstract concept, consciousness magnified to new levels. Yet for all that he was godlike in his omniscience here, he felt more human than ever before.

The image of Mark in the hospital bed with an IV's stainless-steel needle plugged into his tiny arm kept coming back to him, reminding him how easily joy could be taken from his life.

Sure, the doctor all but said that he would be fine, that Mark's seizures were just a reaction to the fever he'd had, and he had let the boy go home, but Jay had *felt* the icy specter of death brush past, coming not for him, but one of *his.*

Maybe everything was fine today, but—what about tomorrow?

He no longer lived in a world that felt under his control, where he could write off misfortune to himself as experience earned.

Come on, Gridley, focus.

This VR scenario, possibly the most complicated in which he had ever been involved, demanded a very high level of concentration.

He and Bretton had gone back to basics looking for the leak in the military's computer network. The formula was simple: Pick a VR metaphor, structure it to your strengths, and run it.

It had taken them a while to come up with it. The dataspace used for simulating multiple nuclear explosions in the full-world sim that Bretton had programmed was so huge that finding a relevant metaphor was a challenge in itself.

But then Jay had remembered a science-fiction book he'd read that described a Dyson sphere. First postulated by Freeman Dyson in the middle of the last century, a Dyson sphere was a huge and hollow globe, constructed of the star's planets, crushed into cosmic cement and somehow glued together. Such a shell then surrounded the sun, to capture *all* of its radiant energy.

Dyson had proposed the construct as the ultimate answer for the energy needs of an ever-expanding civilizations—a monstrous bubble that would catch everything the star emitted, wasting nothing. It would be useful for millions of years, and by the time the star went nova and burned out, a race sufficiently advanced to have built the sphere in the first place could probably figure out a way to move to a more hospitable neighborhood.

Such a sphere would necessarily be very, very *large*.

So he and Bretton had remapped the dataspace of *all* the known infected military computers as a Dyson sphere, locating themselves outside it, looking for the break in the wall that had let the virus inside. Their model wasn't a long-time scan, that wasn't possible with the machineries at their command. What they had built represented but two or three seconds that they had calculated when the virus must have been released into the system. They hoped.

The Chinese guy Chang would love this—too bad they couldn't show it to him, but the military was a little touchy about allowing foreigners this deep into their heart and brain.

That's just the way it goes. . . .

Focus, Jay!

By checking the entire surface of the sphere during that period, they would examine every possible place their leak could be, and would therefore find it.

In theory, at least. Eventually.

The second part of developing the scenario was tailoring it to their strengths. Jay was an expert at looking for system weaknesses. If anyone could figure out where the break was, it was him. The only problem was that it could take *years*, even in an accelerated time frame, to search the sphere.

The solution, they figured, would require both of them.

Bretton, the military VR jock, was a master of AI programming. In his warfare simulations, he created large-scale interactions of software systems to represent the entire world at war. His complex systems interacted at both a macro and a micro level, representing a repeatable reality.

In this case, Bretton had created a huge army of robots. Each one was over a mile long, with thousands of magnetic millipedelike legs. Each was loaded with full spectrum sensors that could read every kind of radiation, chemical, sound, and texture that mankind had ever encountered. Millions and millions of these snakelike creations crawled across the sphere, sampling, testing, looking.

Bretton had made them, but the robots were under *Jay's* control.

Jay's normal VR sensors had been rerouted through the robots, each machine giving him data, millions of points of information combining into his senses.

He hung in space, an immense figure, the sphere appearing to him about the size of a large beach ball. He reached out and rotated it, running his hands over its surface, feeling for imperfections, looking for the place that wasn't like the other places, the spot that was weaker.

As he did so, huge arrays of robots fanned out on the sphere covering every spot that his fingers touched, using their sensitive legs to send information to his tactile sensors. He felt a uniform pattern on the sphere, a pattern that fit with the geodesic nature of the construct.

Every location that his fingers passed changed color after it had been scanned, a bright red that seemed to seep from his nails like blood. The marker helped track his progress and would let him know when he'd completed this stage of the search.

He closed his eyes to focus on the tactile sensors—and for a moment he saw Mark in the hospital bed. He remembered standing there with Saji after the doctor had finally come. Mark had been asleep by this point, far more relaxed than his parents.

Oh, my God, Jay, I was so scared, he remembered Saji saying, and the squeeze of her hand.

He opened his eyes and saw that he had covered most of the globe in red. He carefully brushed his fingers over the rest.

Nothing.

He pulled his hands back, and traced a sign in the air.

The stars blanked out, leaving the sphere darker than before. The scene was almost black now, only a faint metallic gleam on the sphere, barely enough to still see it. His eyes shifted slightly, and the globe became blacker as the radiation sensors in the robots came on-line.

He reached for the sphere again, this time checking it for any light leaks. Such a leak would indicate the data hole he was searching for, whether it was in any part of the emittable spectrum or not.

It was larger now, about the size of a hot-air balloon, representing the scale change necessary for this test. He worked slowly, feeling the massiveness of the sphere as he turned it, carefully staring at each piece on the macro level while legions of robotic sensors scanned it at the micro.

His eyes had adjusted to the darker light, and now the segment of the sphere he looked at appeared brighter, almost silver. . . .

Like the needle in Mark's arm . . .

No. Focus.

Jay blinked twice to shake the image, and continued to turn the globe. He had to be sure to hold it in each position for three seconds so that he could see all of the surface within the three-second window that the sphere represented. A tiny turquoise bar-graph at the edge of his vision constantly counted off the time, filling up with gold and then reverting to blue at the end of each interval.

A wire-frame model below the bar showed his progress. Two segments left.

Jay completed the search.

Nothing.

He started his next check, a chemical examination of the sphere, using his olfactory sensors. The globe had shrunk now, to a basketball. He pulled it close to his face and started to sniff.

As he did this, the robot armies, now germ-sized on his scale, deployed spectral analyzers, checking the atomic makeup of the sphere, looking for variations that could not be explained. There was a slightly pinelike smell, almost antiseptic.

Like the hospital.

This wouldn't do.

Jay activated a control and the smell shifted to a more pleasant cedar, taking him away from thoughts of Mark.

He turned the ball, sniffing, a bloodhound looking for something that didn't smell right.

A bell chimed, and he realized that he'd completed the search.

Nothing.

Nothing at all.

He hadn't found anything. But he should have. The interface had been tested, the robots' AI performed flawlessly, and the metaphor was good. There was the tiniest chance that they'd gotten the time frame wrong for the sphere, but it seemed unlikely.

Which left *him* as the weak link.

It's me.

Jay let out a long breath. He'd been distracted, thinking about Mark. He must have missed something, some factor.

He was going to have to try something else.

23

Queens, New York

After they alighted from the cab, Thorn said, "See that lot over there?"

Marissa nodded.

"Holds two hundred cars, and it's full. That's the parking for Tials. See all those people at those outdoor tables, under those ratty umbrellas? That's the dinner crowd."

It looked like a busy evening at a country fair's food plaza. Maybe three hundred people in the warm summer night, at long rows of wooden picnic tables set end to end. The diners were laughing, talking, eating.

"Come on."

She followed him around the corner. There were three lines of people queued up in front of what looked like a market stall, a pole barn with counters and a dozen men and women inside it, no walls, just a roof. Fragrant smoke rose from the place in a thick cloud.

Behind it was a stubby, rectangular building the size of a small two-bedroom house—that held a refrigerator, freezer, and a lot of storage space.

"Looks like the waiting line for a ride at Disneyworld," she said.

He nodded. "The long line is for new customers, the medium-long line for regulars. The short line is for cops and firefighters only."

"And this is enforced how?"

"If you are in the regulars or cops line and somebody doesn't recognize you when you get to the counter? You don't get served—you have to go to the back of the new-customer line."

"And these dedicated people are lined up to eat what?"

"Chiliburgers."

Marissa shook her head. "This is it? Lord, Tommy. I was guessing maybe you were taking me someplace where they served fugu or some weird Tasmanian snail or something. You flew us all the way to New York—to Queens, of all places—to have *chiliburgers*?"

"Best in the country, maybe best in the world," he said. "So how come a crack CIA operative like you doesn't know about Tials?"

"I don't even know what kind of *name* that is," she said.

"Acronym, actually," he said, heading toward the cop/firefighter line.

"How do you rate the short line?"

"Well, I was a regular, but Bruce decided that becoming Commander of Net Force made me a cop. Best perk I've gotten from the job so far, present company excluded."

"Uh huh. You were explaining the name of this place?"

" 'There is always a Larry somewhere.' The first letter of each word—T-I-A-L-S."

They reached the end of the line. The man in front of them turned and saw them. "Hey, Thorn," he said.

"Hey, Mickey. Marissa, this is Mickey Reilly, Detective Third, NYPD. Mickey, Marissa Lowe. Marissa is an operative for one of those, ah, federal agencies usually known only by their initials."

"Pleased to meetcha," Reilly said.

"Likewise."

She looked back at Thorn. "Explain the name, please."

"What? Mickey?"

"I *will* hit you, Tommy."

He smiled. So did Mickey. "Well, Bruce used to work in Hollywood. He was an up-and-rising screenwriter, wrote a couple movies for guys like Tom Cruise, Brad Pitt, like that. But it got to him after a while, all the Hollywood crap, so he took his money and quit. He bought a secret family chili recipe from some Greek guy back in the old country, then set up shop here."

"And?" she asked.

"The story Bruce tells, he would go into meetings with studio executives to pitch a script. And they'd go back and forth, but nobody ever wanted to make a decision right there and then. They always had to check it with somebody first. Only a handful of folks in La-La-Land can actually greenlight a movie. So they'd tell him, 'Baby, *I* love it, it's great, a fantastic idea, but before we can go ahead, I have to run it past Larry, you know.' "

"Ah."

Thorn nodded, grinned. "Bruce said there was always a 'Larry' somewhere—down the hall, up the stairs, on vacation in Mexico. It was one of the ways studio guys avoided having to ever say 'No.' They could look like they were on the side of the angels, because *they* never rejected anything, never had an unkind word for anybody. It was always *Larry's* fault."

She shook her head.

"All they serve is chiliburgers and soda. You get to the counter, you say how many of each you want, that's it. Nine dollars for the burger, a buck for the soft drink. They don't take checks, Visa, Mastercard, or American Express, cash only. They also don't make change—you give 'em a ten, you break even. A twenty, you either want two burgers and drinks, or you tip them ten dollars."

He paused, but she didn't say anything, just waited for him to continue.

"On an average night," he said, "there will be ten or fifteen thousand dollars in small bills in the cash drawer. And, in case you are wondering, no, nobody has ever robbed them. If anybody ever tried, most of the cops in this line would happily shoot them and step over the body to get their order."

Mickey nodded at that, and threw in a wink.

"You want it your way," Thorn went on, "you go to Burger King—you don't alter anything here. What you get is half a pound of ground sirloin on an oversize burger bun, slathered in the special Greek chili, wrapped in a piece of aluminum foil, and a wad of napkins, which you'll need, and whatever soft drink they got the best deal on this week. You don't want to know how many calories and fat and cholesterol is in Bruce's burger."

"Right," Marissa said.

"Forty years ago, there used to be a place in L.A. with a similar setup, it's where Bruce got the idea, but they franchised it, and it wasn't the same after that. Tials is one of a kind. Open twenty-four/seven. Come by here at two A.M. on a weekday, it's this crowded. People bring their families here for Christmas dinner. Tials never closes. I think Bruce must live in the refrigerator—which occupies a good section of that building behind the stand."

"Wow. It's that good?"

"It's better than that. Just wait. After Tials, you'll never be able to eat a burger anywhere else without frowning at it."

"Two surprises in one evening. What else have you got up your sleeve, Mr. Thorn?"

He smiled and winked at her, but didn't say anything else.

Twenty minutes later, they were sitting at a stained picnic table, each with a chiliburger and a Coke. Thorn watched her take her first bite, and smiled at the look on her face as she chewed and swallowed it.

"Lord. This is *great!*" she managed.

"You're a cheap date," he said, waving his burger. "Well, except for the ride."

"Shut up and eat," she said.

They did, chili dripping. Thorn watched her as he ate, and at that moment, figured this might be as good as dinner ever got, in which case, he'd have no complaints.

Rue de Soie
Marne-la-Vallée
France

Seurat admired the woman's sleeping body, taking great pleasure in looking at every exposed millimeter without having to pretend he wasn't staring, without the need for a social pretext that what he saw didn't attract him and draw him in completely.

Ah . . .

She lay on her side, her rich, long hair dark against his ivory silk sheets, her tanned skin lightly dotted with freckles, each of which seemed utterly fascinating. Her head was turned toward her chest, her chin tucked in, and the rise and fall of her chest seemed to raise her breasts to almost touch her face, sheltering it with every breath.

Her hip rose from the bed, a graceful arc that beckoned him to put his hand on it, a call that he had answered many times already this night. One long leg was hooked over his duvet, and he admired its utter smoothness, its grace.

He realized he was looking at her with the intensity he usually reserved for paintings, and grinned. She was a beautiful artwork that was all the more amazing for being *real,* and all the more exciting for being in *his* bed. He grinned again when he realized how much the comparison would amuse her.

And an American. *Who would have thought?*

The last day had been full of surprises. To think that he'd very nearly missed this one!

He had been outrageously irritable since the most recent attack, which had crashed the local CyberNation node, lashing out at his staff, wanting answers, pushing them to work harder, when they all wanted the same thing he did, and very nearly as much as he wanted it. *Le boss* was being the ass, and everybody knew it, no one more so than the boss himself. . . .

In his last communication with Gridley, the man had obliquely hinted at a brute-force approach that was being tried on the attack, designed to find the mechanism by which their network had been compromised. Seurat had not been surprised, since it was the approach he would have expected from the Americans anyway. Never use a scalpel when a chain saw will serve. . . .

But his own team had not been able to suggest a better approach.

He liked to think of himself and of CyberNation as smarter, more able to figure out the linchpin, the keystone of a problem, and to use that knowledge rather than force to achieve victory. A dagger rather than a blunt instrument.

And when they had failed him, and he, himself, had not been able to solve the problem either, he had left work in a foul mood.

On the way home, as he looped around the Boulevard Périphérique, his calendar had chimed to remind him of a showing at his aunt's house, just out of the city. His family had for years managed to use the influence of their name and of their various connections in the art world to arrange for private showings of his ancestor's works whenever one was on tour and passed through Europe. The events reinforced the bond of blood, and had helped reconcile the disparate branches of his family line, legitimate and not. Plus, they were usually a good time, a respite from the work world, and indeed a reason to take one.

But he'd been angry and had slapped his PDA, silencing the reminder, and accelerating toward his home. Art could not help him now, he needed science.

It had taken a few more kilometers of driving for him to laugh at himself, and to acknowledge that art *was* what he needed. Even if it did not inspire a solution, it would provide a different focus for the rest of the evening. Besides, the painting coming was a study for *La Grande Jatte*, one that had been out of the country for decades. Surely it was not going to be back soon.

So he had kept driving past his exit, heading toward his aunt's, another thirty kilometers outside the city. By the time he had arrived, it had grown dark. The gathering was in full swing, the old chateau lit brightly from within, the color of the electric light the only difference from what might have been seen several hundred years before.

His uncles and aunts had greeted him warmly, and he'd grabbed a glass of wine from one of the family vineyards, a delightful '08 that had sweetened his disposition considerably.

He had enjoyed the interaction, and had gradually worked his way toward the back of the house, to the old parlor where Aunt Sophia displayed paintings for events such as this. The rococo stylings of the house had soothed him, taking away the pain of the difficult day through their familiarity and sense of continuity.

Things have been worse and gotten better before, they seemed to say.

And there, in the back of the room, several of his older cousins staring at it, was the painting.

It was large, and Seurat recognized it immediately as one of the last studies for *La Grande Jatte,* nearly full-size, with the majority of the pantheon from the final painting laid out on it, albeit somewhat differently.

He stepped closer, feeling the warmth of that distant day, enjoying the serenity of the figures in the painting as they did also, taking pleasure in the consummate skill of his ancestor, acknowledging the careful planning.

And this was not even the final painting.

He felt a touch at his sleeve and returned to the world, the noise from the party washing back over him like an ocean tide, not realizing he'd completely tuned it out until it returned.

Standing there was good old Aunt Sophia, wearing one of her opera gowns, dressed, as usual, to deny detractors the pleasure of disparaging comments.

"Ahhh, Charles, *mon cheri,* there you are! I wanted to introduce you to Mademoiselle Millard, who is here with the painting. She travels with it on the tour, and was good enough to grace us with her presence."

He thought he'd heard his aunt emphasize the woman's status as single, and made a note to tease her about it later, which he promptly forgot as he turned and saw Millard.

She was tall, and wore a low-cut dress that covered enough to satisfy propriety, but which revealed enough to encourage imagination. She smiled, a graceful movement of her lips. Surely anyone could do such a thing—but if that were so, how come he'd never seen them poised just—*so?*

Sophia had completed the introduction.

"Michelle Millard, this is my nephew, Charles—also a Seurat."

He remembered feeling a sudden thrill rush through him as he heard her name.

Michelle. How beautiful.

"Mademoiselle, it is a pleasure to meet you," he said, thinking how inadequate it was. But somehow she brightened, and when she spoke her words seemed to tell him something deeper, something more.

"The pleasure is mine," she'd said, and then, "I understand you have some of your ancestor's works that are not publicly shown?"

He wasn't sure, but he thought he'd heard Sophia chuckle before she walked off.

Seurat was no schoolboy. He'd been with women—many women. But he had had such chemistry with only a handful.

They had talked until late in the evening, about surface things—paintings, favorite artists, and even the weather. But beneath their words an understanding simmered, cascades of meaning that spoke of a deeper interest, deeper meanings to the nods and smiles.

He had offered to drive her back to Paris, of course.

And when she had asked if they could perhaps stop by his house to see his paintings, he had said, "Of course."

Truly she was beautiful—and more.

Seurat couldn't remember the last time he'd spent so much time with anyone without talking about CyberNation. Had he even told her what he did?

"Do you like what you see, Monsieur?"

He started. Had she been awake the whole time?

"If I had any clothes on, your eyes would have burned through them the way you were looking at me!"

He chuckled. "If *I* had any clothes on, they would have been burned off just by looking at you. Does that answer your question, Mademoiselle?"

"*Oui.*"

She reached over and slid her hand down his body, stopping at just the right place.

"As does this."

He put his hands on her as well, and her breathing increased to match his.

An American, he thought, as they started to move together, and then, *She is wonderful beyond belief.*

It could be that he was going to have to reevaluate his feelings about the United States. Surely a place from which she had come from couldn't be quite as bad as he had thought. . . .

24

San Francisco, California

Colonel Abe Kent glanced at his watch. It was pushing midnight, and Natadze was buttoned up tight. The motel room he was in had no rear exit, and there was no reason for him to be crawling out through a window—assuming he hadn't spotted Kent tailing him.

From his rented van, thirty yards away and parked facing Natadze's door, Kent considered his strategy and tactics. Natadze wasn't going to step out into the parking lot with his eyes closed—he'd be wary, looking for anything unusual. He knew Kent by sight, so there was no way he could just stroll in the killer's direction and make it close enough to get the drop on him. He could park his vehicle a bit nearer, but even so, opening a car door would draw Natadze's attention in a hurry.

Yes, Kent had the advantage, but it wasn't so great as all that. Taking down an alert and cautious enemy wasn't as easy as they made it look in the movies.

A smart man would have called in the experts—SWAT, SERT, FBI Tactical—and let them deal with the situation.

Kent was a man of war; he knew battlefield tactics, he could shoot and hit his target, and you could call this war on a small scale. Still, there were people better equipped for this particular scenario. He knew it.

He also knew that, smart or not, this was a personal thing. Him against Natadze, however wise that might be. There were some things a man took care of on his own, if he wanted to keep looking at his face in the mirror when he shaved.

Kent was adept at what he did, and his luck was better than average—at least it had been so far—but even so, a plan of action would be a good idea.

Of course, everybody knew it was better to be lucky than good.

Kent smiled. That brought another old memory up. That seemed to be happening to him more and more these days. Maybe it was a product of age. The older you got, the more you had to look at behind you than ahead of you.

This particular echo involved a conversation he'd had with John Howard, as they'd sat in a camper waiting for Natadze at Cox's estate—when they'd lost him. They'd been yakking about growing up, and about luck, the kind of thing you did when you had time on your hands and nothing pressing to fill it.

Howard had told a story about his first serious girlfriend, and how they had missed by seconds being caught by her father in a compromising position, and how a stuck hook or zipper would have made the difference. Could have short-stopped his entire career.

Kent had laughed, then told his story: He had an older brother he'd spent a summer with when he was twelve. Martin was married, going to school at LSU, down in Baton Rouge, where it was hot, damp, and rained a lot. Must have been around 1965 or '66. Martin had lived just off campus in an apartment with his wife, a gorgeous redhead with whom Kent had fallen in love at first sight.

Howard had smiled, one old soldier to another. The joy of older women.

"Anyway," Kent had continued, "my brother gave me

the full campus tour. The school's mascot was a Royal Bengal tiger, traditionally named Mike. The first tiger arrived in the forties, and there have been five or six since. When I visited my brother, they were up to Mike III, I think. The cat lived in a cage just outside the football stadium, next to the parade grounds where the ROTC marched. You could walk right up to it."

Kent smiled again, picturing the scene. "LSU was a land-grant college, so all male students who were physically able had to do two years of Army or Air Force ROTC. They had classes, even in the summer, and they marched early, before the heat got too oppressive. Bright and early, there would be hundreds, sometimes thousands of male students in their ROTC summer khaki uniforms at attention out there, yelling 'Good morning, Mike the Tiger, sir!' "

Howard smiled, too, and Kent continued. "The tiger used to be pulled in a cage around the stadium before football games. The story was, every time he roared, that meant the team would score one touchdown. They called the stadium Death Valley. Loudest place in the city on a Saturday night during football season. The police would one-way streets heading toward the campus before the game, one-way them in the other direction afterward."

"A tiger's hard to keep in a cage," Howard said.

Kent nodded. "Every now and then, Mike would somehow get out of his cage. Pranksters broke the locks off once, or somebody forgot to shut the cage. Mike got out, and naturally, he went exploring. Imagine how you'd feel if you were walking to the local market for a carton of milk and you looked up to see a four-hundred-pound Bengal tiger padding down the sidewalk toward you."

Howard laughed. "I'd need new underwear."

"Me, too. Luckily, nobody ever got eaten when the various Mikes took their strolls. Good thing, because if the cops or animal control people had ever had to shoot the big cat, the city would probably have lynched whoever pulled the trigger. Everybody loved Mike. The first one? After he died of old age, twenty-something, they stuffed and mounted him in the school museum, and you could listen to a tape recording of his roar. My brother took me to see him. Kind of spooky, that old stuffed tiger standing there."

He paused for a moment, remembering. "The point is, when you have a wild animal, he's only safe to be around as long as he's under control. And it's real easy to lose control of such a creature. One small slip, he gets you. Remember that magician who got attacked onstage in Las Vegas ten or twelve years ago? By a cat he had raised and trained?"

"Yes."

"So, you always have to be careful."

Howard said, "I hear that."

And yet, here was Kent, three thousand miles away from that camper and conversation, being reckless. Waiting for a wild animal—one that could shoot back, no less—to emerge from his lair.

Killing Natadze would be easy: He steps out the door, you line your sights up, don't say squat, and cook off two .45 auto rounds into the man's heart, bam, bam, end of story. But that wasn't how he wanted it to go down. He wanted the man alive and talking. It wasn't about *killing* him, it was about *defeating* him—

Natadze's door opened. There was no light behind him to silhouette him, but enough illumination from the parking lot and outside lamps to get a good view. He had the guitar case in one hand—his left—with his other hand free.

Kent frowned, liking this less and less. He couldn't let the man get into his car, not and risk losing him. Where was he going at this hour?

Never mind that, Abe. Go!

He pulled his Colt and thumbed the safety off—he was already cocked and locked—put his trigger finger outside the guard, took a deep breath, and opened the van's door.

Natadze spotted the motion immediately. He had taken several steps toward his car, was almost there, although he hadn't dug his keys out yet. Kent would have been happier if the man had both hands occupied.

Kent kept his pistol behind his leg as he started toward

Natadze. Still far enough away so the man might not make him—

At the back of his car, Natadze set the guitar case down, as if he was going to put it into the trunk, then straightened and suddenly broke into a sprint at a right angle to Kent, heading toward the open hallway to the north where the ice and soda machines were.

Kent snapped his pistol up, but Natadze was already ten feet farther away pumping fast and gaining speed. He hadn't gone for his gun, and Kent didn't want to shoot him. Plus a miss would put a round through a motel door or wall, and maybe hit somebody sleeping inside.

"Stop!" Kent yelled.

That was a waste of breath. Natadze sped up.

Kent ran, chasing the fleeing man.

The corridor opened up into another section of parking lot, around which there was a short chain-link fence. Too short a fence to slow Natadze down. He vaulted it, hit on the other side—another parking lot, for a fast-food place—and kept running.

All that training on the obstacle course paid off as Kent sailed over the fence without catching or breaking anything.

Natadze had twenty yards on him and was gaining more. Even full-out, Kent wasn't as fast. If this kept up, Natadze would run away from him in a few minutes. He might have to shoot the guy anyway.

But Natadze doglegged to his left, into the parking lot of a small strip mall. Thirty yards back, Kent watched his quarry make a mistake. He rounded a corner, and when Kent reached it and glanced after the runner, he realized it was a dead end—windowless buildings on either side and a brick wall of a third building at the end.

Natdaze spun, and came up with a handgun—

Kent dodged to his left and took three steps, out of Natadze's line of fire, behind the corner of the building. He didn't want to shoot the man, but neither did he want to get shot himself—

Cover, he needed *cover*—!

Behind him was parked a pickup truck with a florist's logo on the door. Kent backpedaled toward it, keeping the mouth of the alley covered.

Game over, Natadze. I have you now!

"It doesn't have to be this way!" Kent yelled.

They were only half a block away from the motel where Natadze had been staying. Kent was behind solid cover, since even the cab of a full-size pickup truck was proof against most handgun rounds, to say nothing of the engine compartment. It was possible that Natadze might skip a round low, off the concrete, but a standard pistol bullet wasn't going to have much steam—if any—after it ricocheted off the parking lot and went through two steel-belted truck tires, especially if it was a hollow-point, even semi-jacketed. But to try a shot that risky, he'd have to show himself, and Kent was ready for that.

"I'm afraid it does have to be this way!" Natadze called back.

He was behind the corner of the building, and Kent didn't know what the walls were made of. It looked like adobe, but that could be a thin layer over concrete block, or styrofoam panels. The difference was concealment versus cover—you could shoot through the former but not the latter. Since Kent wasn't sure exactly where the other man was, he wasn't going to try and perforate a wall and hope that he hit the bad guy—and maybe generate a ricochet into some little old man five blocks away walking his Pomeranian.

Besides which, he wanted the man alive. There were a lot of questions still hanging, and Natadze knew the answers. Dead men told no tales.

More than that, dead was too easy.

Kent shifted his grip on his pistol. He was lined up, aiming over the hood of the truck, covering the corner of the building. There was one in the tube and seven in the magazine. He had two more full magazines, and if he needed more than two dozen rounds, he was gonna be in deep trouble anyhow.

Right now, they were in a standoff. The alley behind Natadze was a dead end; he wasn't going anywhere unless he came out the way he went in, and that meant he'd have to get past Kent. On the other hand, Kent couldn't go in after him, because there was no cover between the truck and the building—an animal clinic next to a dog-grooming shop and a Mexican restaurant—no concealment, nothing.

The first man to leave cover would be the first one exposed to the other's fire. It was about twelve or fifteen meters from the truck to the building, and even a crappy shooter could make a body shot at that range; Kent had to assume that a professional killer knew how to shoot straight—thinking otherwise could get you dead in a hurry.

Time was on Kent's side, though, and they both knew it. In a neighborhood like this at night, a little strip mall on the edge of a fairly upscale area, somebody probably would have heard the chase and the shouts. The local police would show up eventually, and while they might not be SWAT-grade officers, they would be cops with guns.

He could have called and warned them about how dangerous Natadze was—if he hadn't left his virgil on the seat in the rented van. He should have had it on his belt.

Yeah. And if he had X-ray vision and superpowers, he could see Natadze and fly over there and capture him, too. No point in going down the "if only" road.

"You could have shot me back in Nebraska," Kent called. "Why didn't you?"

"Why would I have done that? All I wanted was my guitar. I got it and left—no reason to kill you."

Kent nodded to himself. Yes.

"Cops'll be coming," he said. "You can't get out."

"And what will they see when they arrive? A man crouched behind a truck, holding a pistol. They are just as likely to shoot you as me."

"I'll explain it to them."

"You have command presence, yes. But how long will it take? Once your gun is lowered, then it is me against a local policeman or two. My chances are passable."

Kent sighed. The man was right. A local cop, even two or three, would show up, see Kent, and immediately order him to drop his weapon—only cops and bad guys had guns in this city, and they couldn't tell which Kent was at first glance. They'd have to disarm him. Even if he convinced them he was on their side and there was a bad man with a gun hiding behind the veterinarian's office, Natadze could come out blazing and take them down before the real danger sank in. Kent didn't want that.

"You could back off. Allow me to leave. Save the lives of those police officers. They could be men with families. A woman officer. Do you want that on your conscience, Colonel?"

Kent almost grinned. Here was a man with brass balls. A killer, attempting to negotiate his way free by threatening to blame his future killings on the man trying to capture him.

"Cops know the risks of their job," Kent called. "No deal."

Natadze laughed. "I did not think so. Still, no harm in trying."

He was going to make a run for it!

Kent *knew* this—how he could not have said, but he knew it.

He took a deep breath—

Natadze burst from behind his cover much faster than Kent was prepared for—he must have backed up to get a running start—because he was sprinting like a champion. Before Kent could line up his sights, Natadze was halfway to the truck, and firing, one-two-three—!

Kent ducked as the bullets *spanged* off the truck's hood. He had maybe a second before Natadze blew past, and even with spray-and-pray, the man could hit him—

He dropped prone, looked under the truck, and saw Natadze's churning legs. He led the runner and squeezed off four rounds, tracking the movement.

The first two missed. The third bullet hit Natadze's right leg, just above the ankle—Kent *saw* the hole appear in the cloth—

Natadze went down, his speed causing him to skid as he

hit on his hands and knees. His gun was in his right hand, and he couldn't get it into shooting position because it was pressed against the concrete, grinding away as he skidded—

—Kent rolled away from the truck, still prone, keeping his own pistol extended as he angled out. Two revolutions and he was clear of cover and lined up for a body shot—

"Let it go! Let it go!"

But Natadze collapsed onto his right side and tried to thrust his handgun out at Kent.

"Don't do it—!"

Time, already running slow, nearly stopped altogether. He had him, no question, and Natadze had to see that, but he still kept moving, bringing his piece around, a bug mired in molasses—

"DON'T—!" Kent screamed.

In that bullet-time slo-mo, he saw the other man grin, and he read his mind: *Shoot me or die, Kent—that's the choice.*

Kent's breath was already held and his front sight was dead-on Natadze's center of mass.

He fired twice—

The .45 slugs hit Natadze right over the sternum and the impact was enough so that his muscle spasm curled him into a fetal ball.

The gun fell from his hand. He managed to roll onto his back.

By the time Kent got there, there wasn't much left in Natadze's clock.

He had enough air and energy to say, "Good shot. You . . . you t-t-take the guitar. S-s-souvenir . . ." He exhaled his last breath. Kent had heard enough death rattles to recognize this one.

He squatted to make sure. No pulse.

He heard the police sirens dopplering in. He stood, tucked his gun into his holster out of sight, and moved away from the dead man. He stood there with his hands held wide, by his shoulders, as the first SFPD car screeched into the parking lot. He stood very still.

25

**Hanging Garden Apartments
Macao, China**

Wu was not a man given to rash action. He had never been
one to just leap off a cliff in the hope that the river below
was deep enough to keep him from breaking a leg. No, Wu
was the kind of man who climbed down the escarpment,
waded into the water with a long pole, probed to find the
exact depth, marked the spot, and judged whether or not he
could hit that precise place when he jumped. If he could
not, he stayed on the cliff.

And yet, here he was, lying on Mayli's bed as she finished her shower, enjoying the fragrance of sandalwood in-
cense and the memory of their recent actions, considering
telling her things that a careful man would never reveal.

Why was that? *What has happened to you, Wu, that you
would even dream of taking this road?*

Well, Mayli was more than passing adept as a lover. She
already knew what Shing was up to, of course. That was
part of her job, to get Shing talking about anything and

everything. That and keeping an eye on him, and keeping him happy.

But she had also been probing, albeit subtly so, to find out what Locke was up to, and even carefully working Wu himself. Nothing blatant, nothing slap-your-face obvious, but it was apparent. She wanted to know what was really going on.

He could keep her in the dark. Take her along and continue to enjoy her company without ever filling in the blanks. But she was a smart woman, and eventually, she might figure things out, and then she'd be dangerous. He might have to . . . take care of her, and that would be such a waste. She was the best Wu had ever been with when it got right down to it.

But: The thought of not seeing her again, of her being married to that smug idiot Shing had, oddly, become . . . repellent. Why should Shing have such a delicious treasure? Why should that narrow and shallow lout be polishing Mayli's pearl, when Wu was a man much better able to appreciate her in all her dimensions?

He was not a man to delude himself—love was not a factor here, nor did he want it to be. But he knew exactly what she was. She was a trophy woman worthy of a great man. With her close at hand, she could be valuable in so many ways—not just as a lover, but as an ally he could rely upon—as long as their interest lay in the same direction, of course.

A man wanted a mate who not only would help him, but who *could* help him. Mayli was nothing if not wise in the ways of men.

As rich as he was going to be, she would prefer his company to that of the callow computer-nerd Shing. Yes, Wu was older, but he was fit, adept, and a woman like Mayli would always be drawn to such as himself. He could buy her houses, cars, yachts, cover her in precious gems, give her anything her heart might desire. And if she wished a lover on the side? What did that hurt? She would be happy, and it would not detract from their time together.

Did he not deserve a way to relax, to keep the tensions at bay? It was a small thing against the totality of what lay ahead. Great men had burdens, but they were not bound by the same constraints as the ordinary.

But—Mayli was far too clever a woman to stand by blissfully ignorant. She would wonder, and if she was going to be more than a bedmate, he needed for her to understand why he wanted her. How important he must think she was to *tell* her.

And in truth, Wu *wanted* to tell somebody. No one knew the full details of his plans, not even Locke, who knew some, but not all.

If it all came off the way Wu planned, it would be a thing of major importance, and the secret was Wu's alone. There would be more than a little satisfaction in telling somebody, in putting them in awe of his genius. She would certainly be impressed. She was worldly enough to appreciate the magnitude of it.

Was it a foolish leap into unknown waters? Wu thought he had a pretty good idea of Mayli's basic character. She was, like him, pragmatic. She served her own interests first, doing whatever was necessary to obtain her own desires. She was skilled. And, of course, she was beautiful, smart, and ambitious. If she knew what Wu knew, who on earth would be a better match?

Betraying him would gain her nothing, and linking with him, the possibility of the world at her feet? A shrewd woman would look at her choices, realize there was little risk, and go with the flow. Mayli was not a Taoist per se, but she was smart enough not to try to swim against the current of a huge river.

The shower cut off—it had been a selling point when Wu had rented this apartment, the water's pressure was great, and a long, hot, needle spray possible. A cloud of vapor wafted from the bathroom as Mayli slid the shower's curtain open and stepped out. She stood framed in the doorway, slick and gorgeous, and turned to smile at him as she reached for a towel. She knew she was beautiful, and she knew men liked looking at her.

Wu felt his interest stirring as he watched her dry off.

She glanced at him. "Ah," she said. "It appears I may have to shower again."

He smiled. "It is possible," he said. "Come here and let us see if that is the case."

They could always talk later, he thought.

Tell her? Or kill her? It might come to that. Which would it be?

Washington, D.C.

The Dyson sphere had come up empty. It was discouraging, but Jay wasn't going to lie down and die, so he shifted his search.

First, he sneaked into one of the black-ops systems nobody was supposed to know about—but, of course, Jay Gridley wasn't just anybody. He had heard they had a very nasty program running that kept track of all kinds of e-mail it wasn't supposed to keep track of, and this was his first chance to take a look at it. You never knew but that some idiot might think he was secure when he wasn't and say something stupid, like, "Hey, didja see how I screwed up the military's VR war games?"

Jay didn't really believe his prey could possibly be that foolish, but stranger things had happened. People said things when they didn't know they were being watched that they would never say if they thought somebody was peeking over their shoulder.

He went in, popped the firewall and encrypted password open, and looked around. He didn't see anything useful. He left. This was a top-level system, supposedly bulletproof, but that was a joke against a man of Jay's caliber.

He smiled at the metaphor.

Then it was back to CyberNation. Maybe something new there.

Behind the Scenes at CyberNation

Jay stared at the hole in the fence, a small, irregular-shaped blank space in one of the planks making up the stockade wall in the small abandoned mining town. This was where players came to pan for gold, and the idea was that the local streams and rivers had played out, but that there was still at least one bonanza claim waiting to be found here, one missed by earlier panners.

Something was not right about that hole in the wall.

Of course a lot of things seemed odd here. Little things—the details in the programming, the quality of sensory input. It wasn't bad—most people wouldn't ever notice it—but most people weren't Jay Gridley. However, as Jay was a guest, he had to stick fairly close to their existing VR scenario.

Another attack had hit CyberNation recently, this time an on-line SCA enclave. The SCA was the Society for Creative Anachronism, a group that enjoyed harking back to the good old days, and pretending that they were knights and ladies in medieval times. In the RW, they spent much time cooking authentic foods and beating the daylights out of each other with padded swords and sticks.

In VR, their battles and lifestyles could go farther, including interaction with elves, unicorns, and other creatures from myth. Which meant that when the combined elf/unicorn attack had come, it had completely shocked the SCA members. Particularly when the avatars used by the hackers had proceeded to perform acts with each other that pretty much negated the whole had-to-be-a-virgin-to-ride-a-unicorn thing.

The attack had then escalated into violence as the attackers engaged some of the SCA members in combat, proving yet again that in video games the computer always wins.

Apparently it hadn't all been bad, however. Although the peaceful elf-loving contingent had pulled out of VR in shock, the more physical SCA·warrior-types had actually expanded its membership.

Jay had backtracked the troop of attackers to this small hole. They had apparently entered the CyberNation system here, and then taken what resources they needed to expand their numbers before the attack.

But there was really something wrong with that hole.

He tabbed his visual input control and instantly he was in full Raptorvision. He ran his new glasses at low rez most of the time, because at high rez he found he sometimes had to reinterpret details that seemed too blocky or fuzzy when sharpened. Which meant that going to high rez was kind of like putting on X-ray glasses. Kind of.

The scene before him shifted. He could still see the hole, only now there were faint gridlike lines around it.

A patch!

Someone had hidden the network details on the incursion space.

Jay extended his forefinger and a small probe shot out. He slid it around the now visible hairline crack surrounding the hole, separating the code that wrote the patch from the VR code that made the hole.

The patch slid off into his hand, and Jay popped it into the satchel strapped over his shoulder, a small VR analyzer.

This could be good news—he hadn't found anything like this before. If this virus had been programmed to cover its tracks, there might be something interesting about this access node that would give him more information about how it worked.

The analyzer chimed and a code window opened up at eye level. He scanned it and frowned.

It was a patch designed to conceal part of their network interface. He'd been given access to their system, all right—but they hadn't wanted him to see everything, so they'd tried to cut off from the bits they didn't want him to know about.

What, did they think he was that stupid? Didn't they have a clue who they were dealing with here?

He scanned the woods nearby. If you knew where and how to look, it wasn't that hard to find. . . .

There it was—a programming back door, concealed as an old tree stump. Easy to hide if you weren't looking for it, because it was an integral part of the environment, not anything added, like the hole.

Well, he'd pop the lock on it, and show these CyberNation jerks what a real VR coder could do. Once he was in there, he'd give himself all kinds of access—

Ping! Ping! Pingpingpingpingpingpingpingping!

Something had gotten caught in Jay's snare. Ah.

His anger forgotten for the moment, Jay ran back the way he had come. As he had traversed the woods, backtracking the attack, he'd laid traps for code remnants that might still be around. It happened sometimes. A virus mutated and didn't reach full functionality, left a bit of itself running around in the bushes, as it were.

It was one thing to see the traces of where an attack had come from, but to see a still-working example was far better.

He jumped a small creek, running hard, bare feet lightly treading the earth, long black braids flying behind him. He reached down and drew the tomahawk from his belt.

Just because he was in a medieval forest didn't mean he had to *be* medieval. He was Jay Gridley, last of the Mohicans. Or at least, last of the movie version of them . . .

There.

Up ahead he saw a large fox in the trap he'd left. It moved strangely for a fox, examining the trap, as if trying to figure out how it worked.

As he watched, it looked up and saw him coming.

It opened its delicate fox jaws and then huge teeth

sprouted, like in some werewolf or vampire movie, huge, *metal* teeth. Its mouth opened impossibly wide and it lunged for its own leg, caught in the trap.

No way, pal—!

Jay threw the tomahawk, a hard overhand toss, and watched it twirl end over end toward the fox. The hickory handle smacked into the side of the fox's head; it yelped and fell over, stunned.

Now, that's what I'm talking about: Jay Gridley has come into the forest, booyah!

He pushed a button on the satchel and it expanded. Quickly, before it could recover, he slid the fox, trap and all, into the analyzer.

A few seconds later a chime sounded, announcing that the virus had been analyzed.

Before he'd come to CyberNation, he'd uploaded the latest virus encyclopedia from the Center for Virus Research in Beaverton, Oregon. A special tri-split screen appeared showing him in the first pane the code for the virus, broken down into segments. In the second window was a representation of an insect. The insect metaphor had become the de-facto ideogrammatic standard for depicting viruses; various parts of the insect were colored to highlight the separate codes making them up, and the body parts always represented similar abilities. The legs showed its ability to spread; pincers or mandibles its ability to attack; the overall size could indicate ease of detection, and so on.

The CyberNation virus looked like no real insect Jay had ever seen, nor would he want to. It had large wings, indicating speed, and a huge stinger plus pincers. The venom reservoir was split, indicating that it could sting for several functions—to paralyze, and replicate.

Nice.

But the third pane of the split screen was what he was most interested in. The CVR had spent years tracking down viruses to their origin countries and, when they were lucky, to their earliest programmers. Since most computer attacks were based on similar methods, there was a synergistic effect to coding, where a hacker might steal an idea from another, or be inspired to create something new.

It looked as if this virus had been developed from code that had origins in Europe, with pieces of USA ancestry.

Jay tabbed a control and called up the reconstruction of the virus that had attacked the military network. Since they hadn't caught it in its entirety, it was more of an identikit version, based on its effects. He compared the two.

They were similar. It was the delivery system that seemed to be the same—the speed, along with the venom replication. The military bug had some of the same code, but there were South American influences as well.

Interestingly, there were no influences at all from what could be called Asiatic countries. No Japan, no Taiwan, and no China.

Which by itself meant nothing, but combined with his earlier clue about China, it reminded him of his second favorite Sherlock Holmes adage. The one about the dog not barking in the night.

There were no Chinese dogs barking here.

And somehow, Jay knew that was a clue. No logic or reason to the knowledge, but a certainty nonetheless.

Which brought back a fleeting memory of an old movie farce about a superagent in the 1960's, Derek Flint. In one of the funniest scenes in that picture, Flint walks down a hall past a couple of military guards. Suddenly Flint attacks the guards, uses his martial arts abilities to take them out, then picks up a fallen weapon and cooks them. When the head of the agency runs up behind Flint and whacks him, thinking he's gone mad, Flint explains why he did it. They were imposters. What gave them away was, they were wearing Battle of the Bulge ribbons. Cramden, the agency head, says, "There aren't any Battle of the Bulge ribbons."

"Exactly," Flint says. . . .

If it took the rest of his life, Jay was going to get this guy. You could take that to the bank.

But it wasn't going to happen today. He logged out.

26

Somewhere in the Air over Kansas

The dead man's guitar—his now, if Natadze's dying wish was to be honored—was stowed in the luggage bin over Kent's head. The commercial jet droned along, somewhere over the Midwest—Kansas, maybe. Once, there had been websites you could access that showed the progress of every commercial flight in the country. Log on, type in the flight number, and you'd get a nice visual of a little aircraft superimposed on a map, showing you exactly where it was, where it had been, and its projected flight path to where it was going.

Those days were long gone. After 9/11, a lot of such information had been shut down. Too risky. Even National Parks data was restricted. And if you started trying to run down where the nation's water supplies were, or the exact geographic locations of military bases, nuclear power plants, or chemical factories, you might well hear a knock on your door with a curious federal agent behind it wanting to know just why you needed such information.

Interesting times, that was the Chinese curse, and certainly that's what had come to pass in the United States. When he'd been a boy, you could catch a bus downtown, wander around alone all day, and your parents didn't need to worry about you. You could walk onto a plane carrying a loaded pistol in your pocket and there weren't any metal detectors between you and the aircraft because nobody ever considered hijacking the craft to Cuba, or flying it into a building and killing thousands. Things you might conceivably put into your mouth were not protected by security seals with instructions that, if broken, you shouldn't eat it. Terrorists didn't sit around planning ways to release poison gas, blow up bridges, or set off an atomic bomb in an American city, except in the movies or in books. And you didn't need to stamp warnings on the barrels of guns that they were dangerous.

Of course, you could still get polio, and his mother had warned him against playing in ditches because she still thought that was how you caught it. The shadow of nuclear war loomed large, and they told schoolchildren to hide under their desks if the Russians dropped the bomb, as if that would help. And institutionalized racism and sexism were still the norm.

No men on the moon back in the 1950s—but also no AIDS.

A lot of things had changed during Kent's lifetime, most for better, but some for worse. Things didn't sit still, that was a given, and the good old days were always better in memory than they'd actually been, but still, now and then, Kent wondered if the new millennium really was much better than the one just past.

He got reflective like this after a battle. And even though it had been just him and Natadze in this one, it had ended with guns working. Yes, he had walked away, which was always better than the alternative, but he hadn't won the victory he'd wanted. If he had been a little sharper, if he had really known what he was doing, it might have gone better.

He remembered his grandfather. Paw-Paw had been in the Second World War, had been on the islands in the

South Pacific fighting against the Japanese—that's where Kent had gotten the samurai sword and the interest in it. But Paw-Paw had also been a master craftsman when it came to building things.

When Kent had been a kid, his parents moved into the first house they ever owned. It was a small place, and his room had been converted from a den—it had no closets or shelves. His grandfather had come to the house with a yardstick—one of those cheap wooden things the paint companies used to give away if you bought a gallon of paint—and a pencil and spiral notebook.

Paw Paw talked to Kent's mother, then went into the den and made some measurements with that old yardstick, jotted down some notes, then went back to his shop and started cutting plywood.

When he came back a week later, he put together a desk, two closets, and a bunch of shelves, using a screwdriver and a handful of wood screws. When he was finished, you couldn't slip a piece of paper into any of the joints—everything fit together as tightly as a Swiss watch.

The man had known what he was doing. He had been an expert at it.

Going after Natadze alone had been a mistake. Kent hadn't had the skill necessary to pull it off. An expert would have figured out a way to bring him back alive. Yeah, Kent had resolved his earlier mistakes, in that Natadze wasn't running around loose anymore, but it was like burning down a barn to get rid of rats. It had cost a lot more than necessary.

Kent sighed. Well. There was nothing to be done for it now, save to go back to work and explain it to his commander. Who might decide to fire him for it, and if so, Kent wouldn't blame him. He had screwed up. And if you can't do the time, you don't do the crime. . . .

* * *

The Summer Festival Marathon Race
Beijing, China

In China, the VR marathon races in which Chang ran were always run at night, and usually in the fog or rain, with the visibility never more than a few meters. It was a long race, a marathon, twenty-six miles, 385 yards, supposedly the distance a long-ago messenger had run in Greece on the plains of Marathon to deliver some important news, just before dropping dead from exhaustion. Over forty-two kilometers, and these days, crippled men, old women, and nine-year-old children ran it regularly, and few of them ever died.

When Chang ran here, he was faster than many, but still slower than some. Now and again, he would pass a runner close enough to see him in the gloom. Occasionally, one would pass him near enough for him to make out. There could be hundreds or even thousands of others in the race. Sometimes he felt them out there, but he didn't see them, didn't hear their footsteps. Now and again, Chang might stumble over something in the darkness—something he couldn't detect until he was too close to stop.

Chang had equipped himself with a flashlight that could extend his vision a few more meters. It would be so much better were these contests held on bright and sunny days, but he had grown used to the fog and rain and moonless dark, and had learned to navigate it, albeit sometimes he was more tentative than he would have liked. It was hard to run full-out, knowing you might trip over something you couldn't spot waiting in the road ahead. But, it was what it was, and there was little to be done about it.

So now, as he stood at the starting line, amidst a crowd of which he could see but a few close to him, he was familiar with the situation.

But: The American, Petrie, had added a wrinkle to the fabric of night. Now, in this scenario, Chang wore a special headset, with goggles that slipped over his eyes, a device that approximated sixth-gen spookeyes—starlight scopes that would gather the faintest light and intensify it, amplify it, transmit it to the lenses, and in doing so, also computer-augment colors to an approximation of normal.

That was the theory, anyway.

As he stood there, waiting for the signal to start, Chang touched a control on the headset. . . .

Light flared brightly, causing him to blink against it. When his vision cleared, he beheld a miracle:

He could *see*!

It was as if he had stepped into a football stadium in the dark and someone had switched on the lights. The colors were perhaps a hair too intense, but before, where he had been able to see but a handful of those lined up with him to run, now he could see nearly all of them! The road ahead was visible for blocks, the buildings lining the street, the sky, everything was open to his gaze.

The beauty of it was awesome.

The starter's gun fired, and the crowd surged. Chang ran with them, marveling at his ability to take it all in.

He looked at a runner fifty meters ahead—a man in a purple unitard that covered him from his knees to his neck, leaving his arms bare. Here was a man Chang would have never known was there before, for he was moving at a pace that Chang normally did not match. Once ahead, Chang would never catch him.

Chang sped up, fell in behind the man, matching his pace, staying two meters back. It was a bit of a strain, but he could manage it for a short time. Long enough to manage something he'd never managed before.

Who was he? Chang didn't know, but he could deduce much from all those details he observed. The man was fit—his muscles lean and hard. He ran easily, denoting a serious amount of training. He was wealthy or he had a sponsor—the shoes were the latest Adidas SmartShoe, with a computer built in to adjust the foot cushion, and those cost four times what a normal pair of decent running shoes would run. The unitard was a Nike wind-cheater, custom-fitted, made from polypropyl and cloned silk, and cost nearly as much as the shoes. The man wore a Rolex watch or a well-made knockoff. He had a tiny Optar-plus pulse monitor strapped to the other wrist—another expensive toy—and even though it was nighttime, he sported top of the line Ferami photogray RunnerShades, and they didn't give *those* away, either. A thousand, maybe twelve hundred U.S. dollars for his outfit, easy—not counting the Rolex.

So much knowledge from just being able to *see* somebody.

Before, in the dark, even if Chang had been within a few meters, he could not have gathered all that, not in such fine detail. And he would have never known where to look.

Chang's game had just improved in a major way. Knowledge was power, and with the new software that Petrie had supplied him with, he was going to have options he'd never had before. He'd be able to see individual racers, notice patterns in the crowd, he'd know who was gaining and who was falling back. Runners ahead of him he'd never known were there? He could spot them, track them, maybe catch them.

This was going to make things a lot different in his job. Men who had counted on the fog and rain and darkness to cloak them were about to lose that protection.

Now, Chang was going to be able to find them, chase them down, and catch them. Soon, there were going to be some very surprised computer criminals in his homeland.

Allah be praised for such a gift.

Washington, D.C.

Chang sat in his hotel room, staring at the program minidisk he had just tried for the first time. It was tiny—the size of a U.S. quarter. He could slip it into his pocket and walk through a dozen airport security checkpoints and nobody would know he had it. He could stick it in an envelope and *mail* it to himself in a normal-size letter, and nobody would bother to worry over it. But—he did not *have* to do these things, because it was a *legal* purchase. It would vastly improve his ability to find miscreants in China, but it was not forbidden for him to own, to take home, because it was old-hat here, something anyone living here could get for his home computer if he had the money to buy it.

Amazing. Americans truly did not know how good they had things. What they took for granted that other societies would see as a miracle.

Chang looked at his watch. He had a few hours before he was supposed to see Gridley, at Net Force. Might as well use the time productively. He would go back into VR, log into his system at home, and do a little hunting. Now that he had this, who knew what manner of crook he might find?

Ah, how wonderful this was!

Net Force HQ
Quantico, Virginia

Abe Kent sat at his desk, staring at nothing. The meeting with Thorn couldn't have gone better. The Commander had listened to his story, then shrugged it off. "This guy was a killer, Abe. You went out there and took him down. A man like that? He wasn't going to give us anything if you'd brought him back alive. He was a bad man, and in a just society he would have paid for it with his life in court. You saved us all a lot of time and money to the same end."

Kent had nodded, relieved some, but still troubled. It wasn't a total personal failure, but it hadn't been up to his standards. All he could do was try to do better in the future.

His secure line cheeped.

"Abe Kent."

The voice on the other end was low, calm, and quiet. He hadn't heard it in a while. He listened, made a comment, and listened some more. Finally, he said, "I'll take care of it. I owe you one."

"No," the voice had said. "I'm paying back one I owe you. We're even."

Kent discommed. After a long moment he shook his head and tapped his intercom button. "Would you see if you could get Jay Gridley to drop by here?" he asked his assistant.

When Jay got the call to drop by Colonel Kent's office, he was surprised. RW face time was mostly unnecessary, but Kent was the same generation as Jay's parents, and they had never been as comfortable with VR as somebody who grew up in it as Jay had.

Kent's secretary smiled and waved him in. Kent was in his chair, not doing anything Jay could tell but sitting there.

"Colonel."

"Jay. Have a seat."

"I heard you got Natadze," Jay said. He plopped onto the couch facing the desk. Hard, not very comfortable. Perfect for a Marine guy. "Congratulations."

"Not the way I wanted, but as the Commander has pointed out, at least he's not still on the street."

Jay nodded. "What can I do you for?" he asked.

Kent took a deep breath. "I got a call from an old friend of mine, used to be a spook in the Company. He's, uh, moved to another agency. It was regarding your breathing."

"My *breathing*?"

"Yes. Whether or not you are going to keep doing it."

That got Jay's attention. "What?"

"You went somewhere you weren't supposed to, and you were noticed."

"I left a footprint somewhere?"

"Not a footprint—you left an image detailed enough to show the size, shape, and number of your freckles. I don't care that it was illegal—I suspect you stopped worrying about that a long time ago. But where you walked was in a black-ops system that isn't supposed to exist. They don't want anybody who isn't supposed to know about them to even dream they are there."

Jay was stunned. Probably looked it, too. Then he started to get just a little irritated.

Kent saw something in his face. He paused for a moment, then said, "Long ago and far away, when I was very young and stupid, there was a foolish game we used to play. On a Saturday night, a bunch of boys would pile into somebody's car and go cruising. We'd hit all the local water holes—drive-in restaurants, bars that would let underage teenagers sneak in, empty stretches of road where they'd drag-race hot cars. And all the time looking for girls to try and impress. We smoked cigarettes because we thought it made us look older. Of course, what that made us look like was a bunch of sixteen-year-old boys trying to pass for eighteen. We thought we were so *cool*."

Jay laughed politely. Where was *this* going?

"Anyway, the game was this: We'd head out into the suburbs away from town and look for a guy walking alone. If we spotted one, we'd go past a hundred yards or so, as if we hadn't seen him. Whoever was driving would pull the car over, and a couple of us would hop out and lift one of the guys out of the car, as if he were dead. We'd haul him to the side of the road and put him down, just as if we were dumping a body. The guy would lie there not moving. We'd start back to the car, then one of us would look up, and pretend that we'd just noticed the pedestrian back there.

"Look!" We'd yell. "He *saw* us! Git 'im!"

Jay grinned and shook his head. "There used to be a television show like that. They'd set somebody up with some kind of scenario just to scare the daylights out of him, then record it. I forget what it was called—I used to watch it when I was in college. Funny stuff."

"Funny, but really, really *stupid*. What we did was back in the days before video cams were around or we'd probably have taped it, too. We thought it was a hoot—we did it four or five times, chased guys a little ways, amazed at how fast somebody who thought he'd just seen a body dumped could run from what he thought was a bunch of killers. Then, once the guy was gone, we'd all hop back into the car and head back to the bars. If the guy reported it, the cops must have laughed pretty good—they'd have heard the story every summer."

Jay smiled and nodded.

"We were lucky beyond measure. All it would have taken would have been for one of our prey to have been a security guard on his way home, a new, off-duty cop who'd never heard the story, or maybe just a guy worried about being mugged. Somebody packing a handgun and deciding he could become a hero by dropping four or five murderers dead in their tracks. It was dark, he wouldn't have seen us smiling as we ran at him, and if he had, probably thought we were homicidal maniacs. No jury in the world would have convicted him for mowing us down—we would have gotten what we deserved."

Jay thought about that for a second.

"If kids tried that game these days, more than likely they *would* get shot—there are a lot of concealed weapon permits out there, a lot more than when I was a teenager."

Jay said, "So you're saying what?"

"I'm saying that just because you have these great abilities to dance in and out of high-security computer systems without worrying that you'll get caught, it is sometimes a mistake." He paused for a moment, letting that sink in, then went on. "It happens some people there know me, and it just happens one of them owes me a favor, so I got a call and I fixed it. But you're lucky—just like we were on those hot summer nights back in my day. Nobody will show up at your door in the middle of the night and disappear you. This time."

Jay's eyes went wide. "No."

"Yes. It doesn't matter that you work for the government. If you go somewhere you shouldn't go, you had better make damn sure you don't get seen. There are some nasty things out there in the world, meaner, hungrier, and some of them are smarter than you are, Jay. I know you don't think so, but it's true, and if you cross one of them at the wrong time, you could leave a widow and child alone and always wondering what happened to you. If I hadn't been here, if somebody hadn't owed me, you'd be in deep trouble. Keep that in mind."

Jay blew out a sigh. He felt a chill ripple through him.

"Jay, remember this: If you get to thinking you're Superman, you *will* eventually find a guy with a barrel full of kryptonite."

And all Jay could think of to say to that was, "My God."

"Amen, son."

27

Marissa dropped by the office unannounced, which pleased Thorn no end. And one of the first things she did when she got there was to ask him about fencing, which pleased him even more. She was curious about what he did. That must mean something.

He hoped.

He escorted her down to the gym on the theory that it was always better to show than to tell. On the way there, he tried to tell himself that no, he wasn't showing off at all.

The Net Force gym was empty. Thorn opened his locker and started removing his gear, very conscious that Marissa was watching him. He'd been fencing for a long time, he was comfortable with it, but most of the women he'd been with—save for the few who were fencers themselves—hadn't shown any particular interest in it.

Marissa had.

"So," she said as he finished suiting up, "other than knowing that the Germans used to scar each other in places like Heidelberg with these things, and D'Artagnan and all, I don't know from swords. Tell me about them."

"Well," Thorn said, "in Western, or collegiate, fencing, there are three different weapons: foil, épée, and saber. Eastern fencing, like kendo, uses a *shinai*, and other martial arts use a variety of weapons, but for now we're going to focus just on the Western version."

She nodded.

"Some of what I'm going to say comes from books I've read over the years, some from conversations with other fencers and history buffs. I've said most of this at one time or another over the years, putting on fencing demos and such. I don't swear that everything I'm going to say is one-hundred-percent accurate, but it's how I see it."

She nodded again.

"I have also found that I can go on at length about this, so let me know if your eyes start to glaze."

She grinned at that. He smiled, too, and began. "Fencing goes back pretty much to when they first outlawed dueling as a sport—if you could say that it ever was a *sport*. A lot of people don't know it, but most duels were not to the death; they were to first blood: Whoever drew blood from his opponent, no matter how much or where the wound occurred, satisfied his honor and won the duel."

She frowned. "They didn't have much in the way of medicine back then. Was infection much of a problem?"

He raised an eyebrow. Few people thought of that. "Yes. In fact, most sword-related battle casualties were from infection, not from the actual sword cuts."

Thorn picked up the foil. "This was the first practice weapon they came up with. They wanted a system to teach people to parry, to respect their opponent's attacks. After all, it might settle honor for you to prick your opponent first, but if you nicked him on his wrist and, a moment later, he stabbed you through the heart, you would have won the duel but lost your life."

"Not much of a trade-off," she said.

"Exactly. So, they came up with the foil. A lighter weapon, with a smaller bell guard than the épée, but the biggest difference was that this weapon had restrictions."

"Restrictions?"

He nodded. "Yep. Two kinds. One was the target area. In épée, the entire body—your head, the little finger on your off hand, your back, even your toes—are all valid targets. With the foil—which, remember, was designed as a practice weapon, not as a simulation of the real thing—the target area is the jacket"—he gestured to the one he was wearing—"excluding the sleeves. Everything else on the jacket—the back, the groin flap, the sides—is all valid. When you fence competitively—or even in practice, in many clubs—you wear a vest made of metal mesh, called a lame, that exactly covers your target area."

She reached out and touched his foil. "And how do you score?"

He moved the blade to show her the tip. "The foil, like the épée, is a point weapon. See this button here at the end of the blade? It takes five hundred grams of pressure to set that point. Fencing electrically, that opens a circuit through a wire embedded in this groove in the top of the blade, which connects to a body cord running through your sleeve and out the bottom of your jacket, to a floor reel and then to a scoring machine. Pressing the button against your opponent's lame sets off your colored light, usually green or red. Hitting him off-target—like on the leg, say—sets off a white one. Hitting him flat, with the side of the blade, or having your point slide along the target area, does not depress the point, and so those count as misses."

She nodded. "Interesting," she said. "But you said there were two differences. Target area is one. What's the other?"

He grinned. "Rules," he said. "Specifically, something called right-of-way. In épée, whoever hits first wins the touch—and bouts used to be to one touch only, just like real duels. In foil, if your opponent has right-of-way, defined as his elbow straight or in the process of coming straight, and his point on line with your target or in the process of coming on line, then you have to respond to his attack before you can claim right-of-way and make an attack of your own. You can parry it, or evade it, or retreat out of distance, or do something to make him break the definition of right-of-way—pumping his arm, for example, so his elbow is no longer straight or coming straight. If you do that, you can counterattack and, if you both hit each other, you win the point. If you don't deal with his attack first, however, and simply counter into it, you would lose the touch if you both hit."

"And épée?"

He replaced the foil and brought out an épée. "This is the closest to a 'real' weapon in Western fencing. Note how much heavier the blade is than the foil. That's to make it more like the rapier, which it's modeled on. A larger bell guard protects the hand and wrist because, unlike foil, those are valid touches. Also, it takes a heavier touch to score—seven hundred fifty grams instead of five hundred to depress the point. No rules. Whoever touches his opponent first wins the point. If you both hit within a twentieth of a second, you both lose a touch. Used to be, back when a bout only had one touch, you could both lose the bout on a double touch."

He paused. "The épée is my weapon of choice, by the way."

"Mine's a handgun," she said with a smile, "but to each his own, I guess."

He grinned. "The last weapon is the saber, and it's not much like the other two. Patterned after the cavalry saber, it's an edge weapon. You can use the point, and do, sometimes, in a bout, but mostly for a change of pace or a surprise move. Historically, the valid parts of the blade were the entire front edge and the top third of the back edge. The flat of the blade was not legal, and hitting your opponent with that did not score a touch. That changed a couple of decades ago when they electrified the saber, and now the entire blade is valid. Personally, I prefer the old way."

He pulled a saber out and made a couple of quick cuts with it, whipping the air. "It has essentially the same right-of-way rules as foil but, since it's designed to replicate a cavalry weapon, and assumes that the combatants are on horseback, the target area is everything from the waist up."

"Wouldn't do much good to hit your opponent in the thigh if he's riding a horse."

"Exactly," he said. "He might die later, of infection, but that wouldn't stop him from taking your head off with his counterattack."

She touched his saber, then looked over at the foil and épée he'd pulled out. "So," she said, "feel like giving a girl some lessons?"

He smiled. "Absolutely."

Washington, D.C.

There was nothing he had to do at the office he couldn't do from his home system, and Jay was rattled enough by his meeting with Kent that he wanted to go home. More than that, he *needed* to go home.

When he got there Saji was sitting *seiza* on the floor, just finishing her meditation. She looked up at him and smiled.

"How's the boy?" Jay asked. He was still shaken, both from being spotted when he had been sure he'd been invisible, and from the idea of being "disappeared." That somebody could do that. That they *would*.

"Fine," Saji said. "Been alert, smiling, perky all day. No fever, ate like a pig. Sleeping like a rock at the moment."

That was what he wanted to hear, of course, but the serpent was in the garden, and things were never going to be the same. Before, he had known it intellectually, but now, he knew it in his soul: His son would always be at risk. Worse, past a certain point of prevention and basic first aid, there was nothing Jay could do about that. It was an awful feeling.

The baby monitor on the coffee table was quiet, the viewscreen showing Mark asleep in his crib, so everything was all right, but . . .

Jay smiled. "I'm going to go check on him."

He walked down the hall and crept into Mark's room. There he was, an angel, out like a light. Jay leaned down and made sure he was breathing. The boy had that healthy, clean-baby smell. Later, when they went to bed, Mark would sleep with them. If he woke up in the middle of the night, they'd both be with him. They had been doing that since he'd been born.

The thought of something happening to his son, or that he wouldn't be here to see him grow up? Bad juju.

Jay moved quietly out of the room and back to where Saji now sat on the couch. He sat next to her.

"How are you doing?" he asked.

She smiled. "I'm fine. It was unexpected, all that happened, but it brought home what I already believed."

"Which is?"

"The Four Noble Truths," she said.

Jay shook his head. He knew what those were, at least: There is suffering in the world. The cause of that suffering is attachment to things that will all ultimately pass. There is a way to stop this suffering. The way to that attainment lies in the Eightfold Path. Simple. Not *easy*, but simple.

Part of what had drawn him to Saji in the first place was her Buddhist philosophy. It wasn't really a religion, in that the existence of a God wasn't necessary to the precepts. You could believe in a deity or not, but Buddhism was about morality and ethics in the here and now, not whatever afterlife there might be. But this was their son!

"Saji—"

She cut him off, gently. "I know what you're going to say. This is Mark, our baby, our child. How can we *not* be attached to him?"

"Took the words right out of my mouth."

"Nonattachment does not mean that we don't love and cherish Mark as much as humanly possible. I would step in front of a bus to save him, and I know you would, too. But unless we can let go of that craving, that clinging, we'll always be in fear for our son. All things must pass."

Jay shook his head again. "With any luck, we'll pass before he does. That's how it is supposed to work."

She reached out and took his hand. "But sometimes it doesn't work that way. What if Mark had died?"

"I don't want to go there." That thought on top of the rest of his day made him feel ill.

"Nor do I," she said. "I was never so terrified in my life as when I saw our baby convulsing and I thought he might leave. And he didn't go. But it is possible. And if that moment had come—if it comes within our lifetimes . . ."

"No," Jay said. "I couldn't deal with it."

"You could. You would have to. You wouldn't be the first parent who had to deal with it."

"And you believe the Eightfold Path will provide the tools."

"Yes."

Jay stared into space. He had learned those ideas from her, too. They weren't complicated—the parade of rights, he thought of them: right view, intention, speech, action, livelihood, effort, mindfulness, concentration. They were supposed to help you develop in turn a blend of wisdom, conduct, and spiritual development. Not as simple as "Just do it" in application, of course. There were all kinds of exercises—meditation, not harming people or animals, not drinking or screwing around, and dozens of others. Over time, you would develop a strength that would shield you from desire and attachment, and thus free you from suffering. The idea was that you hurt because you don't get what you want. If you don't want anything that bad, it doesn't hurt if you don't get it.

That was the theory as Jay understood it. But he couldn't see it applying to his son. If Saji could, she was far and away superior to him along the path to serenity.

Of course, he already knew that. Even as upset as she had been before, she had recovered faster, and done better about it than he had. Still, it was a big leap. He didn't see how he could ever manage it. He wasn't at all sure he *wanted* to manage it. If your son dies, how could you just . . . shrug it off? You ought to feel grief, pain, suffering. . . .

"Let it sit," she said. "You can come back to it later."

He nodded. "Yeah."

"So, how was your day?"

He smiled. To jump from dealing with the possible loss of your child to how-was-your-day? Funny.

He decided that the meeting with Kent didn't need to be mentioned. He could talk about other stuff. No point in worrying her—it was history.

"Terrible," he said. "The Chinese hacker is a ghost. No tracks, no shadows, nothing. We haven't been able to figure out how he's doing it, much less who he is."

"You will. I have faith in you."

He laughed. "I want this guy, bad. Which, I know, is a not-good desire and all, but I am definitely *attached* to getting him."

She laughed. "You don't say."

"Bretton and I have come at this from every which way we can think of, and still zip."

"Not really. You know he is Chinese."

"I *believe* that. I don't have any *proof*. My latest foray into CyberNation confirms it, in a bass-ackward way— something I didn't see as much as something I saw—but it doesn't seem to have helped overall. I don't know what to do from here."

"Just keep on truckin'," she said.

He smiled again. He was a fan of the great underground cartoonist R. Crumb, and he had managed to buy a vintage poster with that funny walk by the man. He also had a small statue of Crumb's Catholic School Girl, which had set him back a week's pay ten years ago. She was right. Sometimes that's what you had to do—just keep on truckin'. . . .

Only, from now on, he would do it more carefully. He wanted his son to have a father when he grew up.

In that moment, Jay remembered that he had an appointment with Chang at Net Force HQ that afternoon.

He pulled his virgil from his belt. He had Chang's number; he probably wouldn't have left for the meeting yet. He could call and cancel it. No, wait, Chang was in the District—why not meet him somewhere? Or even have him come here?

"Babe? I was supposed to meet the Chinese guy at the office this afternoon, and I forgot. Would it be okay if he came by here? We could stay in my office and do some VR there."

"The place is pretty messy," she said.

Jay looked around. "Looks fine to me."

She laughed. "You wouldn't notice a dust bunny until it was big enough to trip over. But, okay, bring him by. I'll run the vacuum cleaner."

"You don't have to do that."

"You must have never been a housekeeper in any past incarnation," she said. "Of course I have to do that."

Jay shook his head. "Call Chang," he told the virgil.

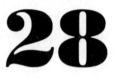

28

Palace of Prosperity
Macao, China

Jack Locke walked out of the casino, slightly lighter in the
wallet than when he had arrived two hours earlier. He had
played blackjack, small bets, winning for a time, then losing. It didn't matter. Gambling was not the point, familiar-
izing himself with the place was. Knowing where things
were, how many steps it took from the front doors to the
men's toilets, where the gift shop was, the number of
stools at the bar, all these were minor details.

Locke had been around long enough to know it was in
the minor details where the devil lived, and if you didn't
pay him proper attention, he *would* mess up your plans. Today, it was the Palace of Prosperity; tomorrow, he might
stop by the Golden Wheel, or the Diamond, or the Sands,
the Kam Pek, the Lisboa. He could lose at baccarat or
boule or fan-tan, or play the slots. And if he dropped a few
thousand MOP or HKD? Nothing.

Locke's cell phone rang. Although they weren't supposed to, some of the casinos, and that included the Palace

of Prosperity, used phone jammers. Nothing like a big base station that would be easy to spot, but guys walking around with tiny ones disguised as pagers or pens or calculators that would kill digital phone signals coming or going within twenty or thirty meters.

There were a couple of reasons the casinos did this. First, they didn't want customers thinking about the outside world as long as they still had money to lose. That was why there were no clocks in casinos. If a man on a losing streak gets a call from his wife, he might decide to cut his losses and go home if she got demanding enough. But if his phone didn't ring, that possibility wasn't there.

Second, there were players who would use every angle they could to beat the house. Card-counting, for instance, wasn't illegal, but it was prohibited by all casinos, and if you got caught doing it—and winning—you'd be banned from play. The house always won in the end, but it hated to lose anything anytime.

Counters sometimes worked in teams, talking via tiny wireless phones with earplugs so small nobody knew they were there. Jamming those signals made it harder for teams to communicate. Some of the blackjack counters were pretty good. There had been a group from some American school a few years back—MIT?—that had hit Las Vegas and Atlantic City, and even a few European casinos, for millions before a security man finally figured it all out.

The casinos were smart enough not to kill all phone calls. If you were in the lobby or waiting for a table at one of the restaurants, your phone might work just fine. There were dead zones all over, and if there were a few more than usual in a casino, at the tables? Who could prove anything?

"Locke," he said into his phone.

"You have a problem," said the voice. No names, but Locke knew who it was. Leigh.

"Do tell."

"Not on a phone."

"Our conversation is protected."

Leigh laughed. "Right. And I'm the King of England. I

can probably decrypt your phone program, and I'm not particularly good at it. Come to my place."

Leigh disconnected.

Locke snapped his phone shut and tapped it against his chin. Leigh wouldn't have called if the problem was something piddly. He could still walk away from everything if an unsolvable problem cropped up. The plan had not progressed to the point where he was committed, where retreat was not an option. So, they would reach that point, and pass it, but not yet.

Best to find out what Leigh had come across before they reached the point of no return.

Locke waved at a taxi. He wasn't worried about being followed, but he would change cabs at least once. No sense in taking foolish risks.

The cabbie pulled over, and Locke entered the vehicle.

Washington, D.C.

Chang arrived at Jay Gridley's condo, feeling most pleased with himself. He had something to bring to the table. No way was he Gridley's equal, but at least he came with information that he felt the Net Force operative did not have.

Of course, Gridley had not told him the particulars of his business to the point were it would be considered a breach of security; still, Chang had not just fallen off the rice cart. Gridley had dropped enough hints for him to be pretty certain he was chasing a Chinese player of more than passing cleverness and skill, for some reason of major importance. And Chang had an idea as to why.

Perhaps the tidbit he had would be but a small morsel against the sumptuous feast at Gridley's table. Maybe it was no more than a little seasoning. Still, it was better than coming up empty-handed.

A beautiful woman answered the door. "Mr. Chang?"

"Yes."

"I am Saji—Jay's wife. Won't you come in?"

He inclined his head in a slow bow. "My honor to meet you," he said.

She led him past a sleeping baby to a room where Jay Gridley was powering up a VR system. "Hey, Chang. Come on in. I have something to show you."

"And I, you," Chang said. He smiled.

Hanging Garden Apartments
Macao, China

After meeting with Leigh, Locke went directly to another meeting with Wu. Locked had called this meeting, on his cell in the cab from Leigh's place.

He hadn't even bothered changing cabs. This was important, and there was little time for games.

Wu, in his uniform, answered the door. Locke nodded and followed Wu into the kitchen.

"Nice place," Locke said.

"Which we both know you have seen before," Wu said. "Along with the occupant."

Locke smiled, one man of the world to another, and didn't bother to try and deny it. "Is that a problem?"

"No," Wu said. "It doesn't affect our business. What she does on her own time does not matter to me." This was not strictly true, but better Locke should think so. One did not show the chinks in one's armor to an armed man, even if he was an ally.

Alliances changed.

Locke bowed his head.

Wu gestured at one of the two chairs next to the small table. There were two glasses set upon the table, along with a bottle of very good Australian red wine. Locke sat, picked up the bottle, read the label, then poured, filling Wu's glass first before his own.

After they had both sipped at the wine, exchanged a few

meaningless pleasantries, and remarked upon the hot and wet weather, Wu leaned back in his chair.

"We have a situation," Locke said.

"Which is . . . ?"

"Shing."

Wu raised one eyebrow. "Shing?"

"He's a gambler."

"This I already know. I have been supplying him with money."

"Not enough money, apparently. He has . . . incurred debts."

Wu frowned. "How much? And to whom?"

"About forty-five thousand British pounds, to Water Room; another twenty thousand to Flexible Bamboo."

"To triads? He owes this much money to criminals?"

"Yes."

"How do you know this?"

"I have dealings with another computer expert. He has access to Li Ho Fok's accounts, as well as those of the loan shark Firecracker Jiang. These accounts are private and there would be no reason to show Shing in them if he did not owe this money."

Wu's frown increased. Why did he not know of this? Could Shing have kept such information from Mayli? If so, he was not as stupid as Wu thought.

As if reading his mind, Locke said, "Maybe the boy has more on the ball than we figured, keeping this from us."

Wu sighed. "Yes. Go on."

"The gambling debts began several years back, before Shing's association with us. He started losing money in college. He has added to these losses lately, but according to my source, most of these are bets on sporting events, through Fok or Jiang Wei's bookies. A call on a cell phone would be enough. I don't expect Mayli would have any way of knowing about them."

Wu nodded. A man who would brag to his woman about winning money on a soccer game might not be so quick to tell her that he had lost his shirt betting on others. No man liked to lose face in such a way.

"And your source is not only reliable but . . . trustworthy?"

"Yes, though of course he knows nothing about our plan," Locke said.

Wu nodded again. He was not surprised that Locke had his own ways of tracking important information. He would have been surprised if he did not.

Wu considered the datum. What did it mean to his plans that his computer genius owed the tongs money? Sixty-five-thousand pounds was serious business. Shing would have to pay it, one way or another. If things went as planned, Shing would have no trouble covering his debts. He might be holding them off with promises. And how much would he have to tell them to get them to believe these promises?

Wu didn't like it.

Locke said, "It's a complication."

"Yes. We still need Shing. Not for much longer, but for the moment he is necessary."

Locke nodded. "Yes. I considered bringing my man in, but without Shing's help, he wouldn't be able to do the job right."

"Shing could be persuaded to help," Wu said.

"Too risky. If my man flubbed, it might be a problem for us. Maybe not, but I wouldn't want to chance that."

"No."

"We could pay off Shing's debts."

Wu said, "Yes. I could manage that. But that would do nothing against what he might have already revealed to the triads. If they had the slightest clue what we intend, they would see that Shing's debt was but a drop in the bucket. They would want to be involved. Too many people would know."

"Loose lips sink ships," Locke observed.

"Exactly."

"So, what do you think we should do?"

Wu sipped from his wine again. Australia was the new France when it came to such things. "I am open to suggestions."

Locke said, "One comes to mind. What if the triads suddenly found themselves the object of major law enforcement attention?"

Wu permitted himself a small smile. Locke was clever, too clever by half, but in such a venture, a man with a sharp wit was much better than one whose blade was dull. "A distraction? As is being done to the U.S. military and CyberNation?"

"Why not? A wolf running from a forest fire doesn't stop to catch mice. If we give the wolves something else about which to worry, Shing becomes a mouse. Even if they think he might be something bigger someday, survival comes first. And pretty soon, we won't need Shing. He could disappear."

Wu allowed the smile to increase a hair. "Then go and start a forest fire and drive the wolves before it."

Locke raised his glass. "Muddy roads to our enemy's army," he said.

Wu raised his glass. "And a great pox upon their generals."

29

The Yellow River
Shaanxi Province
North Central China

Jay stood in the middle of the sampan while Chang worked the long oar at the rear, sculling the wooden pole back and forth in a machinelike rhythm. The little boat was twelve or fifteen feet long, weathered wood, with a cloth-and-bamboo-covered hoop that formed an arc-roofed cabin running most of the boat's length. They were going with the current, and Chang's efforts were more to keep it lined up with the flow than to drive it.

The water did have a yellow color to it.

"Comes from the Loess Plateau," Chang said. "The earth there turns this shade when it becomes sediment in the water. Half as big as Texas, that plateau. Haung Ho—the Yellow River—is also called 'China's Great Sorrow.'"

Jay looked at him, squinting against the bright sunlight.

"From all the misery the river has caused over the years," Chang said. "Floods, destruction, so many deaths.

Chinese civilization began here on its banks, you know. All the major dynasties."

Jay nodded.

Ahead of them, behind them, other boats floated on the muddy water, small sampans like the one they were in as well as ones that were larger, with sails. A few were so tiny that they seemed like children's toys, probably made from sheepskins. The smell of fish hung in the damp and warm air. Some of the boats held bamboo cages with big black diving birds in them. Cormorants, Jay knew, used to catch fish.

"We're not far from the ruins of Banpo Village," Chang said. "More than six thousand years old. In Xi'an, that's the capital of this region, there are other ancient wonders—the Goose Pagoda, the Forest of Stone Tablets, the Qin Terra-cotta Warriors and Horses."

"Very scenic and historical," Jay said. "And a well-built scenario."

"You honor me."

"I call 'em like I see 'em. What's the time line?"

"About 1800 CE," Chang said. "There, just ahead, to your right, see the boat with the red eyes?"

Jay saw the one Chang meant. The same sampan-style, a bit bigger than their boat, with a single man in it, in one of those straw coolie hats—unless somebody was hidden in the little cabin.

"Why are we watching him?" Jay asked.

"Because he is watching somebody else," Chang said. "The junk, ahead and to the left."

Jay looked at the larger boat. He didn't see anybody on the decks. The boat had an anchor line out, holding it still against the current.

"Who's on it?"

Chang shook his head. "I don't know. They have not revealed themselves. But the man in the red-eyed sampan has kept the junk—one of the old Grand Canal designs—under close observation since I spotted him."

"What does it mean?"

"Again, I do not know. Before my recent software acquisition, I didn't know either of these two existed. The man in the sampan—there's a sexual metaphor in that name, did you know?—is a computer operator of some skill. I did not have the tools to see him before. When I happened across him, I was surprised. As adept as he is, his interest in the other player is by itself most interesting."

"And you think this something I need to know?"

Chang stopped working the oar. He lifted a heavy anchor tied to a long rope and tossed it over the side. It disappeared in the muddy water and the line sank rapidly, paying out until the anchor hit bottom. The boat drifted a short ways, then slowed to a stop.

"Perhaps this would be a good place to fish," Chang observed.

"It's your scenario," Jay said with a shrug. "But, again, why would I find this particularly interesting?"

"Please pardon me if I offer an observation that is completely incorrect," Chang said. "But if I had to guess, I'd say you are looking for somebody who has caused something of a stir in military computer circles of late. I also understand that CyberNation has had some difficulties."

Jay blinked against the glare from the water. Too bad they couldn't wear polarized sunshades in this scenario. "How did you hear about that?"

"Even China does not exist in a vacuum. Rumors travel. I am not entirely without access to the West."

"Assuming you're right, why here?"

"Because I believe you are seeking a Chinese operator. Little things you have said during our acquaintance indicate this. My apologies if I am wrong."

Jay shook his head. "No apologies necessary. You aren't wrong."

Chang said nothing.

Jay said, "Without getting into details, you nailed it. I'll take all the help I can get."

"I will give all that I can," Chang said.

"Got a telescope on this boat?"

"In the trunk inside the cabin. I'll fetch it."

"Good. Then we can get a closer look at this guy."

Both men smiled.

Net Force HQ
Quantico, Virginia

"General Hadden would like to speak to you," Thorn's secretary said over the intercom. She sounded nervous.

"Sure. Which line?" Thorn asked.

"Uh, he's here, sir. In the office."

Thorn frowned. The Chairman of the Joint Chiefs was *here*?

"Send him in, please." Thorn fought to keep his composure. People like that didn't just go places without letting folks know in advance. What was he doing here?

Four-Star Army General Patrick Lee Hadden stepped into Thorn's office. He was in uniform, his jacket's breast covered with ribbons and medals. He was a genuine war hero. Hadden was awarded two Purple Hearts in Vietnam, along with the Bronze and Silver Stars, and served with distinction in Bosnia, First Iraq, and the Syrian campaign. He was a tall man, iron-gray hair that was once black in a brush cut, still fit for a man of sixty-four, his face tanned and creased with laugh lines. His nose, broken at least once and set a hair crooked, gave his face a certain lopsided character.

Thorn stood, feeling as if he needed to come to attention.

"Commander," Hadden said. He smiled, a high-wattage expression, with natural but nearly perfect teeth.

"General. Please, have a seat." Thorn gestured at the couch.

Hadden sat, his back straight, but not stiff. Thorn also sat.

"What can I do for you, sir?"

"I, ah, just happened to be in the neighborhood," he said. He smiled again, to show he was kidding. "I wanted to check and see if you've made any more progress on our problem."

Thorn had told Jay to keep the military liaison posted and up to date, so anything he could offer now wouldn't be new, but he also had heard that Hadden was a hands-on guy when it came to things he considered important. He wanted to hear what was what from the man running the investigation, and Thorn could understand that. When something reflected on you up the chain of command, when it might eventually be your head on the block for any reason, it was a good idea to track those things.

Still, it irritated Thorn a little. The military was hearing it as soon as Net Force had anything to tell them, Hadden had to know that, so he had to be here for something else as well. To prod them a little? To check out Thorn personally?

Or to put the fear of God into him?

"Our best people are on it," Thorn said. "We are making progress."

Hadden leaned forward a little. "And the sun is shining, the birds are singing, and all is normal with the world? That's a little . . . nonspecific. The service is bleeding money every time this snafu hits us, Commander. I want to know how close we are to catching this terrorist and stopping his attacks."

Here was a powerful man, used to command, and accustomed to getting his way. Thorn could feel that radiate from him. He understood it, but he didn't like being the focus of it. He was used to doing things his way, too, and nothing got his back up faster than somebody who didn't know what he was talking about telling him how to do his job—or hinting that he didn't know how to do it.

"Do you think it's going to rain in Sydney next Thursday, sir?" he asked.

"Excuse me, what does that have to do with—?" Hadden stopped. "Ah."

Thorn saw that the general had gotten it, he wasn't slow, but Thorn wanted to make sure. "My crystal ball doesn't work any better than yours, General," he said. "You're getting our best effort. This isn't like tracking an elephant across damp ground. We'll find the guy. Could be tomorrow, could be next week, could be a month from now. It takes what it takes."

Hadden smiled. "You're not afraid of me, are you, Commander?"

Thorn didn't hesitate. "No, sir," he said. "All you can do is fire me. I don't need the job."

Hadden's smile grew bigger. "I could do a lot worse than that, actually, but that wouldn't help me solve my problem, would it?"

"Not unless you have somebody better to replace me."

"And you doubt that."

Thorn shrugged. "Me, maybe. My technical people? You can't find better."

Hadden's smile had gone away. "And they are loyal to you."

"I can't speak to that. Fire me and find out."

The general frowned. "Commander, I don't think you want to get into a power struggle with me. I could draft your people and keep them right where they are."

Now Thorn was really getting angry. "You don't really believe that, do you? Face it, General, the most you could do is to keep their butts in the chair. That's all. And you know as well as I do that if you did that with threats, you could kiss any chance of solving your problem—or your next problem, or the one after that—good-bye. These are creative and independent people. Push some of them too far and hell will freeze over before they give you squat. They will look real busy, but they won't be doing anything useful."

Hadden leaned back a little. "You're part Native American, aren't you?"

"I don't mind the term 'Indian.' Yes, sir, I am."

"You know, I had a great-great-grandfather who served with Custer. An ordinary trooper. He died at the Little Bighorn."

"None of my relatives were there," Thorn said. "Different tribe. But Custer got what he deserved. And if your grandfather was part of what he did to the innocent women and children along the way, then he got what *he* deserved, too."

Hadden laughed. That puzzled Thorn, overriding his anger.

"If a man doesn't have balls, I don't need him working for me," Hadden said. He stood and extended his hand. "Keep giving me your best efforts, son, and I'll stay out of your hair. But if I think you're dogging it, you'll be rejoining the private sector PDQ."

Thorn stood, surprised. "Fair enough." He extended his own hand.

The two men shook. Hadden said, "I'll talk to you later."

And with that, he turned and left. Not quite a march, but not too far from it.

After he was gone, Thorn shook his head. Well. That had been . . . unexpected. And he wasn't sure of what he had heard. It sounded as if the man was giving him slack, but that he'd shown up here and pushed him to see how he'd react was a little irritating. Thorn would just have to see how it went. If this was all Hadden was going to do, fine. If he decided to come back and apply pressure again? That wasn't going to work. Thorn didn't have to put up with that.

Washington, D.C.

As he ate, Jay pondered his realization. It was the middle of the night—actually closer to two A.M., and Saji and the boy were asleep. Chang had packed up and gone back to his hotel a couple hours ago. Jay hadn't stopped for supper, and it was early for breakfast. What was the nighttime equivalent of brunch? Dinfast? Supbreak?

The meal, whatever it might be called, was simple: a

couple of boiled eggs he'd found in the fridge, an apple, and some cashews. Not the most exciting food, but at least it was something.

He sat at the kitchen table and went over it again, checking his reasoning.

He had gone at the problem every way he knew how, and it was the dog not barking in the night, he was sure.

Sherlock Holmes's dictum once again—everything else had been eliminated, and there wasn't anything left—at least not that Jay could figure out. He had run down every possibility except one:

There was a back door in the basic software—one that had been there since before the military—or CyberNation—ever got their hands on the programs. Put there by somebody looking far ahead.

In an interlinked multiple-affect synergistic software system this big, with its layers upon layers and wheels within wheels, figuring out where the hidden door was made looking for a needle in a haystack seem like a walk in the park on a nice spring day. It was more akin to finding a particular grain of sand on a big honkin' beach. It *could* be done, if you knew *exactly* what you were looking for—and you had lots and lots and lots of time to spend on it. . . .

Many million lines of code would have to be searched, and even with a dedicated Super-Cray or a Blue whale running full-blast looking, if you didn't have a pretty specific idea of how to frame your search, you could *still* miss it. Like putting the word "the" into a big Internet search engine—you came up with more than five and a half billion hits, and it only took two tenths of a second to get those, but *reading* all those for content? You wouldn't live long enough to do it.

There was another way to maybe get to the "who," and he was pretty sure that Chang's help had already put him on that track. Amazing what the guy could do even when he had almost nothing to work with. Chang said he would identify the man in the sampan, the one they had seen in the joint scenario. Jay had a gut feeling that this guy was involved, though he didn't know how.

Jay had already done the obvious—he had run a search for Chinese programmers on the original software crew, then the revision crews, even the marketing team, anybody who might have been able to embed a few clever lines of code where they'd leave unauthorized access to the system. Along the way, hundreds of programmers had worked on the beast, some extensively, some for only a few loops and lines. The score of Sino-sounding names still in the U.S. that had come up would be on a visit-now list for the FBI, but none of them looked like promising candidates. Jay's instincts, which had no basis in any kind of logic, told him that the guy had gone home.

Of course, it might be—was likely, in fact—that the Chinese op hadn't done the deed himself, but had socially engineered a programmer with a name as far away from China as Iceland. . . .

More, just being able to get into the system wasn't the whole answer: Once there, the guy doing the rascal had to manage it in such a way that it wouldn't be spotted, and it wouldn't point straight back at the hidden door even if it was picked up. Since none of the program's built-in virus-, worm-, or trojanware had caught the attacking sequence, the slashware either had to be piggybacked on something where nobody had thought to look, or so smooth that it looked harmless on its own.

Jay would bet that the slashware had been installed at the same time as the back door, and in such a way that the program didn't see it as anything but part of its normal OS. It wasn't a foreign invader, it was part of the body. Whatever it did, the program would think it was merely doing what it was *supposed* to do. And even so, it still had to be convoluted enough that the diagnostic safeware couldn't see it.

The sucker could even be on a timer. . . .

Jay himself could do something like this, assuming he'd

been one of the original code-writers with access early on. There was more than one way to go about it, though, and how Jay would manage it could be far different than the way it had been done.

This guy was good, no question, but now, at least, Jay had a handle on him.

He hoped.

Jay had four options, as he saw the situation.

One, he could find the door and close it, then find the built-in disguised slashware and deep-six it.

That could take slightly less than forever.

Two, somebody—and it wasn't going to be Jay—would have to go over every line of code and verify it. That would take forever—and then some.

Three, the military—and CyberNation—would have to junk their infected programs and any other programs that interfaced with them, and start over with new software. Neither one of them was likely to do that, since that would cost a king's ransom, and take major systems off-line for a long time. The cure would be nearly as bad as the disease—worse, even, like cutting off your hand to get rid of a wart on your little finger. And the wart's virus could *still* be in your system. . . .

Or four, Jay could find the guy responsible and then have somebody lean on him hard enough so he'd give up the door and slashware. Somehow, Chang's guy on the boat was in it. Maybe he was the player, maybe not, but he was in it. Somehow. Chang had a better handle on his country's system, even though Jay was worlds better generally.

Of the options, the only one that made any sense to Jay was the last. The best way to find a well-hidden body was to get the man who buried it to take you there.

The military program had, fortunately, been entirely written in the U.S., no outsourcing allowed for this level of sophistication. So whoever had screwed with it had been in the States during the creation of the program. It had taken three years and some to build and vet, and since Jay couldn't be sure that the Chinese op had actually laid his own hands on it, he was going to have to take the long road to find him from this end. The guy had to be a player—even if he bribed another programmer, he'd have to know what to tell him to do, and in great detail. And Jay was sure by now that the guy was Chinese, so the way was apparent, if not easy:

Jay would have to run down every computer expert from China who had been in the U.S. during the years that it had taken to build the infected program. Chang could help, and he would—it would go a long way to building a bridge between his organization and Net Force, and Chang would also know that Net Force would certainly be grateful. Such gratitude could manifest in a lot of hardware and software for Chang, and the military would happily foot that bill if Chang helped them solve their problem, no question at all. They'd bury the guy in gold dust if he pulled their fat out of the fire.

Meanwhile, on this end, Jay could start by finding all the Chinese students in computer science programs, as well as any Chinese visitors who listed anything connected with computers on their passports or border entry logs. That alone could be tens of thousands, maybe hundreds of thousands of people, he had no idea. It wouldn't be as hard as verifying multiple millions of lines of computer code, though. Even so, he was going to need major processing time. If they could track the guy down from Chang's end, Jay didn't have a problem with that, no, sir, not at all. He'd rather do it himself, of course, but the point was to catch the bad guy, to win. Everything else came second.

He chewed on a mouthful of boiled egg. With enough pepper, it wasn't so bad. . . .

30

The Yellow River
Shaanxi Province
North Central China

Chang watched through a telescope. The man from the sampan definitely had something to hide.

Chang was a long way off, and mostly behind the cover of a rickety boathouse on the river's south shore, two hundred meters, easy, so the telescope was necessary. At this distance, Chang would be virtually invisible to his quarry, but the telescope was of sufficient quality so that he could clearly see the man's expressions. Holding the scope steady was tricky, but the gray and splintery boathouse wall made a good enough support to mostly manage this, though the wood smelled of dead fish and soured waterweed.

The man from the red-eyed sampan sculled his boat to the shore, well downriver from where Chang had first seen him. He tied the boat to a post, shouldered a small kit on a short pole, and started to walk along a muddy path toward the houses in the nearby village. He never stopped glancing around, looking for anybody who might be watching him.

Sampan-man had no fish, for he had not been fishing, even though that was his disguise. Another reason to think he was hiding something.

Chang smiled, remembering an incident in Beijing some years ago. A man had attempted to rob a high-end jewelry store, owned by a Vietnamese. Before he could pull it off, the clerk had become suspicious of him and pushed a silent alarm, so when the man pulled a knife and demanded gold, the police were waiting just outside the shop's door. He walked right into their arms.

Why had the clerk become worried? Well, he said, it was the man's appearance. His clothes were ragged and of poor quality, indicating that he did not have the money to be buying expensive jewelry.

Plus, he had a black eye patch and a wooden leg.

Chang smiled again. That would-be thief was never going to blend in anywhere, save maybe at a pirates' convention. . . .

This was not as blatant, but if sampan-man was a simple fisher, Chang was the son of two turtles and the brother of a sea snake.

Chang closed the telescope and hurried away from the boathouse, circling away from his subject. Following him directly would be risky; the quarry would be looking for anybody behind him, so better that he was in front of him. He had to be going to the village—there was no other place around, and on foot, dressed in fishing clothes, he wasn't going to be hiking very far, not this late in the day.

There was a small outdoor market in the village, open for business, and Chang moved to stand with two women, three children, and a couple of old men in front of a fish-seller. Next to that stall, other patrons attended a man selling tubers and carrots, and past that, a third stall offered herbal medicines and acupuncture treatments, with several patients lined up there. Chang, dressed as the villagers, would not stand out.

Chang was careful not to look directly at sampan-man when he passed, but only watched him peripherally.

Sampan-man continued walking for half a block, then turned to his right into a narrow lane between two rows of small houses.

Chang hurried toward the lane. He slowed, and walked past, again using his peripheral vision only.

Sampan-man was not in sight.

Chang walked a bit farther, then turned around. So, the man had gone into one of those houses. Which one?

An old woman emerged from a house, carrying a broom. She began to sweep dust and pine needles from the packed-earth walk leading to the road.

"Good evening, Grandmother," Chang said.

The old woman smiled, revealing a mouth missing more than a few teeth.

"I wonder if you might help me?" Chang continued. He pulled a copper coin from his pocket. "I was at the river, and I saw a fisherman drop this as he left his boat. I would return it to him, but I don't know where he lives. His boat has red eyes, he is tall and thin."

The old woman nodded. "Li," she said. "That house, there, with the tall bamboo fence around it."

"Thank you, Grandmother. May the gods smile upon your family."

"Call out loudly," she said. "Li does not like visitors and his yard is full of brambles and traps."

He bowed, and she went back to her sweeping.

I know your name, sampan-man, and where you live. Now I will find out exactly who you are and what you are up to. . . .

Gridley would be pleased with his news, Chang knew. And it would be more than a little pleasing to have helped Net Force in this matter. A matter of no small pride.

*   *   *

Macao, China

Locke stood outside a fan-tan parlor north and east of the reservoir, a small place that catered to those with less than sterling backgrounds. The gambling den was next to a pocket park, not much more than a large lot with trees and a trimmed lawn, and neither was prey to tourists or idle passersby.

Locke had dealings with the triads, going all the way back to his Hong Kong days, and the triads were not somebody with whom you wanted to get crosswise, so this would have to be done with care.

At this point, he wasn't really sure they still needed Shing, certainly not as much as Wu seemed to think. Of course, Wu had longer-range goals, past the casinos, ambitions that he had not filled Locke in on completely, but that anybody with half a brain could figure out. Wu was doomed to fail in these, Locke was certain, but that wouldn't be *his* problem, he'd be out of it by then. Living in luxury on an island off the coast of Spain, perhaps, or maybe New Zealand. Both—he'd be able to afford that and a lot more.

Still, Wu thought Shing was necessary, and if Wu did fail, it wouldn't be from anything Locke had done.

The night was warm and humid, and rain was moving in. He could smell it in the air. He looked at his watch. Almost eleven, and Three-Finger Wei would be on time—he was always on time.

Wei was an information broker, and this included being a police informer. Wei did very well at it. The police listened to him, for he was right more often than not. The man moved around a lot—he had enemies who would put a hatchet into his skull given an opportunity—but Locke had more than a few contacts, and he and Wei had done business in the past.

The trick with Wei was not to give him a tip, which might make him suspicious, but to point him in a direction without him knowing that was what you were doing. Locke had already set up part of the sting, and if he did this right, Wei would take care of the rest of it.

At ten seconds before eleven o'clock, Locke saw Wei strolling across the little garden toward him. He smiled. Dependable as the sunrise, Wei.

They exchanged polite greetings, talked about the weather, the state of the world, and local politics for a few moments.

Finally, Wei got to it. "What can I do for you, old friend?"

Locke said, "I need some information on a big police action upcoming against the triads," Locke said. "Regarding the smuggling of surplus Russian guns into the district."

"What exactly do you want to know about it?" Wei asked, never hesitating a beat. Locke wanted to laugh. Wei couldn't know anything about such an action, because there was no such action being contemplated, given as how Locke had just made it up. But one did not make money as an information broker by looking puzzled when a question was asked. Any question.

"I know there are shipments on the way, but I don't know when or where the police are going to do their main raids. I have some . . . business that might be affected by the law showing up at the wrong place and time, and I want to avoid that. The date is more important than the place."

"I am to meet a man about this very subject in the morning," Wei said. Butter wouldn't melt in his mouth. "I'll have more specific information after I speak with him. We can get together again tomorrow."

Locke nodded. "That will do. Thanks, Wei."

"I live to serve."

Locke headed one way, Wei another, and Locke allowed the smile he had been suppressing to break free. Wei's go-to guy on the major crimes strike force was a clerk who had a weakness for expensive prostitutes. Locke had, through a cutout, approached this clerk and bribed him. The clerk would be able to indulge himself in three-hundred-pounds-a-night call girls for a couple of weeks if he would tell Wei that the police would be mounting a major operation against the triads in four days. Hundreds of agents, scores of locations, smashing down doors and arresting anybody who so much as looked at them crooked.

Once Wei had this information, he would find a triad buyer and sell it to him. Word would get out, it always did, and the triads would button up faster than a sailor expecting a typhoon. The effect would be the same as if the police actually *did* launch the raids—the triads would be hunkered low, keeping their heads down, and it would not be business as usual. Shing would hardly be on anybody's to-do list for a while.

But the real beauty of it was, once the criminal organizations went to ground, the police would pick up on it immediately. The good cops were like hounds, they could smell something in the air, and that would instantly bother them. What was going on? What do we need to know that we don't know?

They'd hear a rumor about gun-running, and since the triads were obviously hiding something, then the police *would* roll.

It was bootstrapping at its best.

In the end, nobody would find any guns, and things would eventually go back to normal, but Locke's purpose would be served, and nobody would ever be the wiser. Wei would come out smelling like a rose with the police and the triads, since what he'd sold both would have happened. That the triads were able to keep the smuggled guns hidden would just be part of the game, and not Wei's fault—unfortunate, but what can you do?

The only person who could gainsay it would be the clerk with the addiction to high-class snatch, and even if he wanted to tell somebody, his contact was an anonymous go-between, a former member of Locke's street gang who had been imported from Hong Kong, and who was already back there.

And if Locke wanted to be absolutely sure? Locke could arrange for the clerk to have an accident. A similar misfortune could befall his old running buddy in Hong

Kong, too, and then there would be nobody who knew anything about anything. . . .

Washington, D.C.

Jay met Chang in VR, a little scenario Jay had built of a red
sand beach in Fiji. The sun was shining, the breeze warm,
the sea birds wheeling and calling.

Chang said, "His name is Bruce Leigh."

"You're kidding."

"Different spelling, L-e-i-g-h. He's British, living in a
house in Macao. I asked a friend in the People's Special
Police Investigation Unit to check him out. There is not
much to see, he keeps a low profile, but my investigator indicated that he uses more electricity than anybody else in
his neighborhood, and that he has disguised communication gear on his house, which house also boasts unusual security. What does that tell you?"

Jay said, "He's growing dope or he's a hacker."

"Yes, my thought as well. I expect the only reason I was
able to follow him is that he doesn't believe anybody can—
certainly not in China. He is very cautious."

"So you think this might be our man?"

"No."

Jay shook his head. "Why not?"

"Because he is not doing anything that seems connected
to your problem. He is spying upon somebody else who is
Chinese. I think this man is a watchdog, and since he
would have had to go to no small amount of effort and expense to put himself in that position, and he is obviously
more adept than most in my country, then whoever he ob-
serves is likely of large importance."

Jay watched a particularly large gull settle down on the
sea, just outside the breaker line. "Go on."

"So far, I regret that I have been unable to find out anything about the junk, or who, if anyone, is actually on it,"

Chang continued. "I cannot find a way to approach it unde-
tected."

"You think maybe our quarry could be on the junk?"

"My skills are humble, but I cannot imagine there are
that many computer experts in my country who are so
much better than I that I had no clue they exist. Especially
when one of the best I've seen is busy carefully watching
another. There may be no connection at all. But still . . ."

"It's something we need to know," Jay said.

"Exactly."

"Thanks, Chang. I guess I'll be taking a run at that big
boat on the Yellow River, to see if I can figure out what's
what."

"Let me know what you find out."

"Oh, yeah. We owe you, man."

Chang smiled. Yes. He knew.

31

Hanging Garden Apartments
Macao, China

"You are a great man," Mayli said when he was done speaking. She said it quietly, with what seemed to Wu to be real admiration.

She was dressed—Wu had not wanted to have this conversation in the raw—and they sat at the same table where he had discussed Shing with Locke only a day earlier. He had watched her face as he'd told it, and her amazement was genuine—or the best acting he had ever seen.

"No need to flatter me," he said.

"Not at all, Wu," she said. "I have never heard any idea so bold. If a man can accomplish such a thing, 'great' would be the least of his accolades."

Wu resisted the smile. This had been a major step, to tell her, but the warmth he felt in his heart now justified it. "You must point out what you see as flaws in the plan."

She shook her head. "What you say about Beijing's reaction seems valid, but I am not political. And if the Republic does not act as you hope . . ."

Wu nodded. "The Taiwanese will. For the ROC to turn down the chance at collecting all that a most-respected general of the People's Army can bring with his defection? No, they will offer me asylum. Even if I do not grease the ramp—which I will—they could not pass it up."

"And the North Koreans?" she said. "You believe they will go forward?"

"They have been poised at the gate too long. The madman who rules them would kick it open tomorrow if he thought he had the advantage. With a couple of operational nuclear weapons in his hands? He will leap on the South as a starving tiger does a deer."

"The Americans—"

"—will have enough distraction that they won't know what is going on until it is too late. Their military computers will be crashing, and they will not be focused on the Koreans. They won't be altogether asleep, but their current President is a cautious man. With the long and slow drain of Iraq and the problems with Syria still fresh in their memory, he won't be in a hurry to get into a shooting war in Korea."

"Even if the North uses atomic weapons?"

"I don't think the Koreans will use them—not unless the battle turns against them, and even so, they will not aim those at American troops, but against their Southern kin. Many old hatreds there, and jealousy. Ever see a satellite picture of Korea after dark? The lights of the cities in the South are easily seen; the North is very nearly dark."

He paused, thinking, then shrugged. "Of course, the Americans have the capability to squash the North Korean Army flat, albeit at a huge cost, but—I do not believe they have the *will* at this point in history."

"And if you are wrong?"

He smiled now, most pleased. "That is the best part—if they do, it does not matter to my plans. If the Americans are willing to join the battle with serious intent, the North Koreans will find themselves mired in a great and stinking pigsty, and they will suffer large misery. Too bad for them.

None of it will be linked to me. The bombs will be surplus Soviet Union, from one of the hungry and broke countries that still has them—but delivered by people who won't be around to speak of the deed afterward. By the time the bombs are transferred and the Koreans ready to move, I will be on Taiwan, with hundreds of millions of British pounds at my disposal, nobody will be the wiser, and the path to power before me without obstacles I cannot overcome."

"What of your family?"

"They will remain here," he said. "Beijing will know what I have done, but they will lose so much face if it is known in the West that they will try to keep it quiet. My family will be safe enough—Beijing will be informed that if anything happens to my family, I will reveal all. I can show a Chinese link to the nuclear bombs, and I will let that fact be whispered into certain ears as well. The last thing Beijing will wish is that the United States believes they had *any*thing to do with the Koreans' attack. Beijing will swallow it and say nothing. The casinos lost money? Too bad for them. They can make more."

She shook her head slowly, and was impressed, he could tell. "So you will be rich and respected and alone, living in Taipei?"

"Not alone," he said. He reached across the table and took her hand.

They both smiled.

It was good to have a helpmate such as Mayli. A formidable woman who did not even blink at the idea of using a little nuclear war to cover one's tracks.

The Cherry Blossom Pleasure House
Edo, Japan, 1700 C.E.

Jay drank warm sake and watched the men—mostly samurai, but he was sure there were a couple of *daimyo* in disguise, and at least one ninja—as they laughed and flirted with the courtesans and geisha. Behind a screen, somebody played a *shakahashi* flute, something simple but bright.

Thunder rumbled in the distance, and the thickening clouds made the lamps in the large room necessary as the sky darkened. Rain soon.

This was the place that Leigh was watching. His quarry, and Jay's, was in here.

Jay, also disguised as a samurai, shifted his position a little and smiled at the young woman attending him. She wore a flower-patterned kimono, and her face and neck were made up to be chalk white, with cherry-red lips painted on. When she smiled, her teeth were stained almost black. It was the look, but it wasn't one that appealed to Jay. She was just cover, so that he could figure out which of the men in the pleasure house was his prey.

It was a good metaphor, Jay thought. There were people who lived in fortresses, massive, well-protected constructs that were so solidly built that getting into them took great skill. There were few such places that Jay couldn't eventually crack, one way or another—stealth, bribery, even direct assault—though some would take a lot longer than others. If his quarry was inside one of those, that was the disadvantage. The advantage was, such forts were usually not that hard to find. The bigger and more elaborate they were, the easier they were to spot. You had to give up one thing to have another.

Harder, in Jay's mind, was the quarry who lived in a small shack amidst hundreds or thousands just like it, with nothing to set it apart from those around it. The only way to find the man you wanted was to open each door and look inside. While the doors were flimsy and opening them was no problem, doing it a hundred or a thousand times was no small job. And a clever enough prey might step outside just before you kicked in his door and found an empty room, then sneak back in after you were gone.

A ranked samurai swaggered down the street arrogantly for all to see, the two swords in his sash, able to chop off the head of a lesser man—a farmer, artisan, or merchant—

with impunity, if he so desired. Easy to see such samurai and mark them.

A ninja, on the other hand, never wore his black suit in public—the ninja's stock in trade was stealth. He would be disguised—as a samurai, farmer, artisan, merchant—and the best of them would offer no clue as to their real identity. The ninja suit was worn for night assassinations or spying, and designed to blend into the darkness unseen. If you saw a ninja in this mode, he wasn't very good at it.

If you could penetrate the disguise, however, you were halfway to defeating a ninja. Yes, they had weapons and dirty tricks, but if you knew that, you had the advantage. A man pretending to be a sake merchant on a rainy Edo street would have to go for a hidden weapon, and Jay could pull out his *katana* and lop off the man's head before the ninja could come up with a *shuriken* to fling at him.

First man to move had the advantage.

Somewhere in this collection of warriors was a fake, and as soon as Jay figured out which one it was, he would have the Chinese hacker. A mistake would give Jay away as well, however, and so he had to be very careful before he moved.

He had managed to sneak onto the Chinese junk on the Yellow River, but the boat had been empty. Somebody had been there recently, there were signs of occupation, but Jay had just missed him. And because the boat had been easy to clamber up and into, he did not figure that the man who'd been there would be coming back. He was more certain than ever it was the hacker he sought.

It was easier to find Leigh, and once he found him, he knew his real target couldn't be far away. He was right. Leigh had led him to this place, and the hunt was back on.

Jay had asked Chang to hold off having Leigh arrested and sweated, for two reasons. First, Jay wanted a shot at finding the hacker on his own. Second, if the Chinese got the guy, they would pry things out of him that the U.S. military surely would not want them to have.

If this didn't work, he'd have to give Chang the go-ahead—if he hadn't already decided to do it anyhow—and they'd get the ID from Leigh, who surely must know who it was he had been watching.

But Jay wanted his chance first. It wouldn't take long—he'd either pass or fail in a hurry. Pass—and it would go a long way to making him feel as if he'd done his job; fail—and they could always take the other road. But they'd have to give up some things to do it. If Jay could catch him, it would be better.

Jay didn't intend to fail. He sipped at his sake, and watched the men in the room. Which one?

The front door opened, revealing the gloomy outside. Rain began to splatter against the tile roof at that same moment. A samurai on the porch stepped into the building, and as he did, a fierce gust of wind blew in as a nearby lightning strike strobed and a loud boom of thunder vibrated the room. The wind blew the lamps out, and for a couple of seconds, the room was dim. The patrons laughed and cracked jokes as one of the serving girls relit a lamp.

When the lights came back up, it took Jay a moment to realize that one of the samurai, a short and somewhat swarthy fellow sitting to his right, near the door, was gone.

Jay scrambled to his feet and hurried for the door. The guy was onto him!

Outside, the storm raged; hard winds drove rain almost horizontally at Jay, blinding him. Where was the guy?

Jay caught a peripheral movement. He turned and saw the samurai running, splashing through puddles already ankle-deep, one hand holding his swords steady as he sprinted away.

No doubt about it, that was him!

Jay took off after the fleeing man.

He started gaining immediately. The guy was slow compared to Jay—of course, so were most people—and already Jay was grinning. Guy might look like a samurai, but he was a fake, and in this scenario, Jay was on a par with Miyamoto Musashi. He'd slice the guy into hamburger, figuratively, anyway—

The rainy air ahead of the ninja *rippled* and it was as if the man had stepped through time and space—he just . . . *vanished,* as if running behind a curtain—

What ninja trick was this?!

Jay skidded to a stop just short of the rent in the air, which, even as he watched, faded back into the rainy night.

Jay looked around, wiping the water from his eyes, hoping to spot some clue—

And there one was: a scrap of what looked like blue silk, flattened and soaked by the downpour. Jay moved to it, bent, and picked it up. A scarf of some kind. There was a tag in one corner, tiny, with writing on it, so small he could barely read it.

It said, "CyberNation."

Jay shook his head. Somehow, the guy had slipped away from him by using CyberNation protocols. Shouldn't be able to do that, but there it was.

Bag that. "End scenario!" Jay said.

He wasn't out of moves yet.

Washington, D.C.

Jay grabbed his virgil from the desk—he was still fully suited—and said, "Call Charles Seurat. Priority One."

32

Seurat was most unhappy about the insistent demand of his cell phone. There was a naked woman in his shower, a woman that he was, he was sure, in love with, and he was about to join her—when the phone started playing "Love Is Blue," the Paul Mauriat instrumental version. Since that was his Priority One ring, he couldn't just let it go. *Merde!*

The caller ID was blocked, but since anybody who knew his private number was somebody he would usually—usually—want to speak with, he answered it. Not all that graciously:

"What?"

"I need full access to your system, no playing around with pitfalls and hidden stuff, I need your security code and I need it now."

Gridley. Seurat recognized the voice—who could forget

that arrogant tone? Not a hello-how-are-you? Just a demand for something he should not have.

"*Va te faire foutre!* Why should I do that?"

"You want *me* to get stuffed? I have the guy who
screwed your network in my sights! He ran into your system to hide and the longer it takes me to get after him, the
more likely it is he might get away!"

"My people can—"

"—get stuffed themselves! We don't have time for this!
Give me the number!"

"Listen, Gridley, if you think—"

"Seurat, the clock is running. The guy is Chinese. He is
in China. The Chinese are about to have a guy in custody
who can give them the hacker's name—what do you think
they'll do once *they* know who he is?"

Seurat felt a cold roiling in his belly. "*Merde—*"

"Exactly. They will grab the guy who was able to penetrate CyberNation *and* United States military hardware and
give both of us all kinds of grief. You think they won't
squeeze everything he learned since he was born out of
him? You *want* the Chinese to do that?"

Seurat had not gotten to where he was by dithering
when he needed to move. He rattled off his personal security code, one that would allow the bearer to go anywhere
in CyberNation.

"Got it. Thanks."

"Go, go! Let me know!"

"Bet on it."

Seurat discommed, and put the phone down. He looked
into the bathroom at the fogged-up shower glass. The future of his company might be riding on what Gridley could
do. How could a man relax under such worry?

Then again, there was a beautiful, sexy woman in the
shower waiting for him. There was nothing he could do to
help Gridley at the moment anyway, *non*? He stood and began to undress.

C'est la vie. . . .

* * *

Los Angeles
2105 C.E.

The Japanese village was gone and now Jay found himself in a gritty Los Angeles ninety years in the future. It wasn't exactly like *Blade Runner*, but it was not a world anybody wanted to live in—the streets were grimy, the people dirty, and it looked more like Saigon in the '60s than L.A. a hundred odd years past that. It was very noisy, crowded, and it stank of something Jay couldn't identify exactly—like some combination of mold, dust, synthetic lube, and sweaty humanity.

It gave Jay some hope that maybe—maybe—he could still find this guy. A true pro—not one just with experience in VR and with rascaling scenarios, but one who was used to playing cat and mouse with the police—would not still be in this scenario. A true pro would have bounced once, twice, three times already, leaving no trail for Jay to follow.

Jay grinned bitterly and shook his head. A true pro, he realized, wouldn't have done that at all. No, he would have simply ended the scenario, unjacking and leaving VR entirely, and giving Jay absolutely no way to track him.

But if this guy wasn't a pro, if he wasn't smart enough—or scared enough—to bail, this would be a nice place to hide. Who'd want to come here looking for you?

And Jay had one other small hope to cling to: He knew what he would have done in the guy's place. Even knowing the smart thing, Jay would have stayed, playing with his chaser, confident in his own abilities.

He already knew this guy wasn't as good as Jay Gridley. No one was, after all. But he could hope the guy was every bit as confident.

Ahead of him on the street, two men who looked to be in their early fifties were talking about some disaster. The taller man was dressed in an orange coverall with some kind of high-tech sandals that flashed red and blue diodes with each step; the second man wore a silky cape over shorts, and what looked like sprayed-on booties.

"—Ivan Noskil Aisee was just outside the Red Zone when the comet smashed into Oakland," Booties said. "He dropped round yesterday and talked about it."

"Terrible thing," Sandals said. "So many people." He said it as if he was talking about a fender-bender on the freeway.

"Crater was almost a hundred miles in diameter. Anybody within that range was vaporized immediately. Outside that, for another hundred miles, you got killed several times—the heat wave from the fireball fried you where you stood, the earthquake shook your building down, the ejecta buried it all, and the wind blew anything still standing on top of the mound flat."

"Could have been worse," Sandals said.

"Yeah, how?"

"Could have hit here."

"I grok that."

Jay shook his head. He did science-fiction and fantasy scenarios now and then, though he preferred to avoid the stuff with dragons and trolls and wizards and all. Too easy.

Jay had seen his quarry move, and he had a handle on what he'd look like, no matter what disguise he adopted here. And he was close, Jay was sure.

He rounded a corner and saw some kind of street theater. A magic show, and a gory one—somebody was lopping arms and legs off three people, blood flying everywhere, but the crowd—and the victims—were all laughing. It was a pretty good trick, Jay thought.

"I'm new here," Jay said to a woman who looked as if she had been tattooed and surgically altered to look like a two-legged cat. She had feline features, body hair so thick it looked like pale gray fur, for God's sake, and save for that, wore no clothes. "What is going on?"

"Public Vengeance," the cat-lady said. "The guy with the sword, his cube was retinal-burned by those three. He gets to kill them any way he wants."

"Why are they laughing if he's killing them?"

She stared at him as if he had turned into a giant cockroach. "Why wouldn't they be? How far away are you from, Dizzy?"

Jay shook his head again. Not a magic trick, and he didn't understand anything she had said. Apparently retinal-burning was bad, whatever that was. Definitely not a world he'd want to inhabit.

Jay moved off, scanning the crowd. Too much time had passed. Seurat had delayed too long in giving up the code. He was starting to lose what little hope he had of finding his quarry.

Wait. There, ahead, on the fringe of the crowd, watching the killings . . . there he was! A short, very Chinese-looking man in his late twenties, laughing at the gore.

The time for finesse was past. Jay sprinted toward the man as fast as he could. The guy didn't see him until Jay was three feet away. Before he could do more than blink, Jay was on him. He grabbed him, whipped his arm around the man's neck, and applied a triangle-choke, shutting off the carotid blood supply to his brain. The guy struggled, but after a few seconds, he went limp, out cold.

"You're mine, now, sucker!"

Figuratively, anyway.

Net Force HQ
Quantico, Virginia

Thorn said, "You're sure."

"No question, Boss. But Chang will pass the watcher on to his security people, if he hasn't already, and the Chinese will beat us to him. I'm trying to hold him off with promises of gear and programs he can't get over there, but I don't know how long that will work. He'll have to give the guy up sooner or later and they'll grab him."

"Maybe not." Thorn waved his hand over his virgil, moving his fingers in a command sig. "Call General Hadden, Priority One. Patch him into the holoproj on my desk."

The connection took all of three seconds, and General Hadden appeared over the desk in three-dee at quarter-scale.

"Commander. You have something for me?"

"Yes, sir. Jay Gridley has the ID on the computer hacker."

"Outstanding."

"The problem, sir, is that the man is Chinese, and in Macao, China, at the moment. And the local authorities will likely have his ID fairly soon."

"Give me his name and information," Hadden said.

"We have people in Macao?" Jay asked.

"Son, these days, we have people *every*where."

"This could be tricky," Thorn began.

"Not in the least. We aren't going to let the Chinese get their hooks on this guy—he knows too much about us."

"I'm uploading the file now," Jay said.

"Good job," Hadden said. "We'll let you know how it goes. Hadden out."

The image disappeared.

"So that's it? We have some M.I. ops or spooks over there who drop by and collect this guy Shing and what? Somehow sneak him out of the country and back here?"

"Your guess is as good as mine, but, yeah, I expect something like that. Maybe they debrief him there, but I don't think they want to leave him in Macao to tell stories to the Chinese."

Jay nodded.

"Of course, this is just the first part of it," Thorn said.

"Huh?"

"We know who he is and, pretty soon, probably how he did it, thanks to you. But the big question is . . . *why* did he do it? That's what we really need."

Jay blinked, and Thorn realized he probably had never even considered that part of it. That was the thing about technical people—turn them loose on a problem and they could move heaven and earth to solve it, but they sometimes didn't see the big picture.

Somebody had attacked the U.S. military computer system and done bad things to it. You found out *who* so you could find out *why*. Otherwise, what was to stop the brains behind it from trying again? You had to get to the source.

If Hadden's people got to the guy before the Chinese did, Thorn was pretty sure this fellow Shing would tell them what they wanted to know. Once upon a time, the United States would have played it differently. These days, whatever it took to protect the country was what got done. Scary, in some ways, but it made would-be terrorists realize that being captured by Americans when you were a danger to them was not going to be a walk in the park anymore.

33

Hanging Garden Apartments
Macao, China

When Locke got to Mayli's apartment, Wu opened the door before he could knock.

Wu led him into the living room. Mayli sat on the couch. Here was a surprise. Why . . . ?

"Tell him," Wu said.

Locke looked at her.

"Men came and took Shing," she said. "Three of them. Two were Chinese, one was a Westerner. He did not speak, the Westerner, but he was in charge."

"What did the Chinese say?"

"They pointed guns and told Shing he was coming with them. Shing did not resist. They left."

"That's all?"

"They knew who he was, they did not ask him to identify himself. They told me to sit still, and that was just what I did."

Locke looked at Wu. "Police? Triad?"

Wu shook his head. "Not police. And I don't think tong—his debt is not ripe enough for this."

"Then who?"

"Who else would be looking for Shing?"

"Americans. Possibly the French."

Wu nodded.

"How could they have found him?"

"Other than that he made a mistake? There are but four of us who knew what he was working on," Wu said. "And three of us are here now."

Locke pulled his cell phone and thumbed in a number. After a beat, a male voice he didn't recognize answered, in English: "Yes?"

Locke broke the connection, slid the back off the phone, and pulled the battery, just to be absolutely sure the untraceable phone didn't hold any secrets. "That was Leigh's secure number and somebody else answered it. They have Leigh—that's how they got Shing."

"How did they get Leigh?" Wu asked.

Locke shook his head. "Doesn't matter."

Wu said, "We'll have to move the schedule up."

"I don't like that idea," Locke said. "The fuse is still burning in the Americans' computers, even if they have Shing, right?"

Wu said, "Shing will crack faster than an egg dropped on a sidewalk. He will tell them what he did, how he did it, and how to stop it. He is more American than Chinese."

"I thought Shing said it couldn't be stopped, short of shutting down their entire system."

"I think we can safely assume that Shing lied. His arrogance would not let him give up that much control. We cannot chance that. We must move soon, or not at all."

Locke tried again: "Shing knows nothing of our plans." He glanced at Mayli. *But she does. Why?*

"She knows," Wu said, confirming what Locke had just figured out. "But while Shing doesn't know what I intend, he does know who he works for. If the Americans have him, they will eventually be coming to pay me a visit, one way or another. We must be finished by the time they get around to that."

Locke nodded. He didn't like it, but Wu was right. "All right. How soon can your men be ready?"

"They are ready now."

"Yes, right, of course they are. How soon? Realistically?"

"Three days."

Locke sighed. "Three days. I'll go see the managers."

He looked at Mayli, who wore a Mona Lisa smile. Here was an interesting development. No more fingers in that honey pot, not for him, he knew. Wu had claimed her for his own. Well. No matter. He could have a different woman every day for the rest of his life, given the money he stood to make. Mayli was not that special. Wu could have her, and he'd better watch his back, too.

Net Force HQ
Quantico, Virginia

Thorn looked up to see Marissa smiling at him from the doorway.

"Hey."

"Hey," he said. "Come on in."

She did. "What did you do, Tommy? I'm getting rumblings from something transpiring on the Chinese front."

"Jay ran down the Chinese hacker. My, uh, new boss thought it would be better if agents of the U.S. government got to him before the local police had a chance to talk to him."

"Smart man. I thought it was something like that. This last day has seen more spooks than a big-city graveyard zipping around in the Orient. Did they get him?"

"I don't know, I haven't heard yet."

"Maybe I can find out. So, I have a few minutes. Do you have time for another fencing lesson?"

"Always."

He stood, and his secure line rang. The ID showed that it was Hadden. He held a hand up toward Marissa.

"Thorn here."

"We have collected our bird, Commander. And he is singing like a canary. I need to see you, Colonel Kent, and your computer wizard whatshisname in my office at your earliest convenience."

"Yes, sir."

Thorn set the phone back into its cradle. "I'm afraid we'll have to postpone that lesson for another time. Hadden wants to see me stat."

"I understand."

Office of the Chairman of the Joint Chiefs of Staff
The Pentagon
Washington, D.C.

Jay had expected something a lot more posh than what it turned out to be, but what the office looked like was not as important as why they were here. He, Colonel Kent, and Commander Thorn sat at a conference table watching a recording of an interrogation, and the holoproj was sharp and clear.

A man sat at a table: Shing, he was called. He was dressed well enough, in yellow silk slacks and a blue pastel Izod shirt, and if he had been physically coerced or threatened or drugged, these things did not show. Off camera, somebody asked questions in English and the man, who was young and apparently unworried to the point where he smiled and nodded a lot, answered them without any hesitation that Jay could see.

At the end of the table, Many-Star General Hadden waved at the image and said, "Here's the part we found most interesting."

"And the name of the man who paid you to engage in these activities?"

"General Wu, of the People's Army," Shing said.

Hadden touched a button and the holoproj froze. He

said, "Comrade General Wu's current assignment is the security of the former Portuguese colony of Macao. He's an
old hard-liner, survived Mao and the Cultural Revolution,
and is well placed and well respected by the military and
Communist Party bigwigs. A patriot."

Thorn nodded. "And you don't suppose he hired Shing
there to screw with the U.S. military computers just for the
pure fun of it?"

Hadden smiled. "Sowing confusion among the ranks of
one's enemy is not generally a bad thing in itself, but that is
usually done as a prelude to something else."

"But you don't expect to see the Chinese Army storm-
ing the docks in San Francisco anytime soon," Thorn said.

"That would give the tourists on Pier 39 something
more interesting than harbor seals to look at, sure enough,
but—no."

Colonel Kent said, "So the question becomes, why
would Comrade General Wu be screwing around with U.S.
military computers?"

"Oh, yes, indeed. And here's something that makes us
really curious. CIA operatives in Asia have passed along a
little tidbit that may or may not have anything to do with
this: Somebody has been poking around in a couple of the
former Soviet republics trying to buy tactical nuclear
bombs. Which in and of itself is not that big a deal, since
Third World operatives have been trying to do that since
the evil empire broke up; only this time, the word is that
the would-be buyer might have a Chinese connection."

"Ah."

Jay frowned. "I don't understand. Why would the Chinese do that? They already have nukes, don't they?"

"Good question," the general said. "And yes, they do."

"I'm still not connecting the dots," Jay said, shaking his
head.

Kent said, "Suppose you had a neighbor who really irritated you, to the point where you want to throw a brick
through his front window. And you've got a pile of old red
bricks right there in your driveway. But down the street a

few houses, there's another neighbor who has a pile of white bricks in his backyard."

"Oh," Jay said, getting it. "You, ah, *borrow* one of your neighbor's bricks and throw that. Guy finds a white one in his living room, he doesn't charge over to your house."

"Exactly."

Thorn said, "But the real question here is, and assuming one thing has anything to do with the other, if Wu wants to throw a brick, whose window is he going to toss it through? And when?"

Jay blinked and shook his head.

"We don't even know if this is the case," Hadden said, "but we do know that Wu is a big fan of Sun Tzu and Miyamoto Musashi, and both of *them* are big on misdirection and sneaky business."

"Wu is up to something unofficial," Kent said.

Hadden nodded. "Our man Shing here knows only what he was paid to do and it's all computer gobbledygook. He does not have any idea *why* Wu wants it done." He looked at Jay. "I'm sending this recording with you. Shing gets into the technical stuff a little later, and I need you to run it down and fix things—our people will assist as necessary."

Jay nodded. "Yes, sir."

Hadden said, "That will take care of the immediate problem with the software, but I'm guessing that's just the tip of a nasty iceberg. Meanwhile, the Chinese authorities have collected Mr. Leigh, courtesy of Mr. Chang, and we don't know what Leigh knows, if anything, and what he will or won't give up. So we are in something of a quandary. For Wu to risk what he's risking by screwing around with us, we aren't talking about a bunch of fraternity guys on a panty raid risking a demerit on their records. If this isn't official—and we can't see how it could be—and his government finds out, they'll crucify him, since they are trying very hard to become a world power and, until that happens, be our best friend. They would lose great face, not to mention a boatload of trade, if it turns out Wu has some plan that involves blowing up something that belongs to us. We might blame them and drop a few big fire-crackers of our own on Beijing to indicate our displeasure."

"We wouldn't, though, would we?" Jay asked.

Hadden looked at him. "I would hope not, son, but I answer to a civilian, and given the nature of life in the world today, you never can tell. The thing is, given the stakes at risk, we have to know what Wu is up to, we don't particularly want his bosses to know if they don't already, and we can't mess around with ambassadors and protocol to find out. If he's warned, he might be able to cover his tracks."

Colonel Kent spoke up. "Don't you think grabbing Shing and Leigh will alert Wu?"

Hadden nodded. "Of course, but it couldn't be helped."

"Frighten a man holding a loaded gun and he also might pull the trigger," Kent said.

"That thought had crossed our minds," Hadden said. He looked at Kent. "How's your Chinese, Abe?"

"Worse than my Portuguese, sir, and that's pretty bad."

"Brush up, Colonel. How soon can you be ready?"

"To get my team in the air? Forty-eight hours."

"Which means you need half that, minus another thirty percent. The clock is ticking, Colonel."

"Yes, sir."

Outside, on the way back to their car, Jay said, "You're serious? You are going to fly to China and kidnap a Chinese general?"

"That's the idea."

"But—why doesn't the Army just use the spooks who got Shing? Or put a bug in the Chinese authorities' ear?"

"Because Shing was easy. He had no security, and no reason to think he needed it. But you can bet that Wu knows we have his man, and that we know something, so a couple of CIA ops aren't going to just waltz in and point guns at Wu and get him to come along with them."

Commander Thorn added, "And remember, we don't want the Chinese to know about this if we can help it. Our friendship with them is both new and iffy."

"But why us? Why Net Force?"

Kent shrugged. "We're qualified. I have the right people to do the job, and I'm already in the chain of command regarding this mess. The fewer people who know about it, the better. Bring in somebody else, that's just more tongues that might accidentally wag someday."

"Can you . . . ?" Jay stopped.

"Get him? Probably. Thirty years ago, I built a deck for my aunt. Took me four days, morning to evening. I had to use a power saw and sander, square, level, posthole digger, measuring tape, and a lot of nails and screws, not to mention a bucket of sweat. About forty hours of solid work. The deck lasted for twenty years, then started to rot, so, then I went back to take it down for her." He paused.

"It took me less than two hours and a pickax to turn the deck into a pile of scrap lumber."

Jay looked puzzled. "Which, uh, means what?"

"It's a lot easier to tear something down than it is to construct it. We can get to Wu. But it's a whole bunch less work to shoot him than capture him in one useful piece."

"You have to take him alive?" Jay said.

"If it comes to a choice of killing him or letting him get away, better dead than fled. Whatever he's up to, if Wu joins his ancestors pushing up daisies, he won't be causing us any more problems."

"But if he's not alone in this . . ." Thorn said.

"Which is why we would rather take him alive," Kent said. "To be sure."

Jay shook his head. "What a mess."

"Welcome to the military, son," Kent said. "Situation normal—all fouled up."

34

Kent was going over his checklist, being methodical, but not dragging his feet. He had a lot of things to get done and not much time to do them.

His virgil bleeped. He answered it without looking at the caller ID.

"Kent."

"Abe. John Howard."

"General. What can I do you for?"

"I, uh, heard about your mission. I'm sending over a little something I thought you might find useful. Ought to be there any minute."

"I appreciate that, John. I can use all the help I can get."

"Break a leg, Abe. Preferably not your own."

He discommed, and Kent did the same. He looked up to see a man in Net Force blues striding between the stacks of ammo boxes three meters high on either side of the row.

"Julio?"

"Colonel."

"You have something for me from John Howard?"

"Yes, sir. That would be me, sir. If you want to reactivate me from reserve status, I have a leave of absence from General Howard to tag along."

Kent grinned. "Consider yourself reinstated to active duty, Captain."

"Yes, sir. Where shall I start?"

Kent handed him the list. "Here. Finish this, there's plenty more to do. Welcome back, son."

"Glad to be here, sir. Being a consultant was getting a little slow."

"I hope you haven't lost too many steps."

"Me, too. But when it comes to shooting, I can still beat you, sir."

"Now and then, son. Only now and then."

Kent grinned again and hurried off to make sure his team was on schedule.

Comrade General Wu's Office
Military Base Annex
Macao, China

Locke made a number of phone calls. These conversations were very nearly the same, save for the names of the casino managers:

"Honorable Chan?"

"Yes?"

"This is Colonel Han, in charge of the local antiterrorist unit of the People's Army. I have been instructed by Comrade General Wu, who, as I am sure you know, is honored to command the division of the People's Army that protects Macao, to call you."

"Wu, yes."

"We have received intelligence, Honorable Chan, that indicates a terrorist plot to attack certain casinos."

"What? When? How?"

"Unfortunately, sir, the specifics have yet to be determined. However, General Wu desires that a general warning be given to those who might be involved. Our information indicates that the terrorists, who are members of a secret and well-armed cabal, could launch an attack within weeks, perhaps even days."

"We will increase our security immediately!"

"Sir, Comrade General Wu directs me to tell you that such a measure might be unwise. The terrorists are particularly violent and likely suicidal, and they will have weapons far superior to casino security officers or even those of the local police. Resistance by your security personnel could result in a bloodbath. None of us want to see dead tourists piled on the floor; that would be bad for international relations, and bad for business. Rather, in the event of such an attack—which we, of course, hope to thwart—your wisest course of action would be to call the Army. We have special antiterrorist teams standing by for instant deployment, stationed in hiding near the casinos. I have here the phone number, which is manned around the clock."

"I see."

Locke knew at this point the casino manager to whom he was speaking would perhaps be raising an eyebrow in skepticism. Anybody could call him on the telephone and make such a claim—terrorists might attack, and if they do, don't resist them—and how stupid would you feel if you did that and it was some kind of trick?

One did not get to run a multimillion-dollar endeavor by being slow of wit.

So Locke set the hook: "Please feel free to call Comrade General Wu's office if you have any further questions about this matter, sir. The general would, of course, be more than happy to speak personally with a man of your standing. I have here his private number. . . ."

Nearly all of the casino managers made that call, which was indeed to a private number established for Wu, and any telephone checks would show it thus. The general hastened to assure the casino managers that yes, Colonel Han of the antiterrorist squad was acting under his direction. The situation was being addressed.

Later, Locke went to the casinos in his official uniform, and spoke in person to the managers. Word, of course, quickly filtered back to the police, but that had been the *first* call he had made—to tell the local authorities the same thing he'd told the casino managers. So if some forgetful security guard called the police? Well, they would know that this was a military operation and to stay away. The Army always ranked above the police force; no one questioned such things.

Locke was just a bit worried. Since he was certain that Leigh was in somebody's custody, there was a chance that the man might reveal something of the plan. True, Leigh did not know all of it. He did not know how, neither did he know when it would happen, since the date had been moved up, so even if he spilled what he knew to a questioner, they would be late to the party. Still, it was vexsome, since he had told Wu that Leigh knew nothing of their scheme. It was better that way—no need to add to Wu's worries. Nor to have him angry at Locke for letting Leigh know anything.

Of course, Wu himself had babbled the entire plan to his spy and mistress, and while she could be trusted to go along, hoping for a big payoff, if something went crooked, Locke didn't trust her as far as he could spit. That she would give them up to save herself was a given.

Well. One had to play the cards one was given.

Ah, but here was an unexpected trump card, one that demonstrated where the beauty of having the local military commander in on the plan came forth. Mere hours after Locke visited this worry about Leigh again, his fake antiterrorist line had rung. The call was from a local senior police official. They had received a communication from the Chinese computer authority, and as a result, had arrested a British national here in Macao. Questioning had revealed nothing of use so far, but it might be possible that this man, a foreigner; was involved in the terrorist plot, yes?

Locke had almost laughed aloud. Yes, he had told the policeman, it was possible. The Army would like to question this prisoner. They would send men to collect him and transport him back to the base for interrogation. It was not a request.

The police were only too happy to comply.

Locke pulled in a couple members of his personal team, already outfitted as soldiers, wrote transfer papers on Wu's official stationery, and sent them to collect Leigh. How perfect was that?

The police were going to turn the only man who could blow the whistle on Locke's operation over to him!

Leigh, unfortunately, would have an accident shortly after he came into Locke's custody. He was a loose end Locke had planned to wrap up anyway, and this just made it easier.

That done, there was nothing else to stop them, nothing.

35

Washington, D.C.

Jay removed his rig, stripped the casters and sensor gear and mesh off, and just let it drop on the carpet. Later, he'd shove the sweaty mesh into the ultrasonic cleaner, and use dry-clean wipes on the bits that he couldn't immerse in the ultrasound's liquid, but for now, he just wanted to go and take a shower himself.

It hadn't been pretty, but it was, at last, done.

No matter how good a scenario you could spin, running down the rascals that Shing had caused to infest the military and CyberNation computers was dull, grinding work. Like pulling crab grass up by the roots, or scrubbing a dirty floor, or maybe chipping barnacles off a ship's hull. Each bit had to be done manually, and once removed, the place where it had been had to be sanded, smoothed, wiped, repainted—remade so that the chunk removed didn't leave a gap or hole or whatever.

It was scut work, and not Jay's thing, but it had to be done, it had to be done *right,* and it was his project.

But, finally, it was finished. As far as Jay could tell, all

traces of the tampering done by Shing and his allies were
no more.

His virgil beeped in its computer dock. Seurat.

"Good evening," Seurat said when Jay accepted the
connection.

"Hey."

"How goes it?"

Jay managed a tired grin. "We got the guy, we got his
modus, and I just finished cleaning it out. The military system—and yours—are as clean as new pennies. At least as
far as this hack is concerned."

"*Très bon,* Gridley! Excellent!"

"Just part of the job, Mr. Seurat."

"But you must call me Charles, *mon ami.*"

"I must?"

"*Oui.*"

The man sounded way too happy, even though Jay had
done him a good turn.

"Do you like Paris, my friend?"

"Sure."

"Then you must come and visit. To a wedding."

"Somebody getting married?"

"Yes. Me. I have met a wonderful woman—an American, no less. She is perfect, the most beautiful and intelli-
gent and funny woman in the world."

"Save one," Jay said.

"Ah, you are married?"

"Yep. Got a baby son, too."

"This is wonderful, no?"

"Yeah. It is. And after I take a shower, I'm going to go
and spend some quality time with them. This has been a
bastard of a case."

"But you have solved it, and all is right with the world,
no?"

"As close as it gets for me," Jay said.

After he and Seurat broke the connection, Jay smiled.
For him, all was right with the world. Or would be, right
after he took a shower. . . .

36

In the Air over the South Pacific

The Net Force 747, an old workhorse but one that still did the job, droned along six miles up. Kent came awake and looked around. About half of his unit was napping, the others reading or working on their battle laptops.

Kent had four squads, ten troopers each, and thus a single platoon. Each squad would be deployed in different parts of the operation—security, communications, transportation, with the actual strike team being six or eight strong. No way could he take enough troops into China to get into a shooting engagement with the Chinese Army.

In fact, the unit would technically be spies if they were caught, because they were all going to be in civilian clothes—an uninvited, uniformed force on foreign soil was sometimes necessary, but in this case, a bad idea.

Next to him, Julio Fernandez, who looked as if he were asleep, said, "General Howard is gonna be sorry he missed this."

"Only if we don't screw it up."

Fernandez grinned. "Well, at least we can blame it on the jarheads if that happens. Sir."

Kent shook his head.

The plan, hurried as it was, seemed pretty reasonable. They wouldn't be flying into China, but to a military base in south Taiwan, where they would transfer to a seaplane that would rendezvous with a boat in the sea south of Macao. The final leg in would be the most tricky, but supposedly, that was covered with enough bribes to make it relatively safe.

CIA and Military Intelligence, along with some intel from the Brits, would, Kent hoped, tag Comrade General Wu so that they could approach him away from his military base. They'd grab him, spirit him back to the boat, and, all things going well, haul him back the same way they'd gotten in.

All things going well . . .

Pan China Airlines Flight #2100
Somewhere over the Arctic

Chang had a bank of three seats to himself, a rare luxury, and he had lifted up the dividing arms and made himself a short couch, upon which he was lying. He kept the center seat belt loosely fastened around himself, just in case they should hit rough air while he was asleep. It was a long flight, and sleep would be welcome.

As he dozed, he considered his trip to America. It had gone well, much better than he could have expected. He had not only seen how Net Force operated, he had done them a large favor, one which was already paying dividends. He had hardware and software he would not have been able to buy on his own, and the good will of Jay Gridley, Net Force's top computer operative, which was worth more than gold.

More, Chang's government had in custody a man connected to the attack on the U.S. military, and, with luck, would soon be privy to what he knew about the situation, a thing that would stand Chang in good stead with his bosses.

Who would have thought it? God, Chang realized, indeed worked in mysterious ways. . . .

A pleasant feeling altogether as Chang drifted off to the land of dreams . . .

Warehouse District
Macao, China

Locke stood in the small warehouse, checking supplies. Everything seemed to be in order. This was where the operation would begin staging, less than forty-eight hours from now. Wu's strike team—and a couple of Locke's own men— would gather here, collect their gear, dress for their roles, and set things into motion. Once that die was cast, there would be no turning back. It would succeed or it would fail. Failure meant imprisonment or death; success meant a life of luxury beyond the dreams of most men, the ability to go almost anywhere and do almost anything Locke could desire.

The encrypted phone on his belt, smaller than his thumb and voice-operated, beeped. Locke unclipped the phone and raised it to his ear. "Yes?"

"Are things in order?" It was Wu, of course.

"Yes."

"Good. I will see you at the rendezvous at the appointed time."

Wu discommed, and Locke clipped the phone back to his belt. His belly tightened, the flutter in his bowels a familiar sensation, though one he hadn't felt since he'd killed that guard in America, and not for a while before then. A mix of fear, anticipation, and . . . joy.

Jack Locke was about to put himself on the line, risking his life for another run at the sweet, sweet taste of a plan well made and executed.

It didn't get any better than this.

37

Thorn wasn't exactly sure what he'd expected, but whatever it had been, Marissa's new townhouse wasn't it.

The place was in a nice enough neighborhood, in a row of two-story condos that looked pretty much the same— not rich folks, not poor, a little above the middle of middle-class. No yard to keep up, at least not in front, just a sidewalk on the street and a couple of small trees in big pots.

There was an alarm system, and one that needed both a thumbprint and vox-ID to unlock the door—which appeared to be steel painted to look like wood. He also noticed wrought-iron grills over the windows, very artistic, but serving as bars to keep all but the most serious of would-be burglars out.

Thorn's security wasn't bad; Marissa's was better.

"What do you have in here, gold bullion?" he asked, as she opened the door.

"Something better, I think," she said.

When he got inside, he saw what she meant:

There were two paintings in the living room. They were fairly large, five feet by three or so, on opposite walls, directly facing each other—oils or acrylics, Thorn couldn't tell for sure.

One was of a large, muscular black man, shirtless, in stained overalls half held up by one strap, with a red handkerchief in a front pocket, sitting in an unfinished wooden glider hung by iron chains under a wide front porch. There was a thick book on the swing's seat next to him. The man was sweaty, and looked very warm; the painter had captured a kind of nobility in his position, as if he were royalty, but a king who worked with his hands. He had a smile that Mona Lisa would envy.

Across the room, the second painting was of a black woman. She was lean, dark, and naked, one arm stretched wide to show a muscular definition, her breasts high and small, belly flat. The artist had shaded the figure so that her sex was in deep shadow, barely hinted at. Her hair was plaited in long braids that flared and reached to the middle of her back, hung as though a strong wind stirred them to her right. She stood against a background of green land, blue mountains, and a cloudy sky, with the sky going darker and into a star field behind her head.

Both of the subjects looked to be about thirty, though it was hard for Thorn to judge—black people had always seemed to him to age better than paler-skinned folk.

"The artist is Rick Berry," Marissa said. "You might have seen his work on some book covers, he has done a lot of that."

"Impressive," Thorn said. He knew quality when he saw it, and this was definitely that.

He looked at her. Caught a hint of something in her smile. "What else?" he said.

"The man is Amos Jefferson Lowe. The woman is Ruth Lewis Jackson Lowe."

Thorn nodded. "Your grandparents, on your father's side."

"No points for that one, Tommy."

He smiled. "I think my grandmother would spin like a gyroscope in her grave if she knew I had a picture of her without clothes on my wall."

"Not mine," she said. "My mother's parents died when I was a child—a car accident in Alabama—a drunk in a truck crossed the centerline and hit them head-on. But Grampa and Grandma Lowe tried to make up for that. Amos was a machinist at a mill who read Shakespeare and published articles about the Bard. Ruth taught third grade for forty years, but had been a champion runner in her youth—held the state record in the mile for twenty years after she graduated. Salt of the earth—with a few other spices mixed in."

Thorn nodded.

"They decided when I was a little girl that whenever I had a birthday, or for Christmas, or other special occasions, they weren't going to give me toys or clothes, they would give me adventures. They took me to museums; to see sailing ships; to the tops of tall buildings where I could look down upon the world. The summer I was ten, we visited a diamond mine in Arkansas. At eleven, the Carlsbad Caverns. At twelve and thirteen, the Atlantic and Pacific coasts. I took lessons and scuba-dived the oil rigs in the Gulf of Mexico when I was sixteen. When I graduated from high school, they paid for a trip to Spain; when I graduated from college, they sent me on a month-long walkabout in Australia."

She paused, remembering, a small smile on her face.

"My grandmother taught me how to shoot a .22 rifle, how to skin and cook a squirrel, and how to run within my breath. My grandfather taught me how to ride a bicycle, to call quail right to the back door of their house, and how to strip down a lawn mower engine. And also about sonnets and plays. He did a mean Othello."

She paused again. "I can't imagine any better grandparents than Amos and Ruth. These pictures capture their essence for me. Who they were—who they still are."

He looked at her, eyebrows raised. "Around here?"

"They live on a little farm down in Georgia. You'll get a chance to meet them pretty soon. I thought you'd want to know a little bit about them first."

Thorn felt a thrill, an almost electric sensation flash up his body—this conversation meant something more than family history. It took his breath away for a moment as he understood just what it did mean.

Then he said, "So, now is it okay to bring up that subject I wasn't supposed to talk about?"

She grinned. "I like a man who can keep up. Go ahead."

"You want to get married?"

"To you? Yes."

He thought his face might break, he grinned so big.

Later, when they were lying on the floor between the two pictures in a state of dress the same as the painting of her grandmother, Marissa said, "So, how's the thing in China going?"

"In the grand cosmic scheme of things, it really doesn't matter to me right now. Not in the least. Not at all."

She laughed. "You are waay too easy, Tommy."

He laughed with her. She was smart, funny, and beautiful, and she wanted to be with him.

He didn't see how it could get any better than this.

Penha Hill
Near the A-Ma Temple
Macao, China

The rendezvous was at the warehouse where Locke waited, but even with what was supposedly an unbreakable cipher program in Wu's and Locke's telephones, the general never said anything that could identify them, or specific times and places, over a wireless connection. What was not spoken could not be intercepted.

Wu was in his command car, and the driver was one of his hand-selected elite robbery team. Too bad the man would be dead soon. He would last longer than some of the others—all the way to Taipei, but then, alas, he would have to become food for the worms. Regrettable, but necessary. The new Wu did not need any such baggage.

True, the People's Government would want his head, but he had already begun making sure that anything they said about him would fall on less-than-interested ears in Taiwan. Of course they would offer all manner of slanders. He would be, after all, a defector. And if his new friends believed the story of the theft of millions—and certainly some of them would—one could buy a lot of goodwill with enough well-placed bribes. It was a very large pie, after all, and the reason he had baked it was to share it.

There were things that money could not buy, but poor and venal officials were seldom among these things. There was always a man who wanted more than he had, and you had but to find him and determine his price to make him yours.

Wu glanced at his watch. He was a little nervous—who wouldn't be? His life was about to change, very much and forever, no matter what happened. If things went badly, then he would suffer. Prison would be the best for which he could hope, death a much more likely end. But if all went well—and it should—then Wu would be one giant step farther down the road to greatness, with the sun shining and not a tiger in sight.

He had found one weakness in the technological might of the United States. Shing was captured, and that secret lost to Wu, but what he had found once, he could find again, with enough money and power at his beck and call.

Wu was a man with large mountain ahead of him, and in his heart, he knew he would not fail to reach and climb it. To stand in the dragon's lair . . .

He smiled as the driver honked at a wooden cart crossing the road ahead of them, a cart with automobile wheels and bald tires on it, being drawn by a pair of oxen, driven by an old man in a straw coolie hat. Here they were, in the twenty-first century, in a city thick with all the aspects of modern civilization, just down the hill from the Ritz Hotel, where a good, but not the best, room would cost HK$2,000 a night, and still such things as ox carts were not only possible, they were not even uncommon.

Wu laughed. He was on his way to becoming the man he was always destined to become, a man of the future, and here he was slowing for something out of history. How amusing.

Life did not get any better than this.

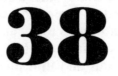

38

Zhujiang Kou Bay
East of Macao, West of Hong Kong

The plane was an old PS-1 ASW Flying Boat, a Shin
Meiwa, made in Japan forty or fifty years ago, but registered to a Chinese tourist-transport company owned by the
CIA. It wasn't the most spacious craft for a full platoon,
but it worked well enough, and it was what was available.

The Chinese pilot landed the plane in the bay not three
miles away from Macao, and did a slow taxi to a dock on
the northeast side of the city. Macao was small geographi-
cally, even with something more than half a million locals
living there—but the plane's dock was out of the way, and
Kent and his team were able to leave in plain sight, disguised as tourists. They were strung with cameras, they
carried overnight bags or day packs, there were women and
men, and they looked like any other group of Westerners
on a charter flight, come to lose money at the casinos.

The officials at the dock who were to check passports
belonged to the Company, Kent had been told, and a uniformed and armed guard smiled and waved at them as they

walked along the dock to where a chartered bus awaited them, so that seemed to be true.

On the bus, which was not air-conditioned, and which had all the windows down to allow the semitropical heat and breeze in, Fernandez, dressed in a bright blue Hawaiian shirt and khaki shorts and sandals, said, "That seemed awful easy."

Kent shrugged. "Who wants to sneak *into* China?"

"I guess."

The CIA liaison, a tall and thin man with carroty red hair who called himself Rusty, dropped into the seat in front of Kent and turned to look at him. "We have your staging area set up, Colonel."

"Any problems?"

"With the Chairman of JCS and the Director of the Company breathing down our necks? Not hardly. If I had a red carpet, I'd have rolled it out for you and saluted as you strolled by."

Kent smiled. It was good to have a boss with clout when you needed it.

The ride didn't take long, and ended at a small hotel, the Golden Road.

"Company owns this, too?"

"Enough of it so the co-owners don't complain when we book conventions of rich tourists."

"And we are . . . ?"

"American dentists," Rusty said.

"Dentists?"

"It was that or lawyers."

Fernandez shook his head. "My mother wanted me to be a lawyer. She was afraid of dentists."

"Everybody is afraid of dentists," the CIA man said. "Given a choice, most people would rather sit on a hot stove than go to the dentist. People are less afraid of death than dentists. Makes good cover."

"Any word on Wu?" Kent asked.

"The last we heard, he had left the base with his driver in his staff car. But we lost him in the warehouse district, and we don't have electronics on his vehicle. He'll turn up again pretty soon. It's not that big a town."

"Good."

Kent and his troops went into the hotel and were assigned rooms. He arranged to meet backup with the unit in a meeting room reserved for them in an hour, which gave everybody time to settle in and drop off their gear.

An hour later, as Kent strolled toward the meeting room, he was stopped at the door by Fernandez.

"Sir, I just got word from the spooks. We, uh, have a . . . situation on the ground here."

Kent looked at him. "Which is . . . ?"

"Apparently there has been some kind of terrorist attack on several of the local casinos. The Army has moved in to deal with it."

"And . . . ?"

"Wu himself is leading the troops."

Kent nodded. "I can understand that. Some men don't like to be armchair commanders."

"It appears they have the problem in hand, but we can't tell for sure—all communications from the sites have been jammed."

"That would be standard—" He stopped. "Oh, my God."

"Sir?"

"I can't believe it."

"What is that, Colonel?" Fernandez looked puzzled. Kent himself was feeling more than a little stupid.

"Wu. That's what it's all about. The misdirection—the computer attacks, trying to buy bombs—those were *cover*."

"To do what? Rob some casinos?"

"Exactly!"

"Are you sure, sir?"

"Yes. It makes perfect sense."

Fernandez frowned. "It seems like an awful lot of trouble just to knock off a few casinos."

"We're not talking about lunch money, are we? Got to be tens, maybe hundreds of millions involved."

Kent could see as it sank in.

After a moment, Fernandez said, "He can't get away with it."

"Who is going to stop him, Captain?" Kent asked. "*He's* the Army! He can outgun anybody who'd try—at least in the short run. Damn, why didn't I see this before?"

Fernandez didn't say anything.

"Get the teams ready," Kent said. "He'll have to move the money somehow. If we follow that, we can get him."

Fernandez hesitated, then asked, "Do we really *need* to get him?"

Kent looked at him. "What are you talking about, Julio?"

"Well, Colonel, if all the computer attacks were to set up a robbery, we know what he's up to now, don't we? It's not our money."

"True. But he still pulled off those attacks, which means he could do it again, if he had a reason to. And a man this complicated has to have more on his agenda. What is he going to *do* with all this money?"

Fernandez shrugged. "Buy a new car?"

"Not around here, he won't. And if he's the guy trying to get hold of surplus Soviet nukes? We sure need to know about that. No, Captain, it was a good thought, but we continue with the operation. We have questions, and this is the man with the answers."

"Yes, sir."

"Go!"

"Gone, sir.".

Once Julio was in the wind, Kent considered his next move. He could make a secure uplink with a Marine comsat and put in a call to General Hadden, though he knew what the man would tell him. You don't stop in the middle of a battle because you *think* you know what the enemy is planning. Yes, it would be wise to apprise the commander of the situation, but Kent was the man on the ground and he had the best picture. What the general didn't know wouldn't hurt him. No point in stirring up those waters just yet.

39

House of Good Fortune Casino
Macao, China

The House of Good Fortune—now there was an appropriate name. The question was, of course, *who* enjoyed the good fortune. At the moment, it wasn't the House—and they had no idea how bad it was yet to become.

Locke grinned. So far, his plan had worked like a fine Swiss watch. So simple, when you knew how. Almost an anticlimax.

When the heavily armed paramilitary "terrorists" had started their assaults on two casinos, firing submachine guns into the ceilings and throwing flash-bangs all around, it had been bedlam. The two casino security heads, who had been carefully primed earlier by Locke in his colonel's disguise, warning of this very thing, had taken one look and done just as they had been told—they called the People's Army antiterrorist hotline. They believed that the local police would be outgunned, just as Locke had told them. And even if they *had* called the police, Locke had that covered as well.

Everything was covered.

A few guards were killed or wounded, but then the People's Army charged in and saved the day, shooting, spraying tear gas, capturing the dozen terrorists in the House of Good Fortune, and being ever so heroic in the process. And how fortunate, no tourists had been slain!

When the second casino—the Palace of Jade—was hit, Wu had declared a state of emergency, then quickly surrounded and occupied the Jade and three more of the major casinos with his troops. The second "terrorist" team was captured as easily as the first. Then Wu had explained to the casino managers that such a large-scale raid indicated a major threat, and that it was better to be safe than sorry. Nobody argued with him.

The owners and managers had been more than grateful. It never occurred to them that Comrade General Wu was the one about whom they should be worried—that the "terrorists" were no more than a sham.

With the cooperation of the security people and the blessings of the owners, Wu temporarily shut down all casino and hotel communications from the gambling palaces, so, he said, any hidden confederates inside could not aid the robbers. Massive and powerful jammers blanketed each place so that not even cell phones would work.

Time was critical. A few hours was all they would have, and then higher powers would want to know what the devil was going on.

For now, Wu had control of the buildings, and even if those inside had worried and thought to call for help—which they would not—they couldn't make that call.

So they held five casinos, with an average of over sixty million dollars U.S. each on hand: yen, dollars, euros, pesos, pataca, pounds, dinars, rupees, rubles. . . . Most of the money was used and unmarked, some of it in computer-accessible draw-upon accounts or certified flashmem deposited in the casinos' computers.

A third of a billion dollars, at least.

It could not have gone any better. Locke was ecstatic.

But, of course, this was the easy part. The hard part—

getting away with the loot? That was where Locke was going to earn his money. And his cut, a mere twenty percent, would be enough to let him buy first-class accommodations in a number of countries around the world by the time they did figure it out.

The plan was pure genius, if he did say so himself.

The only small beetle left in the pudding was Net Force. Leigh was recently buried in a shallow grave in a local park, and would aid no one. But Net Force did have a faint trail, and Locke wasn't sure how far along it they actually were.

They almost certainly had Shing, who knew that Wu was behind the military computer attacks, but Shing *didn't* know about this part of it. Locke didn't think they were that close—and what could they do against Wu's trained troops anyhow?—but he couldn't be sure—he'd been more than a little busy here, setting up the score.

Well. He'd worry about Net Force later. Even if they knew more than he thought, knowing it and *proving* it were two different beasts. By the time they might be in position to cause any problems, the party would be long over.

Locke's com button chirped. He tapped the tiny button on the device, which was small enough to fit entirely in his left ear. It operated on one of the very few frequencies not blanketed by the jammers.

"Here."

"Stage Two?" came Wu's voice.

"Yes."

Locke tapped the com device's control again. He went and found the casino's manager.

"Ah, Colonel," the man said, his face full of relief. "We are forever in your debt. Is everything okay?"

"Actually, no, sir," Locke said. "We have uncovered a major problem. The terrorists claim they have set dirty bombs in several of the casinos."

"Set what?"

"Explosive devices rigged with small amounts of radioactive material."

"An atomic bomb? *Here?*"

Locke thought the man might bolt in a dead run for the doors.

"No, sir, not an atomic bomb—it's a conventional explosive, probably C-4, could even be dynamite. Low-yield. It probably wouldn't begin to knock your building down, or even cause major damage by itself. But around the explosive core is something radioactive—medical-grade material, or low-level uranium, most likely. If those go off, they will contaminate the buildings—everything—and everybody—in them. Nobody will be able to come back into any of the casinos for a long time, and nothing in them will be salvageable."

Locke didn't know if dirty bombs worked exactly that way or not, but the story sounded both plausible and dramatic, and that was all that mattered. Besides, it was highly unlikely that the casino manager was any kind of expert in radiation poisoning and contamination.

Locke let the manager get there ahead of him, and it didn't take him long. "Our money! We've got to get it out, to a safe place!"

The idea of sixty million dollars that nobody could touch, much less spend? What a horrible idea to a casino manager!

"Yes, sir. Get your guards to help my men. We'll move all the cash and credit tabs to a secure location and come back to find the bomb. We'll force the terrorists to tell us eventually, but we might not have much time—"

"Yes, yes, of course. Wong!"

The head of the casino's security hurried to where Locke and the manager stood. "Go with the colonel—there's a radioactive bomb here, we need to get our money out, now!"

"And have your people evacuate the building," Locke said. "If that bomb goes off, everybody in here could be contaminated."

Wong pulled his walkie-talkie and began speaking rapidly into it.

Pure genius, Locke thought. The best plan he'd ever come up with.

"Where will you take the funds?" the manager asked.

Locke pretended to think. "There is a small steamship in the harbor that belongs to the People, a cargo freighter used for Army supplies. It will be easier to guard with water all around it, and the river is upwind from the casinos. If there is an explosion at one of the casinos, the money will be safer there than anywhere else. We'll take it to that ship. Your security chief will stay with it."

"Yes, yes. Hurry!"

Hurry and steal all our money! Locke had to hold his smile in check. Indeed, he would hurry.

The freighter was a red-herring—the money would indeed go up a ladder on the starboard side—but without pause, it would go down another ramp on the port side, where a trio of fast boats would be waiting. These in turn would go but a short distance to a makeshift airfield where much faster airplanes were standing by.

Wong the security man would be clouted on the head and dumped into the bay, as would the other security people invited along to allay even the most remote suspicion. The boats would be roaring away as soon as they were unloaded, and the freighter rigged with explosives—nothing radioactive, just enough to make a very large bang and to sink it—and when eventually someone came looking for their money, the freighter would blow up.

After transferring the money to the aircraft, the empty boats would head for Taiwan. These might or might not escape detection, and too bad for the men running them if they did not.

The money by then would be flying along just over the sea, in stealth-gear-ensheathed airplanes painted to match the sky from below and the water from above.

All of this had been put together like a fine Swiss watch, every cog in place, jewels at every friction point, as slick as a film of oil on glass.

Wu had a hundred men in the operation, hand-picked and trained, and loyal to him, most of whom believed they would receive a quarter of a million U.S. dollars each for their help in the heist. In truth, ninety of them—including the twenty or so who played the role of terrorists—would get jacketed metal machine-gun bullets instead of money. Of the ten survivors, most thought *they* would get a million each. Eight of those would eventually join their fallen comrades, leaving only two who expected to receive *five* million apiece.

Greed was a wonderful motivator.

Wu would dispatch those last two, and then there would be none.

Well, save for Locke, and he had no intention of turning his back on anybody. He had his own plan. He would divert a portion of the money for himself—for there would be *four* fast boats opposite the freighter, instead of three, as well as a helicopter hidden elsewhere with a range sufficient to reach Taiwan or maybe even India—and Locke would be gone before anybody knew it, including Wu.

Especially Wu.

By the time whichever authority in charge got it all sorted out, Wu would be in Taipei, and Locke halfway to somewhere far, far away, the first leg of several flights and passport changes to leave a cold trail behind him.

Locke's plan was so bold, nobody had ever considered it before. And, as everyone knew, fortune favored the bold. . . .

Locke went to direct his team, who would be helped in the theft by the casino's own guards and the blessing of its manager. In a few moments, Army trucks full of money were going to roll through the streets of Macao, with the enthusiastic assistance of those who were unknowingly being robbed.

Pure genius. No doubt about it. . . .

40

"Sir, it looks as if Wu's men are clearing roads in the direction of the docks. Some from each casino. There also appears to be some kind of activity around a small freighter in the harbor."

Kent frowned. "He's planning to escape on a *boat*? That's not very smart."

"No, sir, it isn't," Fernandez said. "All this, just to get blown out of the water by the Chinese Navy? He's got to have something else up his sleeve."

"My guess is he does. Go get first squad on the way back to our aircraft and float it out where they can see what's going on. Tell the CIA guy to get the cars here now, then load up second and third squads and get them rolling, radios on opchan alpha. Get us some other watercraft."

"Yes, sir." Fernandez started talking into his radio, issuing orders.

Kent considered his options. Julio was right, the money wasn't important—let the Chinese worry about that. What they needed was Wu, and they needed to get him and get away before any of the locals figured out what was going on and who they were. They had to move quickly.

"Captain, which casino is Wu in?"

"The House of Good Fortune."

"Get fourth squad and let's go. Three cars. We are going to have to run and gun. No time for anything else."

"Yes, sir."

Kent grabbed a tactical radio unit and made sure it was tuned to the right opchan. He'd have to make it up as he went along. Sometimes that was the best battle plan you could manage. You had to make do with what you had.

"All squads, listen up. Here's what we are going to do. . . ."

41

House of Good Fortune Casino
Macao, China

"I'll see you at the airfield, comrade," Wu said to Locke.

"Right."

"Travel safe." Wu clapped him on the shoulder, smiled, and turned to leave.

As soon as he was gone, Locke and his assistant loaded up the last six bags of loot into Locke's Toyota Land Cruiser. That much money was heavy, even in large bills. About as much as what Locke was supposed to get for his part, he reckoned. Maybe a bit less, but he wasn't going to get greedy about it. Stopping to pick up that last dime could get you caught or killed.

They climbed into the SUV and headed for the harbor. They'd beat Wu and the other trucks there—Locke would take the shortest route, do it at speed, and the official police light flashing on the vehicle's dashboard would see that nobody stopped them. They'd be there ten minutes ahead of Wu. Plenty of time.

Locke's assistant was actually Wu's man—Locke knew this—but that didn't matter. Not yet.

"Five minutes," Locke said, looking at his watch. "We'll be alone on the ship, first to get there. I want to be gone by the time the first truck arrives."

The assistant was a muscular Mongolian named Khasar, which meant "terrible dog." A tradition in that backward land, to name children for ugly things, to protect them from evil spirits. That trick wasn't going to be enough keep him safe in this, though.

Khasar said, "Yes. We will hurry."

He stepped on the gas pedal and the car surged forward.

The Streets of Macao
China

Kent pulled his car—a Volkswagen beetle, of all things—next to Fernandez's car, a Korean compact he didn't recognize.

Kent said, "Set up here, Captain. You've got three, maybe four minutes. I'm going on to the freighter, just in case."

"Yes, sir."

"Good luck, Julio."

"You, too, sir."

Kent revved the VW's engine and took off. Despite the hurry, and the absolute lack of time to do things properly, he realized he was grinning as he drove. A battle joined, plans unfolding fast, the end not at all certain, and lives on the line—but he was doing what he knew how to do best.

It didn't get any better than this, did it?

42

Aboard the Freighter **Shengfeng Hao**
Macao Harbor, Macao, China

As part of his colonel's uniform, Locke had a pistol. This
was a QSZ-92, a no-nonsense black metal and plastic
handgun made in a People's Liberation Army arms factory
outside Beijing, and chambered for the proprietary 5.8mm
Chinese round, with the bottlenecked and pointed bullets.
The gun held fifteen cartridges in the magazine, plus one
in the chamber, and there was a spare magazine on his belt,
so he had thirty-one shots. It was a semiautomatic double-
action weapon, and all you needed to do was disengage the
safety, aim, and pull the trigger each time you wanted it to
go *bang!* A well-made military pistol, and if not the best in
the world, certainly not the worst. Sufficient for his needs
here, this gun.

Locke drew the side arm from its holster and clicked the
safety off. He took a deep breath.

In front of him, Khasar, who was every centimeter Wu's
man, was not yet ready to begin his assigned task. The
would-be assassin was halfway down the ramp from the

freighter to Locke's powerboat, with the last bags of cash in hand.

Wu would have told Khasar to hold off, to wait until they got the diverted money onto the getaway boat, to be sure of what Locke planned. To be certain the wily criminal did not have something nasty rigged to cover his escape. For Wu knew that Locke would try to sneak off, and well that he should—Locke had left plenty of clues lying around to make sure the general figured it out.

Locke shook his head. Did Wu really think he was that stupid? With Locke knowing that Wu would kill his own troops, that Locke would never think that *he* might be a target? Did Wu expect him to believe in honor among thieves?

Wu had his own kind of honor, but his goals did not include letting Locke—or anybody else—remain alive to be a potential problem. Wu was a burn-the-fields, salt-the-earth kind of general. If there was nobody left behind, there would be nobody to sneak up on you someday when you might not be expecting it.

Not that Locke himself had a problem with that. He just wasn't about to be a victim of it.

Locke waited until Khasar had stepped onto the boat. It was twelve or fifteen meters from the deck of the freighter, at a steep downward angle, but an easy shot.

Locke lined up the sights square between the man's shoulder blades and fired twice.

Khasar the Mongol fell, no doubt surprised, and the last bags of cash thumped down onto the power boat's deck. Neat.

But the Mongol was a big and strong man, and the bullets were small. Locke took careful aim at Khasar as he came unsteadily to his feet, and squeezed off one more round—into the man's head.

It didn't matter how strong he was, Khasar wasn't going to shake that one off.

The Mongol fell again, going boneless in that way only the dead can achieve.

Locke lowered the pistol. He would descend the ramp now, shove the body into the bay, and be gone. Ten minutes away, his helicopter awaited, and once he got there, he would be essentially home free.

"Don't turn around, Colonel," came an unfamiliar man's voice from behind him.

Locke froze. The speaker spoke badly intoned Chinese, and Locke guessed that whoever it was was probably British or American.

Another small boat churned into view then, and upon the craft, five men, dressed as tourists!—but armed with pistols and submachine guns—approached Locke's getaway craft.

Locke's heart fell.

Nobody down there but a dead man to stop them.

Who were they? They weren't Chinese, he could see that.

And he had just murdered a man in plain view of whoever was behind him. This was bad.

He'd never be able to get down the ramp and outshoot those men below, who, even as he thought it, reached Locke's boat and pulled alongside to board it.

Locke sighed.

It wasn't the money so much. It stung, of course, knowing he'd had it in his grasp and now would not be able to collect on it, but then he hadn't joined Wu for the money. Locke had enough—more than enough—for his own needs.

No, he had joined Wu for the challenge, for the thrill, for the knowledge that he had been able to stand up to the United States and to CyberNation, and to win.

But to do that he had to get off this boat alive.

This all ran through his mind very fast. He had to leave.

But first he had to deal with the problem behind him.

"Down put the gun," came the voice, again in fractured Chinese.

"You're CIA?" he asked, in English.

"Close enough," the voice said in that same language. "Put your gun down, please. Slowly and carefully."

An American. They weren't ruthless, the Americans, they believed in fair play. The man wouldn't shoot him in the back.

He had a chance.

Locke began to lower the pistol, slowly, as instructed. He marked the voice, guessed the speaker was no more than five or six meters directly behind him. The man would be aiming his weapon at Locke's back. If he dropped and spun fast enough, it would take the American a second to adjust his aim. Locke knew how to shoot. He hadn't done much of it in a long time, but it was like riding a bicycle, you never forgot how. Especially when your life depended on it.

"Take it easy," Locke said. "Don't shoot, I give up—"

With that, he dropped and turned at the same time, ending up in a tripod on the deck, on his knees, stretched out and supported on his left hand. He brought his right hand up and around fast, thrust the pistol out and fired—one-two—!

But even as he fired, he knew it was wrong—the man behind him wasn't standing—he was prone!

Locke's shots missed by a meter, too high, too *high*—!

The American was on his belly, his own handgun extended in front of him. Locke had time to see that the man was also dressed like a tourist—a bright orange and yellow shirt, shorts—and that he was old and gray-haired.

He tried to adjust his aim downward—

An icy hammer smashed into his chest, just below his neck. The shock was so unexpected that Locke's supporting arm collapsed and he fell on his face. He had to let go of his pistol to push himself up, but halfway there, his strength failed, and he sprawled again.

The wooden grate over the metal deck felt very cold against his face.

This couldn't be happening. Everything had been going so *well*!

He saw the man's feet—he wore sandals, no socks—as he approached. Saw the shooter kick the fallen handgun away, then squat down.

Locke's vision went gray, then faded. And it was suddenly so very, very cold. . . . "All . . . wrong . . ." he managed.

"Colonel Abraham Kent of Net Force and the United States Marines," he heard the man say.

And that was the last thing Jack Locke heard as the spirit fled his body.

43

The Streets of Macao

Wu's car rolled through the streets, heading for the docks. It was incredible, he still couldn't quite believe it, but it was all going exactly as they had intended. This was something new: a battle plan that survived first contact with the enemy!

Things could not have gone any better. Here he was, riding behind a heavy Daewoo truck made in Guangxi—and wasn't that amusing? A Korean/Chinese venture—and that truck was full of money, a rich man's fortune, all of which was his.

Locke expected one-fifth of the haul, and deserved as much for his excellent work in setting up and executing the plan. And Locke's cut was not so much, not when such a vast sum was at hand. But even so, Locke was yet another loose end that had to be tied off, and besides, an extra fifty or sixty million dollars U.S. would go a long way to making sure Wu's rise to power went smoothly.

Wu cared nothing for the money itself, nor the toys it could buy him, only the power that would allow him to do big things. It was but a tool. A very large hammer with which he could bludgeon any who stood in his way.

Wu's terrible dog the Mongol would deal with Locke, and then Wu himself would deal with his dog. Hard, but necessary. A man sometimes had to do things for the greater good that were . . . distasteful.

Eventually, he would rule Taiwan. Eventually, he would have an army at his back. Eventually, he would find the precise place upon which to stand and insert his lever, and with it, he could topple the base government that ran his homeland. And then? Well, then, eventually, it would perhaps be time to test the Achilles' heel of the Americans' technological superiority in ways that really mattered.

Lofty goals, to be sure, but possible, possible—

Ahead, he could see the bay. Not long now—

The streets weren't crowded—he'd had his men mostly clear this one, shoving pedestrians away from the street and moving vehicular traffic aside. But standing on the corner ahead and to his right were two Westerners, a man and a woman, tourists wearing cameras and those silly shorts and loud shirts and stupid, vacant expressions that marked them as such. Fools! Did they not see there were important things being done here?

One of the tourists, the woman, bent down and made a motion as if rolling a ball.

What was she doing—?

Just ahead of his car, the Daewoo truck lurched to one side. There was an orange flash, a loud explosion, and the truck skidded and stopped.

Wu's driver slammed on his brakes, and Wu's car also slewed to a halt, centimeters short of hitting the truck's back bumper.

The two tourists ran off.

Yet another man in loud Western clothes came from around the corner of a building, and what he had on his shoulder was not something any tourist should have—it was a rocket launcher, looked like an old PF-89, an 80mm light antitank weapon—

Wu had time to frown, and then the tourist fired the launcher.

The money truck exploded.

The air was suddenly filled with colorful graffiti.

The most expensive graffiti the world had ever seen.

Wu reached for his pistol—

Yet *another* pair of tourists appeared from nowhere and stood next to his car, submachine guns pointed at him.

"Don't try it, General," one of the tourists said, in English.

Wu's driver pulled his own submachine gun from the seat, but before he could fire it, the man who had spoken fired his own weapon, a quick, three-round burst, 9mm.

The empty cartridges sparkled and fell in slow motion in the afternoon sunshine. . . .

Wu's driver jerked and slumped against the driver's-side window, blood oozing from his shattered head.

This couldn't be happening! Not in the middle of the street in Macao! Not in Wu's own command territory! Not this close to victory!

"Step out of the car, sir. Now!"

Stunned, Wu obeyed.

Around him, various paper currencies fluttered like a flock of wounded birds, flying and wafting and settling upon the street and sidewalk.

There was no stopping people from rushing out to gather it in now.

44

The pilot said, "Boy, it sure hit the fan back there. The Chinese Air Traffic Control guys are going nuts on the air. They want everybody on the ground to stay there, and nobody is going to be landing any time soon."

Kent, who stood next to him in the cockpit, said, "Can we get away?"

"If I can get us another couple of klicks away from shore before we take off, yeah," the pilot said. "Their Navy hasn't checked in yet, and I don't think they have anything close enough to run us down."

The Japanese seaplane's engines were rumbling loudly, and the craft was bouncing along, jarring Kent's teeth with every hit.

"Kinda choppy," Kent observed.

"We can take off in three-foot waves, no problem," the pilot said. "Better go sit down, though, it might get a little rough."

Kent nodded and worked his way back to his seat.

Next to him, General Wu sat, staring out through the window.

He turned to look as Kent sat.

"You are in the American Army?"

"Marines, sir, working for Net Force's military unit."

Wu nodded. "Net Force. Shing. The idiot and his computers. They gave us away. Such things are not to be trusted."

"Between you and me, yes, sir."

Wu nodded again. "I was so close."

Kent didn't reply.

Wu frowned. "What now?"

"We have people who want to talk to you."

"I won't tell them anything."

Kent shrugged. "If I were in your place, I'd consider it, sir. Your government will eventually sort out what happened in Macao. They'll want to talk to you worse than we do. Probably more, uh, harshly."

"And if I cooperate with the U.S. authorities, I'll be allowed to stay in your country? Is that what you are saying? People died during this operation, and I am responsible—you would excuse that?"

"No, sir, I can't make that promise. A Chinese general would have a lot to give us, and I'd expect that somebody from the State Department will eventually get around to making an offer to you, but that's politics, and not my area of expertise."

Wu smiled. "I have seen your area of expertise, ah . . . I did not get your name and rank . . . ?"

"Abraham Kent, sir, Colonel."

"A well-played operation, Colonel."

"Thank you, sir."

"One must admire skill wherever one sees it, even in an opponent. How long did you take to set up your operation?"

Kent was embarrassed to tell him, but there was no point in lying. "We got to Macao today, sir. We didn't know you were going to hit the casinos until we got there, so we had to develop our options on the fly, as it were."

Wu's face showed his surprise. "No! Our plan was many months in the making, and you just swept in and destroyed it with no preparation?"

"Better to be lucky than good, sir."

Wu smiled, but it was bitter. "Your gods must be stronger than mine. I had dreams, Colonel. A new and better China. I would have gotten rid of the Communists. I might have done it."

"Yes, sir."

"Well. Sometimes the dragon flies, sometimes the dragon dies."

Kent thought he was speaking metaphorically. He didn't have a chance to move before Wu pulled his uniform shirt up and bit off the top button—

"General, don't—!"

Wu smiled. Kent heard the crunch as Wu's teeth crushed the poison tablet disguised as a shirt button.

"Medic!" Kent yelled. He grabbed at Wu, tried to open his mouth, but he knew it was already too late.

Comrade General Wu had been right. He wasn't going to be telling anybody anything. Wu was on a one-way voyage to . . . elsewhere.

Damn.

45

General Hadden sat at one end of the conference table, Thorn at the other, and along the sides were Jay Gridley, Abe Kent, General Roger Ellis, and a couple of Hadden's men from the Pentagon, along with the Director of the CIA.

Kent finished his recitation. It had been clean, crisp, and to the point. He ended it with an apology for allowing Wu to commit suicide.

"Not at all, Colonel," Hadden said. General Ellis nodded. "That old poisoned-button trick went out before Mao, nobody does that kind of thing anymore. No reason to expect it. Besides, whatever grand schemes Wu had died with him. That's what we were really after."

Kent nodded. "Yes, sir."

The CIA Director, who had held the job less than a year, said, "The Chinese recovered most of the money from the thefts. Some of it was, ah, destroyed in an explosion, and a few hundred thousand dollars grabbed by looters at that location, but apparently somebody tipped off Beijing as to the whereabouts of the transport planes and they were stopped before they could take off."

He looked around the table, his eyes coming to rest on Colonel Kent. "Although it seems at least one of the gang might have managed to escape," he went on, "for there is an estimated six and a half million dollars that has been unaccounted for. There was a leased Chinese helicopter discovered on a beach in Taiwan only a day or so after the heist. No sign of the pilot or any passengers was found, but a local farmer says he saw a beautiful woman he didn't know in the area shortly before the helicopter came to light. Taiwanese authorities have not been able to locate this woman—if she actually exists. Could be the farmer conked the pilot over the head and stole the money."

Nobody had anything to say about that. It was not their problem in any event.

Thorn looked around. It was his meeting. "Anything else?"

Nobody said anything.

"Then I guess that wraps it up," Thorn said.

"Oh, one other thing," General Hadden said. "Roger?"

General Ellis reached into a pocket and came out with a small box. He grinned and slid it across the table toward Abe Kent.

Ellis said, "We know you have a closet full of ribbons and medals you seldom bother to wear, Abe, but we thought you might like these."

Kent opened the box.

Inside was a pair of small silver stars.

"Congratulations, *General*," Hadden said.

The stunned look on Abe Kent's face was, Thorn thought, priceless.

EPILOGUE

Washington, D.C.
The Mall

The sun shone brightly, but a recent thundershower had cooled the air a bit, so that it was muggy, but not too hot.

Thorn and Marissa walked along the edge of the Mall, looking at tourists, enjoying the day and each other's company.

"So, are you going to stick around at Net Force, Tommy? If I'm going to introduce you to my family as my intended, I have to tell them whether you're unemployed or not. My mother always worried that I'd marry some shiftless, no-account bum I'd have to support."

Thorn smiled. "I'm sure I can convince them I can take care of you."

"Perhaps. But I'm not sure they'd approve of a ne'er-do-well who can't hold a job, even a rich ne'er-do-well."

"I expect I'll stay where I am for a while," he said. "So far, the military hasn't stuck its nose too far into my business. They're happy with the job we did on their problem. With luck they won't get too hands-on."

"Good. Maybe we can go down to Georgia on a long weekend soon, see my grandparents."

"That'd be fine. I'll brush up on my Shakespeare and squirrel-skinning."

"My grandfather's favorite play is *A Midsummer Night's Dream,* and he prefers the Fisher printing over the Roberts."

"Duly noted. Any hints on squirrel stew?"

"Only one—first, catch a squirrel."

"Thank you so much."

"You'll do fine. My mother is so desperate for grand-children, as long as you have a pulse you'll be acceptable. My father trusts my judgment, though I have given him oc-casion to wonder. My grandma and grandpa will see the real you through whatever facade you hold up, and that'll be good enough for them."

"You think?"

"It's good enough for me. That's all that really matters."

Thorn grinned. Earlier, he had thought that life couldn't get any better. He'd been wrong.

He squeezed Marissa's hand. Life was getting better all the time.

Other titles by Steve Pieczenik

THE MIND PALACE
BLOOD HEAT
MAXIMUM VIGILANCE
PAX PACIFICA
STATE OF EMERGENCY
HIDDEN PASSIONS
MY BELOVED TALLEYRAND

For more information on Steve Pieczenik,
please visit www.stevepieczenik.com and www.strategic-intl.com.

*   *   *

Books by Alexander Court

ACTIVE MEASURES
ACTIVE PURSUIT